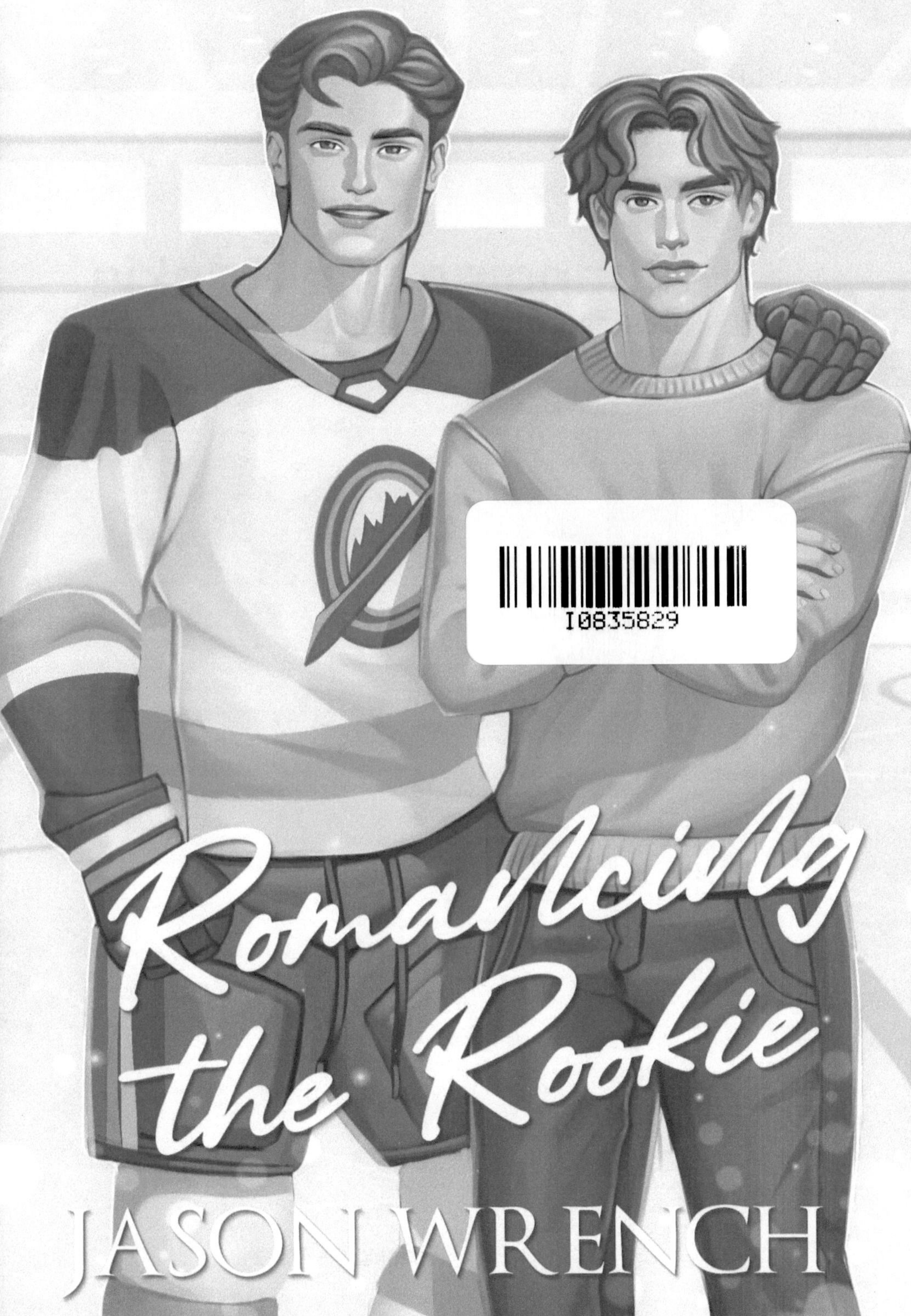
Tales from the Crease: Book 2
Romancing the Rookie
Jason Wrench
I0835829

Romancing the Rookie

Tales from the Crease - Book Two

Jason Wrench

Pink Sloth Books

Book Cover by Janjan Arts: https://www.facebook.com/janjan.arts.2024

Print Book ISBN: 978-1-971739-05-2

Ebook ISBN: 978-1-971739-04-5

Contents

Chapter 1
The Cold Read

Rowan

The air in the visitor's locker room tasted of old sweat and cold cement. Not a bad smell—familiar, an anchor in a world that had felt untethered too long. I dragged it in deep, letting the familiar smell of a locker room fill my lungs as I taped the blade of my stick. New team, new barn, same ritual. One full wrap around the toe, overlapping strips down the blade, a final pass of wax to keep the snow from building up.

Control what you can control.

My gear was a mismatched collection. Skates from a clearance sale, pants I'd had since juniors that somehow still fit, and a helmet—one good knock away from retirement—I'd found at a garage sale over the weekend. Everything black. Unbranded. Anonymous. Blending in was the whole point. For years, I'd been a walking billboard, every piece of equipment dictated by contract and color-coded for the camera. Now, for the first time in a decade, I wasn't Chase St. Clair, the kid from the cereal box and the front man for a hockey movie franchise. I wasn't number seventy-three, I was just a walk-on hopeful with a transfer transcript and a prayer.

Oakridge University had lost a player at the end of the fall semester. They needed a body to fill the roster. When the call went out for walk-ons, I thought, might as well.

I'd chosen Oakridge for a reason. Six hundred miles from Los Angeles, buried in the northern California redwoods, small enough to stay invisible but still close to the ocean. That's what I needed. A place where I could finish my degree. Playing a sport I'd once before the industry hollowed it out, would be the icing on the cake.

A guy a few stalls down, younger and built like a vending machine, was retaping his stick for the third time, hands trembling. The sound of ripping cloth echoed off the low ceiling. A freshman. He had that particular brand of terror in his eyes that only came from having your entire identity wrapped up in a game you weren't sure you were good enough to play at the collegiate level. I knew the feeling. I'd had a five-year head start on it.

"You Calloway?"

The voice came from my left. I glanced over. A player with Maddox stitched onto his gloves was leaning against the lockers, already dressed. He wasn't a walk-on; his gear was pristine, all matching Oakridge University Ospreys navy blue and orange. A junior, maybe a senior, here to help run the tryout drills and size up the new meat.

I smoothed the wax on my blade. "Yeah."

"Great." He placed a mark next to my name on the clipboard. "I'm Reece Maddox, team captain." He didn't extend his hand. His eyes did a quick, dismissive scan of my equipment—the mismatched black, the worn padding, and the garage-sale helmet. I watched him file it away: nobody.

He flipped through a few pages on his clipboard. "So, it says here you've played a little before."

"A little." The truest and most dishonest thing I could say. The league I'd played in before going to Hollywood had been dismantled, my stats scrubbed from the internet along with my career. All that was left were the ghostship fan sites and the grainy YouTube clips from Ice Kings 3: Dynasty's End.

Maddox grunted, a sound that wasn't quite a welcome. "You seem a bit old for this."

"I'm not that old," I said. Twenty-three felt ancient in this room, but I'd seen thirty-year-old rookies grind their way onto NHL rosters. Age was just a number if your body cooperated.

Maddox grunted again. "So, why? Why do you want to be a walk-on?"

"Just transferred. Finished my associate's degree in December at Alpine County Community College. Finishing my BA in journalism here."

"Yeah, I don't really care about your life story. Why do you think you're better than the six other guys trying out for the same position?"

"I have experience. I know how to handle myself on the ice. I want to be a team player."

Maddox rolled his eyes like I'd given the worst answer on a job interview. Turning to the freshman. "That means you're Davies."

"Yes, sir. Captain, sir." The hulking kid's voice cracked on the second sir.

The guy seemed way out of his depth. Maddox was a shark, and the tank was about to become his chum. I'd skated with guys like Maddox before—alpha dogs who needed to rub others' faces in it to feel big. I wanted to stick up for the young kid, but that would go against keeping my head down. I finished waxing my blade and ignored the rest of their conversation.

"Coach expects you on the ice in five. Don't be late," Maddox said after finishing up with the tank. Maddox pushed off the lockers and headed for the tunnel, his new skates leaving clean white slices on the rubber matting.

I pulled on my helmet, the worn foam compressing against my temples. I fastened the cage, and the world snapped into a grid.

I stood, my knees protesting the shift from a crouch. At twenty-three, I was the old man in the room. Most of these kids were coming straight from juniors or high-level U-18s, their whole lives still ahead of them.

The walk down the tunnel was short. Concrete walls gave way to padded boards, and the muffled sounds of the locker room were replaced by the vast, hollow echo of the arena. I stepped through the gap in the boards and onto the ice.

For a second, I stood there.

The cold hit my face like a baptism—clean, mineral-sharp, almost sweet. The arena wasn't a pro barn. I'd grown up in those, with their Jumbotrons and endless tiers of seats that climbed into darkness, the roar of fifteen thousand strangers who thought they knew me. Oakridge's rink was different. Smaller. The opposite of wide, it was tall. The stands rose from the glass at a steep angle, like the walls of a canyon carved by some ancient glacier. When this place filled with bodies, they'd be right on top of you, breathing down your neck, close enough to hear the scrape of every edge and the grunt of every check. The effect was borderline claustrophobic.

I loved it immediately.

Half a dozen other walk-ons were skating tentative laps. The ice was freshly flooded, a perfect, unbroken sheet of white under the bright lights. No logos yet—just pure, clean surface waiting to be marked. My blades bit in with that first stride, the sound a crisp tear that echoed off the high ceiling. I pushed off, gliding, letting my legs remember the rhythm. Left, right, crossover, glide. The knot in my stomach loosened with every stride.

This was why I was here. Not for the degree, not really. Not even for the anonymity, though that mattered. I was here because the ice was the one place I'd ever felt like myself. Before the cameras, before Chet Finlay turned me into a brand, before the Ice Kings franchise made my face into something that belonged to everyone but me—there had been this. Just this. The cold air, the smooth surface, the physics of blade and momentum. On the ice, I wasn't a product or a disappointment or a cautionary tale. I was my movement. My edges, my speed, my choices.

The head coach, a man named Sterling with a face like a worn catcher's mitt, blew a whistle that cut through the murmur of skates and sticks. We converged at the center circle.

"Welcome to Oakridge." His voice was a low gravel that carried without effort. "For the next two hours, you're not freshmen or transfers. You're hockey players. We need skaters who are smart, disciplined, and relentless. We're a defense-first program. If you want to be a hero, you're in the wrong barn. We win games in the corners and in front of our own net."

His gaze swept over us. I kept my eyes forward, my posture neutral—just another hopeful, just another number.

"We're watching everything. How you skate, how you listen, how you finish a drill. Show us you belong here. First up: laps. On the whistle."

The whistle blew, sharp, and we were off.

A test. Not of speed, but of conditioning and control. Forward, backward, crossovers, pivots. My lungs burned, the cold air scraping my throat. I settled into a rhythm, keeping my strides clean and efficient, my upper body still. I wasn't the fastest guy out there. A few of the younger kids shot out like they were spring-loaded, all frantic energy, burning themselves out in the first five minutes. I let them go. I found a pace in the middle of the pack, focused on the skater in front of me, on the clean, rhythmic scrape of my own blades.

Don't stand out. Don't disappear. Just be solid.

After the skating drills came puck handling. Weaving through cones, stickhandling in tight spaces. My hands felt good—too good. The puck snapped to my blade like it was magnetized, responding to the smallest adjustments of my wrists. Muscle memory buried deep, a language I hadn't spoken in years but hadn't forgotten. On one sequence through the cones, I felt my body wanting to add a flourish—a quick toe-drag, a behind-the-back pull—the kind of flashy move of great cinematic closeups. I caught myself, forced my hands to stay simple, and finished the drill clean but unremarkable.

Control what you can control.

I kept my head up, eyes scanning the ice even when there was nothing to see. Habit. Or maybe self-preservation.

Always know where your exits are.

It was during a one-on-one drill that I felt it.

A shift in the air. The low-grade hum of being observed sharpened into a single, focused point. I wrote it off at first. Of course, we were being watched—that was the whole point of a tryout. Coach Sterling and his assistants stood by the boards, clipboards in hand, faces unreadable. A few assistant coaches were scattered in the first rows behind the bench, men in team jackets with stoic expressions.

I was skating back to the line, heart pounding from the drill. I'd made a decent play—didn't score, but I'd protected the puck, maneuvered around the defenseman with a sharp cut to my forehand, and put a hard, low shot on net that the goalie had to scramble for. A good, solid, unremarkable play. The kind of play that kept you employed but didn't get you noticed.

As I came to a stop, I chanced a look up into the stands.

The seats were mostly empty, a sea of dark-blue plastic rising into shadow. But halfway up, right on the center line, a single figure sat alone.

He wasn't wearing a team jacket or holding a clipboard. Just a guy in a gray hoodie, leaning forward with his elbows on his knees, hands steepled in front of his face. The steep angle of the canyon walls made it feel like he was hovering directly above me, a gargoyle perched on a cathedral ledge. Even from this distance, I could feel the weight of his stillness. He wasn't scanning the group. He wasn't watching the drill.

He was watching me.

A cold spike of adrenaline, entirely separate from the athletic burn in my muscles, shot through me. My stomach clenched. Old instincts—ones I'd thought years of therapy and six hundred miles had buried—flared to life. The reflexive cataloging of a face. The assessment of a threat. Is that a camera? A phone? Does he recognize me? How did he find me here?

He was just some student, bored, killing time between classes. Maybe a friend of one of the other players. Nothing to do with me. I was in a helmet, hiding behind a cage.

The whistle blew. Another drill. Three-on-twos, rushing the net. I fell back into the rhythm, my mind screamed at me to focus. Read the play. Find the open man. Backcheck.

My body went through the motions, but a part of my awareness stayed snagged on that figure in the stands. Like skating with a burr in my sock—a constant, irritating point of pressure.

On the rush, I found myself with the puck in the high slot. Open ice ahead. The goalie cheating to his glove side, leaving the five-hole vulnerable. My hands knew what to do—a quick fake, a snap shot low—but my brain screamed don't. Don't make a highlight. Don't give anyone a reason to look twice.

I dumped the puck into the corner and peeled off for a line change.

Sterling blew his whistle. "Water break. Two minutes."

We skated to the bench in a loose cluster. I grabbed a bottle from the rack, tilted my head back, and lifted the bottom of my cage just enough to get the nozzle underneath. The water hit the back of my throat. For those few seconds, the world narrowed to just breath and hydration and the burn in my legs.

I squeezed the bottle, sending a stream of water across my overheated face, then lowered the cage back into place. The grid snapped over my vision—steel bars sectioning the world into manageable pieces.

I tossed the bottle back and pushed off toward center ice.

The scrimmage was the last part of the tryout. Full ice, two teams of cobbled-together hopefuls. I was on the "skins" team, the cold arena air biting through my base layer. I played my game. Kept it simple. Dumped the puck in deep, finished my checks, got back on defense. I focused on being a two-hundred-foot player—pressuring the puck carrier, clogging the passing lanes, backchecking like my roster spot depended on it.

Solid. Dependable. Forgettable.

Maddox slid a pass to me as we crossed the blue line, too hard, too far in front. I stretched, my stick tipping the puck, redirecting it. I chased it down, a defenseman hot on my heels.

I checked my shoulder, mapping the ice in a split second. I saw the defenseman overcommitting to the body hit, eyes on my numbers rather than the puck. Instead of trying to force a play to the net, I saw our third man, Davies, streaking toward the far post. I stopped hard, my edges biting deep to spray up a wall of ice, and feathered a backhand pass—using just the right amount of soft hands to ensure it landed flat on his tape.

He had a wide-open net. He buried it. And I got slammed into the glass.

A good play. A smart play. The kind of play that won teams games. An assist is better than a selfish shot—the words of one of my peewee coaches shot through my memory. I peeled off toward the boards, and despite every cell in my body screaming not to, my eyes flicked up to the stands again.

The guy was still there. Still leaning forward. But now his hands were down, and I could see his face more. He hadn't moved a muscle. Who the hell was he?

Maddox skated past, bumping my shoulder. "You ever gonna shoot the puck, Calloway? Or just donate it?"

"I made the smart play," I said, without glancing at him.

"You dumped it." His voice dripped with condescension. "There's a difference."

He was right. And the fact that he was right—that this cocky college kid could see what I'd done, could see the fear dressed up as strategy—made my skin crawl.

The coach's whistle blew. Over.

A wave of exhaustion so profound it was almost peaceful washed over me. We skated to center ice, gathering around Coach Sterling one last time. My thighs screamed. My lungs felt scraped raw.

"Good work today." Sterling's eyes were dark chips of granite, his expression giving nothing away. "We saw some things we liked. We saw some things we didn't. The roster will be posted outside the locker room tomorrow morning at eight. If your name is on it, practice is at three. If it's not, thank you for coming out."

That was it. No feedback. No encouragement. A clean, brutal cut. I appreciated the efficiency.

We tapped our sticks on the ice in a ragged salute and drifted toward the exit. As I skated off, legs like lead, I couldn't help it.

One last look.

The figure in the gray hoodie was moving. Arms stretched overhead as he stood—taller than I'd thought, lanky, with a mess of dark hair visible even from this distance. No longer watching the ice. Turned toward the exit at the top of the aisle.

A student. Just a student who'd wandered in, watched for a bit, and left when he got bored. I felt a wave of relief so strong it made me lightheaded. I'd built the whole thing up in my head—a phantom from my past projected onto a stranger. The pressure I'd felt wasn't his. It was mine. A ghost I'd brought with me to Oakridge.

I shook my head, disgusted with myself, and stepped off the ice onto the rubber mats, the familiar clomp of my skates grounding me. First the vending-machine kid, now me. Everyone was terrified of their own shadow today.

In the locker room, no one talked much. We were all rivals, but we'd shared something—a two-hour trial by fire. We stripped off our gear in near silence, the only sounds the rip of Velcro and the clatter of equipment being tossed into bags.

I worked methodically, reversing my earlier ritual. Wiping down my blades. Stowing my helmet. The smell of sweat was stronger now, mixed with the damp chill of the ice. I was one of the last to the showers, the hot water a blessed relief on my aching muscles. I stood under the spray for a long time, forehead pressed against the cool tile, letting the water wash away the grime and, I hoped, the lingering paranoia.

By the time I was dressed—jeans, black T-shirt, old Bruins hoodie—the locker room was almost empty. The vending-machine freshman was sitting on a bench, staring at his phone, face pale. I slung my bag over my shoulder.

"Calloway, right?" His voice was quiet.

"Yeah."

"Jayceon Davies." He extended his hand. I gripped it and immediately regretted it—the guy's grip could pulverize concrete. He seemed oblivious to his own strength. "You played well. That pass on the three-on-two was sick."

"You finished it. That's the part that matters."

He offered a small, grateful smile. "Hope I see you tomorrow, man."

"You too." I meant it.

I pushed through the door and walked out into the main corridor of the arena. Empty now, the lights dimmed to a pale amber glow. My footsteps echoed off the concrete. My beat-up hockey bag felt like it weighed a thousand pounds. All I wanted was my apartment, a microwaved burrito, and twelve hours of sleep. The anxiety from the tryout had been replaced by a deep, physical weariness that was almost peaceful.

I'd done it. I'd survived.

I rounded the corner toward the main exit, already thinking about the walk across the quad, the chilly January air, my empty apartment waiting with its blank walls and careful absence of anything personal—

And stopped dead.

Leaning against the wall, right beside the doors, was the guy from the stands.

My relief evaporated. The exhaustion vanished, replaced by a sharp, cold clarity. He was waiting. He'd come down from the stands, found the exit, and positioned himself where I'd have to pass.

Up close, he was all sharp angles and deliberate presence. Tall—maybe six feet—and lean in the way of runners or dancers, people who used their bodies as instruments. The gray hoodie read OAKRIDGE THEATRE in faded letters across the chest. His hair was a chaotic mess of wavy black. His face was the kind you'd call interesting before you'd call it handsome—strong nose, defined jaw, dark eyes that caught the dim light and held it.

Those eyes were fixed on me. Had been fixed on me since I'd stepped into the corridor.

He pushed off the wall. A slow, deliberate movement. Controlled. The way an actor moves when they want you to watch them move.

"Seventy-three." His voice was a low tenor. "I was wondering when you'd be done."

Chapter 2
The Character Study

Elliot

"Hold it! Elliot, stop. Just . . . stop."

The voice of Professor Andrew Albright, sharp and weary, echoed through the empty Black Box Theatre, cutting through the heavy silence of the room. I stood in the center of the stage, my skates—the ones the department had spent fifty dollars on at a thrift store—clunking awkwardly against the reinforced plywood floor. I was supposed to be portraying a man who lived on the ice, but right now, I felt like a newborn giraffe on stilts.

"You're doing it again," Albright said, stepping out of the shadows of his makeshift desk in the third row of the theatre. He was a compact man in his fifties, all sharp edges and a sharper tongue, with a gray beard he stroked when he was thinking and tugged when he was frustrated. Right now, he was tugging. "You're acting like a person who thinks they know how a hockey player behaves. You're giving me . . . cliché. The heavy shoulders, the Neanderthal brow, the choreographed aggression."

Behind me, I heard Lucas Reed shift his weight. He was playing Tyler Mitchell—my scene partner, my character's secret, my dramatic foil. Lucas had the physicality down cold. He'd played lacrosse in high school, wrestled in college, and moved through the world like someone who'd never once questioned whether his body belonged in a space. When he put on the hockey pads, he looked like he'd been born in them. When I put them on, I was a kid playing dress-up in his father's closet.

"I'm trying." I let out a frustrated breath, the sound loud in the cavernous space. "I'm already off-book. I spent my entire break watching hockey on YouTube."

"The script is words on a page, Elliot. Acting is what happens between the words." Albright walked closer, his eyes—too observant, always—searching mine. "This character, Diego Santos, is carrying a secret that could destroy his family's legacy. He doesn't move like a brute. He moves like a man who is constantly bracing for an impact that never comes. There's a coiled energy there. An economy of movement. A profound, terrifying stillness."

He gestured to my feet. "You're just stomping. A hockey player doesn't stomp. They glide. Even when they aren't on the ice, their center of gravity is different. They own the space without trying to crush it."

"Show him the thing," Lucas said from behind me, his voice carrying the easy confidence of someone who'd already figured out his character. "The thing you showed me."

Albright nodded and walked to center stage. Without warning, he dropped into a slight crouch, knees bent, weight forward on the balls of his feet. He didn't move, but somehow his whole body communicated readiness—a coiled spring waiting to release. Then he took three steps, and even without skates, even on the dusty plywood, he glided.

"I played in college," Albright said, straightening. "Division III, nothing special. But the body remembers. Diego Santos has been on skates since he was four years old. That's not something you can fake with YouTube clips and good intentions."

"I don't know how to do that," I admitted. The honesty tasted like copper in my mouth. "Before this play, I'd never even seen hockey." I thought about it for a second and added, "Well, not real hockey. I've seen Hollywood hockey. You know The Mighty Ducks, Ice Kings, Go Figure, MVP . . . You know, Disney hockey!"

It was the understatement of the century. I was not naturally athletic. Sure, I had great genes and a workout regimen that kept my cheekbones sharp, but I've never played a sport in my life.

"Then go watch real hockey," Albright said. "I read in The Oakridge Observer this morning that the campus hockey team is holding walk-on tryouts this afternoon. Go sit in the stands. Don't take notes. Don't seek 'motivation.' Just watch. Find one person. Not the best one, not the star. Find the one who is trying to disappear. Figure out why he can't."

I started to protest—I had a shift at the Brewed Awakening, the campus coffee shop; I had lines to memorize; I had a reaction paper due for my media studies seminar—but Albright held up a hand.

"This role matters, Elliot. You know that."

I knew that. The Penalty Box was the department's prestige production this semester, the one that would bring in reviewers from San Francisco and talent scouts from the regional theatre circuit. Diego Santos was one of the leads—the terrified one, the one who couldn't stop hiding, the one whose need to remain invisible ultimately forces a reckoning when Tyler refuses to disappear. It was so the exact opposite of who I am as a person. I was obnoxiously out loud and proud. I was a theatre major. But the role could define a career. Or end one before it started.

The department had taken a chance casting me. I knew what they said about me in the green room, in the hallways, in the careful silences when I walked into a room: Elliot Vega is talented, but he's too much. Too intense. Too hungry. Too desperate for attention. In a program full of people clawing for attention, I was apparently the one who clawed too hard.

But being too much was better than the alternative. The worst fate wasn't failure—it was being forgettable. Being the actor whose name no one remembered, whose face blurred into all the other faces, who graduated and disappeared into community theatre and dinner shows and the long, slow fade into nobody.

I would not be nobody.

"I'll go," I said.

Lucas clapped me on the shoulder as I gathered my things. "Find someone good," he said. "Someone who moves like they've got something to lose. That's the secret, man. It's not about the muscles. It's about the weight."

"Before you all take off," Dr. Albright said from his table, "The PolyGlide flooring should be in next week. We will have ice skating calls then. I know you all have some skating experience, but they say skating on PolyGlide is a bit different."

The way he said "all" seemed more like a personal attack. Sure, I'd lied during auditions and told them that I had skated as a kid. Thankfully, they hadn't tested that lie. I spent most of my winter break learning lines and seeing how many bruises I could rack up on my body. But at least now, I didn't look like a complete idiot, just mostly.

I left the theatre with my messenger bag slung over my shoulder. Oakridge Falls in January was a study in grays and blues, the air smelling of pine needles and the damp salt blowing in from the coast. I cut across the quad, my footsteps the only rhythm on the concrete, and headed toward the arena.

I'd never stepped foot in the place. I knew we had a hockey team, but it just didn't seem to be my scene. I know there are people who love sports. People who yell at their televisions and root for the home team. About the only time I rooted for anyone on television was during the Tony's. Even then, it's not like I thought I won an award when a show I liked took home best play. I just didn't get the whole fandom climate thing.

When I walked in the main doors, no one was there to greet me, so I followed the sound of voices and entered onto the mid-tier area. Below me, there were about ten rows of seats before the ice. I turned and climbed.

The Oakridge Arena had some pretty steep seating. I climbed halfway up to Section 112, Row M, Seat 8—dead center, staring down at the white expanse of the rink. By the time I chose a seat I felt like an Olympian observing the Grecian people from my place in the sky. I hovered over the players. I guess this ensures there's no bad seat in the house.

Below me, guys skated around on the ice. Some of them were clearly part of the team already, they had the requisite orange and blue jersey of the Oakridge Ospreys. I did look it up, it means "bird of prey" in Latin. Some original naming on someone's part there. The other guys on the ice were a mess of mismatched jerseys and equipment. I slung my arms over the seats on either side of me and stared down from on high. I kind of wish I had my opera glasses. No one was nearly as clumsy as me on the ice, which I guess should be expected. I mean, I'm more of a lounge at the beach kind of guy.

A kid in a too-new jersey cut straight across the middle, nearly clipping another skater, yelling "Here! Here!" like someone was actually going to pass to him. Two others raced side-by-side along the wall, elbows out, their skates carving loud, angry lines as they tried to get ahead of each other. Someone dropped a pass and slammed his stick on the ice—the crack echoed all the way up to my seat. Another guy tried some kind of spinning move near one of the blue lines, lost control of the puck, and had to scramble after it while a coach on the bench scribbled something on a clipboard. The whole thing was exhausting. Like watching people audition for a role they were pretty sure they wouldn't get.

And then I saw him.

Random guy in all black. He looked like a villain right out of a hockey movie—he might as well have been wearing a black cowboy hat. No branding, no flashy colors, no "look at me" gear. He was a shadow moving across the ice. But while the other kids were fighting the surface, he was part of it. There was a fluidity to his movement that made everyone else look like they were skating on gravel.

He wasn't trying to stick out. When the coach blew his whistle and the players started skating in circles, the guy in black didn't shoot out to the front; he just hung in the middle. He was trying to be invisible.

Find the one who looks like he's trying to disappear.

I leaned forward, elbows on knees, hands steepled in front of my face. The script stayed in my bag. Pure observation. The guy in black held his stick like it weighed nothing, like it was just another part of his body. Every time he passed one of those painted lines on the ice, his head turned—just a quick glance—like he was checking the exits in a theatre before the lights went down. He moved like someone who'd spent a long time learning how to be exactly where he needed to be without anyone noticing he'd gotten there.

But there was something else. A tension in the line of his shoulders. Every time he made a play, he shrank immediately afterward, trying to pull the light back into himself. Other guys became all macho and "look at me" when they did anything even slightly impressive on the ice. This guy was doing a job.

The coach blew his whistle. Water break. The players skated to the bench in a loose cluster. The man in black grabbed a bottle from the rack, tilted his head back, and lifted the bottom of his cage just enough to get the nozzle underneath.

And there it was.

The angle of his jaw. The slope of his nose. The exact architecture of a face I'd seen dozens of times in freezeframes and screenshots; not to mention my dreams. Hell, the face that had hovered over my bed throughout middle school, torn from a magazine and taped to the ceiling where I could stare into his eyes every night before I fell asleep.

Older now. Sharper. Stripped of the soft edges and manufactured innocence of adolescence. But unmistakable. You don't spend years memorizing every millimeter of your first crush's face and then fail to recognize it in the flesh.

He squeezed the bottle, sending a stream of water across his face, then lowered the cage back into place. The grid snapped down. He tossed the bottle back and pushed off toward center ice.

I sat perfectly still, my pulse a steady drumbeat against my ribs.

Chase St. Clair. The "Ice Prince." The star of a franchise that had made him a household name at fifteen and then, apparently, spit him out. I'd watched the press junket footage a hundred times—the moment he'd refused to say the catchphrase, the way his jaw had clenched, the light dying in his eyes. The picture that surfaced of him kissing a costar in a hot tub. I'd read the fan theories, the speculation, the digital eulogies from people who'd built shrines to a boy who'd simply . . . vanished. I thought he was dead. Well, that was one of the internet theories.

Yet, there he was. Skating at a walk-on tryout in a nowhere college town, wearing black gear and trying to disappear.

I spent the rest of the audition cataloging details. The way he moved. The way he shrank from attention. The careful, deliberate anonymity of his gear. Every choice he made on the ice confirmed what I was seeing: a man in hiding. A man who had once burned so bright he'd been visible from space, now desperately trying to dim himself into darkness.

Figure out why he can't.

As soon as the final whistle blew, I didn't head for the exit. I went to the lobby, found a bench tucked behind a vending machine, and pulled out my phone.

The search was simple: Chase St. Clair hockey.

The results loaded. A Wikipedia page, long abandoned. Fan sites frozen in time. YouTube clips with comment sections full of digital ghosts asking where he went. Ice Kings 1, 2, & 3. A franchise that had made him a household name at fifteen. Then nothing. He fell off the planet at eighteen years old. A gap of five years. No interviews. No social media. No public appearances.

Just silence.

I scrolled through the image results. Publicity stills. Red carpet photos. A kid with perfect teeth and camera-ready charm, wearing gear that probably cost more than my entire tuition. The smile was different then. The man I'd just watched on the ice hadn't smiled at all.

I glanced up from my phone, toward the corridor that led to the locker rooms. Chase St. Clair was here. At Oakridge. Hiding in plain sight.

The question wasn't who he was. The question was why.

I pocketed my phone and headed for the main exit. The corridor was empty now, the lights dimmed to that institutional amber glow. I found a spot right beside the doors and leaned against the wall.

And waited.

I looked down at my watch. A couple of guys I recognized from their auditions walked past me. I knew locker-room stuff would take time. Showers, the post-audition rituals, the slow process of convincing yourself you'd done enough. I had patience. I'd spent three hours in a theatre practicing the weight distribution of a single step. I could wait.

My mind was already racing ahead, building the architecture of an approach. Why was he here? Why did he audition for hockey at a small university in upstate California? He was hiding from something—that much was obvious. Maybe he was hiding from the mob? The anonymity, the restraint, the way he'd flinched every time his skill threatened to shine through. He wasn't just playing small; he was performing smallness, constructing a character called "nobody special" and wearing it like armor. Maybe he was researching a role? A comeback?

I knew something about that. About the exhausting work of being someone you're not. About the terror of being seen for who you really are.

The difference was, I wanted to be seen. I craved it like oxygen. And he was suffocating himself to avoid it.

Footsteps echoed down the hallway. He rounded the corner—jeans, black T-shirt, old hockey team hoodie. His beat-up bag slung over his shoulder. Hair still damp from the shower. Shoulders slouched. A slowness to him after hitting the ice hard.

Then he saw me. I smiled and watched as a mask slammed down. His face went blank—a beautiful piece of stagecraft, deliberate and practiced and utterly hollow. I recognized it because I'd done it myself, a thousand times, when the world got too close.

I pushed off the wall. Slow. Deliberate. Let him clock me—the theatre sweatshirt, the messy hair, the lack of athletic bulk. Let him understand I wasn't a scout or another player. Let him realize I was something else entirely.

"Seventy-three." Using his old hockey jersey name from the Ice Kings series. My voice carried in the empty hallway, pitched to fill the space. A performer's voice. "I was wondering when you'd be done."

His hand tightened on the strap of his bag.

"Do I know you?" Clipped. Harsh.

I smiled. "No." I took a step closer, claiming the space between us. "But I know you."

I let the pause stretch. Watched his eyes flicker—calculation, fear, the desperate hope that he was wrong about what was coming.

"Chase." I said it soft, almost tender. Then, with the precision of a blade: "St. Clair."

The name landed like a body check. I watched the ripple effect—the whitening of his knuckles, the hitch in his breathing, the way his whole body braced for impact.

"I think," I said, trying to be as nice and inviting as possible since he looked like a bear who'd been backed into a corner, "we should talk."

"I don't know what you're talking about," he said. The lie was flat, uninspired. "My name's Calloway."

"Come now." I leaned against the wall, projecting casual interest. "I think you do. Everyone under a certain age saw Ice Kings 1, 2, & 3. Then you just . . . disappeared. And now here you are, in the flesh. Smaller than I expected. Less shiny."

"I'm not who you think I am."

He pushed past me, shoulder brushing mine. The contact sent a small electric shock through my skin.

"Let me buy you a coffee," I called after him. "Or a beer. We could talk about what you're running from."

"No."

The word was final. He turned and walked away, his footsteps a percussive rhythm against the concrete. I watched him go—the set of his shoulders straightened, the pace fast. He didn't glance over his shoulder at me, but I'm sure he wanted to. I mean, how could you not want to stare back at me?

Chapter 3
The Fortress

Rowan

I walked. That was the only thing I could do. Out the double doors, into the January evening, my footsteps a flat, percussive rhythm against the concrete of the arena parking lot. The weight of my gear bag, which usually felt like a grounding anchor, was now just dead.

I reached my car—a beat-up SUV that didn't scream "Hollywood royalties"—and fumbled with the keys. I threw the bag into the back, the clatter of my sticks against the trunk liner sounding like a gunshot in the quiet lot. I scrambled into the driver's seat and slammed the door, locking it instantly.

The silence of the car was worse than the hallway. In the hallway, I'd used my old paparazzi script—deny, deflect, disappear. Here, in the dark, I was just a twenty-three-year-old whose worst nightmare had called him by his dead name.

Chase St. Clair.

The name echoed louder than my own heartbeat. Five years since anyone had seen the "Ice Prince" when we met. Five years of scrubbing my digital footprint, using my real name as a shield, avoiding anyone who might have seen a movie poster in the twenty-teens. And now, a guy in a theatre sweatshirt—a guy who didn't even look like he could tie a pair of skates—sent me running like a kid with my head between my legs after getting scolded.

I leaned my forehead against the steering wheel, the plastic cool against my overheated skin. I couldn't breathe. The air in the car felt recycled, thin, insufficient. My vision tunneled, the dashboard lights blurring into staccato flashes of paparazzi bulbs. My chest was a fist clenching around my lungs.

Fucking panic attack! I'd dealt with these before. The words of my old therapist ran through my head. Deep breaths. Control what you can control.

I gripped the steering wheel until my knuckles turned white. Counted the beats of my heart. One, two, three, four. The roaring in my ears faded to a dull static. It was just one guy. One student. One person in a town of thousands who happened to have a memory for mid-tier Disney franchises.

When I finally saw out the SUV's windshield without having double-vision, I started the engine. The vibration of the car helped settle the static in my nerves.

My apartment was a fifteen-minute drive from campus, on the second floor of a converted Victorian that had been chopped into student housing sometime in the seventies. I climbed the stairs on autopilot, my body moving through space while my mind replayed the hallway confrontation in an endless loop. But I know you. Chase. St. Clair.

I unlocked the door and stepped inside. The motion-sensor light flickered on, illuminating the carefully curated emptiness of my life.

The apartment was clean. Not just tidy—sterile. A futon against one wall, covered in a plain gray blanket. A desk with a laptop and a single lamp. A kitchenette with exactly four plates, four glasses, four sets of silverware. No posters. No photographs. No evidence that a human being with a history actually lived here. There were no remnants of my life.

I dropped my gear bag by the door and went to the bathroom. Splashed freezing water on my face. Gripped the edges of the sink and forced myself to look in the mirror.

The face that stared back wasn't the one from the cereal boxes. That kid had been soft, camera ready, manufactured to sell something. This face was sharper. More guarded. The jaw had lost its adolescent roundness—the baby fat a distant memory. My eyes had lost their mischievous spark of innocence giving way to learned nothing. I looked like a journalism student trying to finish a degree. I looked like a carefully cultivated nobody.

But theatre kid had seen through it in seconds.

"It's just a fluke," I whispered to my reflection. "He's a theatre major. He probably watched the movie a dozen times as a kid."

The words sounded hollow even in the empty bathroom.

I headed back into the living room. The air in my room was still, but the moment I unzipped the heavy nylon of my bag, the scent of the rink—sour sweat and damp leather—spilled out to claim the space. I moved toward the corner, where the makeshift drying rack I'd thrown together using PVC pipe from a local hardware store stood like a skeletal sentry against the wall. I laid out my gear to ensure it wouldn't mold.

When I finished, I pulled out my phone—a prepaid smartphone with no social media apps, no cloud backup, no connection to anything that could be traced. My contacts list had exactly six entries: my parents, my landlord, the campus shuttle service, a pizza place that delivered, and the number for the university health center. No friends. No history. No digital footprint. No messages.

I sat down at my makeshift desk and opened the laptop browser and typed: Theatre Department Oakridge University.

The results loaded instantly. A quick search confirmed what I'd suspected—Elliot Vega was everywhere online, performing visibility the way I performed invisibility. He was my opposite in every way.

Chet Finlay's voice, smooth as snake oil, slithered through my memory. "You're not a person, Chase. You're a brand." My former agent, with his five-thousand-dollar suits and perfect teeth. Back then he had owned every piece of me. I didn't blink if it wasn't on cue. I could still see his face in that hotel conference room, the day after I'd refused to say the catchphrase on camera. "You think you get to have feelings? You think you get to decide when you're done? You cost us two million dollars in promotional tie-ins. You're going to fix this, or I'm going to make sure you never work in this industry again."

I hadn't fixed it. I'd grabbed my bag and my royalty checks and run.

But I was so tired of running.

I opened a new browser and logged into my bank account—not the main one, which held my meager student budget, but the other one. The royalty account. The money still trickled in from streaming residuals and overseas syndication of the Ice Kings franchise.

The balance was modest now—nothing like the seven-figure paydays of my teenage years—but it was enough. Enough to pay rent. Enough to pay tuition. Enough for the recurring monthly transfer that appeared on every statement:

HENDERSON FAMILY TRUST—$500.00—AUTOMATIC PAYMENT

The transfer had gone out two days ago, right on schedule. Anonymous. Untraceable. The Hendersons had no idea who was sending the money, and I intended to keep it that way.

I closed the laptop.

Outside, the January wind rattled the old Victorian windows. The apartment was quiet, empty. A fortress designed to keep the world out.

I could run. I could be in Nevada by sunrise, Oregon by noon. I could start over again, find another college or university, another anonymous life, another place where no one knew my name.

I couldn't give up hockey. Not again. Not because some theatre kid with good cheekbones had recognized my face.

Let the game save me.

It was the same thought I'd had when I'd first laced up my skates at a public rink in Lake Tahoe, two years into my exile. The game had saved me then—given me something to work toward, something that existed outside the wreckage of my former life. Maybe it could save me again.

Control what you can control.

I couldn't control whether Elliot told anyone. I couldn't control whether he'd already posted something online, already shared his discovery with his theatre friends, already started the chain of exposure that would end with my face on gossip blogs and my inbox full of interview requests.

But I could control whether I showed up to practice tomorrow. I could control how I played. I could control whether I let some stranger's knowledge of my past dictate my future.

Maybe it would be okay. Maybe he'd gotten what he wanted—the thrill of recognition, the power of knowing something no one else knew—and that would be enough. Maybe he'd keep it to himself.

I didn't believe it. People like Elliot Vega didn't keep secrets; they relished them. I was an actor. I grew up around drama queens of a much higher caliber than Mr. Vega could hope to be.

My stomach grumbled. "I should eat something," I said to the emptiness. I dragged myself away from the laptop and opened the fridge. I had two slices of pizza sitting in a box that were a bit drier than they should be after a few days, but it was food. I ate the cheese-covered cardboard—the pizza, not the box—and pulled up an old game on the NHL Network.

Chapter 4
The Final Roster Call

Rowan

The first hint of gray light appeared at the edge of my apartment window. Six-fifteen. I'd been staring at the ceiling since four, watching the shadows shift and lengthen, my mind running the same loop it had been running all night: What if your name isn't there? What if it is?

The bulletin board was outside the main locker room door—I'd scouted it yesterday, so I knew exactly where the roster would be posted. But as I approached, I heard voices drifting from down the hall around the corner. The door was cracked open, spilling a wedge of fluorescent light into the dim hallway.

I should have kept walking. Should have found the board, checked my fate, and left. Instead, I stopped. Coach Sterling's low gravel, and a woman's voice I recognized from the tryout. Coach Okafor, the assistant coach. She'd been running the skating drills, clipboard in hand, expression as unreadable as Sterling's.

"—completely changes the lineup," Okafor was saying. "Taylor's out for the season. Compound fracture. What the hell was he thinking, cliff jumping in January?"

"He wasn't thinking." Sterling's voice was flat, disgusted. "That's the problem. Senior year, starting position locked, and he decides to show off for some girl at the beach. Kid's lucky he didn't break his neck."

"So, we're down two now. Taylor and Rodriguez," Okafor said. Papers rustled. "That's half our Aline. The depth we built all fall—"

"Is gone. I know." Even from the hall, I heard Sterling's long exhale. "We promote Bline to A. Maddox is going to throw a tantrum. C and D lines just aren't ready for B, so that forces the new Bline with the walk-ons."

"Maddox's going to lose his mind."

"He's going to do his job." Sterling's tone left no room for argument. "He's captain. He wants to lead, he can lead from wherever I put him. Besides—" Another pause. "The walk-ons we picked up might surprise him."

"Davies?" Okafor sounded skeptical. "He's raw. Talented, but raw."

"If I'd known Jayceon Davies was on this campus, I would've been recruiting him from day one. Kid was all-state in high school. Led his team to the state championship his junior year." Sterling made a sound that might have been a laugh. "Problem is he doesn't know how good he is. Doesn't trust it yet. You saw him in the tryout—hesitates before every shot, second-guesses every pass. But give him a few weeks, let him settle in, and that kid's going to be something special. Big thing is going to be keeping Maddox out of his head. I'm going to need you watching that "

"What about the other one? Calloway?"

My breath caught. I pressed myself against the wall, heart suddenly hammering.

Sterling was quiet for a long moment. When he spoke again, his voice was different. Careful.

"I know what that kid is capable of."

"That sounds ominous."

"It's not." Another exhale—heavier this time, weighted with something I couldn't name. "I don't know why he's here. Don't know why he's playing DIII hockey when he could be . . . somewhere else. And frankly, I don't care. The kid can play. You saw him out there—he's got hands, vision, hockey IQ that you can't teach. As long as his past doesn't cause problems for the team, he's worth taking a shot on."

"His past?" Okafor's voice sharpened. "What past? His transcript was clean—"

"There was an incident. Few years back. On the ice." Sterling's chair creaked. "The media blamed him for it, but anyone who actually watched the footage knew it was a fluke. Accidents happen in hockey. That's why we're out there in pads and helmets. It's a dangerous sport."

The silence stretched. I stood frozen in the hallway, my pulse roaring in my ears.

He knows. Sterling knows about Henderson.

"The kid carried that weight for a long time," Sterling continued quietly. "Maybe still does. But that's not my business. My business is putting the best players on the ice, and Calloway—" He paused. "Calloway's the real deal. Whatever else is going on with him, that much I'm certain of."

"So, we're taking a gamble."

"We're taking two gambles. Davies and Calloway. But they're good gambles." Papers shuffled again. "Alright. Davies at center, Calloway at left wing, Maddox at right wing. That's our new Bline. Chen moves up to Aline with Kowalski and Park."

"And when Maddox throws a fit about being demoted?"

"Then I'll remind him that captains lead by example, not by privilege." Sterling's chair scraped back. "Come on. Let's get the roster posted before the whole team shows up and starts a riot."

I moved before I could think, sliding back down the corridor as quietly as I could manage. Sterling knew—not everything, but enough.

The media blamed him, but anyone who watched the footage knew.

I'd spent five years convinced the hockey world saw me as a monster. Convinced that anyone who learned the truth would judge me the same way the tabloids had. Sterling knew. And he'd still put me on the team.

I found the bulletin board and stopped, staring at the empty cork surface. I leaned against the opposite wall and waited.

I wasn't alone for long.

Heavy footsteps echoed down the corridor—heavy, slightly uneven, the gait of someone who hadn't slept. Davies appeared around the corner, his young face pale and drawn, dark circles carved under his eyes. He looked up as he approached, surprise flickering across his features when he saw me.

"Calloway, right?" His voice was a hoarse whisper. "You're here early."

"Yep, and Davies?" He nodded. "Couldn't sleep."

"Yeah." He rubbed the back of his neck, a nervous gesture. "Same. I tried to make myself stay in bed until seven, but I just kept staring at the ceiling. Figured I might as well know."

I understood that completely. "Same."

We stood there for a moment, a silent, two-man vigil.

"So," Davies said, his leg bouncing with nervous energy. "What do you think our chances are?"

"I think we've got a shot," I said.

Before he could respond, footsteps echoed from the direction of the coaches' office. We both straightened, shoulders tensing. Amarachi Okafor appeared around the corner, a single sheet of white paper in her hand. She gave us a brief nod—neither encouraging nor discouraging—and walked to the bulletin board.

The paper went up with a single pushpin. Clean. Final.

She turned and walked away without a word.

Davies and I glance at each other. His face had gone pale again, his Adam's apple bobbing as he swallowed.

"You first," he said. "Your name comes before mine."

He was right. C before D.

I took a step toward the board, then another, until I was close enough to read the clean, black sans-serif font. Official. Final. Each entry had a name, a position, and a number.

I scanned past the As, the Bs. My eyes found the Cs.

CALLOWAY, ROWAN—LW—#28

There it was. Calloway. And a new number—not seventy-three, my fake jersey number from the movies, but twenty-eight. A real roster number. A real identity.

"Well?" Davies's voice cracked behind me.

I stepped aside, and he surged forward. His head moved down the page. One second. Two. Then his whole body seemed to deflate, a ragged sigh escaping his lips.

"Shit," he breathed.

My stomach dropped. After everything Sterling had said—

But then Davies turned, and his face was split by a grin so wide it had to hurt—pure, unadulterated joy.

"Holy shit," he said. "I'm on it. Davies, Jayceon. Center. And—" He pointed at the paper, his finger trembling. "We're on the same line. You, me, and Maddox."

I looked where he was pointing. Under the BLINE header:

CALLOWAY, ROWAN—LW—#28 DAVIES, JAYCEON—C—#41MADDOX, REECE—RW—#7

The three of us. The team captain who'd dismissed me as nobody, the nervous freshman who didn't know how good he was, and me—the ghost trying to become a real person.

"Maddox is going to hate this," Davies said, but he was still grinning. "He was on Aline all last season."

"He'll deal with it," I said.

Davies laughed—a bright, surprised sound. "Man, I hope so. Otherwise, this is going to be a really awkward semester."

We stood there for another moment, both of us staring at the roster like it might disappear if we turned our eyes from it. Two walk-ons who'd somehow made the team.

Two guys who had no business being here, who'd been counted out before they'd even laced up their skates.

Davies extended his hand. "Guess we're linemates now."

I took it. His grip was still too strong, but this time I didn't mind.

"Guess we are."

A wave of relief so powerful it left me dizzy crashed over me. I felt the tension drain out of my body, leaving me weightless. I put a hand on the cold cement wall to steady myself. The sound of my own breathing was loud in my ears.

"We did it," Davies whispered, awestruck. "Holy shit, Calloway, we actually did it."

I could only nod, the words stuck in my throat. Two walk-ons who'd survived.

"Practice at three," Davies said, practically vibrating. "You got any classes before then?"

"One. My journalism seminar." The thought of sitting through two hours of lecture when my body was humming with adrenaline seemed impossible. "You?"

"Nothing until two. I'm gonna go call my mom. She's been up all night waiting." He grinned again, that infectious, puppyish joy. "See you at three, man. We're teammates now."

Teammates. The word should have felt good. Instead, it landed with a weight I hadn't anticipated. Teammates meant team photos. Team rosters on the athletic department website. Game footage that could end up on streaming platforms, shared on social media, searchable by anyone with a keyboard and a memory for faces.

Davies clapped me on the shoulder—hard enough to rattle my teeth—and took off down the corridor, his footsteps echoing with barely contained excitement. I watched him go, trying to hold onto his joy, to let it infect me.

It didn't work.

I turned back to the roster, and that's when I saw him.

Maddox was standing at the far end of the corridor, just outside the weight room door, already dressed in his team-issued workout gear. Arms crossed over his chest. Watching.

Our eyes met. He held my gaze for a long moment—five seconds, ten, long enough to become uncomfortable. There was no welcome in his expression. No did you make the cut? Just a flat, challenging assessment, the same look he'd given me during tryouts when I'd dumped the puck instead of taking the shot.

He walked toward me, his footsteps measured and deliberate. Stopped about three feet away, close enough that I had to look up slightly to meet his eyes.

"Calloway." His voice was neutral, but his posture wasn't. "Did you make the roster?"

"Yep."

"I've seen a lot of walk-ons come through here," he said. "Most of them wash out by week three. They can't handle the pace, or they can't handle being at the bottom of the depth chart, or they just decide it's not worth the work." He tilted his head slightly, studying me.

He glanced at the roster—a dismissive flick of the eyes, someone checking a formality. Then, his gaze stopped. Held.

I watched his expression change. The cool superiority flickered, replaced by something sharper. His eyes moved up to the Aline. Chen. Kowalski. Park. No Maddox. Then down to Bline, where his name sat sandwiched between mine and Davies's.

The silence stretched for three long seconds.

"What the hell is this?" His voice had lost its casual authority. He stepped closer to the board, scanning it again like the letters might rearrange themselves into something more acceptable.

I stayed where I was, keeping my expression carefully neutral. But something warm unfurled in my chest—a petty satisfaction I wasn't proud of but couldn't quite suppress. This was the guy who'd seen my garage-sale gear and decided I was nobody. Who'd asked if I was going to shoot the puck or just donate it.

"Bline," Maddox said flatly. "They put me on Bline."

"Taylor's out," I offered. "Broken leg."

His head snapped toward me. "How do you know that?"

I shrugged. "Word gets around."

Maddox turned back to the roster, his jaw tight. I could practically see him doing the math—the Aline he'd anchored all last season, now belonging to other players. His captaincy unchanged, but his position on the depth chart decidedly down.

"This is bullshit," he muttered. "I'm team captain. I should be—" He stopped himself, but not before the words hung in the air between us.

"Should be what?" I asked mildly. "Above playing with walk-ons?"

His eyes cut to me, sharp and dangerous. For a moment, I thought I'd pushed too far. But I'd spent five years being ignored. And here was this kid—younger than me, with his pristine team-issued gear and his guaranteed roster spot—acting like sharing a line with me was some kind of insult.

"He wants to lead," Sterling had said. "He can lead from wherever I put him."

"Sterling put us together for a reason," I said, keeping my voice even. "Guess we'll find out what it is."

Maddox stared at me for a long beat. The anger was still there, simmering just below the surface, but something else flickered across his face. That same reassessment I'd seen at tryouts when I'd made the pass to Davies instead of taking the selfish shot.

"Practice is at three," he said finally, his voice clipped. "Don't be late. And don't think making the list means you've made the team." He jabbed a finger at the roster. "You've got a number now. Doesn't mean you've earned it."

He held my gaze for another beat, then gave me a curt nod and walked past me toward the weight room. The door swung shut behind him with a heavy clunk.

Chapter 5
First Practice

Rowan

The locker room at two forty-five was a different animal than it had been during tryouts. Then, it had been a holding pen for strangers—nervous walk-ons and skeptical evaluators, everyone sizing each other up. Now, it was a living thing, pulsing with music and movement and the particular energy of a team preparing for work. A dozen conversations overlapped, punctuated by the crack of tape being torn and the clatter of gear being assembled.

My stall was in the corner. I'd checked the assignment sheet on my way in—CALLOWAY #28, third from the end, sandwiched between a defenseman named Kowalski and an empty stall that still had someone else's name tape peeling off the wood. The corner was good. Less visible. Easier to observe without being observed.

I fell into the ritual—skates first, then base layers, then pads.

Control what you can control.

The hierarchy was visible if you knew how to read it. Maddox held court near the center of the room, surrounded by three or four other players who laughed too loud at his jokes and deferred when he spoke. The old guard. The core.

The rest of the room arranged itself around them in concentric circles of status. I was somewhere outside all of it—a corner stall next to a guy who hadn't introduced himself.

That guy—Kowalski, according to the nameplate—glanced over as I pulled on my base layer. He was built like a fire hydrant, all shoulders and no neck, with a face that had stopped a few too many pucks over the years.

"You're the new guy," he said. It wasn't a question. "Calloway."

"Yeah."

"Tommy Kowalski. D-man. Third-line." He extended a meaty hand and I shook it, bracing for the same bone-crushing grip Davies had subjected me to. But Kowalski's handshake was surprisingly gentle. "Don't take it personal if nobody talks to you for the first couple weeks. Walk-ons have to prove themselves before we invest."

"Makes sense."

He grunted, apparently satisfied with my lack of offense, and went back to taping his stick. I filed him away—Kowalski, defensive, practical, not hostile—and continued getting dressed.

Across the room, Davies caught my eye and raised a hand in a nervous wave. He was sitting between two other freshmen, both of whom were deer in headlights. I nodded back, a small acknowledgment. His face relaxed slightly, like seeing a familiar face had released some pressure valve.

"Listen up!"

The voice came from near the center of the room. I looked up to find Maddox staring at me directly as he talked. "Coach wants us on the ice in ten. Don't be late." He held my gaze for a beat, then turned back to his conversation without waiting for a response.

I finished dressing in silence, letting the sounds of the locker room wash over me. The bass thump of the music. The rip of tape. The overlapping conversations about classes and girlfriends and last night's NBA game.

I pulled on my helmet, fastened the cage, and felt the world snap into that familiar grid.

Practice ran the same drills as tryouts—laps, stickhandling, board battles—but now I was one body among twenty in matching navy and orange. After fifteen minutes, Sterling blew the whistle and waved us toward the far end for passing drills.

This was where it got dangerous.

We lined up in two columns, partners facing each other across thirty feet of ice. Simple drill: pass, receive, pass, receive. Focus on tape-to-tape accuracy, on soft hands, on the rhythm of give and take.

I was paired with Chen from Aline, compact and quick with a decent first step. He fired a pass at me—harder than necessary, probably testing the new guy—and I caught it without thinking. The puck landed on my tape like it was magnetized, my hands adjusting automatically to absorb the impact and redirect the energy into a return pass.

Too clean. Too smooth. The kind of reception that came from ten thousand hours of practice, from private coaches and elite camps and the relentless polishing of a skill until it became instinct.

I fumbled the next one deliberately. Let the puck skip off my blade and chase it down with an apologetic grimace. Chen smirked, apparently satisfied that the new walk-on wasn't some hidden prodigy.

But I caught Sterling watching me from across the ice, his expression thoughtful. He knows I blew that on purpose.

The drills continued. Breakout patterns, zone entries, cycle plays. I moved through them on autopilot, constantly calculating the balance between competence and excellence. Good enough to belong. Not so good that anyone asked questions.

It was exhausting. Not physically—the pace wasn't that different from the dawn sessions I'd been running for years—but mentally. Every touch of the puck required a decision. Every instinct had to be filtered through the question: Will this make them look twice?

Finally, Sterling split us into two groups for a scrimmage. I was on the white team, lined up at left wing with Chen at center and a junior named Petrov on the right. Maddox was on the navy team.

Of course he was.

The first few shifts were uneventful. I dumped the puck when I should dump it, finished my checks, got back on defense. Sterling's voice echoed off the boards — "Good angle, Petrov!" and "Stay with your man, Davies!" — but he didn't say anything to me. I wasn't sure if that was good or bad.

Then came the shift that mattered.

Chen won the faceoff cleanly, kicking the puck back to our defense. They moved it up the boards, a simple breakout, and I curled into the neutral zone to provide an outlet. The pass came to me in stride—a good feed, right on the tape—and suddenly I had open ice in front of me.

I saw it all in an instant, the way I always did when the game slowed down. The navy defenseman cheating toward the boards, expecting me to dump it in. The gap between him and his partner, wide enough to drive a truck through. Maddox closing from the back side but not fast enough, his angle wrong by three degrees.

I could split them. A quick move to my forehand, a burst of speed, and I'd be in alone on the goalie with time to pick my spot. The kind of play that used to make highlight reels. The kind of play that used to make Chet Finlay's eyes light up with dollar signs.

I dumped the puck into the corner and peeled off toward the bench.

"Change!" I called, even though I had gas left in the tank.

Maddox caught my eye as I skated past. His expression was unreadable, but I could feel him filing it away. Another dump. Another safe play. Another question mark.

The scrimmage continued. I took a few more shifts, kept them simple, tried to fade into the background. But Maddox wasn't done testing me.

It happened in the third period of our abbreviated game. I was cycling in the offensive zone, the puck on my stick, looking for a passing lane. I heard him coming before I saw him—the heavy scrape of his edges building momentum.

The hit was clean but hard. Shoulder to shoulder, my back slamming into the boards with enough force to rattle my teeth. The puck squirted free. I didn't chase it.

Maddox stood over me for a half-second, not offering a hand. "Good battle," he said, his voice flat. Then he skated away.

I pulled myself off the boards and got back into position. My shoulder throbbed where he'd connected, but I didn't show it.

The whistle blew for a stoppage, and I found myself lined up next to Davies for the faceoff. His face was flushed, his breathing ragged. The practice had been harder on him than on most of us—his conditioning was good but not great, and the pace was relentless.

"You okay?" I asked, low enough that only he could hear.

"Yeah." He shook his head. "No. I keep losing the draw. Sterling's gonna bench me if I can't win a faceoff."

I glanced at the opposing center—a senior named Volkov, thick through the shoulders, experienced. Davies had been lining up square to him, trying to match strength with strength. A losing proposition.

"Cheat to your forehand," I said. "Don't try to win it clean. Just get your stick on his and tie him up. Let the wingers do the work."

Davies blinked at me. "What?"

"Trust me."

The whistle blew. Davies shifted his stance, moving his weight slightly to his forehand side. Volkov went for the clean win, trying to sweep the puck back to his defense. Davies got his stick in the way—not a clean win, but enough disruption. The puck squirted to the side, and Chen swooped in to collect it.

Davies looked at me with something like wonder. "How did you—"

"Just something I noticed." I skated away before he could ask anything else.

Practice ended forty-five minutes later. We filed back into the locker room, a sweaty, exhausted mass of bodies. The music came back on—something mellower now, recovery mode—and the conversations resumed, quieter than before.

I sat in my corner stall and methodically stripped off my gear, reversing the ritual. Pads, base layers, skates. Everything in order. Everything where it belonged.

The door opened and Sterling walked in. The room didn't exactly go silent, but the volume dropped. Everyone tracking the coach without obviously tracking him.

He moved through the room slowly, stopping at various stalls to exchange a few words with players. Some got praise, some got corrections, some got nothing but a nod. The hierarchy of attention, doled out in careful increments.

He stopped in front of my stall.

I kept my expression neutral. Sterling's eyes—dark, unreadable—studied me for a long moment.

"Calloway." His voice was pitched low enough that only I could hear. "Solid work today. You read the ice well. You don't cheat on defense."

"Thank you, Coach."

"Don't thank me. Just do it again tomorrow." He started to turn away, then paused. "That advice you gave Davies on the faceoff. Good eye. But," he paused and looked me square in the eyes, "if I see you pull a play again just to avoid attention, I will bench you."

Before I could respond, he was gone, moving on to the next stall.

Chapter 6
The Onstage Shower

Elliot

The Black Box Theatre was a void of matte black paint and heavy velvet, a space designed to swallow the real world so we could build something more interesting in its place. The walls absorbed light, sound, everything—leaving only the performers and the fiction they created. It was my favorite place on campus, the one room where being "too much" was exactly right.

But tonight, the only thing I was building was a massive headache.

"Elliot, for the love of Brecht, don't stare at the floor." Professor Andrew Albright's voice cut through the darkness from somewhere near the tech booth. "You're Diego Santos. You're seventeen, you're terrified, and you're about to kiss your best friend in a locker room shower. You're not calculating the square footage of the tiles."

"I'm trying, Professor," I said, my voice echoing off the black-painted rafters. "It's just . . . the movement is stiff. I'm not a natural athlete."

"That's because you're performing the idea of an athlete instead of embodying the reality of it." Albright stepped into the work lights, his compact frame casting a long shadow across the stage. He stroked his gray beard—the thinking gesture, not the frustrated one. Progress, maybe. "I told you to go to the rink. Did you go?"

"I went."

"Then use it." Albright crossed his arms. "We're running scene three again. From Tyler's entrance. Elliot—this is on you. Diego has been pretending just as long. Three years of not asking. Three years of keeping the line intact. He tells himself he's fine because nothing's happened. But the second Tyler pushes, that lie starts to crack. Don't protect him. Let him feel cornered."

I dropped my bag by locker seven, sat on the bench, and pulled out my AirPods. The blocking was specific—Albright had taped the locker numbers to the set wall in painter's tape, each one a different color so we wouldn't lose our marks. Seven was blue. I mimed putting in the AirPods in and unlacing my shoes. My head bob to nothing.

That was the trick with Diego. He filled silence with music. He made small things—untying a shoe, pulling out a towel—look like choices instead of habits. Albright had said it in the first read through: Diego is performing control. Tyler is performing ease. The audience should wonder which mask cracks first.

"The stage left door bangs open.," the stage manager says.

Lucas crossed in with his hockey bag and stick slung over one shoulder, saw me, and grinned.

"Yo!"

I didn't react. Music. Diego couldn't hear him. Lucas crossed to me and flicked the back of my head—light, practiced, the kind of gesture that had taken us three rehearsals to calibrate so it read as casual instead of aggressive.

I jumped, miming pulling out an AirPod.

"Dick."

"Thought you left," Lucas said, dropping into Tyler's easy grin.

"Nah." I tucked the AirPods away, keeping my hands busy, keeping Diego grounded in routine. "Gotta shower. Mom's picking me up in like forty."

"She still making you do that college tour thing?"

"Every weekend. Last week was BC, this week is BU."

"Look at you, fancy college boy."

"Jealous?"

"Of riding in a car with your mom for three hours listening to NPR?" Lucas dropped his bag, already pulling at his shoes. "Nah, I'm good."

"She plays Reggaeton when I'm in the car."

"That's even worse."

I threw my shoe at him. Lucas dodged, laughing, and the laugh was so perfectly Tyler that I almost forgot it was rehearsal. Almost forgot we were standing on taped marks in the Black Box, that the lockers were flats and the showers didn't exist yet.

The scene progressed through the easy stuff—Tyler complaining about suicides and Coach Reilly, Diego needling him about penalties, the rhythm of two guys who'd been teammates long enough to insult each other without thinking. Lucas and I had found the groove of this section early. The banter was quick, overlapping, alive. Albright barely ever stopped us here.

"Must be nice being rich as shit," Lucas said, kicking off his second shoe.

"He's not that rich."

"Dude, his house has a pool. In New York."

"So?"

"So normal people don't have pools! Your house doesn't have a pool."

"We have a hot tub."

"That doesn't count."

"Why not?"

"'Cause it's a hot tub. That's like . . . rich people who aren't that rich."

"You're an idiot," I said, and grabbed a towel from my locker.

This was where the scene started to shift, and both of us knew it. The banter was still there, but Diego was steering now—pulling out shower stuff, asking about Marcus's party, nudging Tyler toward something social, something normal. Something that might prove they were just teammates. Just friends.

"You going to Marcus's thing Friday?" I ask.

"I don't know. Maybe."

"Maybe? Whole team's going."

"That's the problem."

"Come on. It'll be fun. You need to get out more."

"I get out."

"To practice and work. That's it." I paused, letting the beat land. "You never come to anything anymore."

"I'm busy."

"With what? It's Friday night. Live a little."

"Says you?"

"What's that supposed to mean?"

"Nothing."

And here was the turn. The moment I'd circled in my script with red pen, the line Albright had made me run thirty times until I understood what Diego was actually doing. Because Diego wasn't being a good friend here. Diego was building a wall—brick by brick, girl by girl—trying to construct a version of Tyler that made sense. That was safe.

"Maybe you'll finally talk to Emma," I said. "She's been asking about you."

"Who?"

"Emma. From the dance team. Apparently she thinks you're cute."

"Good for her."

"Dude, she's hot. And she's into you. You should go for it."

"Not interested."

I pushed harder. Diego pushed harder. "Why not? You haven't hooked up with anyone all year."

"So?"

"So everyone's gonna start thinking—"

"Thinking what?"

The air in the room changed. Lucas's voice had dropped—not louder, but denser, the way Tyler's anger didn't explode but compressed. I felt my pulse tick up. This was the edge. This was where Diego realized he'd walked himself to the cliff and couldn't stop.

"Nothing. Just—you should come to the party. Talk to Emma. Have fun."

"Is that what you want?" Lucas said, and something in his delivery made the line land differently than it read on the page. Not accusatory. Searching. Tyler looking for the answer Diego refused to give.

"What?" I asked.

"Me to hook up with Emma."

"I don't care what you do."

The lie sat in the room like a held breath. I could feel it—the weight of what Diego wasn't saying pressing against the inside of my chest. And that was when the image hit, fast and uninvited: Rowan Calloway at the rink water fountain during tryouts, lifting his helmet cage just enough to drink. The sharp line of his jaw. Water catching the overhead lights. A face I'd studied from magazine photos for years—safe at a distance—now real, now close, stripped of anything soft.

I blinked it away. Kept going.

"What about you?" I said. "You could ask out—" I stopped, the way the script told me to, but the hesitation was real this time. "What's that girl's name? Sarah? The one who's always—"

"I don't want to talk about this."

"Why not?"

"Because."

"That's not an answer."

"I'm gonna shower."

"Tyler—"

"Drop it, Diego."

Lucas turned and walked toward the shower area—two strips of tape suggesting a doorway that didn't exist yet. I stood there, Diego's frustration sitting heavy in my shoulders, and I wasn't sure how much of it was his.

"Stop."

Albright's voice cut through the room. Lucas paused at the tape line. I turned to face our director, suddenly aware that my breathing had changed, that something in the back half of the scene had shifted.

"Better," Albright said slowly, his eyes narrowing. "That last moment—there was something real there. Something hungry. What changed?"

I opened my mouth. Closed it.

Rowan, I didn't say. Rowan changed.

I couldn't exactly tell him I'd been fantasizing about a hockey player while pretending to kiss my scene partner.

"I don't know," I said. "I just . . . stopped thinking."

"Then stop thinking more often." Albright made a note on his clipboard. "We're breaking for fifteen. When we come back, I want to run the full sequence from the top. Elliot—whatever you just found, don't lose it."

Albright disappeared into the darkness of the tech booth. The work lights shifted, the stark white giving way to a softer amber that signaled break time. Around me, the small crew—stage manager, lighting designer, the assistant director—dispersed toward the green room and the coffee maker that lived there.

Lucas didn't follow us. He stood on the stage, watching me with an expression I couldn't quite read.

"So," he said, reaching for the T-shirt he'd left draped over a prop locker. "You want to tell me what that was about?"

"What was about?"

He pulled the shirt over his head, emerging with his eyebrows raised. "You've been phoning it in for two weeks. Albright's been on your ass, I've been picking up your slack, and you've had this . . . vacancy in your eyes. Like you're running lines in your head instead of actually being in the scene."

"Thanks for the vote of confidence."

"Oh, I'm not done." He sat down on edge of the stage, patting the space next to him. I sat, reluctantly. "Tonight was different. That last take—you were here. More than here. You were somewhere that actually mattered to you." He tilted his head, studying me with the same analytical eye he brought to every role. "So, what changed? Where'd you go? Honestly, I thought you were about to throw me to the ground and have your way with me."

I let out a chuckle as I picked at a splinter on the plywood, not meeting his eyes. "Albright told me to do research. Observe real athletes."

"Uh huh. I was here." Lucas's voice was carefully neutral. "And? Did you find what you were looking for?"

The question was simple. The answer was not.

Did I find what I was looking for?

I'd gone to the arena for physicality—the weight and movement of a real athlete, something I could borrow for Diego Santos. I'd found Chase St. Clair instead, a ghost from my adolescent ceiling, now flesh and blood and skating on a college rink in Northern California.

"I found a guy," I said finally, my voice pitching upward as heat rose in my cheeks. "A player. He moves . . . differently. Like he's trying to take up less space than he actually occupies. Like he's hiding in plain sight."

Lucas nodded slowly. "Sounds like Tyler."

"Yeah." I swallowed. "Except I'm not playing Tyler. I'm playing Diego. The one who wants to stay hidden."

"So, what's the problem?"

The problem was that I'd spent two days sneaking into the arena to watch Rowan Calloway rehearse, and instead of learning how to play Diego, I'd started wanting to understand Rowan himself. The problem was that when Lucas had pressed his body against mine on that stage, I'd been imagining someone else's breath on my face, someone else's hands, someone else's wall of careful control finally cracking open.

The problem was that I wasn't sure anymore if I was researching a role or chasing something else entirely.

"I don't know," I said. "I think I might be losing the thread."

Lucas was quiet for a moment. Then he laughed—not unkindly, but with the knowing warmth of someone who'd been in the theatre program long enough to recognize the symptoms.

"Elliot Vega, losing the thread. That's a first." He stood, brushing sawdust off his jeans. "I don't know what's going on with you and this hockey player you're 'observing,' but whatever it is, it's working. That last take was the best scene work you've done all month."

"It was?"

"Don't let it go to your head. You've still got a long way to go before you're not embarrassing yourself." He started toward the green room, then paused. "But yeah. There was something real there. Something you actually wanted." His expression was unreadable in the amber light. "Figure out what it is. Then use it."

He disappeared through the door, leaving me alone on the empty stage.

Chapter 7
The Observer Effect

Elliot

Below me, the Ospreys moved through their drills with the synchronized chaos of a well-run practice. Navy and orange jerseys blurred against the white ice, sticks cracking against pucks, skates carving parallel lines into the fresh surface. Coach Sterling stood near center ice, whistle in hand, calling out corrections that echoed off the high ceiling. Though personally, I preferred watching the assistant coach, Amarachi Okafor, she did not suffer fools at all. I once saw her dress down a guy who had to be at least three times her size. When she was done with him, he was ready to crawl into an early grave.

I pulled out my Moleskine and found my pen. The familiar weight of it in my hand settled something in me. This was work. This was craft. I was here to learn how to move like and embody Diego Santos, and if that meant watching Rowan Calloway for hours at a time, that was simply the cost of authenticity.

At least, that's what I told myself.

I found him immediately. Number twenty-eight, positioned on the left side during a breakout drill. Even from this distance, even among twenty other players in identical gear, he was unmistakable. Something about the way he held himself—that particular stillness even in motion, that economy of movement Albright kept demanding I find.

I opened a fresh page and started writing.

The drill ran. Rowan received a pass from the defenseman, cradled it, moved it up the ice. Nothing flashy. He found the open man, delivered the puck tape-to-tape, peeled off toward the bench for a line change.

When I hadn't been watching hockey at the arena, I had been reading up on the subject. I learned that they're not called rehearsals, they're called practices. Who knew? And what I saw the first day wasn't an audition. These people have a language of their own.

Another drill. Board battles this time, players paired off in the corners to fight for loose pucks. Rowan against Maddox, the team captain, who seemed to have it in for Rowan for some unknown reason. Personally, I just thought Maddox was a bully. The puck dropped, and they collided—shoulder to shoulder, stick against stick.

Maddox was bigger, stronger, meaner. He threw his weight into Rowan with the kind of controlled violence that was technically legal but clearly personal. Rowan absorbed it. His knees bent, his center dropped, and he used Maddox's momentum against him, pivoting so that the bigger man slid past. The puck squirted free, and Rowan collected it, protecting it with his body until a teammate could retrieve it.

The scrimmage whistle blew. Sterling shouted something about spacing or lanes—I couldn't quite catch it—and the players regrouped at center ice. The drill reset into another three-on-two rush.

Rowan was on the attacking side, but he didn't start with the puck. Davies—the nervous freshman—was carrying it up the right side, but he didn't have the confidence that some of the other guys had. Rowan skated slightly inside of him, close enough to be an option but not demanding the pass, while the third forward lagged a step behind.

The defense backed up, guarding the middle, and for a second I assumed the play was going to end the same way most of them did: a safe shove of the puck into the corner and a whistle.

Then Davies went down.

It wasn't dramatic—just a clipped edge or a bad shift of weight—but suddenly he was on the ice, sliding, his stick scraping uselessly as the puck squirted loose off his blade. It drifted toward the middle, slow and unclaimed, exactly the kind of mistake Sterling had been yelling about all afternoon.

I thought that was it. A defender was already closing in. Half a second more and the play would be dead.

Rowan moved.

I almost missed it because I was still tracking Davies on the ice. One moment Rowan was coasting, just another body in motion, and the next he cut hard toward the loose puck. His skates dug in, throwing a spray of ice as he pivoted, his body turning faster than seemed reasonable. He reached out and gathered the puck in stride, shielding it instinctively as the defender lunged.

I didn't know enough about hockey to name what he did—only that it was sudden and decisive. His hands were calm even as his body twisted, the puck staying with him like it was tethered.

And then he passed it.

No pause. No windup. Just a quick flick across the front of the goal, the puck lifting cleanly off the ice and gliding over a defender's stick. It landed right in front of the trailing player, who barely had to adjust before slamming it into the open net.

The whistle blew again.

The entire thing couldn't have taken more than two seconds.

My pen stopped moving.

For a moment, I wrote, the words coming slowly, the ghost caught fire.

I stared at the ice, at Rowan already skating back toward center, already shrinking back into himself. The goal was being celebrated by his teammates—Davies, back on his feet, was grinning and clapping the scorer on the back. But Rowan just nodded.

I couldn't hear what was being said on the ice, but from his nonverbal behavior he seemed to just shrug off the play as if what he'd just done was nothing. As if anyone on that ice could have done it.

But they couldn't have. I knew enough about hockey now to recognize the difference between competence and brilliance.

As if he could feel my attention, Rowan looked up.

Shit!

It was sudden—a sharp turn of his head toward the stands, his helmet cage tilting as his eyes scanned the steep rows of seats. I went completely still, my breath caught in my throat, my pen frozen over the page.

The observer effect, I thought wildly. The act of observation changes the thing being observed.

His eyes swept across Section 112, passing over my row without stopping, continuing toward the other side of the arena.

I didn't move. Didn't breathe. I was acutely aware of how this would look if he spotted me. The theatre kid who'd confronted him after tryouts, sitting in the stands during practice, watching him with a notebook full of observations. He would think I was stalking him. Maybe I'm just a little obsessive.

Am I?

The question surfaced before I could stop it, and I didn't have an answer.

Rowan's gaze continued its sweep, found nothing, and returned to the ice. His shoulders dropped slightly—relief, maybe, or just a return to the baseline tension he always carried. Sterling's whistle blew, calling the next drill, and Rowan skated toward his position.

The moment had passed.

He knows he's being watched, I wrote. He just doesn't know by whom.

I sat with that for a moment.

What am I doing?

I was observing someone without their consent.

Below me, Rowan entered another board battle. Another collision, another moment of physical struggle. I watched him absorb the hit, protect the puck, make the smart play instead of the spectacular one.

He's beautiful, I thought, and the word surprised me so much I almost dropped my pen.

I stayed until the end of practice.

When the final whistle blew and the players started filing toward the locker room, I gathered my things and slipped out the back exit. The chilly air outside was a shock after the refrigerated constancy of the arena—somehow sharper because of the breeze. I pulled my jacket tighter and walked fast.

Halfway across the quad, I stopped under a bare oak tree and opened my Moleskine.

I flipped back through the pages, reading my handwriting in the fading afternoon light. The early entries were clinical. Subject. Movement patterns. Behavioral tells. The language of observation, detached and analytical.

But somewhere around the middle of today's session, the language had changed.

Rowan's hands are impossibly soft—the puck seems to float to him.

Rowan moves like he's apologizing for taking up space.

Rowan. Just Rowan.

I hadn't even noticed when I'd stopped writing subject and started writing his name. When the clinical distance had collapsed into something uncomfortably intimate. I might as well have been drawing little hearts around Rowan + Elliott! Inside, I was as giddy as a kid with their first crush. What is going wrong with me?

I closed the notebook and stood there for a long moment, staring at nothing.

Chapter 8
Off-Book Interactions

Elliot

The lock on my apartment door clicked shut behind me. The charged energy from the arena hadn't dissipated; it hummed under my skin, a pleasant thrum of discovery. I tossed my keys into the ceramic bowl on the entryway table and moved into the main room of my loft.

My apartment occupied the second floor of a shuttered bookstore downtown. Bookshelves lined one wall, overflowing with stage plays, critical theory, and actor biographies. A reclaimed wood table served as my desk, its surface buried under stacks of paper and highlighters along with a hundred abandoned projects. Dual monitors glowed in the corner, currently displaying the Oakridge Athletics website.

Then there was the corkboard.

It took up most of the wall opposite my bed—a four-by-six-foot expanse of cork that I'd installed my first week in the apartment. Originally, it had been for production research: character maps, scene breakdowns, costume references.

Now, it belonged entirely to Rowan Calloway.

I'd like to tell you it was subtle. Dignified. The kind of thoughtful character study a serious actor might assemble for a challenging role.

It was not.

The board may be something a detective in a crime procedural would stand in front of while saying, "The pattern is here—I just can't see it yet." Or better yet, "Murder Board! Murder Board! Murder Board!" Pushpins. Red yarn. Index cards with observations written in increasingly frantic handwriting. If my mother walked in right now, she'd either stage an intervention or call the authorities. Possibly both.

This is normal, I told myself. Method actors do this all the time. Daniel Day-Lewis would understand.

Daniel Day-Lewis would absolutely not understand. Daniel Day-Lewis would have me committed.

I pulled my Moleskine from my bag and flipped to today's observations. The notes I'd taken at the arena were detailed, precise—the kind of thing that would seem impressive in a behind-the-scenes documentary about my creative process and damning in a court of law. I found a fresh index card and transcribed the key points, pinning them to the board in the section I'd labeled CURRENT PATTERNS:

Chooses high-percentage plays over high-visibility ones

Economy of movement—never wastes a stride

Dims himself immediately after any display of skill

Performing invisibility as survival strategy

I stepped back, surveying the entire wall. A normal person would have Googled him a few times, maybe watched some old clips, and moved on with their life. A dedicated actor might have kept a journal.

I had built a . . . let's call it a shrine.

The worst part? I couldn't entirely explain why. Yes, there was the role—Diego Santos shared something with Rowan, some quality of deliberate concealment that I needed to understand if I was going to play him truthfully. That was the professional justification, the one I'd give if anyone asked.

But underneath that neat explanation was something messier. Something that had started when I was thirteen or fourteen, watching Ice Kings for the first time, and had never quite gone away. A fascination that felt less like academic interest and more like—

Nope. Not going there.

I sat down at my desk and opened my laptop, grateful for the distraction of research. The blog and subsequent comment thread was long—over two hundred posts spanning three years—and I read it all. My coffee went cold. The light outside my windows shifted from afternoon gold to evening blue. And slowly, horribly, a picture emerged.

Michael Henderson had been a defenseman for the Vancouver Vanguard, a junior team in the Pacific League. Fifteen years old. Highly recruited. The kind of prospect that NHL scouts flew across the country to watch.

During a game against the Vancouver Vanguard—not the cool Canadian Vancouver, the Washington one—Henderson had gone into the corner to retrieve a puck. A body blow from behind had driven him headfirst into the boards. The medical reports—leaked to the forum by someone claiming to be a team trainer—described a fractured C4 vertebra. Career-ending. The posts speculated about whether he'd ever walk normally again.

The player who'd caused the injury was never publicly identified. According to the league, they had lost the game footage, which only spurred on the internet conspiracies. The official report claimed the hit, while tragic, was just an accident—not even a penalty during the game. Two years later, the league quietly disbanded amid financial troubles that may or may not have been connected.

But the forum users had their theories.

I was at that game, one poster wrote. It was #17 on Portland. The Holmström kid. But there was another player involved—he made the pass that set the whole thing up. Kid in the movie, the one with the stupid catchphrase.

Another post: My cousin worked for the Vanguard. Said there was a settlement. Henderson's family got paid, everyone signed NDAs. But that movie kid quit the league like two days later. Guilty conscience?

And another: Holmström and the actor were tight. Like, suspiciously tight. Saw them at a tournament once, always together. Whatever happened to Henderson, they were both in on it.

Then: I don't know who these other morons are, but I played on one of the teams that night. It was an accident. The rest of you are just trying to cause trouble where there isn't any.

I sat back from my laptop, my chest tight.

Here's the thing about anonymous forums: anyone can say anything. Half of these posts were written by people who weren't there, speculating based on other speculation, building conspiracy theories out of coincidence and confirmation bias. I knew that. I understood how misinformation worked.

But I also couldn't unsee it.

The Henderson name appeared nowhere in the official Chase St. Clair narrative. No mention of a career-ending injury, no hint of involvement in anything darker than missed press junkets and refused catchphrases. The Hollywood machinery had either scrubbed it clean or—more likely—it had never been connected to him publicly in the first place.

If there even was a connection. Which I didn't know. Because I was basing this on anonymous forum posts from people who might have been making it all up.

This is exactly how conspiracy theorists start, I thought. First, you're reading old hockey forums, then you're convinced the moon landing was faked and the world is flat.

But Rowan had been there. That much was verifiable—he'd played for the Portland Eagles before going to Hollywood. And two days after the Henderson incident, according to the league records I'd found, he'd stopped playing. Just . . . stopped. The next verifiable appearance was a casting announcement for Ice Kings three months later.

I stared at my corkboard with fresh eyes. The constructed archive of a man who'd done everything possible to disappear. The patterns I'd identified, the behaviors I'd cataloged.

He's not just hiding from fame, I realized. He's hiding from something.

Then immediately: Or you're projecting a mystery onto someone who's just a private person, because you can't accept that your teenage crush grew up to be ordinary.

I pulled out a blank red index card and wrote: HENDERSON—MARCH—C4 FRACTURE—CONNECTION?

The three question marks were a compromise with my conscience. I pinned it to the board, then felt like an asshole.

This was a real person. Henderson. Someone who'd had his life derailed at fifteen. And here I was, treating his tragedy like a plot point in the Rowan Calloway mystery I'd invented.

What are you actually doing here? I asked myself. What do you want?

The honest answer was uncomfortable: I didn't know anymore. The research had started as preparation for Diego—understanding how someone conceals a secret, how that concealment shapes their body language, their relationships, their sense of self. Legitimate actor homework.

But somewhere along the way, the lines had blurred. Was I studying Rowan to understand Diego, or using Diego as an excuse to study Rowan? Was this professional dedication or personal obsession dressed up in artistic justification?

And underneath both questions was, did I want to understand him, or did I just want him?

This is either going to be the start of something real, I thought, or the documentation of my complete breakdown.

Honestly? It could go either way.

Chapter 9
The Library Ambush

Elliot

Despite the absurdity of treating a library visit like a high-stakes audition, I spent far too long costuming myself in a "casual" uniform of a gray henley and rarely worn glasses—the perfect ensemble for a harmless booklover who definitely wasn't stalking anyone. I meticulously crafted the image of an innocent student, even planning to use a stack of heavy books as a method-acting prop for a calculated "accidental" encounter. The goal was to deliver a line that would sound like a clumsy quip to a stranger but would hit Rowan with the weight of a thousand press junkets: "Time to break the ice."

The catchphrase from Ice Kings 1, 2, and 3. The words Rowan had refused to say at his final press junket, the moment everything had unraveled.

I was going to say it to his face and see what happens.

This is a terrible idea, a voice in my head observed. It sounded suspiciously like my mother. You're about to poke an emotional wound just to see what happens. That's not research. That's cruelty. It's for the role, I told myself. Diego has secrets. Rowan has secrets. If I can understand how Rowan works, I can understand how Diego works.

The justification felt thin even inside my head. Like a tissue-paper wall pretending to be brick.

My heart rate was elevated as I walked to Thompson Library—not anxiety exactly, but the heightened awareness that came before any performance. I got the same feeling in the wings before an entrance, when the audience was still just a murmur beyond the curtain and anything was possible.

This is research, I told myself again.

I tired of telling myself that.

The Thompson Library was a brutalist monument of concrete and sickly fluorescent light, its third floor housing the sparsely populated media studies collection where graduate students toiled among rows of film theory and semiotics. It was a quiet, institutional domain, perfect for those seeking the isolation of dusty shelves and niche academic research.

You could still turn around, I thought as I climbed the stairs. You could just . . . not do this. Go home. Throw away the corkboard. Take up a normal hobby, like pottery or murder podcasts.

I kept climbing.

By the time I pushed through the fire door onto the third floor, I'd settled into character. Just another student searching for a book. Nothing unusual. Nothing planned. Nothing that would make a reasonable person question my sanity.

The section was a maze of shelving units arranged in a grid pattern that created natural sight lines and blind spots. I moved through it, scanning the study tables positioned between the stacks.

And there he was.

Rowan sat alone at a table near the windows, his back to the wall. A defensive position, I noted. The choice of someone who wanted to see threats coming. A laptop was open in front of him, but his attention was on a textbook, a highlighter moving in slow, methodical stripes across the page.

His face was softer than I'd seen it before, the constant vigilance relaxed. He looked younger like this. More like the boy in the old photographs. He almost passed for a regular undergraduate.

I positioned myself behind a shelf where I could observe without being seen, my heart hammering against my ribs.

This is creepy, I acknowledged. This is objectively, unambiguously creepy. You are hiding behind a bookshelf spying on someone. If a friend told you they were doing this, you would stage an intervention.

Through the gaps between books, I cataloged details anyway: the curve of his shoulders, slightly hunched over his work. The way he worried his lower lip as he read. The small furrow between his brows that suggested genuine concentration rather than performed effort.

He looked vulnerable. Unguarded in a way I'd never seen him on the ice or in the arena hallway. This was the Rowan who existed when no one was watching.

And I was about to shatter that peace. On purpose. With a scripted line I'd rehearsed in my bathroom mirror.

You could still leave, the reasonable voice suggested. You could walk away right now and he'd never know you were here. You could be a decent person.

I thought about his face yesterday at the arena—that moment of pure, unguarded joy when he'd made the impossible pass. The way the light had come into his eyes before he'd remembered to dim it.

I wanted to see that again. I wanted to know the person who could feel that kind of joy and feel compelled to hide it.

But maybe—and this thought was new, uncomfortable—maybe I didn't have to crack him open to find out. Maybe I could just . . . talk to him. Like a normal human being.

The catchphrase felt like a betrayal. Not just of Rowan, but of whatever I was hoping might happen between us.

So, don't say it, I thought. Just go over there. Drop the books. Make conversation. See what happens without the manipulation.

I took a breath. Adjusted my armload of books.

Then, before I could talk myself out of it entirely, I stepped out from behind the shelf.

And walked right past him.

Keep going, I told myself. Just keep going. You don't have to do this.

My heart was pounding, but my feet kept moving. One step. Two. I was going to walk to the other end of the stacks, pretending to hunt for a book, then leave. I was going to be a normal person who didn't weaponize childhood trauma against unsuspecting strangers.

Rowan chose that exact moment to reach down for his backpack.

I didn't see it happen so much as feel it—the strap of his bag catching my ankle as he swung it up from the floor, the sudden loss of balance, the horrifying certainty that I was going down and there was nothing I could do about it.

The books went first. They exploded out of my arms like startled birds, scattering across the industrial carpet with a series of thuds that sounded like gunshots in the library. The high-pitched squeal that escaped my lips shot my masculinity points to a negative score. Then I followed, my hip catching the edge of his table, my glasses flying off my face, my dignity departing for parts unknown as I sprawled across the floor in a graceless heap of limbs and humiliation.

This was not choreographed. No method acting. Just me . . . eating shit in front of the hottest guy I know.

"Oh, fuck—I'm so sorry!" Rowan was already out of his chair, his voice sharp with alarm. "I didn't see you. Are you okay?"

I lay there for a moment, staring at the ceiling, taking stock. Nothing broken. Pride fatally wounded, but that was probably for the best. One of my books had landed on my stomach. Another was somewhere near my head. My glasses were . . . somewhere.

This is what you get, I thought, for thinking you were in control of anything.

"I'm . . . fine," I managed, though the words came out slightly wheezy. "Just—give me a second to remember how dignity works."

Rowan crouched down next to me and gently grabbed my shoulder. For one disorienting moment, I glanced up at him from floor level—the concerned furrow of his brow, the way his hair fell forward, the surprising warmth in his eyes before he'd had time to put up his walls. He was worried he'd hurt me.

"Here." He grabbed my glasses from where they'd skidded under his chair and held them out. "These yours?"

I took them, brushing our fingers. His hands were warm. I was still lying on the floor like an idiot.

Get up, I told myself. Get up, say thank you, and leave. You can still salvage this.

I sat up too fast, and the book that had been resting on my stomach slid off and hit the floor with another thud. Rowan was already gathering the others, stacking them with the efficient movements of someone used to cleaning up messes.

"I'm really sorry," he said again. "I didn't hear you coming. Are you sure you're okay? That was a hard fall."

"I'm fine. I've had worse pratfalls." I got to my feet, wobbling slightly, and took the stack of books he was holding out to me. "That was entirely my fault. I was carrying way too many and not paying attention."

He almost smiled. Almost. There was a flicker at the corner of his mouth, quickly suppressed. "Eyes bigger than your arms?"

"Story of my life," I said, and then—loss of balance. Nervous energy. Sheer cosmic punishment for everything I'd been planning to do five minutes ago.

"Well," I heard myself say, "I guess that's one way to break the ice."

The words were out before my brain caught up with my mouth. Not calculated. Not rehearsed. Just the kind of stupid joke anyone might make after faceplanting in front of a stranger.

No. No, no, no—

Time stopped.

I watched Rowan's face with horrified attention. For a moment—one eternal, suspended second—his expression didn't change at all. The mask held. The wall stayed up.

Then it cracked.

The color drained from his face, a visible tide of blood retreating beneath his skin. His eyes went wide, then empty—that beautiful, hollow blankness I'd seen in the hallway, but worse now. Rawer. The eyes of someone who'd been punched in the stomach and was trying not to show it.

His throat worked. I saw him swallow once, twice, the muscles jumping beneath his jaw. His mouth opened, but no words came out.

What have you done?

I'd expected a reaction. I'd planned for a reaction. But I hadn't planned for this—this visible, visceral pain that I'd caused on purpose. I hadn't planned for the way it would feel to watch someone's carefully constructed peace shatter because I couldn't resist pulling a thread.

"I—" Rowan's voice came out strangled, barely a whisper. He cleared his throat and tried again. "I have to go."

He was already gathering his things. His textbook went into the bag wrong, pages crumpling. He fumbled with his laptop, nearly dropped it, shoved it in anyway. His movements had lost all their careful grace—this was pure flight response, a prey animal desperate to escape a threat.

A threat that was me. I was the threat.

"Hey, wait—" I heard myself say, some instinct toward damage control kicking in far too late. "I didn't mean—"

Liar, my brain supplied. You absolutely meant it. You planned it for days.

But he was already gone. He grabbed his bag and pushed past me, close enough that I felt the brush of his sleeve against my arm, and then he was walking—not quite running, but close—toward the stairwell. He didn't look back.

I stood there, my arms full of books I didn't need, and watched him disappear through the fire door.

The fluorescent lights hummed overhead. Somewhere in the stacks, someone turned a page.

And I just stood there, feeling like the villain of my own story.

The silence that followed was absolute.

I lowered myself into the chair Rowan had vacated, moving on autopilot. The seat was still warm. His highlighter lay abandoned on the table, cap off, a small yellow stain bleeding into the wood where he'd dropped it.

I picked it up. Turned it over in my fingers. Such a small, ordinary object—the kind of thing you bought in bulk at the campus bookstore without thinking about it.

He'd left it behind because he was too busy fleeing from me to remember it.

Congratulations, I thought bitterly. You got your data. How does it feel?

It felt like shit. It felt like I'd kicked a puppy, except the puppy was a grown man who'd done nothing to me except exist as someone I found interesting.

That morning I'd told myself it was just research. Hypothesis testing. Character study. All the academic language I'd wrapped around what was, at its core, a selfish desire to see what would happen if I pressed the button.

Did you think he was going to laugh it off? I asked myself. Did you think he was going to smile and say, "Oh, you recognized me; how fun?" He's been hiding for five years. Five years of building a new identity, a new life, probably a new sense of self. And you just reminded him that none of it is real.

I set the highlighter down on the table, exactly where he'd dropped it. A small act of . . . what? Contrition? Like leaving it there would somehow undo what I'd done?

I was obsessed with someone who didn't know me. Instead of dealing with that like an adult—like a person who understood that other people weren't puzzles to be solved—I'd turned him into a project.

And the moment you got close enough to connect with him, I thought, you blew it.

Why? Why had I said the catchphrase when I'd already decided not to? When I'd been standing right there, close enough to just . . . talk to him?

The answer was uncomfortable: because talking to him would have been vulnerable. It would have meant risking rejection, awkwardness, finding out that the real Rowan was nothing like the one I'd imagined. The catchphrase was safer—it gave me power, put me in control, kept the dynamic exactly where I wanted it.

Except you didn't want it there, I realized. You wanted something else. And you sabotaged it.

I stood up, gathered my books, and walked toward the stairs.

The library was quiet around me. Students at scattered tables, heads bent over laptops, earbuds in. And despite my yelp, no one had noticed what had just happened. No one knew that the theatre kid with an armload of books had just detonated a small emotional bomb.

This is what you're good at, I thought. Performance. Manipulation. Making people feel things they didn't ask to feel.

On stage, that was a gift. In real life, it was pathology.

Outside, the afternoon light was bright and cold. I walked across the quad toward my loft, my thoughts churning in circles that led nowhere good.

I'd gotten what I wanted. Confirmation that the catchphrase would trigger a response. If this was actual research, I'd be celebrating having proven my hypothesis true. Writing up my findings. Planning the next phase.

Instead, I kept seeing his face.

That moment when the color drained away. The strangled "I have to go," like the words were being pulled out of him against his will.

I'd done that.

What kind of person does that?

The question followed me all the way home, through the door of my loft, past the entryway where I dropped my keys in the ceramic bowl like always. The corkboard was waiting for me on the far wall, that stripped-down version I'd told myself was more respectable.

It wasn't respectable. It was still an obsession. I'd just hidden the most damning evidence.

I walked over to it and stood there, rereading what remained. The timeline of Rowan's career. The photos—old and new. The handwritten notes about his playing style, his body language, his patterns of behavior.

You told yourself this was about Diego, I thought. About understanding your character. But Diego is fiction. Rowan is real. And you've been treating him like he's not.

I pulled down the playing style notes from the corkboard. Then the body language observations. Then, after a long moment, the photos.

When I was done, the corkboard was almost empty. Just the pushpin holes remained.

Better, I thought. This is better.

But it didn't feel better. It felt like it was too little, too late.

I sat down at my desk and opened my Moleskine to a fresh page. The one where I'd written, Library. Third floor. Media Studies section. Afternoon.

Underneath, in the margin, I'd added: No agenda. No script. Just see if he wants to talk.

I stared at those words for a long time. That had been the better plan. The good plan. The one that might have led somewhere real instead of somewhere cruel.

And I'd abandoned it the moment I'd opened my mouth.

Why?

You sabotaged yourself, I realized.

I turned to a fresh page and wrote:

I think I've made a mistake.

Then, underneath:

No. I know I've made a mistake. The question is whether I can fix it.

He would not want to talk to me after this. He was going to avoid me, and he'd be right to. I'd shown him who I was.

You could apologize, a small voice suggested. You could find him, explain, take responsibility. You could try to be better.

The idea was terrifying. It meant admitting what I'd done. It meant being vulnerable, risking rejection, accepting that I might have destroyed any chance of . . . whatever it was I'd been hoping for.

Tomorrow, I decided. Tomorrow, you will find him, and you will apologize.

It was also the only option that didn't make me the villain of this story.

Chapter 10 The Weight of the Mask

Rowan

I didn't remember leaving the library, only the sharp sting of January air as I fled across the quad, my lungs burning and the "break the ice" catchphrase echoing in my skull like a trapped bird. By the time I reached the apartment and slid down the locked door, the familiar I could run spiral had narrowed my world to a cold, gray cell. The anonymous life I'd carefully cultivated felt useless now; I had worn the costume of a regular student, but Elliot Vega had seen right through it.

The closet door was slightly ajar, revealing the darkness inside. I stared at it for a long time before I moved. I knew what was in there. If I opened the box, I knew I'd have to face it. I thought I'd worked through all of this shit in therapy, but I'd been wrong. One stupid catch phrase and I felt like I was eighteen years old again having my first panic attack.

Hearing those words out loud had cracked something open, and I couldn't shove it closed again. The memories were already flooding in.

I crossed the room on unsteady legs and reached into the closet, past the stack of old textbooks, until my fingers found the battered metal of the lockbox. It was heavier than it looked—or maybe that was just the weight of what it contained. I carried it to the center of the room and sat down on the floor, the cold of the hardwood seeping through my jeans.

The combination was my mother's birthday. I'd never changed it. Some part of me had always known I'd need to open it again someday.

The lid creaked as it lifted, revealing the contents I'd been avoiding for five years.

The skate shard was on top. A jagged piece of red and gold plastic, maybe three inches long, with a manufacturer's logo still partially visible on one side. It had come from Michael Henderson's skate—broken in the impact when his head hit the boards, scattered across the ice along with his future.

I picked it up, feeling the edges bite into my palm. I'd found it after the game, when everyone else had cleared out and the Zamboni was running and I'd wanted something, anything, to anchor me to the reality of what had happened. A piece of evidence. A relic. A reminder that I'd been there when a boy's life ended, even if his heart kept beating.

Beneath the shard: the checkbook. Standard blue cover, nothing special. Inside, the register showed the same entry repeated month after month, going back years: Henderson Family Trust—$500.00. Anonymous payments to a fund that helped cover Michael's ongoing medical expenses. Not enough to matter, probably. But all I could afford on a student budget, and the only penance I knew how to pay. I'd stopped sending checks years ago and let the bank handle it from the trust I established. I'd been ensured by the bank officer that there would be no way to trace the account directly to me.

And at the bottom, underneath everything else: photographs.

There were only four. I'd burned the rest during those first wild months of running, feeding them into motel room fireplaces and trash can bonfires, trying to erase any evidence that Chase St. Clair had ever existed. But these four I couldn't destroy.

My parents at my first movie premiere, their faces lit up with pride I'd never quite believed I deserved. A candid shot from the Ice Kings 2 set, me and Anders Holmström laughing at something off-camera, our shoulders touching, our faces young and unguarded. A professional headshot from when I was fifteen, all manufactured charm and perfect teeth. And the last one—a Polaroid, slightly overexposed, of me sitting on the boards at a practice rink in Portland, my helmet off, my hair sweaty, grinning at whoever held the camera.

I didn't remember who'd taken that last photo. But the boy in it appeared happy. Actually happy, not performing happy.

I couldn't remember what that felt like.

The memory surfaced without warning, pulling me under like a riptide.

Los Angeles. The Peninsula Beverly Hills. A suite on the fourteenth floor with floor-to-ceiling windows and white lilies in crystal vases and the kind of aggressive luxury that was supposed to make you feel important but only made me feel small.

I was barely eighteen. It was the press junket for Ice Kings 3: Dynasty's End—the final installment, the one that was supposed to cement my legacy as the franchise's leading man. We'd been doing interviews for three days straight, the same questions repeatedly, the same answers delivered with the same practiced smile.

"So, Rowan, what was your favorite part of making this movie?"

The interviewer was a woman in her thirties, perfectly groomed, holding a tablet with questions she'd probably downloaded from my PR team five minutes before we started. Behind her, a cameraman adjusted the lighting. Off to my left, just out of frame, Chet Finlay stood with his arms crossed, monitoring the proceedings with the cold efficiency of a factory foreman.

"My favorite part?" I heard myself say. The answer was scripted. I'd given it thirty times already. "Getting to work with such an amazing cast and crew. We really felt like a family."

Lies. All lies. The cast barely spoke to each other offset. The crew treated me like a prop to be positioned and lit. And Chet—my agent, my handler, the architect of my entire career—had made it clear that "family" meant "people who did what they were told."

"And of course, the fans are dying to hear it one more time." The interviewer smiled, leaning forward. "Can you give us the catchphrase?"

Time to break the ice.

The words were right there, waiting on my tongue. I'd said them a thousand times. In the movies, in interviews, in promotional spots that aired during Saturday morning cartoons. I'd said them so often they'd lost all meaning, just sounds my mouth made when prompted.

But today, I looked past the interviewer, past the camera, past Chet's expectant face—and I saw it. Through the window. Across the street.

A billboard. Three stories tall. My face, grinning down at the traffic on Wilshire Boulevard. The words TIME TO BREAK THE ICE in letters six feet high, positioned over a movie poster that made me a superhero, a champion, a boy who had everything figured out.

The smile on that billboard wasn't mine. It was something Chet's team had designed, focus-grouped, manufactured from pixels and Photoshop. The person on that poster didn't exist. Had never existed. Was just a product, a brand, a thing to be sold.

And in that moment, something broke.

"I don't have one," I said.

The interviewer's smile flickered. "I'm sorry?"

"A favorite part?" My voice sounded strange—flat, disconnected. "I don't have one."

Chet stepped forward, his face tight with controlled panic. "What Chase means is—"

"No," I said. "That's not what I mean."

The room went very quiet. The cameraman exchanged a glance with someone off-screen. The interviewer's professional composure cracked, revealing something like concern underneath.

"And, I'm not going to say it," I said. The words came out calm, almost peaceful. "I'm not going to say any of it anymore."

After that, everything happened very fast. Chet called for a break. Handlers ushered the interview crew out of the room. Someone on the phone with the studio, their voice low and urgent. And Chet, his brilliant, predatory smile finally gone, replaced by something cold and furious.

"Do you have any idea what you just did?" His voice was quiet, which was worse than yelling. "Three days of press. Forty-seven interviews. And you choose NOW to have a breakdown?"

"I'm not having a breakdown," I said, but I wasn't sure that was true.

"You're going to call her back. You're going to apologize. You're going to say the goddamn catchphrase with a smile on your face, and then you're going to finish this junket like the professional I raised you to be."

"No."

The word hung in the air between us. I don't think I'd ever said it to him before. Not like that. Not meaning it.

Chet's face went through several expressions—shock, rage, calculation—before settling on something like resignation. "Fine. If that's how you want to play it." He pulled out his phone. "We'll call this exhaustion. Heat stroke. Something sympathetic. You'll go to a facility—a nice one, very discreet—and we'll regroup in a few weeks when you're thinking clearly."

A facility. A PR retreat, he'd called it later. A place where difficult clients were sent to be recalibrated, their rough edges smoothed away until they fit the machine again. I'm sure someone in the industry would craft a story about me needing to go to rehab. Even though I'd never drank, didn't do drugs, and only vaped once and decided that was horrible.

I never got on that plane. I ran.

I surfaced from the memory gasping, like I'd been held underwater. The apartment was dark around me—I'd been sitting here for hours without realizing it, the winter light fading to dusk outside my windows. Shit! I missed practice.

The skateshard was still in my palm, its edges leaving indentations in my skin. This was a piece of a boy's destroyed future.

The fame. The catchphrase. Chet Finlay and his machine.

But mostly, Michael Henderson lying on the ice with his neck at an angle that wasn't right, and me skating away because I didn't know what else to do.

The lockbox went back in the closet. The photographs went back in the lockbox. The skate shard stayed in my pocket—I couldn't explain why, but I needed to feel it there, a sharp reminder of what I owed.

I crossed to my gear bag and pulled out my stick. The tape from yesterday was still there, slightly worn from practice. I stripped it off in long, deliberate strokes, the sound of tearing cloth loud in the silent apartment.

Then, I started fresh.

One wrap around the toe. Overlapping strips down the blade. The rhythm was meditation, the same sequence I'd performed a thousand times in a thousand different locker rooms. My hands knew what to do even when my mind was chaos.

Control what you can control.

I finished taping the blade and set the stick against the wall. Tomorrow I'd have practice. Tomorrow I'd step back onto the ice and try to remember how to be invisible.

I sat alone in my empty apartment, the catchphrase still echoing in my skull.

Chapter 11
Opening Night Jitters

Rowan

It'd been more than a week since my run-in with Elliot in the library. Thankfully, I hadn't seen him since, which was good because it gave me the space I needed to focus.

The locker room before a game had a different energy than practice. The air itself seemed charged, humming with nervous anticipation and the particular testosterone-fueled intensity of young men about to go to war.

I sat in my stall, methodically taping my stick for the third time, even though the tape was already perfect. Around me, the team moved through their pregame rituals with the kind of focused casualness that came from repetition. Kowalski, the fire-hydrant defenseman, was stretched out on the floor doing hip flexor stretches while muttering what sounded like Polish prayers under his breath. Maddox had his earbuds in, head bobbing to something aggressive, his eyes closed and his face blank with concentration. Near the center of the room, a speaker pumped out a hip-hop playlist that someone had titled GAME DAY BANGERS with absolutely no irony.

This was my first real game. Not a tryout, not a practice, but an actual competitive contest against another team. The Sierra Coast Condors—a mid-tier Pacific Crest Conference opponent, according to the scouting report Sterling had distributed yesterday. They played a physical game, forechecked hard, and had a goalie who gave up rebounds. Nothing special. Nothing we couldn't handle.

But my hands kept wanting to shake anyway.

Davies dropped onto the bench next to me, his face pale beneath the fluorescent lights. "You nervous?" he asked, his voice pitched low enough that only I could hear.

"A little," I admitted. It was more than a little, but admitting that felt like giving the fear power.

"I think I'm going to throw up," Davies said conversationally. "Like, genuinely. I had a breakfast burrito this morning, and I can feel it trying to escape."

"Don't throw up on the ice. Sterling will bench you for a month."

"Right. No vomiting. Got it." He exhaled shakily. "First game, man. Can you believe it?"

I couldn't, actually. A week ago, I'd been hiding in a library, trying to study while a theatre kid with too much knowledge and not enough boundaries dropped emotional grenades at my feet. Now I was about to play my first collegiate hockey game, wearing a jersey with my name on the back, surrounded by teammates who were slowly—reluctantly—starting to accept me as one of their own.

It felt surreal. I stood on the edge of a cliff and not knowing whether the next step would be a leap or a fall.

The music cut out. The room went quiet.

Maddox stood at the center of the space, his gear already on, his helmet under his arm. He looked around at all of us—the veterans, the sophomores, the new guys like me and Davies—and for once, his expression wasn't challenging or dismissive.

"Alright, listen up," he said. "Some of you have done this before. Some of you haven't. Doesn't matter. When we hit that ice, we're one team. We play our game. We play the system. We don't try to be heroes." His eyes found mine for a moment, held there, then moved on. "We grind. We battle. We make them work for every inch."

He tapped his stick on the floor twice. "Ospreys on three. One, two, three—"

"OSPREYS!" The word exploded from twenty throats at once, a primal sound that echoed off the concrete walls.

The door opened, and Coach Sterling walked in.

He didn't say much—he never did. Just stood at the front of the room, his face as unreadable as ever.

"Defense wins games," he said. "Play the system. Trust your teammates. Everything else takes care of itself."

That was it. No inspirational speeches, no motivational quotes, no chest-thumping declarations of impending victory. Just the simple, brutal truth of the philosophy he'd built his program around.

I respected that. I needed that. A system meant rules, and rules meant safety, and safety meant I didn't have to think about who I used to be.

Sterling nodded once, turned, and walked out. We followed.

The crowd noise hit me as I stepped through the gap in the boards—two thousand people packed into steep seating, right on top of us. The cold air filled my lungs.

And for one terrifying moment, I was fifteen again.

The Staples Center. Twenty thousand people. Cameras everywhere, capturing every angle for the movie's premiere broadcast. A custom jersey with ST. CLAIR on the back, the name lit up on the Jumbotron—

I blinked, and the memory shattered. This wasn't Los Angeles.

The national anthem played. I stood at the blue line with my helmet over my heart, staring at the flag without seeing it, running through the game plan in my head.

Play the system. Stay in position. Don't stand out. Control what you can control.

The anthem ended. The crowd roared. The referee skated to center ice with the puck in his hand.

Game time.

My first shift was a blur of adrenaline and controlled panic.

The whistle blew. Davies won the faceoff—barely—and the puck squirted toward the boards on my side. I chased it down, feeling the presence of a Condors forward closing in on my right. The instinct to dangle, to deke, to make something happen, screamed in the back of my brain.

I chipped the puck around the boards to our defenseman and got back to center ice.

Read the play. Cover your man. Don't overthink.

The Condors cycled in our zone for what felt like an eternity. I tracked my assignment—their right winger, a lanky kid with decent speed but sloppy edges—and stayed between him and the net. When the puck came to him, I was there, stick in the passing lane, body angled to force him wide.

He tried to cut inside. I stepped up, took the contact, and the puck squirted loose. Our defenseman cleared it down the ice.

Whistle. Icing. Line change.

I skated to the bench, my lungs burning, my heart pounding so hard I could feel it in my teeth. Sterling didn't acknowledge me as I sat down.

I'd survived. One shift down. However, many more to go.

The game settled into a rhythm after that. The Condors were physical, just like the scouting report said, but they weren't skilled. They forechecked hard but made mistakes in the neutral zone. They crashed the net but left passing lanes open. Our system was designed to exploit exactly this kind of opponent—contain, counterattack, capitalize on errors.

By the second period, I was feeling almost comfortable.

Almost.

The moment came midway through the frame. A Condors turnover at center ice, the puck bouncing free toward open space. I was the closest player, my legs already moving before my brain caught up. I collected the puck in stride, felt the ice open up in front of me, saw the defense scrambling to recover.

Two-on-one. Me and Maddox against a single retreating defenseman. The goalie was cheating toward Maddox's side, leaving the short side vulnerable. If I drove the net, faked the pass, and went five-hole—

The highlight reel played in my head. The move I would have made ten years ago, when cameras were everywhere and every goal was content for the next promotional spot. The dangle that would have made Chet's eyes light up with dollar signs.

I dumped the puck into the corner and peeled off for a line change.

Maddox's jaw dropped, then closed as his face reddened. The bench was silent as I hopped over the boards.

"Calloway." Maddox's voice, low and flat. "You had the lane."

"I saw the backcheck." The lie came automatically. "Didn't want to get caught."

Maddox stared at me for a long moment, his expression unreadable. Then, he turned back to the ice.

My hands were shaking under my gloves. Not from the cold. From how close I'd come—how close I'd come to letting the old instincts take over, to becoming visible, to giving anyone watching a reason to look twice at the walk-on in the corner stall.

The game continued. We scored twice in the third period, both goals the product of the system Sterling had built—grinding forechecks that forced turnovers, traffic in front of the net, rebounds buried by players who were in position because they'd done their jobs. The final score was 3-1. I wasn't on the scoresheet, but my plus-minus was +1. A solid, unremarkable, completely invisible performance.

The locker room after a win had its own energy—looser than pregame, tinged with relief and satisfaction. The music was back on, louder now, and someone had produced a case of energy drinks that were being distributed with the reverence of championship champagne.

I sat in my stall, stripping off my gear with methodical precision. The exhaustion was settling in now, that bone-deep weariness that came from sixty minutes of controlled effort. My legs ached. My shoulders were tight. But underneath it all, something that felt almost like peace.

I'd done it. First game. First step.

"Calloway."

I followed the voice to find Sterling standing a few feet away, his clipboard tucked under his arm, his expression as unreadable as ever.

"Coach?"

"You played your game tonight." He nodded once, a small gesture that somehow carried more weight than any praise I'd received in years. "Keep doing that."

Then he moved on, pausing at Davies' stall to say something that made the kid's face light up like a Christmas tree. Davies had gotten an assist in the third period—a secondary helper on our insurance goal—and he was practically vibrating with joy.

"First point," he said to me after Sterling walked away. "First collegiate point. Can you believe it?"

"You earned it," I said. "That backcheck in the second period, when you disrupted that two-on-one? That's what got us the momentum."

Davies blinked at me, surprised. "You noticed that?"

"It was a good play."

He grinned, that puppyish enthusiasm I was starting to recognize as his default state. "Thanks, man. You played solid tonight too. That defensive positioning in the first—"

"Just doing my job."

I finished stripping my gear and headed for the showers, leaving Davies to bask in his moment. He deserved it. I remembered what it felt like, that first point, that first real proof you belonged.

The parking lot was quiet when I emerged, the cold January night sharp against my face. Most of the fans had cleared out, leaving behind scattered cars and the distant hum of traffic on the main road. The arena lights cast long shadows across the asphalt, creating pools of brightness separated by stretches of darkness.

I was halfway to my car when I felt it.

That familiar prickle of awareness. The sensation of being watched.

I stopped. Turned. Scanned the edges of the lot.

And there he was.

Elliot Vega stood near the far entrance, just outside the cone of light from the nearest lamppost. He wasn't approaching. Wasn't calling out. Just standing there, watching, his hands in the pockets of his jacket, his breath visible in the cold air.

Fifty feet away. Far enough that I could pretend I hadn't seen him. Close enough that pretending was pointless.

Our eyes met across the distance. The space between us felt charged, electric, heavy with everything we hadn't said since the library. The catchphrase still echoed in my memory—break the ice—and underneath it, all the questions I didn't have answers to.

Neither of us moved.

Then Elliot nodded.

He turned and walked away, disappearing into the darkness beyond the parking lot lights.

Chapter 12
The Blocking Rehearsal

Elliot

The Black Box Theatre felt different tonight. Smaller, more intimate. The work lights cast everything in that flat, honest glow that stripped away theatrical illusion and left only bodies in space, performers without the safety net of atmosphere and shadow.

We were working Act Two, Scene Three. The fight.

Not a stage combat scene with choreographed punches and carefully counted beats. This was something rawer—Diego and Tyler's relationship imploding on the ice, in front of everyone, captured on a dozen phone cameras. The moment when everything they'd been hiding became impossible to hide.

The moment when violence and intimacy became the same thing.

"Alright, let's pick up from the confrontation," Professor Albright called from his usual spot in the third row, clipboard balanced on his knee. The rest of the cast had been dismissed for the night—this scene was just Lucas and me, working through the blocking that would carry the emotional weight of the entire production. "You've just collided. Tyler's stick caught Diego high. Helmets are off. This is where it escalates."

I stood center stage, one hand raised to my face where the imaginary stick had connected. Lucas was a few feet away, hands up in the universal gesture of I didn't mean to.

In the script, this was the moment Diego's fear turned to anger. Three days of Tyler avoiding him, three days of silence after Diego had finally admitted what he felt, and now this—a careless high stick that felt like one more rejection.

You've been avoiding me for three days.

The line was Diego's, written by Cameron Torres for a play about two boys destroying each other because they didn't know how to love each other safely.

Avoidance, silence, someone building walls so high you couldn't see over them, Rowan immediately came into my mind.

The shocked expression in the library, as the colored had drained from his face. The tremor in his hands as he'd gathered his things.

I have to go.

I pushed the image away. Focus. The scene.

"And . . . action."

"What the fuck!" I shouted, dropping my imaginary helmet. The anger came easily—too easily. "You've been avoiding me for three days!"

Lucas stepped closer, his voice low and urgent. "Diego, not here—"

"Then where?" I closed the distance between us. We were inches apart now, close enough that I could see the pulse jumping in his throat. "You can't just ignore me!"

"What do you want me to do?"

"I want you to talk to me!"

"I can't. Not here."

"Then when?"

"I don't know!"

I shoved him. The stage direction called for it—Diego pushes Tyler's chest, hard—but the force behind it surprised us both. Lucas stumbled back, caught himself on the edge of the practice bench.

"That's not good enough!" I heard myself say.

Lucas recovered, came back at me. "It's all I have!"

We were chest to chest now. The stage directions described it as too close, everyone watching, and even in the empty theatre, I could feel the weight of imaginary eyes. The phones raised. The cameras recording. Of course, we'd have to re-block it when we started working with the PolyGlide because this entire sequence would be on skates.

"You said you were done hiding," I said. Diego's line, but my voice broke on it in a way that wasn't scripted.

"I am," Lucas breathed.

"Then why won't you—"

I stopped. Couldn't finish. The script said He stops. Can't say it. Not here. Not with everyone watching. But the words caught in my throat for a different reason.

Because I wasn't thinking about Diego anymore.

I was thinking about Rowan in the hallway after tryouts. The way his face had gone carefully blank. The wall slamming into place. I don't know what you're talking about. When we both knew he absolutely did.

"Because you asked me not to," Lucas said. Tyler's response. Soft, loaded.

And then—according to the script—Diego sees the phones. Panics. Pulls away.

I pulled away.

"Don't touch me," I said, backing up. The fear in my voice wasn't acting.

Lucas's face shifted. Hurt bleeding into anger. "Fine."

"Tyler—"

"I said fine!" He turned to face the empty seats, the imaginary crowd. "Everyone see that? He doesn't want me to touch him!"

"Stop—"

"Why? Afraid of what they'll think?"

This was where it happened. The moment Tyler, hurt and reckless, almost outed them both. The moment he said the word.

"Maybe they should know—" Lucas started.

"Don't you fucking dare—"

"Know what? That you're a fucking—"

He said it. The slur. The word that had started everything in Act One, the word that hung over the entire play like a blade.

I shoved him. Hard.

Lucas crashed into the bench—our stand-in for the boards—and the sound echoed through the empty theatre. Then he launched himself at me, and we went down together.

Here's the thing about stage combat: it's supposed to be controlled. Choreographed. You count the beats, you pull your punches, you fake it to keep everyone safe.

This didn't feel controlled.

We were tangled together on the stage floor, rolling, grappling, and somewhere in the chaos, the choreography fell away. Lucas's elbow caught my ribs—actually caught them, hard enough to hurt. My knee connected with his thigh. We were breathing hard, grunting with effort, and the sounds were too real, too raw.

This isn't a hockey fight, the script said. This is intimate. Personal. Messy. They're tangled together—impossible to tell where one ends and the other begins.

I ended up on top. Fist raised. Lucas beneath me, not defending himself.

Just staring up.

For a moment, the theatre disappeared. The work lights, the empty seats, the production notes scattered across Albright's lap—all of it gone. There was only this: Lucas's face beneath me, breathing hard, his lip actually bleeding where we'd collided somewhere in the chaos.

Except it wasn't Lucas's face I was seeing.

It was Rowan's. Rowan was beneath me. His eyes finally, finally unguarded. All that careful invisibility stripped away, leaving only the person underneath.

"I hate you," I whispered. Diego's line.

"No, you don't," Lucas whispered back. Tyler's response.

My fist unclenched. My hand came down—not to hit, but to land on his chest. Over his heart. The script described it as too gentle, too intimate, for a split second it's something else entirely.

I felt his heartbeat under my palm. Fast. Rabbit-quick.

I wondered what Rowan's skin would feel like under my fingertips. To break through all those walls and find the person hiding behind them. To have him see me the way Lucas was looking at me now—open, vulnerable, seen.

"And . . . hold."

Albright's voice shattered the moment. I pulled back, suddenly aware of how hard I was breathing, how my hand was shaking where it still rested on Lucas's chest.

"That was . . . " Albright paused, making a note. "That was it. That's exactly what this scene needs. The violence and the tenderness, indistinguishable. The audience shouldn't be able to tell if you're about to kill him or kiss him."

I climbed off Lucas, offering him a hand up. He took it. His lip was bleeding—a small cut where we'd collided.

"Shit. Sorry about—" I gestured at his face.

He touched his lips. A trickle of blood on his fingers. He almost smiled. "Method acting. I'll put ice on it."

"Let's take five," Albright said, already standing. "Then we'll run the aftermath—the locker room scene. The 'I love you.'" He headed for the door, muttering something about coffee.

The theatre fell silent.

Lucas sat down on the bench, pressing the back of his hand to his lip. I stayed standing, trying to get my breathing under control, trying to figure out what the hell had just happened.

"So," Lucas said finally. "You want to tell me where that came from?"

"What do you mean?"

He gave me the don't bullshit me look he'd perfected over three years of scene work together.

"I've done enough stage combat to know when someone's actually in the scene with me," he said. "And whoever you were pinning to the floor just now? It wasn't me. But damn, I wish it was. Even as a straight guy, that was fucking hot." He winked.

I didn't have an answer. Or rather, I had an answer I wasn't ready to say out loud.

"The scene worked," I tried. "Albright liked it."

"The scene worked because you stopped acting." Lucas tilted his head, studying me. "When you said 'I hate you'—that wasn't Diego. You were thinking about someone. And when your hand came down on my chest . . . " He touched the spot, thoughtful. "That was not choreographed."

The silence stretched between us. The empty theatre felt cavernous, all that black-painted space swallowing sound and light.

"Is it the hockey player?" Lucas asked. "The one you've been 'researching'?"

"It's . . . complicated," I said, heat rising in my cheeks.

Lucas laughed. "Someone's got a crush." I turned away so he couldn't see as my face continued to turn beet red. "And it's okay. It's always complicated." He stood, grabbing his water bottle from beside the bench. "I don't care who you're pining after. It's none of my business. But as your scene partner, I need to know what I'm working with." He took a long drink, then wiped his mouth. "Whatever's happening with this guy—use it. That's what actors do. We take the messy, complicated feelings and put them on stage where they can mean something."

"And if the messy, complicated feelings are . . . really messy? And really complicated?"

"Then the scene will be even hotter."

He headed for the door, pausing with his hand on the frame.

"For what it's worth," he said, "whoever he is—he's got you twisted up in a way I've never seen. That's either going to make this the best performance of your life, or it's going to destroy you." He shrugged. "Maybe both."

The door closed behind him.

Overhead, the house lights hummed. We finally had the makings of a set from the carpentry shop. They weren't painted or staged yet, but they cast long shadows across the floor—the benches that would become boards, the lockers that would become the architecture of secrets kept and exposed.

I walked to center stage. Stood where I'd been standing when I pinned Lucas to the ground. Where I'd seen someone else's face.

"I hate you."

"No, you don't."

The lines echoed in my head, but they'd shifted. Transformed. Diego's words, Tyler's words, becoming something else entirely.

I remembered Rowan flinching when I said the stupid catchphrase. How he'd shut me out as completely as any security gate at the mall.

I'd hurt him.

"Don't touch me," Diego said in the script.

"I have to go," Rowan had said in the library.

Same panic. Same desperate need to protect himself from something he couldn't control.

And Tyler's response—hurt bleeding into recklessness, the almost-outing, the slur that was pain searching for a target—

Was that what I'd done? Hurt Rowan because I couldn't handle being shut out?

I sat down on the bench and stared out at the empty house.

The thing about playing Diego was that I understood him. Understood the fear that made him push Tyler away, the desperation that made him lash out, the love that was so tangled up in terror that he couldn't tell them apart anymore. Diego was hiding—from his teammates, from his mother, from himself. And that hiding was destroying the one thing he wanted.

"I want to not be scared," Diego said in the next scene. "I want to be brave like you. I want—I just want you."

I wanted Rowan.

The admission hit me like a physical thing, like the elbow Lucas had landed during our fight. Not just fascination. Not just research. I wanted him—the real him.

In the play, Diego learns that the hard way. His fear, his hiding, his inability to trust—it almost costs him everything.

What was my fear costing me?

I pulled out my phone. Opened a new message.

I'm sorry, I typed. For the library. For what I said. You didn't deserve that.

I stared at the words. I realized I didn't have Rowan's number. Didn't even know if he had a phone, or if "Rowan Calloway" had social media, or if there was any way to reach him that didn't involve ambushing him somewhere on campus.

I deleted the message.

Tomorrow, I told myself. Tomorrow, you find him and you apologize. In person. Face-to-face. The way it should be done.

I laid back, feet dangling over the edge of the stage, staring up at the lighting grid. The metal framework crisscrossed the ceiling like a constellation, all those instruments waiting to illuminate whatever happened on the stage below.

"I hate you," Diego said.

"No, you don't," Tyler replied.

Tyler knew that sometimes people pushed away the things they wanted most, because wanting made you vulnerable, and vulnerable meant you could get hurt.

I'd spent weeks studying Rowan from a distance. Cataloging his patterns. Building theories about his secrets.

The theatre door opened. Albright's voice echoed through the space: "Elliot? You ready to run the aftermath?"

I sat up. Took a breath.

"Yeah," I said. "I'm ready." I stood and brushed the dust off my backside.

Lucas trailed Albright and headed toward the stage, a fresh ice pack pressed to his lip.

"Good to go?" Lucas asked.

I nodded.

And as Albright called "Action," and I launched into Diego's desperate confession—I don't know how to do this, be what you need, be what I am—I let myself feel it.

All of it.

"I just want you," Diego said.

I meant it.

Chapter 13 The Westhaven Rivalry

Rowan

The team bus hummed beneath me, a steady diesel vibration that I could feel in my bones. Outside the window, the California coastline unspooled in a blur of rugged cliffs and winter-bare trees, the Pacific a slate-gray presence on our left as we wound south toward Port Calder.

I sat in the middle of the bus. Behind me, Maddox's voice boomed as he dissected a play from last night's NHL highlights. Something about a two-on-one, a missed pass, an opportunity squandered. His analysis was sharp. His hockey IQ was better than I thought. He saw the game the way coaches did, reading patterns and possibilities that most players missed. I filed that away. It explained why Sterling trusted him with the captain's C.

In front of me, Davies vibrated with nervous energy, his knee bouncing so hard I could feel it through the seat back. This was his first real road game too, and he was handling it the way he handled everything: with the enthusiasm of a Labrador puppy.

"I can't believe we're playing Westhaven," he said to no one in particular. "Did you see their highlights from last week? That goal by Miller was insane. Like, physics-defying. Do you think we can actually—"

"Davies." Kowalski's voice cut through from across the aisle. "Breathe."

"Right. Breathing. Good advice."

I leaned my head against the cool glass of the window and let my eyes lose focus. The landscape shifted as we drove—redwoods giving way to scrubby hills, then the first signs of the sprawling coastal city. Palm trees appeared, their fronds swaying in a breeze I couldn't feel. The sun was brighter here, the sky a different shade of blue.

The Port Calder Arena rose from the stadium district like a temple to athletic excess. Everything about it screamed money—the gleaming glass facade, the massive digital displays cycling through highlight reels and sponsor logos, the luxury box windows glinting in the afternoon sun like the eyes of wealthy observers.

"Wow," Davies whispered beside me, his eyes wide as dinner plates. "It's like a pro barn."

"It's just ice." My voice came out steadier than I felt. "Keep your head up and your feet moving. The puck doesn't care about the architecture."

The words were as much for me as for him.

We filed through the visitor's tunnel toward our locker room—smaller than Westhaven's, obviously, positioned in the less glamorous section of the building. But the ice would be the same. The puck would be the same. The game would be the game.

The warmups were a theater of intimidation. The Westhaven Breakers skated with synchronized precision, their crisp navy jerseys catching the light, their movements designed for the highlight cameras that tracked them from multiple angles. They were playing to the crowd before the game even started—flashy stickhandling, theatrical saves in the crease. Sure, the showmanship made for good social media content, but it didn't necessarily translate into a winning strategy once the puck dropped.

I kept my head down. Tight-turn drills to settle my center of gravity. Edge work along the boards, feeling out the ice surface. My eyes stayed on my skates, my stick, the puck. I ignored the Jumbotrons cycling through player headshots. The early crowd filing into the polished seats, were just another distraction. The media photographers setting up along the glass, I turned my head away slightly any time I skated too close.

I am number twenty-eight.

The first period was a high-velocity blur.

Westhaven lived up to their reputation. They moved the puck with diagonal flow patterns that made our defensive positioning outdated, cycling through the neutral zone with a speed that forced scrambles and adjustments. Their top line was talented. Many of their players would go on to pro careers, or at least professional-adjacent ones.

I focused on fundamentals. The two-hundred-foot game that Sterling preached. Relentless puck pressure on the forecheck. Tight gap control in the neutral zone. When I couldn't create, I disrupted. When I couldn't score, I made sure they couldn't either.

"Win the battles!" Sterling's gravelly voice barked from the bench. "Defense first!"

I wasn't looking for the highlight deke. I was winning the grimy battles along the boards, using my low center of gravity to absorb contact and protect the puck. The unglamorous work that didn't show up on stat sheets but kept us in games.

The score was 0-0 at the first intermission. A minor miracle, given how many shots we'd faced.

The second period started the same way—Westhaven pushing, us grinding—until midway through the frame, when everything changed.

A loose puck in the corner of their zone. I read the play before it happened: their center losing an edge, the puck squirting free, a window of opportunity opening. I was already moving, already committing to the chase, when I felt the vibration through the ice.

Their defenseman—a kid built like a small truck, probably 220 pounds of muscle and bad intentions—had been waiting for exactly this moment. He'd seen me coming before I saw him. The perfect predator.

The hit was a dead, brutal impact that rattled through every bone in my body. My vision went white for a half-second, then exploded into staccato flashes of light. My spine compressed against the boards. My teeth clacked together so hard I tasted copper as I collapsed to the ice.

The arena's roar became something else—a distant screech, like tires on pavement, like a sound from a memory I'd buried so deep I'd almost forgotten it existed.

Henderson going into the boards. The crack of his helmet against the glass. The way his body went limp, puppet-strings cut—

I didn't stay down.

I couldn't.

I used the boards to find my balance, anchoring my edges against the ice, refusing to let my body acknowledge the pain screaming through my ribs. The defenseman was already celebrating, already turning away, assuming I was neutralized.

But the puck was loose. And Davies was streaking toward the far post, completely unmarked because everyone had expected me to be finished.

I saw it. The lane. The possibility.

My hands worked on autopilot—muscle memory from a thousand drills, ten thousand hours of practice. A backhand pass, soft enough to land flat, strong enough to reach him. I watched as Davies eyes grew as he saw what I was about to do a fraction of a second before the puck left my blade. My ribs shrieked, my vision still swimming.

Davies one-timed it into the back of the net.

1-0 Ospreys.

The explosion of noise—our bench, the small contingent of traveling fans, Davies's primal scream of joy—washed over me as I finally pushed off the boards. My legs felt like water. My side felt like someone had parked a car on it. But we were winning, and I'd done my job.

As I skated back to the bench, I caught a look from the Westhaven side. One of their veteran forwards—Miller, the guy Davies had been gushing about on the bus—was staring at me. Not with the annoyance of someone whose team had just given up a goal.

With recognition.

It was subtle, barely more than a narrowing of the eyes, a slight tilt of the head. The "where do I know you from" stare that I'd learned to recognize and fear. Miller had played in the Pacific Northwest junior leagues the same years I had. Why he was only now in college like me was anyone's guess. We'd probably faced each other in tournaments, in showcases, in all the places where Chase St. Clair had been paraded around.

I ducked my head and kept skating. My heart hammered against my bruised ribs. But the back of my neck was on fire, and I could feel his eyes following me all the way to the bench.

The third period was an exercise in survival.

Westhaven pushed back with the desperation of a home team facing an upset. Their offense became a frantic, high-tempo siege—wave after wave of pressure, shots from every angle, bodies crashing the crease. We spent most of the final ten minutes pinned in our own zone. Sterling's system was the only thing standing between us and collapse.

I focused on positioning. Cutting off passing lanes. Supporting our defensemen in the corners. My ribs screamed every time I absorbed contact, but I refused to let it show. Pain was temporary and could be compartmentalized.

With two minutes left, Westhaven pulled their goalie for the extra attacker. Six skaters against five. The Port Calder crowd was on their feet, the noise a physical force that vibrated through the arena. This was what they'd paid for—the drama, the tension, the possibility of a comeback.

A point shot blasted toward our crease. I didn't think. I dropped to a knee, making my body a shield, and the puck hit me square in the thigh—a frozen meteor of vulcanized rubber traveling at ninety miles per hour. The pain was transcendent, the kind that existed outside normal human experience. I stayed upright just long enough to sweep the rebound toward the neutral zone, buying precious seconds.

The final buzzer shrieked. 2-1 Ospreys.

We'd won.

Davies was the first to reach me, practically tackling me with enthusiasm that made my bruised everything protest violently. "That assist, man! That pass! How did you even—"

"Lucky," I said. The word came out hoarse. "Good finish on your part."

"Lucky my ass. That was a whole other level of impressive."

I didn't answer. Couldn't answer. Because he was right, and we both knew it, and I didn't have a lie prepared for how a walk-on with no notable history had delivered a professional-grade pass while being pinned to the boards.

We filed toward the tunnel, the team exchanging stick-taps and shoulder bumps, the quiet satisfaction of a road win settling over us like a blanket. Sterling caught my eye as I passed and gave me one of his signature nods.

"Hey! Hey, St. Clair!"

The voice came from above—young, excited, cutting through the ambient noise of the crowd filing toward the exits. I froze mid-step, my blood going cold.

No. No, no, no—

I glanced up.

A kid. Maybe twelve years old, leaning over the railing in the third row, his face flushed with the particular fervor of youthful recognition. He wasn't wearing Westhaven colors. He was wearing a jersey I hadn't seen in five years—faded red and gold, oversized on his thin frame.

Portland juniors. My old team. The jersey I'd worn during the season when everything fell apart. My actual jersey, not even the fake ones created for the movie series.

"I knew it was you!" The kid was shouting now, loud enough that heads turned, people trying to see what the commotion was about. "My dad said you disappeared, but I knew you'd come back! I watched every game on YouTube! I still have all your cards!"

I couldn't move. Couldn't breathe. The tunnel seemed to narrow around me, the crowd noise becoming a roar that had nothing to do with the game we'd just won.

This kid had grown up watching me. This kid had kept my jersey, my cards, my memory alive while I'd spent five years trying to erase every trace of Chase St. Clair from existence. To him, I was still the Ice Prince.

"Can you sign my jersey?" The kid was pulling at his father's arm now, trying to climb over the railing. "Please? Just one autograph? I've been waiting so long—"

Other people stared. A woman with her phone out, already filming. A security guard glancing over to see what the noise was about.

"Wrong guy, kid." I ducked my head, pulled my helmet low over my damp hair, and walked fast—not quite running, but close—through the tunnel and into the darkness of the visitor's corridor. I didn't glance back. I couldn't. I didn't want to see the kid's face fall, see the confusion and hurt of a fan whose hero had just lied to him.

I'd see myself at twelve, standing outside an arena, waiting for an autograph that never came.

The locker room door closed behind me with a heavy thunk, and I stood there in the harsh fluorescent light, my back against the concrete wall, my chest heaving with breaths that wouldn't quite fill my lungs. I was having a panic attack.

The team filtered in around me over the next few minutes, filling the small visitor's locker room with the sounds of celebration. Sticks clattering, gear being stripped off, voices high with the adrenaline of victory. Davies was recounting his goal to anyone who would listen, his hands moving in elaborate gestures that threatened to knock over everything within arm's reach.

I sat in my stall and didn't join.

The face of that kid was burned into my retinas. The hope in his eyes. The worn jersey that suggested years of wear, of watching, of caring about someone who had abandoned him without a word.

To the world, Chase St. Clair had simply vanished. No explanation. No farewell. One day the hockey player-turned-movie star was everywhere, and the next he was gone. The tabloids had speculated—rehab, scandal, mental breakdown—but no one had known the truth. The PR team had handled the disappearance with the same clinical efficiency they'd handled everything else, and eventually, the world had moved on to fresher gossip.

But that kid hadn't moved on. That kid had kept the jersey.

Is this what survival is?

I'd told myself that disappearing was the only option. Chase St. Clair had been toxic. A brand built on lies and exploitation of a boy who'd been complicit in something he couldn't even name. I'd told myself that my birth name, Rowan Calloway, was better—cleaner, simpler, free from the machinery that had consumed my childhood.

But Chase St. Clair had meant something to people. To that kid in the stands. To however many others had worn my jersey, collected my cards, believed in the person they thought I was.

And I'd run away from them all without a single word of explanation. Not that I owed them an explanation.

I reached up and touched the cage of my helmet, which I still hadn't removed, still damp with sweat. This was supposed to protect me. The anonymity, the distance, the careful erasure of everything I'd been. But the past kept finding cracks—Elliot in the library, the kid in the stands, Miller's suspicious gaze across the ice.

How long before the whole structure collapsed?

Kowalski dropped onto the bench next to me, his face flushed with postgame satisfaction. "Hell of a pass in the second period, Calloway. Where'd that come from?"

"Just instinct," I said. The lie was automatic now.

"Some instinct." He studied me for a moment, then shrugged. "Whatever it is, keep doing it."

Chapter 14
The Locker Room Truth

ROWAN

Practice felt different in the days after Westhaven.

Not objectively different—Sterling ran the same drills, barked the same corrections, demanded the same defensive intensity he always did. But something in the air had shifted. The way teammates looked at me during line rushes. Small nods of acknowledgment that hadn't been there before. Subtle repositioning of bodies in the locker room that suggested I'd moved, somehow, from outsider to something closer to accepted.

The Westhaven assist had done that. One play, one moment of instinct overriding caution, and suddenly I was under a microscope.

I tried not to let it change how I moved on the ice. Same low center of gravity. Same safe plays. Same methodical, system-first hockey that Sterling preached and I'd embraced like a religion. The validation of that game had seeped into my muscles, and it was harder to keep the instincts suppressed.

We were running a three-on-two drill, the neutral zone transition work that Sterling loved because it forced quick decisions under pressure. I took a pass from Kowalski at the blue line, two defenders backing up in front of me, Davies and Maddox flanking me on the rush.

The lane was there. I saw it the way I always saw it—the gap between the defenders, the goalie cheating left, the clear path to a high-percentage scoring chance. My hands wanted to make the move. My body wanted to explode through the opening.

I dumped the puck into the corner.

Safe. Smart. Exactly what Sterling wanted.

But as I peeled off toward the bench, I caught Maddox watching me from the far blue line. His expression was unreadable, but something in his posture suggested he'd seen the same thing I had.

The lane I didn't take.

He found me after the drill, skating over with the casual authority of a captain who'd earned his position through years of exactly this kind of observation.

"Calloway."

I stopped at the boards, reaching for my water bottle. "Yeah?"

"You had it." He positioned himself beside me, close enough that the conversation would stay between us. "Clear path, goalie out of position. You could have walked in for a shot."

"I saw the safer play." The lie came automatically. "Davies had a better angle."

"Davies had an angle. You had the better one." Maddox's voice was flat, matter-of-fact. The voice of someone stating an obvious truth that we both knew. "But you dumped it anyway."

I took a long drink from the water bottle, buying time. "Coach wants system hockey. Dump and chase. I'm playing within the system."

"You've had the lane five times this week." Maddox leaned against the boards, his arms crossed over his chest. "That neutral zone rush just now. The two-on-one in yesterday's scrimmage. The power play sequence on Tuesday. Every time, you dump it."

"I see the safe play."

"You see every play." His eyes narrowed. "That's what I'm trying to figure out. You read the ice like you've been doing it your whole life, but then you make the rookie choice every single time. It doesn't add up."

The water bottle was empty. I had nothing left to fidget with. "I am a rookie, Captain. Not trying to be a hero. Just here to contribute."

"Sterling wants smart hockey," he said. "There's a difference between smart and scared."

The word landed like a blow. Scared. The same accusation Elliot had thrown at me in the hallway after tryouts. Coward. Different word, same meaning.

"I've searched for you on the internet," Maddox continued. "Before here, it seems like you've never played hockey in a day in your life. Nothing special. No club team, no junior league worth mentioning. Just a guy who showed up at walk-on tryouts and somehow moves like he's been playing elite-level hockey since he could skate."

I kept my face neutral.

"You're hiding something, Calloway." Maddox pushed off the boards, squaring his body toward mine. Not aggressive, exactly, but present. "I've watched enough tape to know elite training when I see it. The way you protect the puck. The way you read passing lanes. That backhand dish at Westhaven—that's not Division III college hockey. I love my school and my teammates, but I know what we are and what we're not. You're like D1 first draft pick in the NHL type hockey." I opened my mouth to argue, but he raised his hand cutting me off before I could speak. "That's the kind of skill you develop when you're playing real minutes in real games at a level that's beyond what we have here."

"I played pickup," I said. "Rec leagues. Nothing organized."

"Bullshit."

The word hung between us. Sterling's whistle blew somewhere in the distance, calling the next drill, but neither of us moved.

"I don't know what your story is," Maddox said, his voice dropping to a low, dangerous frequency that cut through the hum of the locker room. "And honestly, I don't care. If you've got baggage, that's your business. You can carry that weight until it breaks you for all I care."

He stepped into my space, his shadow falling across the gear I'd just finished hanging. "But if you're sandbagging—if you're intentionally stifling your talent because you're afraid of something—that becomes my business."

He held my gaze, his eyes narrowing as he searched for the "Ice Prince" I was trying so hard to bury. "In this league, sandbagging isn't just poor sportsmanship; it's a goddamn insult to the game. You're playing at 60 percent, hiding a Junior-A pedigree behind a grinder's mask so you can coast through a conference spot without being noticed. It's unethical, Rowan. It's cheating the guys in this room who are actually playing at their ceiling."

He jabbed a finger toward the ice. "We're fighting for a playoff seed. We need every ounce of skill on that roster. If you're holding back while the rest of us are bleeding for a win, you're not a teammate. You're a liability."

"I'm giving you everything I have."

"No." Maddox shook his head. "You're giving us everything you're willing to risk. It's not the same thing."

"Everything good?" Davies asked, materializing at my shoulder. His timing was perfect or terrible depending on your perspective. He was still breathing hard from the last drill, his face flushed, but his eyes were sharp as they moved between me and Maddox.

Maddox's expression flickered—annoyance, maybe, or recalculation. "Just getting to know our mysterious walk-on."

"He's not mysterious." Davies positioned himself beside me, not quite between us but close enough to make a statement. "He's just quiet. Some people are quiet."

"And you're defending him?"

"He fed me the game-winner at Westhaven." Davies shrugged, as if this explained everything. "So, yeah. I'm defending him."

The tension held for a moment—Maddox looking at Davies, Davies looking back, neither of them willing to be the first to break. I stayed silent, watching the dynamic play out. This was new. Davies, the nervous freshman who'd been vibrating with anxiety on the bus ride to Port Calder, was standing up to the captain on my behalf.

Something had shifted between us without my noticing. We'd become teammates. Maybe even friends.

Maddox must have seen it too, because he stepped back, the aggression in his posture softening into something more like resignation.

"We're not done, Calloway," he said. But the edge was gone from his voice. "Think about what I said."

He skated away toward the rest of the team. Coach Okafor was already calling out instructions for the next drill. Davies watched him go, then turned to me.

"What was that about?"

"Nothing." I picked up my stick, tested the tape with my thumb. "Just captain stuff. He's doing his job."

"He was in your face."

"He's suspicious." The truth slipped out before I could stop it. "He thinks I'm holding back."

Davies was quiet for a moment. "Are you?"

I looked at him—this earnest, enthusiastic kid who'd somehow decided I was worth trusting—and I didn't know how to answer. The lie would be easy. The lie was always easy. But something about his expression, the genuine concern in his eyes, made the words stick in my throat.

"I'm playing within the system," I said finally. "That's all."

Davies nodded slowly, accepting the nonanswer. "Well, whatever you're doing, it's working. Wherever you learned to play like that . . . "

He trailed off, leaving the sentence unfinished. An invitation to explain. A door I could walk through if I wanted.

I didn't walk through it.

"Okafor's calling the next drill," I said. "We should get back."

Chapter 15
The Notes

Elliot

By the second week of February, the grind of the semester had settled in, wedged between a grueling game schedule and the looming threat of first-round assessments.

The corkboard was mostly empty now, a field of tiny pinpricks in the cork that felt like scars from a previous life. I'd kept my promise to strip away the obsession, but the digital ghost of the Pacific Junior Hockey League was much harder to exorcise.

It was two in the morning. I sat cross-legged on my bed, the laptop a heavy, warm weight on my knees. The blue light of the screen was the only thing cutting through the shadows of the loft. Below me, the former bookstore was a hollow shell of floorboards and silence. The rows of shelves were long gone, leaving only the pale rectangles on the walls where the tall bookcases had once shielded the plaster from the sun.

The space was filled with nothing but dust and the echo of a business that had folded before I arrived. I was trying to find an ending for my own project—for The Author's Cut—but the "Physicality of Performance" kept leading me back to the same fractured problem.

I wasn't looking for Rowan anymore. I needed the truth about the league's collapse to give the play some historical heft. But the internet is a series of interconnected rooms, and I'd just stepped into a cold one.

The Henderson section of my digital notes grew by the minute. I'd spent three days reconstructing a timeline that no official record wanted to acknowledge. It wasn't a murder board; it was a ledger of a coverup that started roughly six years ago.

March 15: Michael Henderson, defenseman for the Vancouver Vanguard, goes head-first into the boards.

March 16: Leaked medical reports confirm a fractured C4 vertebra.

March 17: Chase St. Clair withdraws from the league. No statement.

August: An unnamed source settles with the Hendersons. NDAs are signed.

June the following year: The league dissolves.

I stared at the dates. It wasn't sociology; it was destruction. A boy's future had been erased, and everyone had agreed to pretend it hadn't happened. My stomach turned not because I'd found a "secret," but because I'd found a tragedy that had been treated like an accounting error.

And then, a name began to surface in the old Sin Bin threads like a curse: Anders Holmström.

The name appeared in the dark corners of the gossip archives I was scouring for costume references. Holmström had been the star forward for the Portland Eagles—a Swedish import with NHL-level talent and a reputation for "physical play" that occasionally crossed the line into something uglier.

The Holmström kid. But there was another player involved—he made the pass that set the whole thing up. Kid in the movie, the one with the stupid catchphrase.

Could Holmström and Rowan purposely hurt Henderson? If so, Rowan wasn't just hiding from fame; he was hiding from a ghost he'd helped create. But as I went deeper into the celebrity gossip archives—the places that preserve the things PR firms try to kill—I found a different type of betrayal.

The photos were grainy, taken from phones at parties that shouldn't have been documented.

Anders Holmström and Chase St. Clair standing too close at a premiere. Another shot of Holmström's arm around Rowan's shoulders at a charity event, Rowan leaning into the touch.

Then there was the hot tub photo. The picture was taken at a house in the Hollywood Hills. The lighting was poor—oversaturated blues from the pool lights clashing with the orange glow of a nearby fire pit—but the composition was devastating. Anders Holmström was perched on the tiled edge of the tub, his legs spread wide, claiming the space with a predatory kind of confidence. He was clearly nude, his wet skin gleaming like marble in the low light.

Tucked between Holmström's knees, facing away from the camera, was a second boy. The shot was taken from behind, showing the sharp line of a pale spine and the curve of a backside just breaking the surface of the water. It was a moment of profound, quiet intimacy captured without consent by some paparazzi. You couldn't see the second boy's face, but the tilt of the head, the specific breadth of the shoulders, and the way Holmström's hand was tangled in those familiar dark curls made the speculation unavoidable.

The digital world hadn't needed a face to reach a verdict. In the toxic ecosystem of the Sin Bin forums and celebrity gossip blogs, the narrative had written itself: the "Ice Prince" hadn't just quit; he'd been caught with his leading man. When I'd first ran across the story, I couldn't find the photo anywhere. Somehow, the photo had been scrubbed from the internet within hours, probably by a fleet of high-priced lawyers. But, as with anything that finds its way onto the internet, the ghost of it remained even if it wasn't easy to find.

Some speculated that Holmström had staged the photo. If that was the case, Holmström hadn't just betrayed Rowan on the ice; he had documented his vulnerability and handed it to a world that was waiting to tear him apart.

Ice Prince is GAY? the old thread titles screamed.

I sat back, my heart hammering against my ribs. A comment buried in a long-dead blog made the final piece click: From some queens in the Hollywood Hills, I hear Holmström hired the photographer who took the photo. The kid wanted to out St. Clair as revenge for something that happened at a game.

No wonder he doesn't trust anyone. I closed the laptop, the silence of the loft was heavy and suffocating. The more I tried to stay away from my "research," the more I just kept finding new threads to pull at in the tapestry that is Rowan Calloway. I had three names: Henderson, Holmström, and Chet Finlay.

Professor Albright's office smelled like old books and pipe tobacco, even though I'd never actually seen him smoke and smoking was banned on campus. It was a small, cluttered space—shelves overflowing with scripts and critical theory, a desk buried under student papers, walls covered with production photos from three decades of academic theatre.

I sat in the chair across from his desk.

"Your work on Diego has improved significantly," Albright said, flipping through his notes. "That last rehearsal—the kiss scene—was the best I've seen from you. Whatever you've been doing is working."

"Thank you." I kept my voice neutral. Professional. "I've been doing field research. Observing athletes, trying to understand the physicality."

"So, I've heard." Albright set down his notes and looked at me over the rims of his reading glasses. "You've been spending quite a lot of time at hockey practices."

The statement hung in the air. Not accusatory, exactly, but weighted.

"Understanding the sport helps me understand the character," I said. "Diego lives on the ice. I needed to see that world."

"And the player you've been watching?" Albright's voice was gentle, probing. "The . . . walk-on."

I felt the blood drain from my face. "I don't—"

"Elliot." He held up a hand. "I hear things. Theatre students talk. Half the cast has noticed you disappearing to the arena. Lucas mentioned you seemed . . . distracted during your scene work. Distracted by something outside the production."

The silence stretched between us. I didn't know what to say. Any denial would sound hollow, and Albright had known me long enough to recognize when I was performing.

"I'm not going to pry into your personal life," he said finally. "That's not my place. But I am going to ask you a question, and I want you to think carefully about your answer."

I waited.

"You're playing Diego—the man being watched. The man being pursued." Albright steepled his fingers. "So, why are you behaving like Tyler?"

The words landed like stones dropped into still water. I felt the ripples spreading outward, touching everything.

"I don't—"

"You're supposed to be understanding what it feels like to be observed. To be hunted. To have someone cataloging your every move." Albright's gaze was steady, analytical. "Instead, you've become the observer. The hunter. You've spent weeks watching this player, taking notes, building some kind of . . . dossier. That's not Diego's experience, Elliot. That's Tyler's."

I opened my mouth to argue, but nothing came out. He was right. I'd been so focused on understanding Rowan—on cracking him open, on documenting his secrets—that I'd lost sight of whose perspective I was supposed to inhabit.

"I thought understanding the subject would help me understand the character," I said weakly.

"And has it?" Albright leaned back in his chair. "Or has it just given you a way to indulge an obsession while calling it research?"

The silence stretched between us. I didn't have an answer.

"Method acting is a powerful tool, Elliot. But it's also dangerous—especially when you're channeling the wrong character." He picked up a pen, tapping it against his desk. "Diego is a man who's been watched his whole life. A man who's learned to hide because visibility means vulnerability. If you want to play him truthfully, you need to understand what that feels like. Not what it feels like to be the one watching."

"How am I supposed to do that?"

"That's for you to figure out." Albright paused. "But I'll tell you this: whatever's happening between you and this hockey player—if you keep approaching him like Tyler approaches Diego, pushing until something breaks—you're going to hurt him. And you're going to lose any chance of understanding what you actually need to understand."

"Think about it," he said. "And Elliot? Be careful. The best performances come from truth. But truth has consequences."

The afternoon shift at Brewed Awakening was exactly what I needed—mindless repetition to occupy my hands while my brain spiraled.

"You're playing Diego. So, why are you behaving like Tyler?"

I poured a leaf pattern into the latte—muscle memory at this point—and called out the order, "Jackson." The afternoon lull had settled over the shop, just a handful of students scattered at tables, laptops open, earbuds in. The perfect environment for an existential crisis disguised as a work shift.

The bell above the door chimed. I glanced up—customer service reflex—my stomach dropped.

Two hockey players. I recognized them even without their gear. The first was impossible to miss: Davies, the freshman built like a semitruck, his shoulders filled the doorway. Behind him was Number 91. Volkov, if I remembered the roster correctly.

They didn't notice me. Why would they? I was just the guy behind the counter, another faceless barista in an apron. Invisible.

This is what it feels like, I thought. To be invisible in front of everyone.

"What are you getting?" Davies asked, squinting up at the menu board.

"Americano. Large." Volkov's accent was slight but present—something Eastern European softened by years in California. "You?"

"I don't know, man. Something with caramel? And whipped cream?" Davies's wide eyes let me know he did not know what any of the words on the menu meant. "I don't really do coffee shops."

"Then why did you agree to come?" Volkov asked.

"Because you said you were buying."

I stepped up to the register, keeping my expression neutral. Professional. "What can I get you?"

Volkov ordered his Americano. Davies eventually settled on a caramel macchiato with extra whipped cream, which he pronounced "mah-chee-AH-toe" with the confidence of someone who had never ordered one before. I rang them up and turned to make the drinks, positioning myself at the espresso machine where I could hear their conversation without appearing to listen.

"So, you're coming tomorrow, right?" Volkov asked, leaning against the pickup counter.

"To the lake? Yeah, definitely." Davies bounced on his heels. "Calloway's coming too. I asked him after practice."

My hands stuttered on the portafilter. I recovered quickly, but my pulse had kicked up.

"Good. He needs it." Volkov crossed his arms. "That guy is wound tighter than anyone I've ever seen. And I'm from Russia, where everyone moves like they have a stick up their ass. Calloway makes my countrymen seem like free-floating hippies. Every practice, every drill—he plays like someone's going to take it away from him if he stops for a second."

"You think so?" Davies sounded surprised. "I just thought he was, like, really focused."

"There's focused and there's . . . " Volkov made a vague gesture. "Whatever he is. The lake will be good for him. Get him out of his head."

I pulled the shots for the Americano, added hot water, tried to keep my breathing steady.

"It's not going to be too cold?" Davies asked. "I mean, it's February."

"We're not swimming, durochka. We're hanging out. Building a fire. Drinking beer that I did not buy for you because you are definitely twenty-one." Volkov's voice was dry. "The whole team goes. It's tradition. Good for morale."

"Maddox is coming?"

A pause. "Maddox is . . . dealing with his own shit right now. But yes. He'll be there. He always is."

I finished the Americano and started on Davies's sugar bomb, my mind racing. The whole team. Tomorrow. Miller Lake.

Rowan would be there. Out of his element. Away from the ice, away from the library, away from all the places he'd built his walls.

"Large Americano and a caramel macchiato," I called out, sliding both drinks across the counter. Though it took all of my effort not to use Davies's creative pronunciation.

Davies grabbed his with a grin. "Thanks, man." He took a sip and his eyes went wide. "Oh, that's good. Why don't I come here more often?"

"Because you're always at the arena or the dining hall," Volkov said, collecting his cup. "Come. We've got film study in twenty."

They headed for the door, already arguing about something else. The bell chimed as they left, and then they were gone, their voices fading into the winter afternoon.

I stood behind the counter, a rag in my hand, not moving.

Miller Lake. What if I happened to be there? Not hunting. Not watching from the shadows. Just . . . present. It's a public lake. Lots of people from campus went there to party on the weekends. It was a good place to chill, build a fire, drink cheap beer while pretending the cold didn't bother you. The local police left people alone as long as they weren't breaking too many laws.

The espresso machine beeped, demanding attention. I turned back to it, already planning what I'd wear tomorrow, how I'd position myself, what kind of "coincidence" would be most believable.

Chapter 16
The Lake Camp

ROWAN

Miller Lake sat in a bowl of redwoods about twenty minutes outside Oakridge, the kind of place that belonged in a nature documentary—pristine water reflecting the gray February sky, pine trees standing sentinel along the shore, the whole scene so perfectly Northern California it almost felt staged. It had several nature trails. I often drove out there when I needed a change of scenery for a morning run or just to breathe in clean air.

I'd barely gotten out of my beat-up SUV before Davies's voice cut through the crisp air.

"You lied to me!"

Volkov was already stripping off his shirt, revealing a chest that had been carved from Eastern European granite. "I did not lie."

"You said we weren't swimming!" Davies stood at the edge of the gravel parking area, arms crossed, looking genuinely betrayed. "You said—and I quote—'We're not swimming, durochka. We're hanging out. Building a fire.'"

"We are building a fire." Volkov kicked off his shoes. "Later. First, we get wet. I said nothing about swimming."

The rest of the team was already in various stages of undress, a chaos of discarded hoodies and abandoned sneakers. Kowalski cannonballed off the floating dock with a whoop that echoed off the surrounding hills. Petrov waded in more cautiously, swearing in Russian—or maybe it was just regular English, hard to tell with the way his voice pitched up as the water hit his upper thighs.

"I didn't bring a swimsuit," Davies said, his voice climbing toward genuine distress. "I don't have—I'm not prepared for this."

"So?" Volkov shrugged smoothing his wet hair back as he tread water. "Go nude."

Davies's face went from pink to crimson in half a second. For a guy built like a vending machine, he could blush like a Victorian maiden. "I'm not—I can't just—there are people here."

"We have all seen—"

"Nope." Davies held up both hands. "Not happening. Absolutely not."

Chen wandered past, already in board shorts. "Just strip to your boxers, rookie. Nobody cares."

"Easy for you to say, you brought actual swimwear—"

"Because I've been to lake day before." Chen grinned. "Consider this your initiation."

I leaned against the Jeep, watching the chaos unfold with something that might have been amusement. This was the team away from the ice—no drills, no coaches, no pressure. Just a bunch of college hockey players acting like idiots at a lake in February.

Davies desperately searched for an ally. His eyes landed on me. "Calloway. Back me up here."

"I brought shorts," I said.

"Traitor."

Volkov laughed. "Is only fifty degrees. In Russia, this is summer."

"This isn't Russia!"

"Come, little Tank." Volkov beckoned with exaggerated patience. "The water, she does not bite."

A chorus of encouragement rose from the guys already in the lake—Do it, rookie! and Tank! Tank! Tank!—the chant building until Davies threw his hands up in defeat.

"Fine! Fine." He yanked his hoodie over his head, revealing a torso that justified his nickname. The kid was built like a brick wall. "But if anyone takes pictures, I'm drowning you all."

He stripped down to a pair of boxer briefs covered in little cartoon hockey sticks—which earned a round of appreciative hooting—and marched toward the water with the grim determination of a man walking to his execution.

The moment his feet hit the lake, he let out a sound that could only be described as a dying moose.

"Cold! This is—why would anyone—cold!"

"Keep going!" Kowalski shouted from the dock. "It gets better!"

"You're lying! Everyone here is a liar!"

But he kept going, wading deeper, his complaints becoming less coherent as the water climbed past his thighs, his waist, his chest. When he finally dunked his head under, he came up gasping and laughing, the shock of it breaking through his resistance.

"Okay," he admitted, teeth chattering. "It's not that bad."

I found myself smiling. Actually smiling. Something about Davies's unfiltered reaction—the genuine horror—cracked through my defenses.

"Calloway!" Kowalski pointed at me from the dock. "You're next! Get in here!"

I held up my hands. "Give me a minute."

"Minute's up! Let's go!"

I stripped off my tracksuit bottoms to reveal a pair of trunks underneath. I folded them into a neat pile as I took my shoes and socks off. Last, I pulled off my hoodie. The water was cold—there was no pretending otherwise. Fifty degrees hit your body like a full-systems reset, every nerve ending firing at once. But after the initial shock, it became something else. Bracing. Alive. The kind of cold that made you feel present in your own skin in a way that was hard to achieve anywhere else.

I surfaced next to Davies, who was now engaged in a splashing war with Petrov that neither of them could win.

"This is insane," he said, grinning despite his blue lips. "This is the best thing ever. But . . . Everyone here is a liar!"

The group of half-naked men burst out laughing.

The next hour dissolved into chaos. Someone produced a waterlogged football and a game of catch devolved into full-contact water wrestling. Volkov and Hedman had a competition to see who could hold their breath longer, which Volkov won by what everyone agreed was cheating. Chen attempted to teach Davies how to float on his back, an endeavor that ended with Davies kicking Chen in the face and both of them going under in a tangle of limbs.

No drills. No coaches. No pressure to perform or prove myself. Just bodies in cold water, laughter echoing off the redwoods, the simple animal pleasure of being young and stupid and part of something.

I caught myself laughing at one point when Kowalski tried to climb onto the floating dock and Petrov shoved him back in. The sound surprised me. I couldn't remember the last time I'd laughed like that.

Eventually, the cold became too much. We staggered out of the water in waves, grabbing towels and hoodies, gravitating toward the bonfire that Maddox and a few of the seniors had built while we were making fools of ourselves in the lake.

The fire was massive—an entire cord of firewood transformed into a blaze that threw heat twenty feet in every direction. I stood close enough to feel my skin prickle as it thawed, steam rising from my wet hair.

Davies appeared at my elbow, wrapped in a towel and shivering. “Okay. I admit it. That was fun.”

“You sound surprised.”

“I’m surprised by everything these days.” He shook his head, sending water droplets flying. “Did you know Volkov can hold his breath for like three minutes? That’s not normal. That’s superhuman.”

“He’s Russian. Different rules.”

Davies laughed—that full-body, puppyish laugh that I was starting to recognize as his default setting. “Come on. Chen brought marshmallows.”

Our bonfire wasn’t the only gathering at Miller Lake. As the afternoon stretched toward evening, the shore had filled with the usual weekend crowd—students from campus sprawled on blankets with textbooks they were pretending to read, a group of townies with fishing poles and a cooler of beer, a couple making out against a tree with the kind of enthusiasm that suggested they’d forgotten they were in public. Most of them had watched our lake invasion with expressions ranging from amusement to concern, but none of them had been stupid enough to join us in the frigid water. Smart people, apparently, came to Miller Lake to relax. Only hockey players came to freeze.

I stayed by the fire for another twenty minutes, making the appropriate noises at the appropriate times, performing the role of “teammate who’s definitely bonding, just quiet about it.” But the effort was exhausting. Every interaction required calculation—what to say, what not to say, how to be present without being visible. Eventually, I muttered something about needing air and slipped away from the group. I walked along the shoreline until the noise of the gathering faded behind me.

The lake curved around a small peninsula thick with pines, and I found a spot where the water lapped against smooth rocks, the trees blocking the view of the bonfire. Quiet. Private. A quiet place where I could just be for a few minutes.

I sat down on a flat boulder at the water's edge and let the silence settle over me.

That's when I saw him.

Elliot Vega was sitting on a rock about thirty feet away, his back against a pine tree, a notebook open in his lap. He was wearing civilian clothes—jeans, a flannel shirt layered over a thermal, the kind of deliberately casual outfit that probably took him twenty minutes to assemble. His dark hair was windblown, curling slightly at the ends, and he was staring at the water with an expression I couldn't read. And as much as I hated to admit it, he was pretty hot.

I'd seen him at practice a few times. He'd done a good job of trying to be unseen, but from the ice it's not hard to see what's going on in the barn.

His attention was on the lake, his pen moving slowly across the page, and for one disorienting moment I could have been watching him the way he always watched me. I was the observer and he was the insect under my microscope.

I should have left. Should have backed away quietly, returned to the bonfire. But curiosity kept me rooted to the boulder.

Maybe it was the way he looked without an audience. Softer, somehow. Less like the crazed fanboy and more like . . . a person. A student with a notebook, watching the water, existing in the world the way anyone else might.

He glanced up.

Our eyes met across the thirty feet of rocky shoreline. I watched recognition flash across his face, followed by something more complex—surprise, wariness, and underneath it all, something that seemed like relief.

"Are you following me?" The words came out before I could stop them. My default defense. The accusation I'd been hurling at him since the beginning.

Elliot's mouth curved in a half-smile. "Yes. But not right now."

The honesty caught me off guard. I'd expected denial. Instead, he just admitted it. Like it was the most natural thing in the world.

"Then why are you here?"

"Environmental dramaturgy project," he said, holding up the Moleskine like it was a shield rather than a ledger of my secrets. "Or ecodramaturgy, if you're feeling particularly pretentious. My professor is obsessed with the idea that we've spent too much time asking Who are we? and not enough time asking Where are we?"

"And that means what exactly? You think where we are is a swamp?"

"Are you talking hockey or the lake?"

There it was. The cheeky response I expected.

"I think this landscape is a character in your team's performance," Elliot said, his eyes scanning the shoreline where the redwoods crowded the water's edge. "Humanist theatre treats the environment as a backdrop—a mere metaphor. But ecodramaturgy foregrounds the crisis. It's about how the terrain dictates your physical vocabulary. You don't move the same way in the water or along the shoreline as you do on the polished ice of the arena, do you? The resistance of the water, the cold of the mud . . . it's de-anthropocentrism in action. You aren't a hockey player here. Sure it's part of your identity, but you're just another organism struggling against an ecosystem that doesn't care about your stats."

I leaned back against a moss-slicked rock, my chest still heaving from the sprints. "That sounds like complete bullshit."

"Oh, it's total, academically defensible bullshit," he shrugged, a smile breaking through his guarded expression. "But it's the kind of bullshit that gets me a passing grade in a class about climate justice and nonhuman perspectives. I'm just here to document how the 'Ice Prince' survives a talking lake."

I didn't know what to do with this version of Elliot. The one who admitted to following me and then immediately undercut his own high-minded excuses.

I didn't know what to do with this version of Elliot. The one who admitted to following me and called his own excuses bullshit. It was disarming in a way his calculated provocations had never been. He wasn't pining for the "star" anymore; he stared at me and how I fit into the trees.

"I'll leave if you want," he said. "I know I've been pushy. Everyone tells me I'm a little extra most days."

The apology—or whatever it was—hung in the air between us. I should have taken the out. Instead, I found myself walking toward him.

I sat on a rock a few feet away, close enough to talk without shouting but far enough to maintain the illusion of control. Elliot watched me approach with an expression of contained surprise.

"You're not running," he observed.

"You're not attacking."

"Fair point." He closed his notebook, setting it aside. "New approach. Less ambush, more . . . presence."

"Presence."

"I'm trying something different." His voice was quieter now, the theatrical confidence dialed down to something more genuine. "The library was . . . I shouldn't have done that. The catchphrase. I was testing a theory, but I wasn't thinking about what it would actually feel like for you."

I stared at him, trying to read the angle. There was always an angle with Elliot—I'd learned that much. But the contrition in his expression seemed real, and I didn't know what to do with it.

"What's the theory?" I asked finally, the cold mud on my skin beginning to tighten as it dried.

"That you're performing a role. That Rowan Calloway is as much a character as anything I play on stage." He met my eyes, his gaze unflinching. "That underneath all the careful anonymity, there's someone who used to be something else."

The words should have felt like another attack, but they were delivered with a clinical, almost academic curiosity.

"Everyone performs," I said, leaning back on my elbows. "Isn't that the whole original basis of Erving Goffman's work? The Presentation of Self in Everyday Life?"

Elliot's eyebrows shot up. "Wait. The jock reads midcentury sociology?"

"I want to be a journalist, Elliot," I countered. "Goffman is one of the patron saints of media studies. We're taught to see the world as a series of 'staged encounters.' Expression given versus expression given off. We all have a frontstage persona."

"True." He shifted on his rock, drawing his knees up to his chest. "But most people don't perform their entire identity twenty-four hours a day. Most people have a backstage—a place where the mask comes off. My problem is, I don't think you ever leave the stage."

"And you think I don't have a backstage?"

"I think I've never seen it." His voice was curious now, genuinely curious. "Even when you're playing—on the ice, I mean—there's always this sense of 'role distance.' Like you're holding something back. Choosing not to do things you could do. Making yourself smaller than you are to maintain the character of a third-line grinder."

"And how do you know what a third-line grinder even is?" I asked, my voice laced with a genuine, sharp-edged surprise. I looked him over again—the vintage cardigan, the carefully messy hair, the fingers meant for piano keys or script pages, not for gripping a composite stick in a goalmouth scramble. "You don't exactly strike me as the season-ticket-holding type."

Elliot didn't flinch. If anything, he leaned into the question, a glint appearing behind his glasses.

"I'm not," he admitted, "but I am the type who does his homework. If I'm going to deconstruct a performance, I have to understand the technical requirements of the role. I've spent the last three weeks submerged in hockey terminology and scouting reports. I know that a third-line grinder is the 'blue-collar' worker of the ice. They're the ones you send out to disrupt the other team's rhythm, to take the hits, to play the 'grimy' minutes so the stars don't have to."

He paused, his eyes narrowing, not as a fan, but as a director analyzing an actor missing his cues.

"It's a specific archetype, Rowan. It's built on the idea of being 'useful' rather than 'exceptional.' It requires a high level of physical sacrifice and a very low level of personal ego. And you play it with a technical precision that is almost . . . too perfect. You don't just play the role; you disappear into it. You check every box of the 'grinder' syllabus, but every once in a while there are these moments where you slip out of that for a fraction of a second and I can see who you are. Admittedly, it's the most disciplined performance I've ever seen, and that's what makes it so terrifyingly obvious that it is a performance."

I looked away, back toward the gray expanse of the lake. I had spent so long trying to be invisible that I hadn't realized my invisibility was its own kind of spotlight to someone who knew how to find it.

"You're overthinking it," I muttered, though the words felt hollow even to me.

"Am I?" Elliot countered softly. "In theatre, the hardest thing to play is 'ordinary' when you're built for the lead. You're essentially a virtuoso trying to play 'Chopsticks' so no one notices you've mastered Rachmaninoff. But the rhythm is too steady, Rowan. You're too good at being average."

The observation landed with uncomfortable accuracy. The lanes I didn't take, the plays I didn't make, the constant, exhausting calibration of how much skill I could show without raising questions.

"Maybe that's just how I play," I said.

"Maybe." He was quiet for a moment, the silence stretching out until the only sound was the wind through the pines. "Or maybe you're hiding what Goffman would call a 'spoiled identity.' Something you think would destroy the show if the audience ever saw it."

The words hung between us. The lake lapped gently against the rocks. Somewhere in the distance, I could hear the team shouting, the splash of bodies hitting water—the normal sounds of people who weren't analyzing the fabric of their own secrets.

"Why do you care?" I asked. The question came out raw, unguarded. "Why does it matter to you?"

Elliot didn't answer immediately. He stared out at the water, his expression thoughtful, and when he spoke, his voice was softer than I'd ever heard it. I moved closer to him, staring out with him. Sitting close enough we could touch, but a clear barrier between us.

"My father tried to make me play soccer," he said. "They put me in front of the net because I could do the least amount of damage there. But I didn't watch the ball. I spent the entire game picking daisies and taking them to my mother on the sidelines." He glanced at me, a self-deprecating smile tugging at his mouth. "That's how gay I was. My one attempt at athletics and I outed myself to the entire stands filled with families and friends."

I laughed. "Sterling would have put you through the boards for that," I said.

"Sterling doesn't understand the theatricality of a well-placed daisy. Besides, he's a teddy bear. I'm way more scared of Okafor. She's downright frightening. I half expect her to pull out a leather whip and start cracking it at some of the younger guys."

A sound came out of my throat. Not quite a full laugh, but the start of one. I couldn't remember the last time I'd made that sound.

"Don't put that idea in her head," I grumbled. "She's intimidating enough as it is. As for your question. I don't think I understand it either. Not the question, I understand that. But an answer, I've spent years trying to figure that out. And trust me, several highly paid shrinks later, and I still haven't figured out life." I turned to him. The natural wave of his lips. The deep brown of his eyes watching me. "But I get the picking daisies part.

Wanting to be somewhere else. Wanting something beautiful while everyone else is trying to hit you."

The words came out before I could stop them, more honest than anything I'd said to another person in years. Elliot's expression shifted—something soft and surprised moving across his features.

"Yeah," he replied. "Exactly that."

We sat in silence for a moment, the lake spreading out before us, gray and still under the February sky. The distance between us felt smaller, though neither of us had moved.

"Why hockey?" Elliot asked. "If you're trying to disappear, there are easier ways. You could have picked a sport no one cares about. Chess. Cross-country. Competitive knitting."

"Is competitive knitting a thing?"

"It should be. Very dramatic needle-clicking."

I laughed again. "Hockey is . . . I don't know. The only place that ever made sense." I stared at the water, not looking at him. "For moments, when I'm on the ice, the performance isn't subterfuge. It's the only time everything else goes away. The noise, the questions, all of it. It's just the game. The puck. The movement. It's the only time I feel like I can breathe."

The honesty surprised me. I hadn't said anything like that out loud since . . . my last therapy session. But something about Elliot's unexpected gentleness, how he'd offered his own vulnerability first, made the words feel safe.

"That's beautiful," Elliot said. Not sarcastic. Just present. "You kind of remind me of a song I learned when I was in Sunday school." I let a corner of my mouth twitch upward in a half-smirk that said I wasn't buying it. "No, no really." He sat for a moment, clearly trying to remember the words. "This little light of mine?" he said, more like a question than a statement. "Yeah, that sounds right. Anyway, there was this part where they talk about not hiding your light under a bushel. Admittedly, as a kid I had no idea what a bushel was, but I remember the part where we would yell 'no' to the idea. That's kind of how I've lived my life. Anytime someone tries to tell me to put out my flame, I scream. No!'"

"I don't think that song was an allegory of coming out, but I get your point," I acknowledged. Before I thought better of it, I added a wink and a crooked smile.

He brushed his shoulder against mine, playfully. “Don’t make fun of my trauma.” The contact was brief, playful, unintentional, but I felt it everywhere. The warmth of another person’s body. The solid reality of someone existing in the same space as me.

Neither of us acknowledged it. But neither of us moved away.

The sky over the lake deepened to a flat charcoal, the clouds pressing low and heavy. The wind picked up, carrying a sharp chill that made me huddle into my coat.

“Storm’s coming,” I said.

“Yeah.” Elliot stared at the rapidly changing sky to the west. “We should probably head back.”

“Probably.”

But neither of us moved. We sat there on our rocks, shoulders almost touching, watching the clouds gather over the water. The gathering noise of the team had faded—they’d probably moved to higher ground already, smarter than us about weather patterns.

When the first drops of rain started falling, they were cold and sharp. I tilted my head toward the sky and let them rush over me like a spiritual baptism from on high. But, the gentle drops soon fell heavier, promising a serious downpour. Elliot stood, gathering his notebook, and I stood too.

“My car’s back at the main lodge,” I said, gesturing toward the path.

“Mine, too.” His hair matting to his forehead. “Pretty far in a storm.”

He was right. The rain was intensifying by the second, the drops becoming a steady drumbeat against the rocks and trees. The sky had gone dark, almost night-dark, though it was barely late afternoon.

“There’s a ranger station,” I said. “Other direction. Closer.”

I didn’t know why I offered it. Didn’t know why I was inviting Elliot Vega to shelter with me from the storm.

“Lead the way,” Elliot said.

We ran.

Chapter 17
The Cabin

Elliot

The rain hit like a wall of cold needles, soaking through my flannel in seconds. We ran along the shoreline path, Rowan ahead of me, his dark hair plastered to his skull, his feet sure on the slick rocks even as mine threatened to slide out from under me with every step.

Lightning cracked somewhere over the lake—close enough that the thunder followed almost immediately, a bone-deep rumble that I felt in my chest. I may have let out a squeal, but thankfully Rowan didn't turn around to check on me, which would have been utterly humiliating. The sky had gone from slightly overcast to apocalyptic in the space of minutes—the joys of the Northern California storms. Unfortunately, these storms could turn a creek bed into a river in minutes, stranding unprepared hikers for days. Which as I watched Rowan's backside running in front of me—because I'm gay, so of course I looked—I hoped Mother Nature would strand us for a week. We could cling to each other for body heat. Surviving only on—

"There!" Rowan shouted over the rain, bringing me out of my wet fantasy as he pointed toward a dark shape between the trees.

The ranger station materialized out of the downpour like something from a fairy tale—small, weathered, its roof thick with pine needles and moss. Rowan reached the door first, shouldering it open with the ease of someone who'd done this before, and I stumbled in after him, gasping, dripping lake water and rain onto the worn wooden floor.

The door slammed shut behind us, muffling the storm to a dull roar.

For a moment, we just stood there, breathing hard, letting our eyes adjust to the darkness. The cabin was tiny—maybe fifteen feet square, with roughhewn walls and a single window so rain-streaked it was nearly opaque. The only furniture was a wooden bench against one wall, a small potbelly stove in the center, and a stack of emergency supplies in the corner: blankets, a first aid kit, a few cans of food that had probably been here since the nineties . . . the 1890s.

It smelled like dust and wood smoke along with a particular mustiness that only comes when a space has been closed up for too long.

Rowan moved toward the window, peering out at the storm. He'd stripped off his hoodie and hung it on a peg that poked out from the wall. His T-shirt was soaked through, clinging to his back, outlining the topography of muscle and bone underneath. I watched a drop of water trace the line of his spine before disappearing into his waistband, and I had to look away.

"Main lodge is at least a half-mile," he said. "We'd be swimming by the time we got there."

"So, I guess we wait it out."

"Yeah." He turned from the window, and for a moment our eyes met in the dim light. "We wait it out. I would hang your flannel over here, just to let it air dry." He pointed to the space next to his hoodie. I crossed the room unbuttoning my shirt at the wrists to make it easier to take off. My henley was soaked through, but the thicker material at least hadn't matted to my chest. Rowan's T-shirt, on the other hand, now didn't even bother to hide his chest and abdominal muscles. I kind of wanted to take my flannel and run it over his washboard abs, but I hung it up instead.

The silence that followed was charged. We were alone. Really alone. No teammates, no professors, no crowds to disappear into. Just the two of us and a storm that showed no signs of stopping.

I shivered—the cold finally catching up with me now that the adrenaline was fading. My clothes were soaked, my fingers numb, my teeth threatening to chatter.

"There should be matches," Rowan said, already moving toward the supply stack. "If the stove still works . . . "

He found them in a waterproof container, along with some newspaper and a few pieces of kindling that someone had left behind. I watched him work—efficient, methodical, the same economy of movement I'd observed on the ice. Within minutes, a small fire was crackling in the potbelly stove, orange light flickering through the grate, heat beginning to radiate into the cold space.

"You've done this before," I said.

"One of the park rangers lives in my house. She's always talking about how they have to stock and restock these places because of lost hikers." He didn't elaborate, but something in his voice suggested there was a story there. One of the many stories I'd been trying to excavate since this began.

I moved closer to the stove, holding my hands out toward the warmth. Rowan did the same, positioning himself on the opposite side, the fire between us.

"Your shirt's soaked," he said. "You should . . . I mean, the blankets are probably dry. If you want to . . . "

He gestured vaguely toward the supply stack, not finishing the sentence. The suggestion hung in the air—practical, innocent, and somehow charged with tension neither seemed ready to admit.

"You first," I said. "You're wetter than I am."

He hesitated, then nodded. Turned away from me and pulled the soaked T-shirt over his head in one fluid motion.

I'd seen him shirtless before. At the lake earlier, during the swimming drills. From a distance, through binoculars of careful observation, cataloging details for my "research." But this was different. This was three feet away, in the warm light of a fire, with no one else around.

His back was a map of athlete's muscles—defined but not bulky, the kind of build that came from functional movement and gym work. A small scar curved along his left shoulder blade, pale against his skin. I wanted to ask about it. I wanted to trace it with my fingers.

I averted my eyes.

"Here you go." A rectangle of foil cloth landed in my lap. When I looked up, he'd wrapped one of the emergency blankets around his shoulders, his wet shirt draped over the edge of the bench to dry. "You should change too. You're shaking."

He was right. I was shaking—from cold, I told myself. Just from cold.

I turned my back and stripped off the flannel, then the thermal underneath. The cold air hit my skin like a slap, and I wrapped that tinfoil blanket around myself before I could think too hard about the fact that I was now half-naked in a cabin with Rowan Calloway.

When I turned around, he stood in a shadow watching me. The light of flame danced across his chest.

"Better?" he asked.

"I will be." I let out an involuntary shiver and sat down on the floor near fire. After a moment, Rowan did the same, settling onto the floor beside me. Close.

The storm raged outside, rain hammering the roof, wind howling through the trees. But inside the cabin, wrapped in our blankets with the fire crackling between us, I wasn't worried and felt myself warming.

"Can I ask you something?" I said.

Rowan tensed slightly—I saw it in the set of his shoulders, the way his hands tightened on the blanket. "Depends on what it is."

"Not . . . I'm not going to ask about that. The stuff I shouldn't know." I pulled my knees up, hugging them to my chest. "I just want to know . . . what's your favorite part?"

"Favorite part of what?"

"Hockey. The game itself. Just . . . why do you love it?"

The question seemed to catch him off guard. He was quiet for a long moment, staring at the fire, and I thought maybe he wouldn't answer.

Then: "The sound."

"The sound?"

"When the puck hits the tape perfectly. There's this . . . I don't know how to describe it. This click. Like everything in the universe aligned for that one second, and you can hear it." His voice had softened, losing some of its careful control. "I've been chasing that sound since I was five years old. Every time I hear it, it's like . . . proof. That something can be exactly right, even if everything else is wrong."

I watched him as he spoke, seeing something I'd never seen before.

"That's kind of beautiful," I said. And I meant it.

He glanced at me, surprised. "You think so?"

"I think you see the game the way I see theatre. When everything comes together, when the performance transcends the mechanics and becomes something . . . more." I hesitated, then added: "That's what I've been chasing since my first play. When the audience forgets they're watching actors. When it becomes real. When we as actors forget that we're reciting someone else's lines and they flow out of us on stage like they are the most natural thing in the world to say in that moment."

"Is that why you do it? Theatre?"

"Partly." I pulled the blanket tighter around my shoulders. "Also, because I'm terrified of being forgotten. Of living an entire life and not leaving any mark on the world. Theatre feels like . . . proof of existence. If I can make someone feel something, then I was here. I mattered. If I can be in a show someone is still talking about decades from now, then I'll have left an imprint on someone's life."

The confession came out easily.

Rowan was quiet, processing. Then: "I used to feel that way about both acting and hockey. About being remembered."

"And now?"

"Now, I think there are worse things than being forgotten." His voice was barely above a whisper. "Being remembered for the wrong things. Having people think they know you when they only know the version you showed them."

The version you showed them. The words echoed in my mind, connecting to everything I'd learned about him—the Hollywood years, the press junkets, the catchphrase he'd refused to say.

"Again, I'm so sorry," I said. "About the library—"

"You don't have to—"

"I do." I met his eyes, holding his gaze. "I treated you like a research subject. Like a puzzle to solve instead of a human being. That was wrong. I knew what I was doing was a total invasion of your privacy and bordered on stalking, but I did it anyway because I wanted to see what would happen." I took a breath. "That's not who I want to be."

The silence stretched between us. The fire crackled. Rain drummed against the roof.

"Why?" Rowan asked finally. "Why did you want to see what would happen?"

"Because I couldn't stop thinking about you." The words came out before I could filter them. "From the moment I recognized you at tryouts, you were all I could think about. Not Chase St. Clair—the person you used to be. Just . . . you. The way you move. The way you're so careful all the time, like you're waiting for everything to fall apart."

I was saying too much. I knew I was saying too much. But the storm and the firelight and the strange, suspended quality of this moment made it impossible to stop, so my mouth kept running.

"I wanted to understand you," I said. "And I convinced myself that understanding meant taking you apart. Finding your pressure points. Using them." I shook my head. "But that's not understanding. That's just another kind of violence. And on top of all that, you were my first crush."

"Okay, that was emotional whiplash," Rowan said, turning to me. "Say what?"

"Oh, I shouldn't have said that," my voice trailed off.

"I was your first crush?"

"I may or may not have had a picture of your face taped above my bed as a young teenager right when my hormones started raging in adolescence."

Rowan didn't respond for a long moment.

"Really? Little Elliot would stare longingly at his ceiling every night and stare at this handsome mug?"

I'm glad I couldn't see the shades of red my face was turning. "You were the epitome of masculinity to me at that age. You were popular, masculine, handsome, famous, everything I was not."

"And?" he asked, his voice getting lower.

"And what?"

"Did you only stare into my eyes dreamily or did you . . . ?"

"I refuse to answer the question. Oh, my God! This is so embarrassing." I pulled the tinfoil blanket over my head so I didn't have to look at him. He let out a soft chuckle. The more I heard that sound come out of him the more I wanted to hear it again. His laughter was like crack.

When he finally spoke, his voice was rough.

"You scared me," he said. "In the library. That catchphrase—it was like you'd reached into my head and pulled out the worst moment of my life. I couldn't figure out what you wanted. Whether you were going to expose me, or blackmail me, or . . . " He trailed off. "I've spent five years paranoid that someone would find me and out me to the world. And then you did, and you were . . . "

"Terrible," I supplied.

"Confusing." His mouth twitched. "You kept showing up. Watching. But you never actually did anything. You just . . . hovered. Like you were waiting for me to make the first move in a game I didn't know the rules to."

"That's because I didn't know the rules either." I laughed, a short, self-deprecating sound. "I'm supposed to be an actor. One would think I would be good at knowing what I want and playing the role that gets it. But with you, I couldn't figure out what I was playing at. What I actually wanted."

"And now?"

The question hung in the air. Direct. Unavoidable.

"Now, I think I want to know you," I admitted. "Not the mystery. Not the puzzle. Just . . . the person who chases the sound of a perfect pass. Who picked daisies too, in his own way. Who's so tired of running that he chose a Division III program in the middle of nowhere just to have somewhere to stop so he could play the game he loves again."

Rowan stared at me. The firelight caught the angles of his face, the scar above his eyebrow, the shadows under his eyes that spoke of too many sleepless nights.

And then something extraordinary happened.

He smiled.

Not the careful, controlled expression I'd seen him give teammates. Not the blank mask he wore for protection. A real smile—crooked, asymmetrical, transforming his entire face. It made him look younger. Surprised by his own amusement. Dangerously, heartbreakingly human.

The storm raged outside, but inside the cabin, the air had changed. Rowan let the blanket slip slightly off his shoulders, less guarded now. I found myself leaning toward him without meaning to, drawn by some gravity I couldn't name.

"So, what happens now?" he asked. "You stop hunting, I stop running. Then what?"

"I don't know." It was the truth. "Maybe we just . . . see what happens. Without the games. Without the ambush and retreat."

"That sounds terrifying."

"Yeah." I smiled. "It does."

He turned and extended his hand to me, "I'm Rowan Calloway, that's my real name. My teammates call me Calloway, but my family and friends call me Ro. You can call me Ro. The only person who calls me Rowan is my mother."

I grabbed his hand and shook it, my blanket falling off my torso. "I'm Elliot Vega. It's nice to meet you, Ro."

The fire crackled. The rain softened from a roar to a steady drum. And slowly, gradually, Ro's posture relaxed in a way I'd never seen before. He wasn't performing anymore. He was just . . . present. Here, in this cabin, with me.

We talked for another hour as the storm wound down. About nothing important—classes we hated, professors we found baffling, the particular hell of on-campus dining options at seven in the morning. Safe topics. Surface-level.

When the rain finally tapered to a mist, we both glanced at the window with something like reluctance.

"Should head back," Rowan said. "Team will send a search party before long."

"Yeah." I stood, gathering my damp clothes. "I should probably not be seen emerging from a cabin with an incredibly hot, half-naked hockey player. Might raise questions."

"Wouldn't want that." But he was smiling again—that crooked, unguarded smile that I was already addicted to. "You go first. I'll wait ten minutes."

I pulled on my still-damp flannel, grimacing at the cold. At the door, I paused.

"See you around, Calloway."

"See you in the library, Elliot." His voice was lighter than I'd ever heard it. Almost playful. "Next time, don't drop the books. Just say hi."

"You tripped me," I said, indignation crossing my face as I pulled the henley over my head.

"Uh huh," he replied. "Any proof of that little accusation?" It wasn't a jab. The tone in his voice was playful.

"You're such an ass," I said without thinking.

"True. But you're the one who keeps staring at my ass."

My jaw dropped. I couldn't come up with a comeback. Ro smiled.

"And on that note," I said dramatically, "I take my leave."

I stepped out into the mist, the cold air sharp against my face after the warmth of the cabin. Behind me, I could feel him watching.

It felt like something else entirely.

I walked back toward the lodge. I hadn't written a single observation. I didn't need to. The image was already burned into my memory: Ro Calloway, wrapped in a shiny silver blanket by a dying fire, smiling at me like I was the first person to make him laugh in years.

Chapter 18
Film Study

Rowan

The film room smelled like moldy old carpet. It was a cross between an old abandoned warehouse and a locker room full of teenage boys. Banks of folding chairs faced a pulldown screen at the front, the projector humming from its ceiling mount, casting a rectangle of light onto the white surface. The tech in this room hadn't been updated since the turn of the twenty-first century. The overhead lights were off, leaving the room in that dim, drowsy half-dark that made everything feel unreal.

I'd positioned myself in the back corner. Three rows behind the main cluster of players, close enough to see the screen but far enough to avoid notice. The chair was uncomfortable—hard metal that dug into my spine and creaked every time you moved. Someone needs to bring some WD-40 down here. The discomfort was useful. It kept me sharp. The squealing sound of the chairs every time someone moved was getting on my last nerve.

Around me, the team settled into various states of attention. The seniors occupied the front rows, obligated by status if not by interest. Maddox sat dead center, his posture straight, his eyes already fixed on the blank screen with the focus of someone who cared about this stuff. Kowalski was beside him, working through a bag of trail mix. Behind them, the sophomores sprawled in their chairs, watched with the casual disregard of players who'd been on enough teams to know they wouldn't be playing this week.

Davies had dropped into the seat next to me, because Davies always found me now.

"I hate film study," he muttered, slouching down until his knees hit the chair in front of him. "Sterling always makes it feel like a pop quiz."

"That's because it is a pop quiz."

"Great. That's great. I'm going to fail a pop quiz about hockey. My parents will be so proud."

Sterling entered before I could respond, moving to the front of the room with the unhurried efficiency that characterized everything he did. He carried a tablet and a remote, his face as unreadable as ever in the dim light.

"Gentlemen," he said pausing the video. "We're going to review the Northridge game. Specifically, the second period breakdown that almost cost us the lead."

A few groans from the middle rows. We'd won that game, barely—a 3-2 squeaker against a team we should have handled easily. The second period had been ugly, a defensive collapse that had let Northridge score twice in three minutes.

Sterling made some movements on his tablet, and the other video showed up. He clicked the remote. The screen flickered back to life, showing frozen footage from the game. I recognized the time stamp: 8:34 remaining in the second.

"Watch the sequence," Sterling said. "Tell me where it goes wrong."

He pressed play.

The footage unspooled in that jerky, overhead-angle way of arena cameras. Northridge had the puck in our zone, cycling it along the boards. Our defense was scrambling, trying to establish position, while the forwards—including me, I noted with a twinge of discomfort—worked to clog passing lanes.

The goal came at 8:22. A cross-ice pass that caught our goalie leaning, a one-timer that found the top corner.

Sterling paused the video. "Petrov. What went wrong?"

Petrov, half-asleep in the second row, jerked upright. "Uh . . . the pass? It was a good pass."

"That's not analysis. That's observation." Sterling's tone was flat. "Chen?"

"The D-man—Kowalski—he got caught watching the puck instead of his man."

Kowalski grunted in acknowledgment. Sterling nodded. "That's part of it. What else?"

Silence. The players shifted in their chairs, most of them hoping not to be called on. I stared at the frozen frame on the screen, my mind already three moves ahead, cataloging every mistake that had led to that goal.

The problem wasn't just Kowalski watching the puck. It was the entire defensive structure. The weakside forward—that was me—had drifted too high, opening a passing lane through the slot. The strongside defenseman had pinched at the wrong moment, creating a two-on-one opportunity that Northridge had exploited. And the backcheck angle of our center was wrong by at least three degrees, which meant he couldn't cut off the cross-ice pass even if he'd anticipated it.

I saw it all. I'd seen it in real time, during the game, and I'd been too slow to correct my own positioning before the damage was done.

"Calloway."

Sterling's voice cut through my thoughts. I looked up to find him watching me from the front of the room, the tablet forgotten in his hands.

"You've been staring at that screen like it owes you money. What do you see?"

Nothing, I wanted to say. I see nothing. I'm just a walk-on who watches a lot of hockey.

But Sterling's eyes were sharp, waiting, and I could feel the room's attention shifting toward me.

"The gap," I said, keeping my voice neutral. "Kowalski's gap was too wide. He was playing the pass instead of the man."

"That's what Chen said. What else?"

The smart play was to stop there. Give a surface-level answer, let someone else take the spotlight. Stay invisible.

But Sterling was still watching me. And something about the way he asked—like he already knew the answer, was just waiting for me to confirm it—made the words spill out before I could stop them.

"The weakside forward was too high," I said. "He should have been at the bottom of the circle, taking away the slot pass. Instead, he's floating near the hash marks, which opens up that whole lane through the middle."

I pointed at the screen, at my own frozen figure in the wrong position.

"That's me," I added. "I should have been lower."

A ripple of surprise moved through the room. Players rarely called out their own mistakes in film study.

"Keep going," Sterling said.

"The pinch on the strong side was premature. The D-man read the cycle and jumped up to create a turnover, but the timing was off by half a second. That pulled him out of position for the transition, which is why he couldn't get back to cover the backdoor man."

I was talking too much. I could feel it, the words coming faster than my caution could filter them.

"And the center's backcheck angle is wrong. He's taking a straight line to the puck carrier, but at that speed and trajectory, he can't cut off the cross-ice pass. He should have taken a wider arc, anticipated the play developing, positioned himself to disrupt the passing lane instead of chasing the puck."

I stopped. Aware of the silence in the room.

Everyone was staring at me. Davies, next to me, had stopped slouching and was staring with his mouth slightly open. Kowalski had turned around in his seat, trail mix forgotten. Even the sophomores, who never paid attention to anything, were watching me like I'd grown a second head.

Sterling's expression hadn't changed, but something in his eyes had sharpened.

"The backcheck angle," he repeated slowly. "Three degrees off. That's specific."

"Approximately." The word came out. Too late to take any of it back.

"Where'd you learn to read the game like that, Calloway?"

The question hung in the air. I felt the weight of every eye in the room, the curiosity and suspicion pressing against me like a physical force.

"I watch a lot of tape," I said. The lie sounded thin even to me.

Sterling held my gaze for a long moment as he cocked his head slightly, which might have been acknowledgment or might have been filing something away for later.

"Let's run the next sequence."

He turned back to the screen, clicking through to the next clip. The room's attention shifted with him, most of the players forgot my little diarrhea of the mouth.

But not everyone.

Maddox hadn't turned around. He was still facing forward, watching the screen, but I could see the tension in his neck. The vein on the right side visibly throbbed, and he was white-knuckling the arms of his chair.

He'd heard every word. One more piece of evidence for his growing assessment of me.

The session lasted another forty-five minutes. Sterling worked through six more clips, asking questions, correcting positioning, building the defensive adjustments he wanted us to implement. I stayed silent for the rest of it, answering only when directly asked, keeping my responses short and unremarkable.

But the damage was done. I could feel it in the way people looked at me differently when the lights came up. Not hostile—just reassessing.

"Dude." Davies caught my arm as we filed toward the door. "That was insane. How did you see all that?"

"I told you. I watch tape."

"Nobody watches that much tape. That was, like, professional-level commentary. My brother played DI at Minnesota State and he couldn't have done that."

"Your brother plays defense. Different perspective."

"Don't deflect." Davies grinned, but there was genuine curiosity underneath. "Where did you actually learn this stuff?"

"I've been playing since I was five," I said, which was technically true. "You pick things up."

"You pick up how to shoot, how to skate. You don't pick up . . . whatever that was. Reading plays three moves ahead. Calculating backcheck angles to the degree. Really?"

I didn't have an answer that wouldn't open more questions. I shrugged, hoping he'd let it go.

"Fine, keep your secrets." Davies punched my shoulder, light and friendly. "But seriously, impressive. Sterling noticed."

"I know . . . So did Maddox."

The words slipped out before I could stop them. Davies's expression went flat, the animation draining from his face as he processed what I'd just said, but before he could ask what I meant, Kowalski appeared at my other shoulder.

"Good eye on the gap analysis," he said gruffly. "I knew I was out of position, but I couldn't figure out why it felt so wrong during the play. The anticipation thing—totally makes sense."

"Just something I noticed."

"Something you noticed." Kowalski studied me for a moment, his broken-nose face unreadable. "You notice a lot of things, Calloway."

He walked away before I could respond. I watched him go, trying to read the interaction. Was it friendly? Suspicious? Just observation?

The paranoia was getting worse. Every conversation felt like an interrogation. Every glance felt like recognition waiting to happen.

I made it to the parking lot before Maddox caught up with me.

He said nothing at first. Just fell into step beside me, his gear bag slung over one shoulder, his breath visible in the cold evening air. We walked in silence for maybe thirty seconds—long enough that I wondered if he was going to speak at all.

Then: "Community college rec leagues."

The words were flat. Not a question.

"What?"

"That's what you put on your transfer application. Hockey background: community college rec leagues. Occasional pickup games. Nothing organized."

I kept walking. "That's right."

"Community college rec leagues don't teach you to read plays like that." Maddox's voice was quiet, controlled. "They don't teach you to calculate backcheck angles to the degree. That's the breakdown coaches do."

"I watch a lot of—"

"Tape. Yeah. You said." Maddox stopped walking. I stopped too, turning to face him. "I don't know what your story is. I don't know why you're here, or what you're hiding, or why a guy with your hockey IQ would end up at a DIII program in the middle of nowhere."

He stepped closer, his face hard in the parking lot lights.

"But I know you're not what you say you are. And as the team captain, that worries me. How I can I trust you on the ice when I know you're lying to me? Lying to all of us."

He held my gaze for a moment longer. Then he walked away, leaving me standing alone in the cold.

Chapter 19
The Rehearsal Invitation

Elliot

I was back in the media studies section, third floor. It was a masochistic choice, really. I was sitting at the same industrial-oak table where the complete debacle with Ro had happened. I just stared at a highlighted passage in a textbook about "maintaining expressive control," but the words were a blur.

The library was quiet, a low-frequency hum of fluorescent lights and distant page-turning.

A shadow fell over my textbook, and the scent of cold air and a lingering trace of arena ice settled around me.

I turned.

Ro was standing there, his hands shoved deep into the pockets of his Ospreys track jacket. And he was . . . nervous. But not the same deer-in-headlights look from when I'd cornered him before—just normal guy nervous.

"Elliot," he said.

"Rowa . . . Ro." I caught myself. I gestured to the other chair at the table as I closed my book, my heart performing a frantic percussion against my ribs that no amount of stage training could quiet. "I thought you avoided this floor. Too many theatrical ambushes."

A ghost of a smile touched his mouth—the crooked one that wasn't for the cameras. "I figured lightning wouldn't strike the same place twice."

He didn't sit down. He just stood there, looking down at me, and I felt exposed. "Something wrong?" Ro asked, his eyes inquisitive.

"No. I just—" I took a breath, trying to summon the "expressive control" Goffman promised. It failed me. "I want you to see something."

Ro's posture shifted, his shoulders squaring. "See what? That sounds ominous."

"A rehearsal. Tonight. The Penalty Box—it's the play I'm doing. The one I used as pretense to follow you around."

I shifted my weight, aware that I was fidgeting with the corner of my Moleskine. "Not the performance. Not the polished version with the lights and the costumes. I want you to see the process. The messy part, where we're still fighting with the script and falling over the blocking."

Ro leaned back against the bookshelf, his arms crossing over his chest. He was studying me the way he studied a defensive line. "Why?"

"Because I've watched you." The words came out raw, stripping away the academic bullshit I usually used as a shield. "At the arena. At the lake. In that cabin while the rain was trying to take the roof off. You've let me see you in your space, doing the thing you love, even when you didn't want me there. Even when I was being an asshole about it."

"I didn't have much choice," he pointed out, though his voice had lost its edge. "You're nothing if not persistent."

"I know." I stepped closer, closing the gap until I could see the flecks of gold in his irises. "But I'm asking now. No stalking, no engineering 'chance' encounters, no ambushes. I'm asking you to come into my world. To watch me do the thing I love, even when I'm terrified of what you'll see."

"You're terrified?" Ro asked softly. "I thought you were the one in control, Elliot."

"Nah, sometimes I like to give up control," I said, my voice barely a whisper. Ro smirked, so the double meaning wasn't lost on him. "Will you come?"

Ro looked at the empty seat across from me, then back at my face. He took a long, slow breath, the kind he probably took right before the puck dropped at center ice.

"Tonight?" he asked.

"Seven o'clock. The Black Box."

He nodded once—a sharp, decisive movement. "I'll be there. But don't expect me to pick any daisies."

I felt the air rush back into my lungs. "I'll settle for you just sitting in the back row."

"Anything you want me to watch for? You know, I do know a thing or two about hockey and acting."

"Just . . . let me know if I seem real."

"Why wouldn't you want me there watching?"

"Because rehearsal is vulnerable." I laughed, a short, self-deprecating sound. "On stage, in performance, there's a wall between you and the audience. The lights, the costumes, the polish—it all creates distance. But rehearsal is different. Rehearsal is where you fail. Where you try things that don't work, where you look stupid, where the seams show . . . "

"I'll be there." Something in his voice made my stomach flip. "Seven o'clock."

The Black Box felt different tonight.

I stood in the wings, wearing my costume, trying to remember how to breathe. The space was small—maybe forty feet square—with black-painted walls and a ceiling hung with lighting instruments. No fixed stage, no permanent seating. Just a flexible void that could be shaped into whatever the production required.

The set crew had outdone themselves: metal lockers lined the back wall of the set, benches bolted to the floor, and in the corner, a working shower setup with actual plumbing. Oh, and the set designer axed the frosted glass partition. No privacy screen. Just three open showerheads mounted to a tile backing, exactly like you'd find in any high school athletic facility.

Authenticity, Albright had said. The audience needs to feel the vulnerability. The exposure. If Diego and Tyler have somewhere to hide, the scene loses its power.

Easy for him to say. He wasn't the one about to strip naked in front of—

I glanced toward the back of the house. The work lights were up, casting everything in that flat, honest glow that made it impossible to hide flaws. A few figures were scattered in the black box—stage manager, assistant director, the lighting designer taking notes. And in the far back corner, half-hidden, a hulking silhouette that hadn't been there ten minutes ago.

My heart stuttered.

The work lights didn't reach that corner, and I couldn't make out features. Couldn't tell if it was Ro or just some random observer who'd wandered in.

He said he'd come. He said, seven o'clock.

It was 7:12.

"We're going to start at Act One, Scene Three," Albright called from his director's chair.

Lucas appeared beside me, his expression professionally neutral. We'd done this scene a dozen times in rehearsal—clothed, blocked, choreographed down to the second. We knew where every hand went, every breath, every beat of the kiss. But we'd never done it like this.

"You good?" Lucas asked quietly.

"Define good."

He laughed, low and nervous. "Yeah. Same."

"Elliot. Lucas."

We both turned. Dr. Marisol Vance was approaching from the wings, clipboard in hand, her silver-streaked hair pulled back in its usual practical bun. She'd been the department's intimacy coordinator for a few years, but she'd worked on Broadway, off-Broadway, a few indie films before she'd decided academia was steadier. She had the calm, unflappable energy of someone who'd seen every possible iteration of actors freaking out before intimate scenes.

"How are we feeling?" she asked, her voice low enough not to carry to the house.

"Terrified," I admitted.

"Appropriately anxious," Lucas said at the same time.

Dr. Vance smiled. "Good. That means you're taking it seriously." She glanced at her clipboard. "Let's do a quick check in. You've both reviewed the choreography for today's run?"

We nodded.

"And you're both still consenting to full nudity with simulated intimate contact, as we discussed in our prep sessions?"

"Yes," I said.

"Yeah," Lucas echoed, though his voice was slightly strained.

"Remember—you can call for a break at any time. 'Hold' or 'yellow' if you need a pause, 'red' if you need to stop completely. No questions asked, no judgment. Albright knows the protocol."

"Got it," I said.

Lucas shifted his weight, his hand going to the back of his neck in that nervous gesture I'd come to recognize over three years of scene work together. "Dr. Vance, can I ask something? It's, uh . . . it's kind of awkward."

"There are no awkward questions in my world, Lucas. Only unasked ones."

He took a breath. "What happens if one of us . . . you know . . . " He made a vague, pained gesture toward his midsection. "Has a physiological reaction?"

I felt my face heat, but I was grateful he'd asked. I'd been wondering the same thing and had been too chickenshit to bring it up.

Dr. Vance's expression remained neutral—warm, even. "That's a very normal concern, and I'm glad you're voicing it. Here's the reality: you're going to be in close physical contact with another warm body, under hot water, simulating sexual intimacy. Physiological responses can happen regardless of attraction. It's biology, not intention."

Lucas nodded. A quick nod was all he managed; his face flushed a deep, uncomfortable crimson.

"If it happens, it happens," Dr. Vance continued. "You acknowledge it privately if you need to—'I need a second'—and we take a brief break. No one's going to make it weird. No one's going to assume anything about your sexual orientation or your feelings toward your scene partner. Bodies do what bodies do. Your body's nerve endings don't understand acting from intimate contact with someone you find sexually attractive."

"And it's happened before?" Lucas asked. "To other actors?"

"To more actors than haven't, in my experience. You're both professionals. You'll handle it professionally." She looked between us. "Anything else before we start?"

I shook my head. Lucas did the same.

"Alright. I'll be in the house, stage left. You see me if you need me." She squeezed both our shoulders. "You've prepared for this. Trust the work."

She walked toward the house, and Lucas and I stood there in our robes, slightly less terrified than we'd been two minutes ago.

"I really hope I don't get a boner," Lucas muttered.

I choked on a laugh. "Same, honestly."

"I mean, you're attractive and everything, but—"

"Lucas. Please stop talking."

"Right. Yeah. Good call."

"Places," Albright called from his director's chair "Remember," Albright said, his voice carrying through the space, "this is the first time they've let themselves do this. The locker room is empty—they think they're safe. I want to see that safety crumble. I want to see the want override the fear." He paused. "And I want to see the fear come flooding back the moment they hear that door."

I nodded, not trusting my voice.

"I'll read the offstage voice," Albright continued. "When you hear me, I want genuine panic. You're naked, you're together, and someone is about to discover you. Find that terror."

Find that terror. As if I needed to find it. It was already crawling up my spine, settling into my chest.

I glanced at the back corner again. The silhouette hadn't moved.

"And . . . action."

The scene started in the locker room. I entered from stage left, hockey bag over my shoulder, stick in hand. I dropped my bag by the locker marked "7," sat on the bench, pulled out my AirPods. Started bobbing my head to music no one could hear.

I let Diego's physicality settle into my body. The way he moved through space—economical, controlled. The way he kept everyone at arm's length while pretending to be open.

I know this person, I thought. I've been watching him for weeks.

The stage left door banged open. Lucas entered—Tyler—hockey bag, stick. I kept focused on the locker.

"Yo!"

I didn't react—AirPods. Lucas crossed to me, flicked the back of my head. I jumped, pulled out an earbud.

"Dick."

"Thought you left."

"Nah. Gotta shower. Mom's picking me up in like forty."

The banter flowed easily—college tours, Coach Reilly being a dick, Carson's new Jeep. We pulled off hoodies, kicked off shoes. The dialogue shifted to Marcus's party, and I felt the tension start to build.

"Finally gonna ask out what's-her-name? Emily?" Lucas asked, keeping his voice teasing.

"Emma. And no." I delivered the line with that slight tension underneath.

"Why not? She's into you."

"How do you know?"

"'Cause she told Jess, and Jess told everybody." Lucas grinned. "You're like the only guy on the team who hasn't hooked up with someone from the dance team."

"Not interested."

"In Emma? Or like . . . any of them?"

"Just busy. College apps, hockey, whatever."

"Dude. You gotta live a little."

"Says the guy who hasn't dated anyone since—" I stopped myself. Right on cue.

"Since what?"

"Nothing."

Lucas sat up. "No, say it. Since what?"

"Since sophomore year. Ashley."

His face closed off. "That was different."

"How?"

"It just was." He stood abruptly. "I'm gonna shower."

"Yeah. Me too."

We grabbed towels and moved toward the shower area. This was the moment. No more clothes to hide behind. No frosted glass partition—just open shower heads mounted to a tile wall.

Lucas got there first. Turned on the water. Steam started to rise.

I pulled off my costume.

The air hit my skin, and I was hyperaware of everything—the stage manager in the wings, the lighting designer, Albright with his notebook, and that hulking silhouette in the back corner who may or may not be watching me strip naked.

This is the job, I told myself. This is Diego.

I stepped into the spray next to Lucas. The water was warm, almost hot, streaming over my shoulders, my chest. We were close—close enough that I could hear Lucas's breathing.

"You think Brennan's actually gonna start me next game?" Lucas asked.

"Maybe. If you stop being an idiot."

"I'm not an idiot."

"You took a five-minute major last game."

"That guy grabbed my stick!"

"So you punched him?"

"He had it coming."

"You're gonna get yourself suspended."

"Since when do you care?"

I paused. Then, quieter: "I don't."

"Liar."

Silence. Just water.

"We play better when you're on the ice," I said.

"Yeah?"

"Yeah."

Lucas held the beat. Then: "You play better when I'm out there."

"What's that supposed to mean?"

"You know what it means."

The silence stretched, heavier now. Lucas shut off his water, stepped out, wrapped a towel around his waist. Stood there watching me, still under the spray.

"You coming to Marcus's party or not?"

"I said I don't know."

"Why not?"

I shut off the water. Didn't come out immediately. When I spoke, my voice was smaller than I intended:

"'Cause I don't want to watch you get wasted and hook up with some random girl."

Lucas froze. Let the moment land.

"What?"

I said nothing.

"What'd you say?"

"Nothing."

"No. You said—"

"Forget it."

"Diego."

Silence.

"Come out."

"I'm getting dressed—"

"No you're not."

I stepped out. Towel around my waist, wet, tense. We were close now. The air shifted.

"Say it again," Lucas whispered.

"I can't."

"Why not?"

"Because."

"That's not an answer."

I tried to move past him. He stopped me—hand on my chest, exactly as we'd choreographed. I looked down at his hand. Back up at his face.

"Move," I said, barely audible.

"No."

"Tyler—"

"Tell me I'm wrong." He stepped closer. "About why you won't come to the party."

My jaw clenched.

"Tell me I'm wrong about why you've been avoiding me."

"I haven't—"

"Yes. You have." He held my gaze. "Tell me I'm wrong about what happened last month. In your car. After the away game."

My breath caught. I closed my eyes.

"Tell me I imagined it," Lucas said, softer.

"We can't do this."

"Why not?"

"You know why."

"Say it."

"Because we're on the same team. Because everyone will—"

"I think about it. All the time," Lucas cut in.

"Don't—"

"About you. About that night."

"Stop."

"Why? Because you don't?"

Silence. I couldn't answer.

"I can't stop thinking about it." He stepped closer still, our bodies almost touching. "About you."

"Tyler, we're in the locker room—"

"No one's here."

"Someone could—"

"They won't."

We were inches apart. Both breathing hard. His hand moved from my chest to my jaw.

“This is a bad idea,” I whispered.

“Probably.”

“If someone finds out—”

“I don’t care.”

I opened my eyes. Stared at him.

“You should.”

“But I don’t.”

Lucas closed the distance. Kissed me. Soft at first—testing. I froze for half a second, then kissed back. My hands came up—one on his neck, one gripping his shoulder.

The kiss deepened. His hands went to my waist, pulling me closer. I made a sound—half gasp, half groan.

We stumbled backward into the shower stall. My back hit the tile wall—cold despite the steam, a shock that made me gasp against his mouth. He pressed against me. The kiss broke—we were both panting.

“Tyler—” My voice was wrecked.

“Shut up.”

He kissed me again. Harder. Hungrier. My hands slid down his back. His towel loosened, fell. Mine did the same.

Skin to skin. The water wasn’t running but we were both still wet. His mouth moved to my neck. My head fell back against the tile, eyes closed.

I went blank.

“Line,” I called quietly, my face still pressed against Lucas’s shoulder.

“We should, someone might,” the stage manager’s voice came from the house.

“We should— someone might—” I repeated, getting back into character.

“No one’s coming.”

The scene continued—intimate, raw, the choreography we’d rehearsed taking over. Hands gripping. Mouths on skin. The sounds we’d practiced—gasps, names, stifled moans.

And then, Albright’s voice cut through the steam, “Hello? Anyone still in here?”

We froze midmovement. Lucas’s hand clamped over my mouth. The panic that flooded my system was real—we were pressed together on the tile floor, naked, wet, and compromised.

“Shower’s running. Must’ve left it on again,” Albright said.

"Footsteps. Getting closer," the stage manager said. "Tyler reaches up blindly, turns on the shower above them. Cold water hits them both. Diego gasps against Tyler's hand. The water runs. Loud. Covering any sound. The footsteps pause."

"Hey!" Albright read from the script. "Rink's closed! Time to go!"

We lay absolutely still. Water pouring over us. I could feel Lucas's heart hammering against my chest. The terror wasn't acting anymore.

"Damn kids . . . "

"The footsteps retreat. Sound: The stage left door opens. Closes. The deadbolt slides home with a heavy CLUNK. They're locked in."

We stayed frozen. Then Lucas's hand fell away from my mouth, and we both started to shake.

"Did he just—" I whispered.

"Lock us in. Yeah."

"Fuck."

"Fuck."

I started to laugh—quiet, almost hysterical. Lucas buried his face in my shoulder, shaking with silent laughter.

Then the laugh turned into something else. My face crumpled. I was crying—real tears, pulling from somewhere deep in my chest.

Lucas pulled back. "Hey. Hey, it's okay—"

"No, it's not." I shook my head, water and tears mixing.

"Diego—"

I pulled away, scrambling up. "Everyone's gonna know."

The rest of the scene poured out of us—Diego's spiral, Tyler's desperation, the horrible argument about hiding, about survival, about all the ways our intersecting identities made this harder for Diego than Tyler could understand.

"BECAUSE I'M NOT LIKE YOU!" The words tore out of my throat—Diego's words, but the pain was mine too, borrowed from somewhere I hadn't expected to find it.

Silence. Lucas stared at me.

"What's that supposed to mean?"

"You know what it means."

"Say it."

"Because you're white! Because when people find out about you, maybe they're surprised, maybe they're not, but when they find out about me—" My voice broke. "I become every fucking stereotype they already think I am!"

The scene played out to its brutal end. Tyler grabbing his clothes. The rough, angry movements. Diego standing in just a towel, water dripping.

"I meant what I said. I love you. But I love myself too. And I'm tired of choosing." Lucas stopped at the exit, not turning around. "But don't ask me to disappear with you."

"Tyler—"

"Call me. When you figure out what you want."

He exits stage right.

I sank to the floor, back against the locker. Pulled my knees up. Buried my face.

The light narrowed to a single spot. My phone buzzed from the locker—once, twice, kept buzzing. I didn't move.

"Distant sound: Skates on ice," the stage manager read. "A whistle. Echoing from another time, another scene."

And the lights dimmed on the stage.

"Scene," Albright called. "Hold there."

The work lights came up. The spell broke.

Lucas appeared beside me with a towel, wrapping it around my shoulders. "You okay?"

I nodded, not trusting my voice. My whole body was trembling—from the cold water, from the adrenaline, from the emotion I'd pulled up and was still trying to put away.

An assistant stage manager brought us big fluffy robes. I pulled mine on, stood on shaky legs, and glanced toward the back corner of the house.

Empty.

The silhouette was gone.

I stood in the wings twenty minutes later, dressed in my street clothes, my hair still damp, my skin still flushed from the scene and the water and the exposure. Albright had given notes—good ones, about the escalation of desperation and the authenticity of the panic—but I'd barely heard them. I kept thinking about the empty corner, trying to figure out if Ro had ever really been there at all.

Maybe I'd imagined it. Maybe I'd wanted so badly for him to see me vulnerable that I'd conjured a phantom out of shadow and wishful thinking.

The stage door opened behind me.

"Hey."

I turned. Ro was standing in the doorway, his hands in his pockets, his expression unreadable. He was wearing the same Ospreys jacket from the library, his dark hair slightly windblown.

"You came," I said.

"I said I would."

"I didn't see you. After the scene, you were—"

"I moved." He stepped into the wing, letting the door close behind him. "During the notes. I didn't want to—" He stopped, his jaw working like he was trying to find the right words. "I didn't want you to know I was there. While you were . . . while you were doing that."

"Why not?"

"Because you would have been performing for me." His eyes met mine. "Instead of just . . . performing."

I stared at him. He was right, of course. If I'd known for certain he was watching, I would have been thinking about what he saw instead of what Diego felt. The vulnerability would have been calculated instead of real.

"What did you think?" I asked. The question came out smaller than I intended.

"Well, I definitely saw more of you than I had expected," Ro said with a smirk.

"Yeah," I let the word draw out. "I didn't realize that was the scene we were rehearsing until I got the theatre. I guess you've seen all of me now."

Ro was quiet for a long moment. "I think I understand now. Why you do this." He gestured vaguely at the stage, the set, the space. "It's not about pretending to be someone else. It's about finding the parts of yourself you're too scared to show any other way."

My throat tightened. "That's . . . yeah. That's exactly what it is."

"The character. Diego." Ro's voice was careful, like he was handling something fragile. "He's hiding. The whole scene, he's hiding—even when he's completely exposed. Even when there's literally nowhere to go."

"That's the point of the staging," I said. "No privacy. Just . . . just him, with nowhere to hide, and someone who won't let him disappear."

Ro nodded slowly. "And Tyler? He's the one who keeps pushing. Who won't let Diego pretend nothing's happening?"

"Tyler is . . . " I hesitated. "Tyler is who I've been. With you. Pushing until something breaks."

The words hung in the air between us. Ro's expression shifted—something complicated moving behind his eyes.

"But you're playing Diego," he said quietly. "Not Tyler."

"I know."

"So maybe . . . " He stopped. Started again. "Maybe you understand something about him that you didn't before. About what it's like to be the one who's watched. Who's exposed."

How could I not? I'm in a theater where my whole body will be naked in every sense of the word, stripped of every defense.

"Yeah," I said. "Maybe I do."

We stood there in the wings, the empty stage behind us, the ghost of the scene still hanging in the air. Ro was close enough that I could see the water droplets still clinging to his jacket—it must have started raining while I was inside.

"Thank you," I said. "For coming. For watching."

"Thank you for inviting me." He paused. "And Elliot?"

"Yeah?"

"You were good. Really good." His mouth curved into that crooked smile. "I believed every second of it."

Something warm bloomed in my chest. "That's the highest compliment you could give me."

"I know." He turned toward the door, then stopped. "See you around, Vega."

"See you around, Calloway."

Chapter 20
Spotlight in the Shadows

Elliot

Section 112, Row M, Seat 8.

I climbed the steep concrete steps to my usual spot, the cold arena air sharp in my lungs, the familiar hum of the refrigeration system a constant undertone beneath the sounds of practice beginning below. The blue plastic seat was as uncomfortable as always—hard, unyielding, designed for function rather than comfort.

But something felt different today.

I settled into my position, Moleskine open on my knee, pen in hand. The ritual was the same: observe, document, analyze. I'd done this dozens of times over the past weeks, filling pages with notes about movement patterns and suppression strategies and the architecture of a man trying to make himself invisible.

But the lens had shifted.

I wasn't hunting anymore. I didn't know exactly when that had changed—maybe in the cabin, watching rain streak down the windows while Rowan talked about the sound of a perfect pass. Maybe at the rehearsal, when he'd sat in the back of the Black Box and watched me strip away every defense I'd built. Maybe it had been changing all along, so gradually I hadn't noticed until suddenly the transformation was complete.

Now I was just . . . witnessing. Present without agenda. Watching because I wanted to see, not because I wanted to use.

Below me, the Ospreys spread across the ice in a wave of navy and orange, Sterling's whistle cutting through the arena's ambient noise. I found Rowan immediately—number twenty-eight, positioned at left wing, his posture carrying that familiar controlled stillness that set him apart from everyone else on the ice.

The patterns were the same as always. I watched him move through skating drills with that economical grace, never pushing to the front of the pack, never lagging behind. Perfect mediocrity. Calculated invisibility.

During a passing sequence, he received a feed from Kowalski and had a clear lane to the net. I watched his body lean into the attack—instinct taking over—and then watched him catch himself, dumping the puck into the corner instead. The safe play. The system play.

I wrote in my notebook: Same patterns. Same suppression. He still can't let himself be seen.

Sterling blew his whistle and called for a scrimmage. "Aline versus Bline. Let's see what you've got."

The team split into white and navy jerseys. The Aline pulled on white—Chen at center, Park on the left wing, Petrov on the right, with Hedman and Chelios anchoring the defense. The top unit, the guys who'd been promoted after Taylor's injury.

I watched Ro pull a navy practice jersey over his gear, settling into position at left wing alongside Davies at center and Maddox on the right. Kowalski and Seibert took their spots on defense behind them. The Bline. The walk-ons and the demoted captain, with something to prove.

Maddox's jaw was tight as he lined up. Being forced to scrimmage against the line that used to be his—that had to sting. But his eyes weren't on Chen or Petrov. They were tracking Ro with that suspicious intensity I'd noticed building over the past weeks.

The puck dropped. Play began.

For the first ten minutes, nothing changed.

Ro played exactly the way he always played—solid, reliable, invisible. He won board battles through leverage and positioning. He made smart passes that kept the play moving. He backchecked with the relentless efficiency Sterling preached.

And every time an opportunity opened up—a lane to the net, a chance to create something special—he let it close. Chose the safe option. Dimmed whatever light was trying to break through.

I'd memorized the pattern so well I could predict it. Pass instead of shoot. Dump instead of dangle. Blend instead of shine.

Then something changed.

It was subtle at first—so subtle I almost missed it. A shift in his shoulders during a line change. A loosening of the tension he always carried. He stepped back onto the ice for a new shift, and his posture was different. Lower. More settled. Like he'd made a decision about something.

The puck came to him at center ice—a routine pass from Kowalski, nothing special. A week ago, a day ago, even an hour ago, I knew what he would have done: chip it into the offensive zone, pursue the dump, grind along the boards.

Instead, he attacked.

The acceleration was explosive—zero to full speed in three strides, his edges biting into the ice with a precision that made everything else on the rink amateur. Hedman, the senior shutdown defenseman who'd been backing up, found himself flatfooted, caught between committing to the body and respecting the speed.

Ro split him.

Not around—through. A quick shift of his hips, a deke to the forehand that froze the bigger man in place, and then he was past, driving toward the net with the puck glued to his stick like it was magnetized.

Chelios tried to close the gap, angling hard to cut off the lane. Ro saw him coming—of course he did, he saw everything—and instead of forcing the shot, he threaded a pass through traffic that found Davies streaking down the slot. The puck landed perfectly on his tape, and Davies one-timed it toward the net.

The goalie made the save. But Ro was already there, following his own play, reading where the rebound would go before it happened. He collected the loose puck, spun away from Chen's backcheck, and fired a wrist shot that rang off the crossbar with a sound like a bell being struck.

The whole sequence took maybe twelve seconds.

Twelve seconds of the most beautiful hockey I'd ever seen.

The arena went quiet. Not silent—there were still the ambient sounds of the building, the hum of the lights, the distant clatter of equipment. But the players had stopped moving. Everyone was staring at Ro, who stood near the crease with his stick still raised from the shot, his chest heaving, his face hidden behind the cage of his helmet, but he turned his helmet toward me.

"What the HELL was that?"

Davies's voice carried up to my seat, high and incredulous. He was skating toward Rowan with an expression of pure bewilderment, his arms spread wide.

"Seriously, dude. What the hell? You've been holding out on us."

Ro shook his head, but he didn't have an answer. Or maybe he just didn't have one he was willing to give.

The team clustered around him, a mix of confusion and excitement and—from some of the veterans—suspicion. I watched Maddox hang back at the edge of the group, his arms crossed over his chest, his expression unreadable. Whatever conclusions he'd been building about the mysterious walk-on, they'd just been confirmed.

Sterling cut through the cluster, his face as impassive as ever. He gestured for Ro to follow him, and they skated to the far boards, out of earshot of the rest of the team.

I caught the movement of Sterling's jaw as he whispered. He nodded once—a firm, decisive motion—and let out a slow, steady exhale, his posture opening up as he tucked his hands into his pockets. And I watched Ro's response—the tension in his shoulders, the slight shake of his head, the eventual reluctant nod.

Sterling clapped him on the shoulder—a gesture I'd never seen him make with any player—and skated back to center ice.

"Alright, enough gawking," he called out. "Run it again. And Calloway—" He paused, and something that might have been a smile flickered across his face. "Do that again."

Chapter 21
Staging the Haunting

Elliot

The evening shift at Brewed Awakening was exactly what I needed after practice—mindless work to occupy my hands while my brain processed what had happened.

The door chimed again, and I glanced up automatically.

Half the hockey team was pushing through the entrance—Davies leading the pack, his bulk barely fitting through the doorway.

"Yo, Caramel Guy!" Davies was already at the register, grinning like he'd discovered a new best friend. "We meet again!"

"Welcome back," I said, forcing my voice to stay professional. "Same order as last time?"

"You remember my order?" Davies went still for a second, his eyebrows lifting in a way that smoothed the tired lines around his eyes. He let out a short, surprised breath. "Dude. That's like . . . really good customer service."

"Caramel macchiato, extra whip. Hard to forget."

Behind him, Kowalski was studying the menu with the intensity of a man planning a military operation. Petrov was texting, barely paying attention. And Ro—

Ro watched me. Not obviously, not in a way anyone else would notice. But I could feel the weight of his attention like a physical thing, the same way I'd felt it in the Black Box when he'd been sitting in the shadows.

I see you, his gaze seemed to say. You saw me tonight.

I took orders down the line. Kowalski wanted a plain black coffee—"None of that fancy stuff"—which made Davies roll his eyes. Petrov ordered something complicated with oat milk that I had to write down. A few of the other guys ordered, their voices blurring together as I tried to focus on the task at hand.

Then Ro stepped up to the counter.

"Hey," he said quietly.

"Hey yourself."

The line had moved past us, the other guys drifting toward the pickup area. For a moment, it was just the two of us, the counter between us, the ambient noise of the coffee shop creating a strange bubble of semi-privacy.

"Good practice?" I asked, because I had to say something.

"Yeah." A pause. "You were there. Thoughts?"

"Impressive." I felt heat creep up my neck.

"I was." His voice was unreadable, but his eyes weren't.

"Cocky much?" I said with a grin. "What you did tonight . . . that took guts."

"That's the job." He tried for casual, missed by a mile. "A little birdie told me I'd been trying to hide my candle under a bushel. Took its advice."

"What can I get you?" I managed.

"Just a black coffee. Large."

I nodded, turned away, grateful for the excuse to do something with my hands. The espresso machine hummed as I worked, but my mind was elsewhere.

I finished his coffee and brought it to the pickup counter. The rest of the team was already clustered near the door, arguing about something—probably where to go next, what to eat, the usual post-practice debates.

Ro reached for the cup at the same moment I set it down.

Our fingers touched.

It was nothing—half a second of contact, skin against skin over a paper coffee cup. But the jolt that went through me was electric, immediate, impossible to ignore. Ro's breath caught, barely audible. His eyes flicked up to mine.

"Thanks," he said softly.

"Anytime."

He held my gaze for a beat too long. Then Davies was calling his name, Kowalski was holding the door open, and the moment dissolved like steam in cold air.

"See you around, Vega," Ro said.

"See you around, Calloway."

He walked out with his teammates, the door chiming behind him. I stood at the counter, my heart hammering, my skin still tingling where we'd touched.

It was nothing. It was everything.

Chapter 22
The Henderson Artifact

Rowan

I told myself I was just getting coffee.

It was almost ten, too late for caffeine if I wanted any chance of sleeping, and I had a perfectly functional coffee maker in my apartment. But my feet carried me toward Brewed Awakening anyway, past the library, past the student union, through the cold February night toward a coffee shop I'd never set foot in before last week.

I wasn't looking for him. I was just getting coffee.

The lie was so transparent I almost laughed at myself.

The shop was quiet this late on a weeknight—a few students hunched over laptops, a couple sharing a pastry in the corner, the low murmur of indie music from the speakers. And behind the counter, wiping down the espresso machine was Elliot.

He glanced up when the door chimed. Our eyes met, and he smiled as he set down the rag.

"Ro." His voice was carefully neutral, but his eyes weren't. "Didn't expect to see you here."

"Couldn't sleep." I approached the counter, hyperaware of the distance between us. "Figured caffeine would help."

"That's . . . not how caffeine works."

"I'm aware."

A smile tugged at the corner of his mouth. "What can I get you?"

"Just black coffee. Large."

He turned to pour it, and I watched his hands—the same hands I'd watched move across a notebook, the same hands that had touched mine over a coffee cup just hours ago. The memory of that contact sparked through me, electric and unsettling.

"Here." He slid the cup across the counter. Our fingers didn't touch this time, but the space between them felt charged. "On the house."

"You don't have to—"

"I want to." He hesitated, glancing toward the back of the shop, then back at me. "Actually, I was hoping I'd get a chance to talk to you. Not here, not like this. Somewhere we could actually . . . " He trailed off, searching for the right word.

"Talk?" I supplied.

"Yeah." He met my eyes. "There's something I want to tell you. Something I should have said a while ago."

The words landed in my chest with unexpected weight. Something I should have said. That could mean anything. It could mean everything.

"What time do you get off?" I heard myself ask.

"Eleven. We close in an hour."

I nodded slowly, my mind racing through possibilities. "I could wait. If you want."

"You'd wait an hour for a conversation?"

"Depends on the conversation."

Something shifted in his expression—vulnerability, maybe, or hope. "It's kind of a big one."

"Then I'll wait."

I took my coffee to a table in the corner, positioning myself where I could watch the door and the counter simultaneously. Old habits. Elliot went back to closing duties—wiping tables, restocking cups, running the register for the last few customers. Every few minutes, his eyes would find mine across the room. A silent acknowledgment. I see you. I know you're still there.

The hour passed. I pretended to scroll through my phone, but mostly I just watched him work. Watched his movements, the easy way he chatted with the last customers, the slight tension in his shoulders that told me he was as nervous about this conversation as I was.

At eleven, he locked the front door and flipped the sign to CLOSED. The last customer had left ten minutes ago. It was just us now.

"My place is a few blocks from here," he said, untying his apron. "If that's okay. It's more private than . . . " He gestured vaguely at the coffee shop.

Six Years Ago

The Portland arena was sold out—three thousand people packed into steep stands that rose like canyon walls around the ice. Semifinals of the Pacific Junior Hockey League. Portland Eagles versus Vancouver Vanguard. Winner advances to the championship.

I was fifteen years old, and I was the best player on the ice.

Not because I was the most talented—Anders had more raw skill, more explosive speed, more highlight-reel potential. But I saw the game differently. Read plays before they developed. Understood positioning and angles and the geometry of hockey in a way that coaches said was rare. Vision that couldn't be taught.

The game was tied 2-2 in the third period. The crowd was deafening, that wall of sound that made everything feel heightened, important, like the stakes were life and death even though it was just a game.

Just a game.

The play started behind the Portland net. I collected a loose puck, my edges biting into the ice as I surveyed the options. The Vanguards were pressing hard, trying to force a turnover. I could feel their forwards closing in, hear the scrape of their skates on the surface.

Anders was open on the far side of the zone. He'd been calling for the puck all period, that hungry look in his eyes that I'd learned to recognize. When Anders stared at me like that, he was dangerous.

Also, he was reckless and willing to do whatever it took to win.

I should have known. I should have seen the setup. Anders had positioned himself just outside Henderson's checking range, the way he was already leaning toward the boards where Henderson would have to follow. We'd run variations of this play a dozen times in practice. Anders called it "the trap."

I made the pass.

It was perfect—tape-to-tape, weighted exactly right, landing on Anders's stick just as Henderson committed to the check. For one frozen moment, everything aligned: the puck, Anders, Henderson closing in with all his momentum.

Then Anders stepped aside.

It was so fast. So deliberate. One second he was there, receiving the pass, and the next he'd pivoted, letting Henderson's body carry past him toward the boards. Toward the corner where the glass met the ice at an angle that was designed for safety but became something else entirely when you hit it wrong.

Henderson hit it wrong.

The sound was—

I can't describe the sound. I've tried, in nightmares, in the long hours before dawn when sleep won't come. It was a crack, yes. But it was also something else. Something wet and final and wrong. The sound of a body doing something bodies weren't supposed to do.

The arena went silent. Three thousand people, holding their breath.

Henderson didn't move.

He was lying on the ice, his body at an angle that made my stomach turn, his helmet cracked from the impact. The medical staff rushed out, their red jackets bright against the white surface. Players from both teams had stopped skating, frozen in place, staring at the boy who wasn't getting up.

Anders skated past me. His face was blank. Empty. Like he'd already decided how he was going to remember this moment.

"Don't say anything," he said, his voice barely audible beneath the chaos. "It was an accident. You didn't see anything."

I didn't say anything.

I stood there on the ice, my stick in my hands, and I watched them load Michael Henderson onto a stretcher. I watched them carry him off the ice, his parents screaming from the stands, his teammates clustered at the bench with their heads bowed.

I watched, and I said nothing.

The coverup started that night.

League officials in our locker room, speaking in low voices with our coach. Lawyers appearing from somewhere—team lawyers, league lawyers, lawyers whose names I never learned. They spoke to us individually, in a small office that smelled like stale coffee and desperation.

"It was a hockey play," they told me. "A tragic accident. These things happen."

"But—"

"Mr. St. Clair." The lawyer—a woman with sharp eyes and a sharper smile—leaned forward. "Your career is very promising. The league would hate to see it derailed by . . . misunderstandings."

They didn't threaten me directly. They didn't have to. I was fifteen years old, I'd just watched a boy slam into the boards head first then get taken out on a stretcher. I'd already heard the words "paralyzed" and "paraplegic" thrown around. Now, I was being told by adults in suits that the best thing I could do was stay quiet.

So, I stayed quiet.

The footage of the hit was "lost" during a server migration two days later. An unfortunate technical error, they said. Very regrettable. The investigation concluded that it was "a clean hockey play with an unfortunate outcome." No disciplinary action. No public statement beyond condolences to the Henderson family.

The Hendersons received a settlement. I don't know how much—I wasn't privy to those conversations. But I know they signed NDAs. I know they stopped talking to the press. Their son went from being a promising young defenseman to cautionary tale.

I left the league two days after the incident. I let Chet Finlay spin it as a strategic decision, a pivot toward Hollywood. The next phase of the Chase St. Clair brand.

The truth was simpler. I didn't have the stomach for it anymore. Every time I stepped on the ice, I saw Henderson's body crumpling. Heard that sound. Felt the weight of the pass I'd made, the trap I'd helped set without even knowing it.

Chapter 23
The Scripted Truth

Elliot

The walk from Brewed Awakening to my loft stretched four blocks. We didn't speak. Ro matched my pace, his hands deep in his pockets, his breath making small clouds in the February air. Every few steps, his shoulder brushed mine.

I'd practiced this conversation a dozen times in my head. I have to tell you something. I've been researching you. The words had seemed manageable in rehearsal. Now, with Ro beside me, they felt like grenades I'd swallowed.

At my building, I unlocked the street door and led him up the narrow stairs. The wood creaked under our weight, each step an accusation. My pulse was hammering so hard I could feel it in my throat.

"It's an old industrial space," I said, fumbling with my keys. "Used to be a bookstore. The landlord cleared out the inventory years ago, but sometimes you can still smell the paper in the floorboards."

Ro nodded but didn't respond. His eyes were scanning the hallway with that careful wariness of someone who'd spent years cataloging exits.

I pushed open the door and stepped aside.

Rowan stepped in. His gaze swept across the room. Then it landed on the binder with his face plastered on the cover. The same image of him I'd had taped above my bed so many years ago.

He stopped.

I watched his shoulders tighten. Watched the careful neutrality drain from his face, replaced by something harder to read.

The binder wasn't a wall of red string and grainy photos. It was a meticulously constructed character profile. Forty pages of notes on a person I'd initially labeled "The Subject" before I'd learned his real name. Sections on physicality, vocal patterns, psychological drivers. Observations about the way he shifted his weight when he was deflecting and the specific, hollow quality his voice took on whenever Portland came up.

It was a blueprint for Diego Santos, the character I was building for my thesis. But it was also a dissection of a person who hadn't consented to be studied.

Ro crossed to the desk. His shadow stretched long across the floorboards.

I stayed by the door, my hands jammed in my pockets to hide the shaking.

He looked down at an open page—the one I'd titled The Ice Prince: Stigma and Shielding. His finger traced the edge of the paper but didn't touch the ink. He flipped through the book before turning to back to me.

"You didn't just research me," he said. His voice was low, almost conversational, but I could hear the tension. "You dramaturgically dissected me."

"I needed to understand the mechanics of the mask." The words came out steadier than I felt. "To play Diego, I had to understand why Chase St. Clair became a ghost. I had to know the 'where' to find the 'who.'"

Ro turned the page. His expression didn't change, but his jaw tightened.

"You have notes on my posture during the national anthem."

"Because you were performing even then." I took a step closer, then stopped myself. "You were playing the part of a man who didn't want to be seen. But for an actor, the interesting part isn't the performance. It's the moment before the curtain goes up—the moment where the real person disappears."

He flipped to another section. The one about his skating patterns. The one where I'd written hides in plain sight—uses third-line grinder role as camouflage.

"This is thorough," he said.

"I'm a theatre student. Thorough is what we do."

"This is beyond thorough." His gaze stayed fixed on my handwriting, his pulse visible in the hollow of his throat. "This is—" He stopped. Something in his expression shifted—from wariness to something closer to recognition. "You're not wrong, though. About the performance. About the disappearing."

I hadn't expected that.

He closed the binder and rested his palm on the cover. For a long moment, neither of us spoke. The only sound was the wind rattling the old windows, a draft whistling through the gap where the seal had worn away.

"You're stuck," he said finally.

"What?"

He tapped the back of the binder. "The 'Resolution' section. It's empty. You've got forty pages of character analysis and no ending."

He'd read that far. Well, he'd skimmed that far.

"I have the facts," I said. "I have the archive. But I don't have the truth. I don't know the ending because I don't know the person who survived it."

Ro was quiet. I could see him processing, the same methodical focus he brought to film study, to skating drills, to everything that mattered.

I walked to the desk and picked up a red pen—the one I'd been using to mark my own assumptions, the places where my research had holes I couldn't fill with forum posts and paparazzi shots.

I held it out to him.

"I'm a theatre student," I said. "I know how to build a character. But you want to be a journalist. You know how to find the truth." I took a breath. "I don't want to guess anymore. Tell me where the profile is wrong. Use the red pen."

Ro looked at the pen. Then at the binder. Then at me.

The silence stretched.

"If I do this," he said slowly, "it's not for your thesis. And it's not for Diego Santos."

"I know."

He reached out and took the pen from my hand. His fingers brushed mine—brief, electric, gone.

He sat down in my thrift-store desk chair, the leather creaking under his weight. He opened the binder to the first page and clicked the pen—a sharp, decisive sound that echoed through the quiet loft.

"First correction," he said. "You've got the timeline wrong on the Henderson incident. It was March fifteenth, not March fourteenth. The Ides of March." A beat. "I used to think that was ironic. Now, I just think it's true."

He bent his head over the pages and wrote.

Chapter 24
Opening Night

Rowan

I told myself I wouldn't go.

For three days after we finished correcting the archive, I told myself that watching Elliot perform was too much. Too close. Too dangerous. Watching him become Diego Santos—watching him use everything he'd learned about me to build a character—would be like watching someone dissect me on stage.

But the night of the opening, I dressed up and walked toward the Performing Arts Center, anyway. Elliot had texted me to let me know that there were two tickets sitting at the box office in my name. He may have also alluded that he chose the seats because they gave me a perfect view of the shower scene. Even though we'd not as much as held hands, the sexual tension had been building between us for days. Thankfully, tonight would be me watching an actor on a stage, and not the two of us hanging out in private at one of our apartments. Alone time with Elliot was becoming dangerous. Well, maybe not dangerous, but eventually, one of us was going to make an actual move, then all bets would be off. Let's just say I've taken a few cold showers and run extra laps out at the lake to vent off the extra stress I've experienced.

The building was alive with the particular energy of an opening night. Sure, this one didn't have a red carpet outside lined by paparazzi, but it still had that electric hum of anticipation and terror that I remembered from my own performing years. People clustered in the lobby, programs in hand, voices pitched with excitement. I kept my head down and went to the will-call booth to pick up my ticket, moving through the crowd like a ghost at someone else's party.

I arrived ten minutes after the house lights dimmed, slipping through the heavy door with practiced silence. The Black Box was gone. In the cold, flat light, the velvet darkness had been traded for battered lockers and stained benches. Every nicked corner and rusted hinge felt permanent, as if the room had existed here for years instead of hours.

I found my seat, which was three rows back from the stage right on the aisle with a direct sightline into the tiled shower. The seat was stuffed but still had that hard and uncomfortable feel, and I kept angling my body to find a comfortable position that didn't encroach on my neighbors.

The lights flickered twice. Okay, here we go.

A woman's voice came over the loud speakers. "Good evening, ladies and gentlemen, and welcome to tonight's world premiere performance of Cameron Torres's The Penalty Box. Before we drop the puck on this evening's show, we have a few quick announcements. Please take a moment to silence all cell phones and electronic devices. Trust us, you don't want to be the one who gets called for interference during a crucial scene. Now's also the time to unwrap any candy, cough drops, or snacks—because once the action starts, crinkling wrappers will earn you a minor penalty from your fellow audience members. Tonight's performance will run approximately ninety minutes with no intermission, so we suggest you make any necessary trips to the locker room now. Don't worry—we promise this show is worth staying on the ice for. Photography and video recording are strictly prohibited and will lead you to taking a major penalty and finding yourself ejected. And remember: in this theater, we all play for the same team. So, sit back, relax, and let's see if love can survive sudden death overtime. Thank you, and enjoy the show!"

The play didn't open the way I expected.

The lights rose on an empty set. Offstage the sound of high heels clacking down a hallway were heard before a middle-aged Latinx woman walked through the door, Elliot following right behind. Both of them tense and guarded.

"You sit by the window," the woman gestured to her son.

"Mom—"

"Window."

The two argue for a minute before a second woman wearing a puffer vest over scrubs, her hair in a ponytail that's come half loose, bursts into the room. She strides over and dumps her overstuffed tote bag onto one of the benches.

She sees the other woman and her demeanor changes in an instant, "Oh. Hi."

"Diane."

This was a masterclass in acting. A cursory glance exposed the women's troubled past.

We soon learned that Diego and Tyler had had some kind of altercation on the ice. The mothers had been dragged in by the coach to figure out what was going on.

I watched the four of them—two mothers, two sons—navigate the wreckage of whatever had exploded on the ice. The tension was immediate, the mothers circling each other with practiced animosity while the boys sat on opposite sides of the room, refusing to acknowledge each other.

Coach Brennan entered, flustered and overwhelmed, trying to mediate something he didn't understand.

Then Tyler mentioned the video. Someone had filmed the fight, posted it on Snapchat. Coach connected Tyler's phone to the TV, and they all watched—the shaky footage, the crowd noise, the garbled audio. I couldn't see the screen from my angle in the audience, but I watched their faces as they watched: Coach wincing, Diane gasping, Maria's face going hard.

Diego's eyes closed. Tyler squeezed his mother's hand.

Whatever they heard on that video, it was enough.

The play unfolded in fragments—scenes that built on each other like pressure under ice, each one adding weight until something had to crack.

I watched the mothers left alone in Coach's office, their hostility giving way to something more complicated. Diane admitting she was scared. Maria confessing the same. Two women who'd spent years in polite competition at fundraisers and carpool lines, finally seeing each other.

Then the lights shifted—golden, warm.

It didn't take the audience long to realize we're looking at some kind of flashback. Diego and Tyler in the locker room, before everything broke. The easy banter between them was startling after the tension of the earlier scenes. Elliot and Lucas performed it with the kind of casual intimacy that only comes from deep familiarity—finishing each other's sentences, the rhythm of old friends.

But underneath, I could see the fault lines forming.

Diego pushed too hard about a party, about Tyler talking to some girl. Tyler deflected, growing defensive. The subtext was screaming, even if the characters couldn't say it out loud.

Then they were moving toward the showers.

The set was brilliant in its simplicity. Steam rose even without water running, some theatrical trick with dry ice. I watched as Diego hung up his towel on a hook right outside the shower. He stepped in and turned on the water and it started flowing down his naked body. Tyler followed. I could tell the brazen nudity made a few in the audience uncomfortable. In the back of my mind, I was like, you people haven't even seen the good part yet.

I'd watched them rehearse this scene. I knew what was coming.

But watching it in front of a full audience was different.

The theater was silent as Tyler and Diego's argument escalated. Voices rising, then dropping to something more dangerous. When Diego stepped out from behind the panel—towel around his waist, desperate—a woman two rows ahead of me shifted in her seat.

Tyler emerged too. They were too close. The air between them crackling with everything they weren't saying.

"Tell me I imagined it," Tyler said.

Diego couldn't answer.

Then Tyler kissed him.

The audience intake of breath was audible.

Elliot and Lucas performed the moment exactly as they'd rehearsed it—the initial freeze, the surrender, the stumbling backward into the shower stall. It was staged carefully. There had a been a few changes since I saw it the first time. But the deep intimacy of two men on the floor of the locker room shower was an amazing mix of passion and fear.

"This is better than porn," I heard someone whisper behind me.

The scene played out—the janitor locking them in, the panicked aftermath, the argument that followed. Diego spiraling about exposure, about loss, about everything he'd worked for. Tyler insisting it was worth it, that he was done hiding.

"I love you," Tyler said, and the words echoed in the small theater.

When the act ended with Diego alone on the floor, the lights fading to black, the applause was uncertain. Scattered. Some people clapping, others still processing.

Act Two moved faster. We're back in the present. And Diego and Tyler are having an argument about who and what they are. Finally, they kiss, this time in full pads, which had to be kind of awkward.

Maria and Diane walked in on their sons. The sharp intake of breath from the crowd, the way people leaned forward. Coach freezing midsentence. The mothers' faces cycling through shock and horror and something that might have been grief.

What followed was a masterclass in family confrontation. Maria's lawyer instincts kicking in, trying to control the damage. Diane's confusion and fear. The boys caught between who they were and who their mothers needed them to be.

Then came Coach's confession—that he'd been in their position once, that he'd chosen hiding, that he'd spent thirty years wondering what if.

The weight of that landed pretty damn heavy with me.

But it was Act Three that broke something open.

The lights came up on a locker room that had somehow transformed. The PolyGlide panels I'd seen the tech crew installing were invisible now, the special polymer surface that let actors wearing modified skate guards glide across the stage as if on real ice.

Tyler and Diego faced each other in full gear, and then they were moving—actually skating, the smooth glide unmistakable. The sound design sold it: the scrape of blades, the thud of pucks, the ambient noise of a game in progress.

I'd used PolyGlide in a showcase once, so I knew the specific technique required to skate on the stuff. Most audiences wouldn't know they weren't on ice.

The fight scene was choreographed with brutal precision. Tyler and Diego circling each other, too close, too physical, the hockey violence bleeding into something more personal. When Diego shoved Tyler and they went down, tangled together, it was intimate and violent at once.

The phone cameras flashing from the audience's perspective made it feel visceral and real. This was how secrets got exposed now. Not through confession but through documentation.

The aftermath unfolded in waves: the note left in Diego's locker, crude and hateful. The mothers processing their terror differently—Maria's rage, Diane's confusion. The team meeting where Diego and Tyler stood in front of everyone (the audience becoming the team in that moment) and told the truth.

"Diego and I are together," Tyler said, his voice steady despite the tremor Lucas let slip through. "We've been together for over a year."

The silence that followed felt eternal.

Then: "So . . . you're still playing, right?" A voice from offstage, uncertain.

The tension broke slightly. Not perfect. But enough.

The final scene was quiet. Diego and Tyler alone in the locker room, processing everything they'd just survived. The conversation was simple, honest, stripped of pretense.

"We're going to be okay. Right?" Diego asked.

"I don't know," Tyler answered. "But I know we're going to try. And that's something."

They stood at the edge of the stage, a single spotlight catching them, and said the words out loud:

"I love you."

"I love you, too."

The light faded to a pinprick on their joined hands.

Blackout.

The applause started slowly, then built. People standing. Some enthusiastic, some more reserved. I sat there, my hands gripping the armrests, my chest tight with something I couldn't name.

Elliot had taken my pain—the photos, the archive, the years of hiding—and turned it into something that might help someone else feel less alone. He hadn't exploited me. He'd understood me. I had tears running down my face. I stood and kept clapping as the cast took their bows. Elliot turned to me. I wasn't sure if he could see me crying in the dark through the spotlights, but he knew I was there.

And somehow, that was more terrifying than anything else.

When the house lights came up, people started filing out around me. I wiped the tears from my cheeks and tried to pull myself together. I was a basket case. Fragments of conversation floating past:

" . . . didn't expect it to be so . . . "

" . . . those actors were really brave . . . "

" . . . that body, I'd be parading around naked on a stage, too . . . "

" . . . do you think it's based on . . . ?"

I needed to leave. I needed air.

Chapter 25
The Phone Call

Rowan

I didn't turn on the lights.

The apartment was dark when I entered, and I left it that way—letting the door swing shut behind me, letting the shadows swallow me whole. The streetlight outside painted pale rectangles on the floor, just enough illumination to navigate by, not enough to make me feel seen.

I dropped onto the futon without taking off my jacket. Without taking off my shoes. Just sat there in the darkness, my chest still tight from the theatre, my mind still cycling through images I couldn't shake.

Elliot's face, transformed into Tyler's desperation. The way he'd moved—my movements, my body language, my careful architecture of hiding—performed back at me with devastating precision. The shower scene, purple light and steam, two naked bodies coming together in the way I'd once allowed myself to want.

He had seen me.

Not the product Chet Finlay had manufactured. Not the ghost I'd become. The actual person underneath the carefully constructed persona.

That should have felt like a violation. In some ways, it did—the exposure of being that visible, the vulnerability of having my pain translated into art for an audience of strangers. Elliot hadn't used what he'd learned to hurt me. He'd used it to understand. To create something that felt true, something that might help other people feel less alone with their own hiding.

The memory of the cabin surfaced, vivid with the sound of rain on the roof and our conversation about picking daisies and the perfect pass. In my mind, I saw his character study of me—the one sitting in his apartment covered in red ink—now transformed from a violation into a collaboration. Even the physical heat of the stick lesson returned to me:

my hands over his, my chest against his back, and the unacknowledged proximity that had made me ache to lean forward and caress his neck with my lips.

My phone buzzed.

The sound cut through the silence like a blade, harsh and intrusive. I'd been ignoring it for weeks—months, really. Ever since I'd landed at Oakridge, I'd treated the phone like a threat, something that might reveal my location or identity if I engaged with it too directly. I checked it for emergencies. I used it to text Davies about practice schedules and Elliot about . . . whatever Elliot and I were doing.

I had hoped it was Elliot checking in on me, so I fished my phone out of my pocket and started scrolling. The screen was too bright. I squinted against it, watching the notifications cascade down—missed calls, text messages from my parents, app alerts I didn't care about. Most of it was noise. Spam numbers. Automated reminders from accounts I'd set up under false names.

But one name appeared in the text thread that made my chest tighten.

'Maybe Anders Holmström,' the screen said.

I stared at the name, feeling the blood drain from my face. I hadn't spoken to Anders in five years. Hadn't heard his voice since the night the photo surfaced, when he'd called to explain—justify, really—why he'd sent it to "a friend" who'd sent it everywhere else.

It wasn't supposed to go public, Ro. It was just between us. Someone leaked it.

I'd hung up on him. Blocked his number. Changed my phone, my email, my entire life. Two days later, I lost it on the set and had run.

But blocking someone on one phone didn't block them on another. How did he get this number?

I scrolled through the messages, my finger trembling slightly against the screen.

Anders (3 weeks ago): Heard you're playing again. We should talk.

Anders (2 weeks ago): I saw a clip from the Westhaven game. That assist was sick.

Anders (1 week ago): You look good, Ro. Really good. Call me.

Anders (3 days ago): I'm going to be in California next month. We should meet up.

Anders (tonight, 2 hours ago): I know you're seeing these. Don't ignore me.

My hand was shaking now. Not from fear, exactly—Anders had never been physically threatening, had never raised a hand against me in all the time we were together. But he represented something worse than violence. He represented the life I'd run from. The person I'd been before I burned everything down.

And he was tracking me.

I scrolled back through older messages, ones I'd missed in my months of deliberate avoidance. Anders had been watching my reemergence with the intensity of someone who'd never really let go.

Anders (6 weeks ago): Saw your name on a roster. Oakridge? Really? You could be playing DI. NHL, even. What are you doing at a DIII school in the middle of nowhere?

Anders (5 weeks ago): I looked you up. "Rowan Calloway." Smart. But not smart enough. I know it's you.

Anders (4 weeks ago): We should talk about what happened. I've been thinking about it a lot. About us.

I closed the message thread, dropping the phone onto the futon like it had burned me.

About us.

There hadn't been an "us" for five years. There had barely been an "us" when we were together—just two boys hiding the same secret, finding solace in each other's bodies, pretending that proximity was the same as understanding.

Anders had never understood me. He'd wanted me, but he'd never seen me.

Every time I had trusted Anders, he had burned me. As the old saying goes, "Burn me once, shame on me. Burn me twice, get the hell out of Dodge."

Anders was my past—the good and the bad.

I know you're seeing these. Don't ignore me.

I turned off the phone.

The screen went dark. The apartment went silent.

I lay back on the futon, staring at the ceiling, the streetlight painting its pale rectangles across the darkness. I lay there in the dark, the phone silent beside me, and I waited for sleep that wouldn't come.

Chapter 26 The Anders Incursion

Elliot

The applause was everything I'd ever wanted.

It rolled through the Black Box in waves—genuine, sustained, the kind of response that told you the audience had been moved, not just entertained. I stood at center stage with Lucas and the rest of the cast, sweat cooling on my skin, stage makeup probably running down my face, and I let myself feel it. The validation. The proof that all those weeks of research and rehearsal had translated into something real.

The cast left the stage as the house lights came up slowly, that gradual reveal that let your eyes adjust from the focused intensity of stage light to the diffuse glow of reality. From the wings, I heard the audience disperse, gathering coats and programs, murmuring about the performance. I heard the low rumble of noise, but not a single voice. I was already moving toward the dressing room, peeling off the hockey pads as I went, laying my helmet and stick on the prop table.

"Elliot!" Professor Albright called from somewhere behind me. "Notes in ten—"

"I'll be back," I shouted over my shoulder, pushing through the stage door into the back hallway. I didn't stop to change. Didn't stop to wipe off the makeup or do any of the post-show rituals that usually grounded me. I just threw my jacket over the sweat-soaked T-shirt and shoved through the door into the lobby.

I needed to find him.

The lobby was emptying, the last audience members filtering toward the exits. I scanned the space—the trophy case along one wall, the poster displays for upcoming productions, the refreshment table still scattered with half-empty cups and abandoned programs.

And then I saw him.

A man was standing by the trophy case, studying the photographs of past productions with the casual authority of someone who owned every room he entered. He was tall—taller than me—with platinum-blond hair swept back from a face that could have been carved from Scandinavian ice. His clothes were expensive in that understated way that screamed money: dark jeans that fit perfectly, a leather jacket that probably cost more than my entire wardrobe, a cashmere sweater visible at the collar.

He wasn't a student. He wasn't faculty. He wasn't a local.

I knew exactly who he was.

Anders Holmström turned from the trophy case, and his eyes found mine with a predatory precision that made my skin crawl. Ice blue, just like the photos in my archive. Cold and calculating and somehow amused, as if he'd been waiting for me.

"Diego Santos in the flesh," he said. His voice was low, accented with the faint Scandinavian undertones I'd read about in forum posts. "Or should I say, Elliot Vega? Very impressive performance."

I didn't move. My heart hammered against my ribs, but I kept my face neutral. Theatrical training for something.

"Thank you," I said carefully. "Did you enjoy the show?"

"I enjoyed watching someone try to understand something they can't possibly comprehend." Anders stepped closer, his movements fluid and controlled. "You've done your research, I'll give you that. The body language, the fear, the particular way someone moves when they're carrying a secret they can't put down. Very authentic. You have him nailed."

"It's called acting."

"Is it?" His smile was thin, almost reptilian. "Or is it something else? Something more . . . personal?"

The lobby was nearly empty now. A few stragglers gathered their things near the exit, but they weren't paying attention to us. We were alone in this strange, charged space between the theatre and the world.

"I don't know what you mean," I said.

"Oh, you do." Anders tilted his head, studying me the way a collector might study a new acquisition. "Once I learned that my old friend was an Osprey, I started paying attention to everything up here. Low and behold, there's a world premiere play about hockey. Well, with my background, of course I followed the production. Then I read that little article in the campus newspaper where you admitted that you had developed your role in 'consultation with primary sources,' I believe you said. Well, I got curious. Did some digging. And I found something interesting."

He reached into his jacket and pulled out a phone, scrolling to something on the screen. He turned it toward me.

It was a photo of me—sitting in Section 112 of the arena, Moleskine open on my knee, watching the ice below. The angle suggested it had been taken from the concourse, maybe with a telephoto lens. Someone had been watching me watch Rowan.

"You've been observing someone," Anders said. "Someone who moves exactly like your Diego Santos portrayal. Someone who disappeared five years ago and seems to have finally resurfaced."

My mouth went dry. "I don't know what you're talking about."

"Don't insult my intelligence," Anders said as he politely patted me on the cheek before pocketing the phone. His expression hardened. "I'm not here to cause trouble. I'm here because an old friend has decided to stop hiding, and I'd like to reconnect. Where is Rowan Calloway?"

The name hung in the air between us. He'd said it so casually, so possessively—Rowan, not Chase St. Clair, not the Ice Prince. The name of someone he'd known intimately. Someone he'd touched. Someone he'd broken.

"I don't know anyone by that name," I said.

Anders laughed—a short, humorless sound. "That's cute, you're protective. That's interesting. The actor defending his muse." He stepped closer, close enough that I could smell his cologne—something expensive and cold, like winter in a bottle. "I understand the impulse, believe me. Ro has that effect on people. Makes you want to shield him from the world, even when he doesn't ask you to."

I held my ground, refusing to give him the satisfaction of making me back up. "I think you have the wrong person."

"Oh, I have the right person." Anders's voice dropped, becoming almost intimate. "I've seen the clips from the Westhaven game. The assist that made the highlight reels. The movement, the vision, the particular way he protects the puck like it's the last thing keeping him alive. That's Ro. My Ro. And I know you know where he is."

My Ro. The possessiveness in those words made something hot and ugly flare in my chest. Jealousy—raw and unexpected and completely irrational. This man had been with Rowan. Had touched him, known him, been allowed past the walls that Rowan kept between himself and everyone else.

And then he'd destroyed him.

"What, need your paparazzi to take another photo of the two of you?" I asked.

The words came out flat, factual. I watched Anders's face for a reaction, some flicker of guilt or shame. But his expression didn't change. If anything, he looked bored.

"Ah," he said. "You have done your research."

"You photographed him without his consent. Then you shared it. You outed him to the entire world."

"I shared a private moment with someone I trusted. That person betrayed that trust." Anders spread his hands, a gesture of helpless innocence that was unconvincing. "Everything I did, I did to help Ro. To protect him. He was suffocating under the weight of his own fame, and I was the only one who saw the real person underneath."

"And yet he ran from you."

The words landed harder than I expected. Anders's composure flickered—just for a moment, a crack in the ice—before smoothing over again.

"He was young," Anders said. "Scared. He made impulsive decisions that he probably regrets now. That's why I'm here. To offer him a chance to come back. To reclaim everything he walked away from."

"A chance." I couldn't keep the skepticism out of my voice. "Out of the goodness of your heart, of course."

"Out of genuine concern for someone I care about." Anders stepped back, reassessing me. "You don't believe me. That's fair. But consider this: I could be useful to you. A theatre student who probably has dreams of working on the stage or in film. I have connections in the entertainment industry—that's not nothing. Your little play could get a lot of attention if the right people heard about it. And that attention could open a lot of doors for you and the rest of your cast."

The offer hung in the air, glittering and poisonous. But it also felt like a threat. He was trying to buy me. The manipulation was so obvious, so calculated, that I almost laughed.

"I don't know where he is," I said again. "I don't know where anyone named Rowan lives."

"But you know who he is." Anders moved closer, his voice dropping to something almost conspiratorial. "You know Ro. You've spent time with him. Maybe you even think you understand him." He let the words land before continuing. "But you don't. Not really. You understand the version of him he's willing to show you. I knew him before he became Chase St. Clair. Before hiding. I knew him when he was still capable of letting someone in."

The jealousy flared hotter. I know him too, I wanted to say. Maybe better than you ever did.

But I didn't. Because that would be giving Anders exactly what he wanted—confirmation that Rowan was here, that I had access, that there was something he could leverage.

"I think you should leave," I said instead.

Anders studied me for a long moment. The predatory amusement was back.

"He'll come back to me eventually," Anders said. "They always do. The hockey world isn't that big, and he can't hide forever. When he's ready to stop playing pretend at this little DIII program, he'll remember who actually understands him."

"Maybe," I said. "Or maybe he'll remember who destroyed his life and decide he'd rather keep running."

Anders's expression flickered again—anger this time, quickly suppressed. "You don't know what you're talking about."

"I know enough." I took a step back, creating distance. "I know what the photo did to him. I know about Henderson. I know about all of it."

As soon as the word Henderson flew out of my mouth, I knew I'd made a calculated error. Anders sneered for second before the smiling facade returned. If I hadn't been watching for it, I don't think I would have seen what was going on behind Anders's eyes and his crafted exterior.

"Whatever Ro told you about Henderson—"

"He didn't tell me. I found it myself." I was talking too much, revealing too much of my own research, but I couldn't stop because when I get nervous my mouth runs on autopilot. "The forums. The coverup. The way everyone protected you while a fifteen-year-old boy ended up in a wheelchair. Rowan didn't run because he was scared of fame. He ran because he couldn't live with what you'd turned him into."

The silence that followed was absolute.

Anders stood there, his perfect composure finally cracked, something raw and ugly visible underneath. For a moment, I thought he might hit me. Or threaten me. Or do something that would prove everything I'd suspected about him.

Instead, he smiled. It was the coldest expression I'd ever seen on a human face.

"You're in love with him," Anders said softly. "That's adorable. And incredibly naive. Rowan doesn't know how to love. He knows how to perform closeness while keeping everyone at arm's length. Ask me how I know."

He turned toward the exit, then paused, glancing back over his shoulder.

"When you see him—and we both know you will—tell him Anders says hello. Tell him the offer stands. And tell him that hiding in Northern California won't change who he is. The Ice Prince doesn't get to just disappear because he's tired of the crown. One way or another, his little secret is done."

He walked out of the lobby without waiting for a response.

I stood there for a long time after he left.

The theatre was quiet now, the last of the audience gone, the cleaning crew not yet arrived.

The door to the theatre opened, "There you are. Albright wants to see you. He has notes before everyone heads off to the party."

"Sorry, got cornered by an unexpected audience member. I'll be right in."

"You're in love with him."

Anders had said it like an accusation, a weakness he could exploit.

But Anders was right.

I was in love with Ro.

I pulled out my phone and typed a message.

Anders Holmström was at the show tonight. I didn't tell him anything.

I stared at the words for a moment. Then I added:

Are you okay? I saw you leave.

I sent the message and slipped the phone back into my pocket. Then I walked back into the theatre and pretended that everything was fine.

Chapter 27
The Archive Revealed

Elliot

I found him at the library.

It was almost noon, and I'd been searching for over an hour. But of course he was in the library. Third floor, media studies section. The same spot where I'd ambushed him with the catchphrase, where I'd dropped books and played games I was now ashamed of.

Ro smiled when I approached. His face told me everything I needed to know; he hadn't gotten my text.

"We need to talk," I said. "Not here." I swiveled my head, afraid Anders was going to jump out of the stacks. "A certain Nordic giant was at the play last night."

The look of shock instantly flooded Ro's face.

"Don't worry. He doesn't know where you are. Well, he knows you're here, but since he didn't show up at your place last night pounding on the door to let him in, I don't think he knows where you live."

He studied me for a moment. Then he nodded, gathering his things with the controlled efficiency that characterized everything he did.

"Your place?" he asked.

I thought about it for a moment, then shook my head. "Actually—yours. Anders has been watching me. He probably knows where I live."

"My place then."

We walked across campus in silence. His gaze stayed out in the margins, snagging on every moving shadow and distant footstep. He walked with a calculated stiffness, like a man moving through a room full of tripwires. It took every ounce of strength I had not to reach out and grab his hand. The day was gray and cold, February asserting itself through low clouds and a bitter wind that cut through my jacket. Neither of us spoke. There was too much to say, and none of it belonged in the open air of the quad. Rowan didn't let his body relax until we were both inside his SUV and heading to his place.

Rowan's apartment was exactly what I'd expected and nothing like it at the same time.

Second floor of a converted Victorian, the kind of building that had been chopped into multiple apartments decades ago and showed its age in peeling paint and creaking stairs. He unlocked the door and stepped inside, flicking on the light.

The space was sterile. Not just clean—empty. A futon against one wall with a plain gray blanket. A desk with a laptop and a single lamp. A kitchenette with what looked like exactly four of everything arranged with military precision. No posters. No photographs. No evidence that anyone lived here.

The only sign of life was the PVC pipe drying rack in the corner, hockey equipment hanging from it like armor waiting for its knight.

This wasn't a home. This was a safe house.

"It's not much," Rowan said, closing the door behind us. He moved to the window, checking the street below.

"It's strategic," I replied, understanding immediately what this space represented. Nothing to connect him to his past. Nothing that could be traced. "How long have you lived like this?"

"Since I fled LA." He let the curtain fall back into place. "Different cities. Same setup. I can pack everything I own in under an hour."

My space was creative chaos; books and scripts scattered across surfaces. The opposite of this cultivated emptiness.

Ro pulled the desk chair over and sat down, gesturing for me to take the futon. We faced each other across the small space.

"Tell me everything."

"He was at the theatre," I said. "After the show. In the lobby. He saw the play. He knows I'm connected to you somehow."

Rowan's jaw tightened. "What did he say?"

"He wanted to know where you were. I didn't tell him. He's been tracking your reemergence. The Westhaven clips, the roster—he put the pieces together." I paused, watching his profile. "He had a photo of me. In Section 112. Someone's been watching me watch you."

Ro closed his eyes. The weight of it—the invasion, the surveillance, the past reaching its fingers into the present—seemed to press down on him physically.

"I got his texts last night," he said quietly. "After I left the theatre. He's been messaging me for weeks. I'd been ignoring them."

"What does he want?"

"To 'reconnect.' To talk about 'what happened.'" Rowan laughed, the sound bitter. "He said he was going to be in California next month for work."

"But he's already here."

Ro stood abruptly, paced to the window, then back.

"He knows about the profile book," I said. "About what I've been doing. He tried to buy me. Offered to help my career in exchange for information about you."

Rowan went very still. "And?"

"I told him to leave."

The silence stretched between us. Rowan was staring at me with an expression I couldn't read.

"Why?" he asked finally. "You could have given him what he wanted. You could have traded whatever access you have for—"

"Because what he wants isn't mine to give." The words came out simply, without drama. I meant them. "You trusted me with your story. You let me see who you really are. That's not something I can sell to the highest bidder."

Rowan snapped his gaze toward the dark window, his jaw working as he audibly ground his teeth together. The muscles in his neck stood out like corded wire. He stayed like that for a long beat, silhouetted against the glass, before he finally forced the words out.

"What did he say? About me?"

"That you'd come back to him, eventually. That the hockey world isn't big enough to hide in." I hesitated, then added: "That he knew you before the masks. Before the hiding."

"He did," Rowan whispered. "He knew me when I was still stupid enough to believe someone could see me and not use what they saw. Anders was safe. He was someone I'd known before the film industry created and marketed me as a product," Rowan said slowly, sitting back down on the chair. "Even knowing how vicious and calculating he was, I thought he wanted me, not the Ice Prince." He laughed, the sound hollow. "Turns out he was just a better actor than most. He saw me, sure. He saw exactly which parts of me he could use to get what he wanted."

"What did he want?"

"To ride my coattails long enough to make himself relevant." Rowan shook his head. "He was a good hockey player, but he didn't have a problem cutting corners if it helped get him ahead. I know it's hard to explain given everything I knew about him, but he always seemed to be the only one in my corner. Come to find out, he was just the best manipulator of those around me. After the film franchise ended, Anders's talent in Hollywood was seen for what it was, mediocre. But dating Chase St. Clair? That opened doors even money couldn't budge."

I stayed silent, letting him speak.

"The difference between him and you," Rowan said quietly, "is that he never asked what I wanted. He just decided he knew best and acted on it. The photo, the outing, everything after—it was all decisions he made for me, without me. Even when he said he was trying to protect me."

"From what?"

"From myself, according to him. From making the 'wrong choices.' From—" Rowan's voice caught. "From telling the world about what had really happened to Henderson. He repeatedly told me it was old news. And if it got out, it would ruin my career. Henderson and his family would be fine, that it was just hockey. For a while, he'd even convinced me that it was just an accident. It was easier to act on the ice when I didn't have that sense of guilt weighing me down."

The revelation landed heavy between us.

"And what would have happened if the Henderson story had gotten out?" I asked.

"Anders had already built the narrative. The official story. Anders's father had connections, resources. He made sure the story stayed buried." Rowan's hands clenched in his lap. "But Anders kept evidence. Photos, texts, timeline documentation. As insurance, he said. In case anyone ever tried to blame us."

"Leverage."

"Always." Rowan met my eyes. "That's how Anders works. He helps you, but he makes sure you owe him. He protects you, but he keeps the receipts. He loves you, but only in ways that benefit him."

I thought about the profile book back at my loft. The pages Rowan had edited, correcting my speculation with truth. A collaboration, not a takeover.

"The photo," I said. "The one that outed you. How did it actually happen?"

Rowan was quiet for a long moment. "We were in a hotel room in Toronto. On the balcony was a hot tub. He convinced me to go for a dip. Of course, we didn't have swimsuits, so he said we should go nude. I was young, naive, and didn't think about the consequences. Plus, we were high up, so there wasn't going to be someone looking at us from a building across the street. One thing led to another, and we started making out. He'd wanted me to do more with him in the hot tub, but I'd put my foot down there. Now, I wonder if he really was hoping for something more scandalous than my back and the two of us kissing. When they were first published in a tabloid, he threatened to sue everyone under the sun."

"And you believed him."

"I wanted to believe him. There's a difference." Rowan's voice was flat. "Three weeks later, it was everywhere. In the press, he refused to say whether I was the man in the image, which only heightened the speculation. He even gave a very public apology, very convincing concern. He asked the media to let the innocent man he was being intimate with enjoy his privacy."

"But you didn't believe him."

"The cracks showed. The photo was too perfectly framed. The lighting on that side of the hotel was perfect for that time in the afternoon. And the timing—right when I was pulling away, questioning everything—it was too convenient." He turned to me. "But I couldn't prove it. And by then, the damage was done."

"He destroyed you to keep you."

"Or to punish me for trying to leave. I've never been sure which." Rowan stood again, paced the small space. "After that, I disappeared. Went back to being Rowan Calloway, buried Chase St. Clair, and moved every few months. I thought I'd finally outrun him."

"Until Westhaven."

"Until you." He said it without accusation, just stating fact. "Your play brought me back into visibility. And Anders has been circling ever since."

I reviewed my conversation with the man in the theatre lobby; Anders's calculated charm, the photo of me in Section 112.

"He's not just circling you," I said. "I think he has most of the puzzle pieces, but not all of them yet. At least not confirmed."

"He'll figure it out." Ro moved to his desk, opened the laptop. "Anders is patient. Methodical. He'll research you, track your movements, map your relationships. And when he has enough information—"

"He'll use it."

“That’s what he does.” Ro pulled up something on the screen, then turned it to show me. A text thread, Anders’s messages unanswered. Weeks of crafted manipulation: I miss you; We should talk; I’ve changed; You can’t run forever; I know you’re in California; We need to discuss what happens next.

The last message was from this morning: Saw an interesting play last night. Small world. We should get coffee this evening.

“He knows,” I said.

“He knows something. He’s testing to see what.” Ro closed the laptop. “This is his pattern. He gathers information, applies pressure, waits for the response. Every reaction gives him more data.”

“So, we don’t react.”

“It’s not that simple.” Ro sat back down, closer this time. “Anders doesn’t give up. He adjusts strategy. If pressure doesn’t work, he tries charm. If charm doesn’t work, he tries threats. And he’s very good at finding pressure points.”

“What’s yours?”

Ro looked at me for a long moment. “You, apparently.”

The words hung between us.

“He saw the play,” Ro continued quietly. “He saw how you translated the story. How you understood things about me I wouldn’t have told you. That kind of insight—it scares him. Because it means I trusted you with something I never trusted him with.”

“What?”

“The truth.” Ro’s voice was barely audible. “Anders had my secrets. My fears. My guilt. But you—you have my story. The real one. The one I’m choosing to tell instead of the one he decided for me.”

I thought about the profile book, the corrections in Ro’s handwriting. The collaboration we’d built.

“So, what happens now?” I asked. “Anders is here. He wants something from you. If this were a hockey match, what’s his play?”

Ro was quiet for a long moment, staring at his hands.

“When I saw your play last night,” he said, turning to stare at me, “I wanted to run. Not because you’d exposed me—but because you’d understood me. You’d taken everything you learned about hiding and fear and the weight of secrets, and you’d turned it into something that might help other people feel less alone.”

He stood up, moved to the window again, looking out at the gray February sky.

"Anders never did that. He used what he knew about me to control me. To possess me. But you—" He turned to face me. "You built a mirror. And then you handed it to me and said, 'What do you want to see?'"

I stood up, moving closer to him. Not touching—we weren't there yet—but close enough to feel the heat of his body in the cold room.

"The profile book is still incomplete," I said. "There's more you haven't told me. More than I could ever find on my own."

"I know."

"So, let me help you. Not by researching or observing or any of the things I was doing before." I took a breath. "Let me help you write the real story. The one only you can tell. The one Anders doesn't own."

Rowan looked at me—really looked, the way he had in the cabin and at rehearsal and the moment on the ice when he'd finally let himself play.

"A collaboration," he said.

"A partnership."

"Against Anders."

"Against anyone who tries to tell your story for you."

The silence stretched between us, charged with something I couldn't name. Through the window, the gray sky was darkening toward evening.

"He's going to come for me," Rowan said. "He's not going to stop until he gets what he wants."

"Then we make sure he doesn't get it."

"How?"

I saw the connection with the play. Tyler Mitchell fighting to be seen on his own terms. Diego Santos learning that hiding was just another form of prison.

"You stop hiding," I said. "Not all at once. Not in a way that destroys you. But you start owning your story. You get ahead of whatever Anders is planning, and you tell the truth before he can twist it."

"As Rowan Calloway or as Chase St. Clair?"

The question hung there, enormous.

"As yourself," I said. "Whoever that is now. Whoever you're becoming."

Ro's breath caught. I watched him process it—the terror of exposure, the exhaustion of hiding, the tentative hope that there might be another way.

"You'd help me with that?" he asked.

"I'd be honored to help you with that."

He didn't answer immediately. But something in his expression shifted—a door opening, just a crack, letting in light that hadn't been there before.

Outside, the February darkness was falling. Inside this sterile apartment, in this space designed for disappearing, two people sat in the lamplight and considered what it might mean to finally be seen.

"The profile book," Ro said finally. "Back at your place. We should probably move it. If Anders knows where you live—"

"We could bring it here."

"Or we could destroy it."

My eyebrows shot up, my gaze locking onto his. I waited for the punchline. "You want to destroy it?"

"I want to stop being afraid of it." He met my eyes. "Whatever story we tell—the one that's true, the one that matters—it's not going to come from your research or my corrections. It's going to come from this."

He gestured between us. The conversation. The trust building in slow increments.

"So, maybe the book doesn't matter anymore," he continued. "Maybe it was just the scaffolding. And now we build the actual thing."

I understood what he was saying. The archive had been my way of controlling the narrative, of processing my obsession. But Ro was offering something different: cocreation instead of documentation.

"We don't have to destroy it," I said. "But we don't have to be bound by it either."

"A starting point, not a Bible."

"Exactly."

Ro nodded slowly. Then he pulled out his phone, and read Anders's messages again.

"He's going to keep pushing," he said. "He'll escalate until he gets a response."

"Then we respond on our terms, not his."

"How?"

I pondered it. About Anders's pattern of manipulation, his need for control, his assumption that he still owned Ro's story.

"We give him nothing," I said. "No meeting, no conversation, no acknowledgment. We don't engage with his reality."

"He'll get more aggressive."

"Let him. Every aggressive move he makes shows his hand. Shows what he's really after."

Ro considered this. "And if what he's after is you? To get to me?"

"Then he finds out I'm not as easy to manipulate as he thinks."

A ghost of a smile crossed Rowan's face. "You really think you can outplay him?"

"I think we can outplay him. Together."

"Okay," Rowan said finally. "We do this together. Whatever comes next."

I put out my hand to shake on it. He grabbed my hand. Instead of shaking it, he pulled me into his orbit. Placed his hands on either side of my face and kissed me.

Chapter 28 The Portland Pilgrimage

Rowan

Somehow both Elliot and I had avoided Anders for a few days. I was sure he was lurking, but it seemed like he'd gone back to LA for the moment. Radio silence was more worrisome than having him here actively. Elliot and I had crafted a plan.

Step one was to deal with my past.

The campus had gone quiet as mid-March arrived, the library and dorms emptying out for Spring Break. A few of the guys—Lindros, Stastny, and Brimsek—had already headed south to San Diego to lounge at Pacific Beach, sending me photos of palm trees and sunshine that felt like a different planet. Their bodies were ridiculously white compared to the tanned bodies around them. I warned them to use sunscreen to avoid turning into lobsters.

For me, the break was less of a vacation and more of a rescue mission for my GPA. Between the tournament travel and the emotional fallout of the last few weeks, I'd fallen behind on a major journalism assignment. Professor Goodall, in a rare moment of mercy, had given me until the end of the break to turn it in.

By the third day, the silence of my sterile apartment was feeling like a cage. I was going stir crazy, the words on my laptop screen blurring into memories of Spokane and Portland. At least Elliot had his show that weekend and his shifts at Brewed Awakening to keep him grounded.

I contemplated all of it in the early morning light, drinking coffee. The skate shard caught the sun through my window, red and gold glinting against the dull metal of the lockbox. I'd been holding it for twenty minutes, turning it over in my hands, letting the edges press crescents into my palm.

Five years. Five years of running, hiding, building walls so thick I forgot there was someone inside them. And now—now, there was Elliot. The character study covered in red ink. The kiss that changed everything. The feeling of being seen by someone who chose not to look away.

But I couldn't move forward while I was still anchored to Portland. To the ice where Henderson fell. To the boy I was when I let it happen and said nothing.

I set the skate shard back in the lockbox and closed the lid. Then I picked up my phone.

Me: I'm going stir crazy. If I stay in this apartment another hour, the walls are going to start talking back.

His response came a few minutes later.

Elliot: The coffee shop is a zoo today, but I'm free tomorrow. We should do something. Something real.

I looked at the closed lockbox. Typed before I could talk myself out of it.

Me: I need to go to Portland. Will you come?

Elliot: When do we leave?

No questions. No conditions. No are you sure? Just presence. Just willingness.

Me: Tomorrow. Six?

Elliot: I'll be there. I'll drive.

I slowly reread the message, something shifting in my chest. This was what it felt like, I realized. Having someone in your corner who didn't need to understand everything but would show up anyway.

The morning was a bruised purple when Elliot's car pulled into my apartment complex parking lot. It was an old Subaru, the kind of practical vehicle that suggested borrowed from a relative rather than purchased for style. The headlights cut through the predawn darkness, and I was already waiting by the curb, my gear bag slung over one shoulder out of habit.

I didn't need the gear. This wasn't a hockey trip. But carrying it felt right somehow—the weight of who I was now, the person I'd become since I stopped being Chase St. Clair.

Elliot got out and circled to the passenger side to greet me. "I know we're taking my car, but if you want to drive, you're more than welcome to. I know some people need that control on road trips."

My hands were doing that jerky trembling again, the kind I couldn't suppress no matter how hard I gripped. "No. I need you to drive."

He didn't ask why. Just nodded, took my bag, and put it in the back with a care that made something twist in my chest. Then he opened the passenger door for me—a small gesture that felt enormous in the quiet of the empty parking lot.

I got in. The car smelled like coffee and something else, something that was just Elliot. It had become familiar over these past weeks. Comforting in a way I didn't expect.

He slid into the driver's seat before leaning over and kissing me good morning. "I got you a large coffee," he said. He adjusted the mirrors and pulled out onto the empty street. Neither of us spoke for the first thirty minutes, the silence filling the space. The town gave way to highway, and the highway stretched north toward Portland.

The redwoods rose on either side of California Highway 199 like cathedral walls, their dark bulk blocking out the early morning sky. I watched them blur past, my forehead pressed against the cool glass of the window and remembered all the times I'd made this drive before. In buses with teammates, in town cars with handlers, in the back of my parents' rental when I was still young enough to believe they were proud of me instead of their investment.

"You're quiet," Elliot said. Not an accusation. Just an observation.

"Thinking."

"About?"

"The last time I drove to Portland." I closed my eyes. "I was fifteen. It was the semifinals. My father had flown in from LA—he never came to games, but this one mattered. The league had scouts in the stands. NHL scouts. Everyone said I was going to go first round in the draft."

"What happened?"

"Henderson happened." I opened my eyes, staring at the trees. "And I left two days later and never played competitively again until January."

Elliot was quiet, waiting. He was good at that—the waiting. Most people rushed to fill silence, to offer comfort or opinions or advice. Elliot just held space.

"Fast forward a few years and three movies later, and I was so tired," I said, the words coming slowly. "That's what I remember most. Not the injury, not the coverup, not even Anders. Just how tired I was. I'd been performing since I was eight years old. First the acting, then the hockey, then the combination of both. I was a brand before I was a person. And I was so exhausted. I was going to escape, or I was going to be another child actor turned addict."

"Is that why you ran?"

"Partly." I watched a raindrop track down the window. "Partly it was guilt. Partly it was fear. Partly it was just . . . the opportunity. The guilt of Henderson had been building. Then Anders released the photo. I saw the walls closing in, and I found a door, and I took it. The coward's way out."

"That wasn't cowardice," Elliot said quietly. "That's survival."

"The line between them is thinner than you'd think."

We crossed the state border around nine, and like clockwork, California gold gave way to Oregon gray as soon as we hit Interstate 5. Before long the gray was accompanied by a fine mist, then a steady drumming against the windshield. Oregon weather. I'd forgotten how much it rained here, how the sky seemed to press down on everything like a weight.

"Can we stop?" I asked. "I need air."

Elliot pulled off at a rest stop near Ashland. The parking lot was mostly empty, just a few semis and a family in a minivan eating fast food with the windows down despite the drizzle. We got out and walked to the concrete barrier overlooking a forested valley, the pine trees disappearing into mist.

The air tasted like damp earth and diesel. I breathed it in, feeling my lungs expand, feeling the tightness in my chest ease slightly.

"Tell me about Anders," Elliot said, coming up behind me and wrapping his arms around my waist.

"What do you want to know?"

"Whatever you want to tell me."

How can I explain Anders Holmström? The first boy I ever loved. The first person who made me feel seen—really seen, not as a product or a brand but as a human being with desires and fears and needs. The person who destroyed me so thoroughly that I was still picking up the pieces five years later.

"He was older," I said finally. "Two years, which doesn't sound like much, but at fifteen it felt like a lifetime. He'd been in the league longer, knew how everything worked. He took me under his wing—that's how it started. Mentorship."

"But it became more."

"Yeah." I watched the rain fall on the pine needles. "He was the first person who ever wanted me for something other than what I could do for them. Or that's what I thought. Turns out he just wanted a different kind of thing."

"What kind?"

"Control." The word came out bitter. "Anders liked having power over people. Liked knowing secrets. The relationship was a secret, obviously—two guys in junior hockey, one of them a marketable child star? That would have ended both our careers. But I think that's part of what he liked about it. Having something on me. Being the only one who knew who I really was."

"How did you navigate your sexual relationship?"

"We didn't," I admitted. "Our relationship was complicated. When we were in Oregon, it was technically legal for us to engage in sexual activity, but in California it wasn't. Anders made the decision that we would have no sexual contact until I turned eighteen. He didn't want to take chances. The last thing he would ever do is allow me to have some kind of hold over him, which is probably how he viewed this. I can't say this for sure because he always sold it as protecting me, but I think it was all about covering his own ass."

"So, you basically turned eighteen and almost immediately the photo came out?" Elliot asked.

"The photo." I laughed, but there was no humor in it. "I was so stupid. That whole situation. I was young and naive."

"Do you think he knew what would happen when the picture got out?"

"I don't know. I've asked myself that question a thousand times." I turned to Elliot. His face was open, listening, not judging. "Part of me wants to believe it was an accident. That he really did just send it to a friend, and the friend betrayed him. But another part of me . . . "

"Another part?"

"I was already pulling away from Anders, already asking questions about things I shouldn't have been asking about. Then suddenly there's this photo destroying my life, giving me something else to focus on, making sure I could never go public about what I saw without appearing to deflect from my scandal."

"But it would have been Anders's scandal, too."

"Maybe, but he didn't have as much to lose and almost everything to gain." I turned back to the rain. "But I'll never know for sure. And honestly, it doesn't matter anymore. What matters is what I do now."

Elliot's hand landed on my shoulder—brief, warm, grounding. "You okay?"

"No." I took a shuddering breath. "But I need to do this. I need to see it. The ice where it happened. I need to stop running from it."

"Then let's go."

In the late morning, Portland emerged from the rain like a ghost city, all gray sky and wet pavement and the silver gleam of the Willamette River. I navigated from memory, directing Elliot through streets that had changed and streets that hadn't, past landmarks I remembered and buildings that were new.

The arena was still there. Of course, it was. You don't tear down a building that size, even if it's been renamed and renovated and slapped with a new corporate sponsor's logo. The Rose Garden was something else now, some tech company's name plastered across the facade, but the bones were the same. The parking lots, the entrance gates, the way it loomed against the gray sky like a monument to everything that happened inside.

Elliot pulled into a spot across the street, and I couldn't move.

The building watched me through the rain-streaked windshield. Inside those walls, I became someone I didn't want to be. Inside those walls, Henderson's life changed forever while I stood frozen on the ice. Inside those walls, I made the pass that set everything in motion and said nothing while the adults built their coverup around me.

"Take your time," Elliot said.

I didn't know how long I sat there. Minutes, maybe. The rain drummed on the roof, a steady rhythm that felt like a heartbeat or a countdown. My hands had stopped shaking, but something else had taken over—a coldness in my chest, a numbness that spread through my limbs.

I could turn around. Tell Elliot to drive back to California, pretend this trip never happened. Go back to my careful life, my anonymous apartment, my DIII hockey and my journalism classes and the comfortable walls I'd built around myself.

But I'd still be running. And I was so tired of running.

I opened the door.

The rain hit my face, cold and clean. I walked toward the arena, trusting that Elliot was following, trusting that I didn't have to do this alone.

The front entrance was locked—offseason, no events scheduled. But there was a side door, and a security guard sitting just inside, bored and scrolling through his phone. He looked up when I knocked on the glass.

"We're closed," he said through the door.

"I know." My voice sounded strange to my own ears—rough, raw. "I used to play here. I just need to see the ice. Five minutes."

Something in my face made him hesitate. He studied me for a long moment—the wet hair, the desperate eyes, the way I was gripping the door frame like it was the only thing keeping me upright.

"Eagles?" he asked.

"Yeah. Long time ago."

He sighed, unlocked the door, stepped aside. "Five minutes. Don't touch anything."

The corridors smelled like concrete and cleaning supplies and the particular mustiness of a building that had been closed up. Our footsteps echoed as we walked—me in front, Elliot behind, the security guard trailing at a distance like he wasn't sure whether to supervise or give us privacy.

I knew the way. My body remembered it even after seven years—the turns, the ramps, the doors that led to the ice level. The closer we got, the heavier my legs felt, like I was walking through water instead of air.

And then we were there.

The arena opened up around us, vast and dark. The ice was uncovered but unlit, a pale gray expanse in the shadows. Empty seats climbed toward a ceiling lost in darkness. No crowd noise. No music. No announcer's voice echoing through the speakers.

Just silence, ice, and ghosts.

I walked to the boards and stopped, my hands gripping the rail. The cold radiated up from the surface, familiar and foreign. I'd skated on hundreds of sheets of ice since I left this place. But this one was different. This one remembered.

"It was here," I said. My voice echoed in the empty space. "Right there, in the corner. Henderson came to check Anders, and Anders stepped aside, and Henderson hit the boards with everything he had, headfirst."

Elliot came to stand beside me. He didn't touch me.

"I was behind the net when it happened. I'd made the pass—the one that set up the play. I saw everything. The way Anders positioned himself, the way Henderson committed to the hit, the way Anders just . . . moved. Choreographed. Like he'd planned it."

My voice cracked on the last word. I gripped the boards harder, knuckles white.

"I heard the sound. The crack when Henderson hit the boards. Then silence—this horrible silence where three thousand people just stopped breathing. And I stood there, my stick in my hands, and I didn't move. I said nothing. I did nothing."

The tears came without warning, hot against my cold face. I didn't stop them.

"He was my friend. Henderson. We roomed together at tournaments, played video games in hotel rooms, talked about what we'd do when we made the NHL. And I watched him get carried off on a stretcher, and I never spoke to him again. Never called, never wrote, never did anything except send checks to a trust fund."

I was sobbing now, seven years of grief and guilt finally breaking through the walls I built to contain it. My legs gave out, and I slid down against the boards, sitting on the cold concrete floor, my head in my hands.

"I should have said something. I should have told the investigators what I saw, what Anders did. But I was fifteen and scared and everyone kept telling me to stay quiet, and I listened. I let them build their coverup, and I walked away."

Elliot sat down beside me. His shoulder touched mine—warm, solid, present.

"You were a child," he said. "Surrounded by adults who should have protected you and didn't. Whatever happened here, you didn't create it. You survived it."

"Survival isn't enough." I stared at the dark ice, at the corner where Henderson fell. "I have to do something. I have to . . . I don't know. Make it mean something."

"Then make it mean something." Elliot's voice was gentle but firm. "But not by punishing yourself forever. That doesn't help Henderson. That doesn't help anyone."

I didn't have an answer to that. I just sat there in the dark arena, crying for the boy who got hurt and the boy who ran away. I cried for all the years I'd lost trying to atone for something I couldn't have stopped.

Elliot draped his arm around me and pulled me closer to him. He let my tears run down my face onto the front of his shirt. He didn't try to fix it. He didn't offer empty comfort or easy answers. He just sat there in the dark, shoulder to shoulder, letting me grieve.

We left the arena as the afternoon light was starting to fade behind the gray clouds. The security guard just nodded as we passed.

In the car, I sat with my hands in my lap, feeling wrung out and hollow. But also lighter, somehow. Like I'd finally set down a weight I'd been carrying so long I'd forgotten it wasn't part of me.

"There's one more thing I need to do," I said.

Elliot looked at me, waiting.

"I need to see him. Henderson." I pulled out my phone. "I Googled his address before we left. He still lives in Portland. His parents' place."

"Are you sure?"

"No." I laughed, a wet, ragged sound. "But I've been depositing money into a Henderson Family Trust for seven years. I've been carrying around a piece of broken skate blade like some kind of penance. I need to face him. I need to know if he hates me."

Elliot reached over and took my hand. "Whatever happens, I'm here."

I typed the address into the GPS. Twenty minutes across town.

The longest twenty minutes of my life.

The Henderson home was a modest ranch-style house in a quiet neighborhood, the kind of place where kids rode bikes in the street and neighbors waved from their porches. There was a basketball hoop in the driveway and a beat-up truck parked out front. Normal. Ordinary. Nothing like the haunted mausoleum I'd built in my imagination.

I sat in the passenger seat, staring at the front door, my heart hammering against my ribs.

"Do you want me to come in?" Elliot asked.

"Yeah." My voice came out small. "Please."

We walked up the driveway together. My hand found his, squeezed once, then let go. I needed to do this standing on my own two feet.

I knocked.

Footsteps inside. The sound of a TV being muted. Then the door opened. A woman greeted us with tired eyes and a kind smile.

"Can I help you?"

"I'm . . . " My voice caught. I cleared my throat. "I'm looking for Michael Henderson. My name is Rowan. I used to play hockey with him."

Her expression shifted—confusion, then recognition, then something I couldn't quite read. "Chase St. Clair?"

"Yes, ma'am."

She studied me for a long moment. Then she stepped aside. "He's in the living room. He'll want to see you."

The house smelled like pot roast and fresh laundry. Family photos lined the hallway—Michael as a kid in hockey gear, Michael at prom, Michael in a graduation cap and gown. My chest tightened with every step.

The living room was warm and cluttered, the kind of space that felt lived-in. A man was sitting on the couch, a laptop open in front of him, spreadsheets visible on the screen. He looked up as we entered.

Michael Henderson.

He was bigger than I remembered—filled out, solid, the gangly teenager replaced by a man in his early twenties.

Not the broken figure in a wheelchair that had haunted my nightmares for five years.

"Holy shit," Michael said. "Chase St. Clair. In my living room." He rose from the couch. There was a slight stiffness to the way he held himself, and when he stood, I noticed a barely perceptible limp.

"It's Rowan now," I managed. "Rowan Calloway."

"Right, right." He gestured to the armchair across from him. "Sit down, man. Dude, you're turning blue. Please don't pass out on me."

I sat. Elliot hovered near the doorway, giving us space but staying close. Michael's mother disappeared into the kitchen, murmuring something about coffee.

Michael settled back onto the couch, studying me with an expression I couldn't decipher. "It's been what, seven years, and you finally show up at my door. What's the occasion?"

"I . . . " I didn't know how to start. All the speeches I'd rehearsed in my head evaporated. "I came to apologize."

"For what?"

The question threw me. "For . . . for what happened. The hit. I made the pass that set up the play. I saw what Anders did, and I said nothing. I let everyone cover it up, and I ran away, and you—"

"Got hurt," Michael finished. "Yeah. I remember. I was there."

"I should have done something. Said something. I should have—"

"Chase, er Rowan." Michael's voice was calm, almost gentle. "Stop."

I stopped.

"I'm going to tell you something, and I need you to actually hear it." He leaned forward, elbows on his knees. "What happened on that ice wasn't your fault. It was never your fault. You were fifteen years old. You made a pass—that's hockey. Anders made a choice. He was a dick, he was always a dick. The league made choices. The adults who covered it up made choices. You were a kid who got caught in the middle of something bigger than any of us understood."

"But I could have—"

"What? Told the truth and gotten buried by the same machine that was protecting Anders?" Michael shook his head. "I've had seven years to think about this, man. Seven years of physical therapy and doctors and learning to walk again without pain. And you know what I never did? Blame you."

I stared at him. The words didn't compute. They didn't fit into the narrative I'd been telling myself for half a decade.

"You were a kid," Michael repeated. "We both were. The only villain in this story was a seventeen-year-old named Anders and the adults who let him get away with it."

"I guess I should say that I'm the one who established the trust," I said.

"I know." Michael smiled, and it was the first genuine smile I'd seen since I walked in.

"You knew?"

"For about a year now." He sat back. "You did a pretty good job of hiding your tracks. The accountant you hired to set this up did a great job. I'm just better. That's what I do now. I'm an accountant. I manage other people's money, so of course I had to investigate on the side. I never touched the money, by the way. Didn't feel right. I didn't blame you for what happened. But my fiancée—" He glanced toward the kitchen, where his mother was talking to a young woman I hadn't noticed before. "She had an idea."

"Fiancée?"

"Emily. We're getting married in June." The pride in his voice was unmistakable. "She suggested we donate the trust fund to the local junior hockey league. I've been coaching there for the past two years—assistant coach for the bantam team. The league's underfunded as hell, can barely afford equipment for half the kids. Your money's been buying sticks and pads and ice time for kids who couldn't afford to play otherwise."

I felt something crack open in my chest. Not pain this time. Something else.

"You've been . . . coaching?"

"Yeah." Michael grinned. "Can't play anymore—not at that level, anyway. My back's never going to be what it was. But I can still teach. Still be part of the game." His eyes were steady. "Hockey didn't end for me that night, Chase. Fuck, Rowan. Sorry, it's hard to call you anything else. Anyway, hockey just changed. And honestly? I'm okay with that. I'm happy. I've got Emily, I've got my team, I've got a life."

The tears were coming again. I couldn't stop them.

"I thought you hated me," I whispered. "I thought you were stuck in a wheelchair, ruined, and it was all my fault. I've been carrying this for seven years—"

"I know." Michael's voice was soft. "I could see it on your face the second you walked in. That's a heavy thing to carry, man. You should put it down."

He stood up, crossed the room, and held out his hand. I took it, and he pulled me to my feet and into a hug that I didn't know I needed until it was happening.

"It's okay," he said. "You can let it go now."

I sobbed into his shoulder—the shoulder of the boy I thought I'd destroyed, the man who had rebuilt his life without a single ounce of bitterness toward me. Seven years of guilt and grief poured out, and Michael just held on, steady and strong.

When I finally pulled back, wiping my face, his mother was in the doorway with coffee and Emily was smiling at us both.

"Stay for lunch," Mrs. Henderson said. It wasn't a question.

I turned to Elliot, who was wiping a tear away from his cheek.

"We'd like that," I said.

Lunch was pot roast and potatoes and green beans from a can. When I had a silver spoon in my mouth, I would have turned my nose up at the very idea of this type of meal. It was the best thing I'd ever eaten.

Michael told stories about his bantam team—the kids who couldn't skate straight, the parents who yelled too much at games, the joy of watching a struggling kid finally score their first goal. Emily talked about wedding plans. Mrs. Henderson kept refilling our plates and calling me "honey" like I was one of her own.

I told them about Oakridge. About the team, about Sterling, about playing hockey again after thinking I never would. I told them about the character study on my wall and the boy who created it—the boy currently sitting next to me, his hand finding mine under the table.

"So, you two are together?" Michael asked, a knowing smile on his face.

"Yeah." Turning to Elliot. "Yeah, we are."

"Good." Michael nodded. "You deserve someone who stares at you the way he does. When I'd first heard you'd been dating Anders, I wondered if it was some kind of Stockholm syndrome thing."

"You're more right than you are wrong. Thankfully, I got this guy now; he's been helping me put the past behind me."

Elliot blushed. I squeezed his hand.

By the time we left, the rain had stopped and the sky was clearing. Mrs. Henderson hugged me at the door like she'd known me my whole life. Emily promised to send a wedding invitation to whatever address I ended up at. Michael walked us to the car.

"Hey," he said, as I opened the passenger door. "Whatever you've been carrying with you all these years, leave it here. I begrudge you nothing. I want you to do the same thing for yourself."

"Thank you," I said. "For everything."

"Go win some games," Michael said. "And stop being a ghost."

Elliot and I got in the car and pulled away from the Henderson house. In the rearview mirror, I watched Michael wave from the driveway until we turned the corner and he disappeared from view.

Chapter 29
Beyond the Boards

Elliot

I watched Rowan in the passenger seat as we drove away from the Henderson house, and I barely recognized him.

The tension that had lived in his shoulders since the day I met him was gone. The way he held himself—hunched, guarded, always ready for impact—had shifted into something looser, more open. He was staring out the window at the Portland suburbs sliding past, but his eyes weren't haunted anymore. They were clear.

"You okay?" I asked.

He looked at me, and the smile on his face was unlike anything I'd seen before. Not the crooked half-smile he used as armor, not the practiced expression from his acting days. This was real. Unguarded.

"Yeah," he said. "I think I actually am."

Rowan reached across the console as we pulled back onto Interstate 5. His hand found mine, fingers intertwining, a touch that was deliberate rather than accidental. He was choosing this, choosing to reach for me instead of pulling away. I said nothing; I adjusted my grip on the steering wheel, driving onehanded, and let our joined hands rest on the console between us. We drove like that for miles. He didn't let go until we were back on Highway 199. The California landscape slid past the windows—gray sky, green trees, and the steady rhythm of the windshield wipers in the early evening. The playlist I'd curated for the drive up didn't feel right anymore, so I left the music off.

We stopped for gas in Hiouchi in the late afternoon. I filled the tank and watched Rowan through the windshield. He stood by the car, stretching his legs and facing the fading light. The coiled tension from this morning had finally snapped. His movements were looser, his posture uncurling from that defensive hunch into something confident and relaxed. We bought coffee and snacks we didn't need and got back on the road. Rowan's hand found mine again, automatically, as if it had already become a habit.

"Ready for an adventure?" Rowan asked as we crossed back into California.

"Dare I ask?" I deadpanned.

"Let's go for a hike." He gestured ahead where the road climbed into the mountains. "There's a trailhead about ten minutes up. The whole hike is maybe two miles round trip to a lookout point over the Smith River. We could see the views, watch the sun start to set, and still be on the road with plenty of time to get back to Oakridge."

I glanced at the dashboard clock. Four-fifteen. "You sure you want to stop?"

"Yeah." He reached over and squeezed my hand. "I want to show you something."

The trailhead was a small pull-off with a weathered wooden sign that read Smith River Overlook—1 mile. A handful of other cars were parked in the dirt lot, hikers probably already on their way back before dark. We got out, and the air hit us—chilly, carrying the scent of wet redwood.

"Thirty, forty minutes max to the lookout," Rowan said, shouldering his jacket. "Easy trail."

"Famous last words," I muttered, but I was smiling.

The trail started out well-marked, winding through second-growth forest with occasional glimpses of the river valley below. Rowan walked ahead of me, surefooted on the uneven ground, and I watched the way he moved. His body was at one with nature. I was sure I looked like a cartoon character in comparison.

"You hike a lot?" I asked between breaths when we came to a bench after about twenty minutes. I sat down and tried to catch my breath.

"Used to. When I was a kid, before . . . " He turned and glanced down at me. "You, okay? You don't look that great."

"This isn't the time for fashion advice or jokes about my physical appearance," I tried to joke. Rowan furrowed his brow with even more concern. "I'll be fine. Just not used to exercise like this."

"But you work out?"

"I run on a treadmill that's flat. This is all—" I gestured wildly at the incline. "Not that."

Rowan tried to suppress a big cheesy grin.

"Wipe that smirk off your face," I said, narrowing my eyes at him.

"Or what?"

"Or I'll leave you here."

"Really?" He cocked his head. "You think you could beat me back to your car?"

Well, damn. He had me there. I pushed myself off the bench.

"Need me to carry you?" Rowan asked. "I could give you a piggyback ride."

I think he was surprised when I took him up on his offer. I threw my arms around his neck and hopped on his back. Rowan had just enough warning to catch my legs. My body adjusted upright as Rowan shifted my weight against his back.

And away he started hiking.

I knew we couldn't do this for long. I wasn't exactly heavy, but I was a full-grown man. After about ten to fifteen seconds of him hiking up the incline with me on his back, I finally said, "Okay, you made your point. You can put me down."

"Nope," Rowan said. "I like you where you are. It's much easier to keep track of you this way. Don't want you getting lost in the woods."

He continued for another thirty seconds before he finally let me back down to the ground. Instead of hiking ahead of me this time, he reached out a hand, and we hiked side-by-side.

We climbed steadily, the trail narrowing as it switchbacked up the hillside. The sun was lower now, maybe an hour from setting, painting everything in amber light. Through the trees, I could hear the distant rush of water.

After about thirty-five minutes, the forest opened up and we stood at the overlook.

The Smith River wound through the valley below us like a silver ribbon, catching the dying light. Mountains rolled away in every direction, ridge after ridge fading into purple distance. The sky was already starting to turn—pale gold bleeding into pink at the horizon, wisps of cloud catching fire.

"Holy shit," I breathed.

Rowan moved to stand beside me at the wooden railing. "Worth the hike?"

"Worth everything."

We stood there in silence, watching the colors deepen. A few other hikers were at the overlook—a couple with a dog, a solo photographer with an expensive camera—but they were packing up, heading back before dark. One by one, they filtered past us down the trail, calling out friendly warnings about the fading light.

Soon it was just us.

"Elliot," Rowan said.

I turned to him and realized he was already staring at me. The space between us felt like too much. I didn't know which of us moved first, but his face was inches from mine, his eyes asking a question I answered by closing the distance.

The kiss was soft and questioning at first. Then Rowan's hand came up to cup my face, and I leaned into him as the kiss deepened. He tasted of bad gas station coffee. I didn't care. His lips were chapped from the cold, but it was the most perfect kiss I'd ever experienced.

We broke apart, breathing hard, the overlook spinning around us.

"We should—"

He kissed me again, cutting off my words. This kiss was more urgent, more demanding. His hands found my waist, pulling me closer, and I let myself melt into it—into him, into this moment suspended above the world.

When we finally separated, the sun had dropped lower. The sky was a riot of orange and pink now, the valley below us filling with shadow.

"We better head back," Rowan said, though he didn't move.

"Okay," I agreed, remaining exactly where I was.

He let out a real, surprised laugh. "You look stoned." He kissed me one more time—quick and sweet—then took my hand. "Come on. We should go before it gets too dark."

We started back down the trail. The light faded faster than I'd expected, the forest swallowing the last of the sunset. The trail that had seemed so clear on the way up disappeared as shadows pooled around us.

"This is the right way, yeah?" I asked after about ten minutes.

"Should be. The trail's pretty straightforward."

But another ten minutes later, we passed a distinctive fallen log that I was pretty sure we'd passed before.

"Ro."

"Yeah?"

"Have we seen that log already?"

He stopped, looking back at the massive redwood trunk covered in moss. "Maybe? All these trees kind of look the same."

"No, I'm pretty sure—there was that weird knot that looks like a face."

We walked back to examine it. Sure enough: same face-knot.

"Okay," Rowan said slowly. "So, we went in a circle somehow."

"How did we go in a circle? It's one trail."

"There must be a junction we missed."

The light was getting seriously dim now, the forest floor barely visible. I pulled out my phone for the flashlight, then checked the signal. "No service."

"Yeah, we're pretty remote." Rowan pulled out his phone too, adding a second weak beam of light to the gloom. "Okay. Let's just . . . go back to where we think we made the wrong turn."

We backtracked carefully, phones held out like amateur spelunkers. The trail forked about fifty yards back—a split so subtle we'd completely missed it in the fading light.

"Left or right?" I asked.

"Left feels right."

"That's not confidence-inspiring."

"You got a better system?"

"We're dead," I said flatly. "They're going to find our corpses out here. I can see the headline: 'Gay Hikers Found in Lover's Embrace.'"

"Lover's, eh?" I couldn't see the smirk that accompanied that, but I knew it was there.

"Yep. Because once I wring your neck, I'm going to use you as a human blanket."

"Oh, so now you're Hannibal Lecter?"

I made that tongue sound he did when talking about fava beans. Rowan couldn't see me, but he laughed.

"Stay close," he said. "Let's use only one cell phone at a time. Just in case . . . "

We took the left fork. Five minutes later, we hit a dead end at a small clearing that was not the parking lot.

"Okay," I said. "Right it is."

We retraced our steps again, took the right fork this time. The darkness was serious now—the kind of darkness that only exists far from city lights. Without my phone flashlight on, I couldn't see my hand in front of my face. Every snapped twig sounded like a serial killer adjusting his grip on an axe.

"I totally shouldn't have made serial killer jokes earlier," I said. "This is fine . . . This is totally fine. People don't get murdered in the woods in Northern California."

"I mean, statistically—"

"Don't finish that sentence."

Rowan laughed, the sound bright in the darkness. "You scared?"

"Of being lost in a forest with no cell service at night? No. Why would I be scared? This is a perfectly normal situation that happens to people who make good life choices."

"We're not lost. We're . . . temporarily geographically confused."

"Oh, that's much better."

I wasn't ready for it, but he stopped and spun around and planted his lips on mine for a second. That was all the reassuring I needed.

We kept walking, our phone lights creating small pools of visibility in the overwhelming dark. Every sound seemed amplified—rustling in the underbrush, the distant call of an owl, what was probably just wind but could have been someone breathing heavily behind a tree.

"You know what this needs?" I said. "Ominous music. Really lean into the horror movie aesthetic we've got going."

"The Blair Witch Project: Hockey Player Edition."

"In theaters never, because we're going to die out here and no one will find our bodies."

"So dramatic."

"I'm a theatre major. It's literally my job."

Then—finally, blessedly—a beam of light that wasn't coming from our phones. The parking lot lights, barely visible through the trees.

"Oh, thank God," I breathed.

"See? Told you we weren't lost."

"You said, and I quote, 'temporarily geographically confused.'"

"Same thing."

We stumbled back into the parking lot, which was now completely empty except for my car. The hike that should have taken maybe an hour total had stretched to nearly three.

"Never speak of this to anyone," Rowan said as I collapsed dramatically against the car.

"What, that we got lost on a one-mile trail?"

"That part especially."

Rowan was grinning, his face illuminated by the parking lot's single flickering light. He looked younger somehow, lighter. Like the weight of five years had finally lifted from his shoulders.

"Come here," he said, and pulled me in for another kiss. We celebrated our survival and the sheer ridiculousness of what we'd just done.

"Still worth it?" Rowan asked.

I looked at him—this man who had carried guilt like a second skin for half a decade, who had finally set it down in a modest ranch house in Portland, who had shown me a sunset and gotten us lost in the woods and kissed me like I was the only thing that mattered.

"Worth everything," I said.

We got in the car and found our way back to the highway. His hand found mine again as we headed south through the darkness.

A dam had burst open on our crazy adventure. We talked about everything on the drive back—the play, the team, what would happen next with Anders. We stopped at a diner outside of Crescent City, sitting on the same side of the booth because being across from each other felt like too much distance. The coffee was terrible and the pie was mediocre, but everything was perfect.

"Michael said something that got me thinking," Rowan said, pushing pie crust around his plate. "You know how he's using the money I kept sending him to purchase equipment and ice time for kids?"

"Yeah."

"I want to do more of that. When this is all over—when I figure out what comes next—I want to help kids like that. Kids who love the game but can't access it." He looked at me. "Is that stupid?"

"That's the opposite of stupid."

"I've been sending guilt money to a trust fund for five years. Turns out it will actually do some good, just not for the reason I imagined." He shook his head. "I want to do it intentionally this time. Make something positive out of all this."

I reached over and squeezed his hand. "I think that's exactly what you should do."

By the time we pulled into Oakridge, it was nearly ten. I parked outside his building, but neither of us moved to get out.

"Thank you," Rowan said. "For today. For all of it. You're the first person I've been one-hundred percent genuine with in a very long time."

"Thank you for letting me be there."

He leaned across the console and kissed me again—a soft promise of more to come. "I've got practice at seven tomorrow."

"I know."

"And I'm done shrinking." He said it like a declaration. Like a promise to himself.

"Good."

He kissed me one more time, then got out of the car. He walked toward his building, turning back to smile once before disappearing inside.

Chapter 30
The 200-Foot Shift

Elliot

Section 112, Row M, Seat 8.

I climbed the concrete steps to my usual spot, but nothing about this moment was usual. We returned from Spring Break to an April sun that was finally starting to warm the pavement outside, but the air inside the arena remained sharp and frozen as we began the final push toward the postseason. The blue plastic seat was the same. The view of the ice was the same. The Moleskine was in my bag.

I settled into the seat and pulled out my phone, scrolling to the text exchange from this morning.

Me: Good luck at practice. There may (or may not) be a sexy stalker in the stands.

Rowan's response had come twenty minutes later: a single thumbs-up emoji.

From anyone else, that would be nothing. From Ro—the man who communicates in careful sentences and measured silences—it felt like a love letter. He doesn't do casual digital communication. Every text I've received from him has been precise, intentional.

A thumbs-up emoji is practically effusive.

I pocketed the phone and watched the ice where the Ospreys were filtering out of the tunnel. The surface gleamed under the arena lights, freshly cut, waiting. The familiar sounds filled the space—blades scraping, pucks clicking against sticks, the inaudible murmur of players warming up.

I find Ro immediately. Number twenty-eight, moving through his pre-practice routine with the fluid efficiency I've memorized over these weeks of watching. But even from this distance, even before the drills begin, I could tell something was off.

Sterling's whistle cut through the arena, sharp and commanding. Practice begins.

The change was visible from the first drill.

Rowan took his position for skating exercises. The hunched shoulders were gone. The constant scanning of the environment—that hypervigilance I'd cataloged as "exit-seeking behavior" in my early notes—had diminished to something closer to normal awareness. He wasn't looking for threats anymore. He was just . . . present.

The skating drill was simple—crossovers around the circles, building speed, testing edges. Rowan moved through it with the same technical precision he's always shown, but there was something different in the quality of his movement. Less careful. More expansive. Like he'd finally allowed himself to take up the space his body was designed to occupy.

The passing drill came next. Sterling set up a sequence that required threading the puck through traffic—a test of vision and timing and the particular hockey sense that separates good players from great ones. I'd watched Rowan do this drill a dozen times. He'd always been competent, always made the safe choice, always had found the obvious lane and taken it without risk.

Today, he threaded a pass through a gap that shouldn't exist.

The puck traveled between two defenders, split the seam perfectly, and landed on Davies's stick with surgical precision. Davies barely had to adjust—the pass was that good. I saw him glance back at Rowan with something like surprise, then grin.

"Nice feed, Calloway!" Sterling yelled.

Rowan nodded and dug his blades into the slush, already pivoting toward the blue line. His shoulders squared as if he'd finally found his footing in a game that had been slipping away.

The shooting drill was where the transformation became undeniable.

Okafor set up a standard sequence: receive the pass, navigate the obstacle, shoot. Simple in concept, endlessly variable in execution. I'd watched Rowan defer in this drill countless times—taking the safe angle, prioritizing accuracy over power, choosing the percentage play over the spectacular one.

The puck came to him on his backhand. A defender slid over to challenge. Rowan had a clear lane to dump the puck behind the net, circle around, try again from a better angle.

He didn't dump the puck.

Instead, he pulled the puck to his forehand with a move so quick I almost missed it—a toe-drag that froze the defender in place—and accelerated into the slot. His release was a blur, the puck rocketed toward the top corner with a velocity that made the goalie's glove snap up too late.

Ping.

The crossbar rings like a bell. The puck ricochets out, but the shot was an inch from perfect. An inch from highlight reel.

The arena was dead quiet, only the sound of a few skates still moving on the ice.

"Holy shit, dude," Davies yelled. "where has THAT been?"

Ro didn't answer. He'd already skated back to the line, his face unreadable behind the cage of his helmet. But everything about his body read, I'm finally ready to stop pretending.

The scrimmage began, and I leaned forward in my seat.

Sterling had the Aline facing off against the Bline—Chen's unit versus Maddox's. It made sense strategically: let the top line push the second line, see how they responded to pressure. Park, Chen, and Petrov lined up in navy practice jerseys. Rowan, Davies, and Maddox wore orange.

Sterling positioned himself at center ice, watching with that impassivity that made him impossible to read. The puck dropped, and the game began.

For the first few shifts, Rowan played within himself—solid, smart, the kind of responsible hockey that Sterling preached. He won a board battle against Park, made a clean breakout pass to Maddox, backchecked hard when Chen turned the play over. Good. Reliable.

Then came the shift that changed everything.

It started in the defensive zone. The Aline was cycling the puck, Chen controlling down low while Petrov searched for an opening up high. Rowan was in position, his stick active, reading the play three moves ahead. Chen tried to thread a pass across the slot to Park. Rowan jumped the lane—anticipating, not reacting—and intercepted it.

He turned up ice. The acceleration was explosive—zero to top speed in three strides, his edges biting into the ice with a precision that made everyone else look like they were skating through mud. Park stepped up to challenge him at center ice. Rowan shifted his weight, dropped his shoulder, and blew past on the outside with a burst of speed that left Park comically grasping at air.

He was in the offensive zone now, carrying the puck with complete control, his head up and scanning. Davies was driving to the net, his massive frame clearing space. Maddox was trailing the play on the back door. The Aline defense scrambled to recover, Chelios and Hedman converging.

Rowan appeared to process all this information in a fraction of a second and kept the puck.

Chelios closed in. Rowan protected the puck with his body, creating space with a spin move that left Chelios reaching. He was alone now, one-on-one with Lindros, the net yawning open in front of him.

His shot was a thing of beauty. Low release, perfect placement, the puck found the corner like it was drawn there by gravity.

Goal.

The arena fell absolutely silent.

Then Davies's voice, loud enough to echo off the rafters: "WHAT THE FUCK WAS THAT?"

I was on my feet. I didn't remember standing. My hands gripped the cold metal railing in front of me, knuckles white. I was watching Rowan accept the congratulations of his teammates—Davies nearly lifting him off his skates, Maddox giving a grudging helmet-tap, even Kowalski nodding from the blue line with something like respect.

He scored. He took the shot, the selfish shot, the one he'd been afraid to take all season, and he buried it.

Sterling's whistle blew. The celebration cut off. The players turned toward their coach, waiting for the assessment.

Sterling stood at center ice, his face as unreadable as ever. He stared at Rowan for a long moment—one of those silences that felt like it lasted forever.

"That," Sterling said, his gravel voice carrying through the arena, "is what a two-hundred-foot player looks like. It's about time you showed up to play, Calloway. I've been waiting all year for you to finally show the team what you can do on the ice."

He turned to the rest of the team. "You see how he read that play? Started in our zone, finished in theirs. Every decision was right. Every movement was purposeful. That's the standard."

He turned to Rowan. "Do it again."

Rowan nodded. "Yes, Coach."

Rowan skated to his position for the puck drop. Before rubber hit the ice, he tilted his helmet in my direction and nodded once.

"Show off," I said to myself, a giant grin spreading across my face.

Practice continued for another forty-five minutes, but the energy had changed.

Ro played every shift like someone had put new batteries in him. He was never reckless. He never intentionally tried to make it about himself. Instead, he was playing within Sterling's system, but he played at a level that made everyone else look like they were playing a different sport. Everything from the passes to the shots were just at a higher caliber and his ability to read the other team was so precise it was almost unfair.

Davies stayed close to him, feeding off the energy, the two of them developing a chemistry that was visible even from the stands. Maddox stopped glaring and started playing, his competitive instincts overrode whatever resentment he'd been carrying about the demotion. Even Chen skated past during a line change and tapped Ro's shin pads with his stick—a small gesture of respect.

Maddox was the most interesting to watch.

The team captain had circled Ro all season, suspicious of the walk-on who played beyond a DIII game. And he was right—Ro had a skill set that was beyond DIII.

I turned my attention to watching how Maddox was coping with this. He may be captain, but he was no longer the best player on the team. Rowan burned past Chelios again to set up Davies for another scoring chance. From my vantage point, Maddox seemed more relaxed.

After the play, I saw Maddox skate toward Rowan and deliver a sharp, brief nod of acknowledgment before turning to reset for the next draw. It was a clinical gesture.

Sterling ended practice with a short speech about the upcoming games—the play-off push, the stakes, the need to play their best hockey at the right time. But his eyes kept drifting to Ro, and there was something in his expression that looked almost like satisfaction. The tension in his forehead smoothed out, his shoulders dropping as if a long-awaited piece of a puzzle had finally clicked into place.

He knew, I realized, watching Sterling watch Ro. He'd been waiting for Ro to stop hiding, and today he finally got what he was waiting for. Part of me wondered if Sterling had known who Ro was this whole time and had just been waiting for him to come out.

The players filtered off the ice, heading for the locker room. Ro was one of the last to leave, exchanging words with Davies that I couldn't hear from this distance. Then he was gone, disappearing into the tunnel, and the arena was empty again.

I sat back down slowly, my legs suddenly unsteady.

Portland had changed everything.

I love him.

I loved Rowan Calloway.

Chapter 31
The Semifinal Siege

Rowan

The locker room was quieter than usual.

Not silent. There was still the familiar soundtrack of pregame preparation, the rip of tape and the click of equipment being adjusted, the low murmur of players running through mental routines. But underneath it all was a tension that wasn't there before.

My phone buzzed. I pulled it out of my locker.

Elliot: Wish I was there. Act One is about to begin. Still mad I don't have an understudy.

I cracked a smile before letting my thumbs type back.

Me: It's okay, babe. I know you're here in spirit as much as I am with you in the black box tonight. Break a leg.

I hesitated for a second before adding,

Me: I'll try not to break someone else's leg . . . but it's hockey!

I actually added a smile emoji. What is wrong with me?

I put the cellphone down and relaxed into my pregame routine.

Tonight, we either win or the season was over. Simple as that.

I sat in my stall, stick across my knees, working through the taping ritual that had been my anchor since I was twelve years old. The movements were automatic now—wrap, pull, smooth, repeat. Control what you can control. Let everything else fall away.

But it's different tonight. The ritual felt less like armor and more like preparation. Less like hiding and more like getting ready.

Davies dropped onto the bench beside me, his own stick clutched between his knees. His leg was bouncing enough to make the entire bench vibrate.

I reached out a hand and put on top of his knee, "Dude." He stopped bouncing.

"You ready?" he asked.

I finished the last wrap of tape and tested the grip. Perfect.

"Yeah," I said. "I think I am."

My phone buzzed in my bag. I pulled it out, already knowing who it was.

Anders: Good luck tonight. Not that you need it. You should be able to sweep the tournament with one hand tied behind your back. Oh wait, isn't that what you've already done with that team of yours?

I groaned.

"What's wrong?" Davies asked.

"Just a snake trying to slither its way back into my life."

I could tell Davies was about to ask me a million questions, but Sterling chose that moment to enter the locker room. The space went silent. He stood at the center, his face as impassive as ever, his eyes raking across each player.

"Redwood State," he said. "You know what they're going to try. Physical. Intimidating. They want to make you uncomfortable, make you play scared."

He paused, letting the words land.

"Don't let them. This is our game. We've earned this ice. Every practice, every drill, every moment of discipline this season has brought us here." His voice dropped, became something almost intimate. "I don't care what the scouts say. I don't care what the rankings say. When that puck drops, the only thing that matters is what happens between those boards."

He glanced at me.

"Play your game," Sterling said before sweeping his head around the room, adding, "every single one of you. Play the game you know how to play. Trust your teammates to do the same. That's how we win."

He nodded once—that sharp, definitive gesture.

"Let's go."

The semifinal game was played on the opposing team's home ice.

The first period was a war of attrition.

Redwood State came to play exactly the game Sterling warned us about—heavy, physical, designed to wear us down. Every whistle brought another scrum, another confrontation, another reminder that they considered us intruders in their arena.

The crowd was hostile in that particular way rival crowds are, feeding off their team's aggression. I hear my name a few times—not Calloway, but St. Clair. Someone's done their research. Someone's trying to get in my head.

A month ago, it might have worked. A month ago, I would have shrunk into my jersey, played smaller, let the noise push me back into the shadows.

Tonight, I let it wash over me like white noise.

My first shift was solid but unremarkable. Won a board battle, made a clean breakout pass, and got back for the change. The system Sterling preaches—position, discipline, trust. I executed it without thinking, my body remembered patterns drilled into muscle memory through countless practices.

But I also looked for opportunities. Read the ice differently than I did a month ago. Saw lanes that existed for fractions of seconds, chances that required risk.

I didn't take them. Not yet. Not in the first period of a semifinal. But I saw them.

The period ended scoreless. Both teams retreated to their locker rooms to regroup.

"They're testing us," Sterling said during the intermission. "Seeing if we'll break. Don't break. Bend when you have to, absorb what you have to, but don't break."

The second period was when the game opened up.

Redwood scored first—a screened shot from the point that our goalie never saw. The arena exploded. The Redwood bench erupted. For a moment, I felt the old familiar pressure, the weight of deficit.

But Davies was already talking, already planning.

"We get it back," he said as we lined up for the next faceoff. "Right now. This shift."

I nodded. "I'll find you."

The puck dropped. Maddox won it back to the defenseman. The breakout began.

I swung through the neutral zone, reading the defense, looking for the seam. Davies was driving wide, pulling his defender with him. Kowalski trailed, offering a safe option.

The puck came to me at the far blue line. I had a choice: the safe play to Kowalski, or the threading-the-needle pass to Davies streaking toward the net.

I threaded the needle.

The puck hit Davies's tape perfectly. He didn't even need to adjust—he just redirected it toward the net.

Ping.

The post. But the rebound kicks out, and Davies was already there, burying it before the goalie could reset.

Tie game.

The celebration was brief—we're too focused for anything more—but Davies found me as we skated back to the bench, his glove tapping my helmet.

"Sick pass, man."

"Sick finish."

The game tightened after that. Both teams played desperate, physical hockey. Every shift felt like a battle. Every whistle brought temporary relief.

I took a hard check in the second half of the period—a Redwood defenseman caught me with my head down, driving me into the boards with enough force to rattle my teeth. I went down, the ice cold against my back, my vision blurred briefly.

The whistle blew. The crowd roared. I heard someone asking if I'm okay.

I got up.

Not because I needed to prove something. Not because I was afraid of appearing weak. Just because I could. Because the hit hurt but didn't break anything, and there's still hockey to play.

Davies helped me to the bench. "You good?"

"I'm good."

And I was. Sore, probably bruised, but good.

The second period ended still tied. One-one. Twenty minutes left to decide who goes to the championship.

The third period was the longest twenty minutes of my life.

Both teams were exhausted. Both teams were desperate. The hits were harder because everyone's too tired to be careful. Half the line spent time in the penalty box at one point or another. The plays were simple because no one had the energy for creativity.

Sterling shortened the bench, riding his top two lines, trusting the players who'd earned the ice time. I was on every other shift; my legs burned, my lungs screamed, my mind somehow was perfectly clear.

The clock ticked down. Fifteen minutes. Ten. Five.

Still tied.

Desperation built with every passing second. Redwood was pressing hard, throwing everything at our net, trying to break through before we could. Our goalie stood on his head, making saves that shouldn't be possible, keeping us alive.

Four minutes left.

Three.

Two.

I was on the ice for what might've been the last shift of the season. Davies and Maddox with me on the line and Kowalski and Seibert on defense. Sterling trusted us with the most important moments of the game.

The puck dropped and was edged into the neutral zone. Bouncing between sticks, neither team was able to establish possession. Bodies flew everywhere. The crowd was a wall of sound.

Then, somehow, the puck came to me.

I was at center ice, facing the offensive zone, two Redwood defenders between me and the net. Davies was on my right, calling for the pass. Kowalski was behind me, offering the safe dump-in option.

Time slowed.

I saw the options laid out like a chessboard. The safe play—dump it in, grind for possession, try to create something in the last ninety seconds. The team play—hit Davies on the wing, let him drive wide, search for the cross-ice feed.

Or the third option. The lane that's opened between the two defenders, narrow but there. A shooting lane that would close in half a second, that required perfect timing and perfect execution. Did I have the willingness to take a shot that everyone in the building would see?

The old Rowan would dump the puck.

The old Rowan would choose the safe pass, choose the team play, choose to disappear into the system rather than stand in the spotlight.

I thread the needle and take the shot.

The release is pure muscle memory—quick, low, the puck coming off my blade before anyone could react. It threaded the gap between the defenders, a black blur against white ice, and I lost sight of it for a fraction of a second.

Then the red light went on.

The puck was in the net.

The horn sounded.

And the Redwood arena goes absolutely, devastatingly silent.

I don't remember the next few seconds.

Bodies crashed into me—Davies first, screaming something unintelligible, then Kowalski, then the rest of the team pouring off the bench. Someone's helmet is digging into my ribs. Someone else is pounding my back hard enough to bruise.

"YOU BEAUTIFUL BASTARD!"

That's Davies. Definitely Davies.

The scoreboard reads 2-1. Under ninety seconds left. We're ahead.

We still must drive down the final minute and a half. Redwood pulls their goalie, throws six skaters at us, desperation made physical. I was on the ice blocking shots, clearing pucks, surviving.

The final horn sounded, and the weight lifted.

We'd won. We're going to the championship.

The locker room was chaos.

Music blasted, players shouted, the particular joy of a team that's accomplished something together. Davies was dancing—actually dancing—in the middle of the room, his equipment half-removed, his smile so wide it looked painful.

I sat in my stall, letting the celebration wash over me, my body finally registering how exhausted I was. Every muscle ached. The hit from the second period had blossomed into a bruise I could feel spreading across my ribs.

But underneath the exhaustion was something else. Something lighter.

I took the shot. Some might consider it a selfish shot, but it wasn't selfish at all. In that moment, I trusted my ability. Trusted in my right to take up space, to be visible, to try.

And it went in.

Sterling appeared in front of me, cutting through the celebration with his particular gravity.

"Calloway."

I looked up. "Coach."

He studied me for a moment, that face as unreadable as ever. Then: "That's the player I recruited."

The words caught me off guard. "I didn't know you recruited me."

Something flickered across Sterling's face—not quite a smile, but close. "I always know who's on my ice. Community college rec leagues?" He shook his head slightly. "I knew what you were the moment I saw you move."

"Then why didn't you say anything?"

"Because you weren't ready." He held my gaze. "You had your reasons, and I didn't need to know them. I knew if I gave you space, you'd stop running and start playing. That was your journey, not mine."

He clapped me on the shoulder—a gesture I'd never seen him make with anyone.

"Championship game. One week. Get some rest."

He moved away. He knew. This whole time, he knew who I was.

Control what you can control.

Maybe Sterling understood that better than anyone.

I was one of the last players to leave the visitors' locker room. The walk to the exit took longer than usual, my legs stiff and sore, my bag heavy on my shoulder. The building was mostly empty, the Redwood crowd long gone, the celebration moved elsewhere.

As I neared the exit, I saw a father and son waiting near the back door. Our bus was parked just on the other side. The kid held a crumpled program and a Sharpie, his eyes wide.

"Chase?" the boy whispered, staring up at me. "Are you really Chase St. Clair?"

A month ago, I had ducked my head and kept walking, the name having hit me like a high stick to the throat. Tonight, I stopped. I looked at the kid, then at his father, and finally at the program.

"Sorry, kid, St. Clair is gone," I said, my voice steady. "I'm Rowan Calloway." The boy's face began to fall, "St. Clair was just a name I used in the movies. Calloway is who I am on the ice." but I reached out and took the Sharpie from his hand.

"But I'd be happy to sign your program," I added, a ghost of a crooked smile touching my lips. "With both."

I scribbled Rowan Calloway in bold letters across the cover, then added Chase St. Clair in smaller script beneath it. I handed it back to the awestruck kid and pushed through the doors into the night air.

The team bus was already humming when I climbed aboard. I found my seat in the neutral territory of the middle rows and finally pulled out my phone. A notification from Elliot was waiting.

Elliot: Just finished the curtain call. The show went perfectly—the audience was actually crying during the third act.

Elliot: More importantly, I just saw the score. 2-1! Congrats on an incredible game, Ro. Congrats on making it to the finals. I knew you could do it.

Something warm and certain settled in my chest as I typed back.

Rowan: I could feel you watching, even from a few hundred miles away. Glad the show went well. See you when I get back.

I was about to put the phone away when one last vibration buzzed against my palm. It was a new message from a number I should have blocked.

Anders: clap, clap, clap

I stared at the three words on the screen. Even without audio, I could sense the dripping sarcasm of his slow clap. As the bus pulled out of the lot and headed toward Oakridge, I realized his "applause" didn't make me flinch anymore.

I deleted the message and blocked the number.

Chapter 32
The Red Pen Review

Elliot

After the show, I went out with the cast to get a late dinner at a local diner. We hung out for about two hours before I finally dragged myself back to my place. I texted Ro and he was about thirty minutes out, so I told him to come on by after he picked up his SUV.

The loft felt different that night. Maybe it was the energy knowing Rowan was on his way. I ran through the shower again, ensuring my stage makeup was off. I had just thrown on a pair of sweats and a T-shirt when I heard Ro pull up in front of the bookstore.

When he walked through my door, he grinned from ear to ear.

"Hey," he said, dropping his bag by the entrance.

"Hey, yourself." He closed the door behind him. "You were incredible tonight."

Ro turned to face me, and that crooked smile surfaced slowly. "I could feel you watching."

"Of course, I watched. Between scenes, I was in the dressing room watching the game on my phone. I think I audibly yelled when you scored your goal. I almost expected Albright to fire me from the show on the spot. Not the most professional thing I've done backstage during a show." I pondered it for a second, "But not the most unprofessional thing I've done either."

"Do I even want to know?" Rowan asked.

"Probably not."

"I was playing the porter in The Scottish Play. Let's just say, Banquo's ghost almost missed his entrance. Glad there wasn't a nude scene in that play. It would have been hard to explain the white stage makeup around my—"

"I don't need to know this," Ro said with a laugh.

Rowan's eyes flicked toward the heavy leather binder sitting on my desk—the character profile. It had been in the same space for weeks, collecting dust. Red ink covered nearly every surface now, his handwriting intertwined with mine, his truth overwriting my theories.

"We should finish it," he said. "Tonight."

"Are you sure?" I asked. "I mean, you've got to be exhausted.

"I slept on the bus." He motioned with his head toward the desk. "Let's do this."

We sat at the desk together, shoulders touching, surveying the work we had done in the dossier. The profile read nothing like it had when Rowan first saw it. The clinical observations had been crossed out and replaced with actual insight into hockey. The speculation had been excised, leaving only facts.

The photographs I had included—those images of a boy I never knew, performing a version of himself that no longer existed—were still there, but they were surrounded now by Rowan's annotations.

This was a bad day. I'd been awake for thirty-six hours doing press. This smile is fake. You can tell by my eyes. This is the only photo from that year where I look like myself.

The Henderson section had been rewritten. My forum-sourced timeline was replaced with Rowan's firsthand account. The speculation about what happened, why he left, and what he knew had all been stripped away and replaced with his truth.

There were a few sections we hadn't touched yet. The future. What comes next? The blank space at the end of the profile that neither of us had been willing to fill.

"This part," I said, pointing to a line I had labeled CURRENT STATUS: HIDING. "That's not true anymore."

Ro picked up the red pen from my desk. He crossed out HIDING and wrote above it: CHOOSING.

"Better," I said.

"What about this?" He pointed to another entry: GOAL: ANONYMITY. "Is that still accurate?"

Ro was quiet for a moment, considering. Then he crossed out ANONYMITY and wrote: AUTHENTICITY. The word hung there, red ink against the white page. Not hiding. Not disappearing. Just being real.

"And here?" I tapped the space at the bottom of the page. "What happens next?"

Ro looked at me. "What do you want to happen?"

"I want to keep seeing you," I said. "I want everyone to know that we're dating."

Rowan took the pen and wrote in that space: WHATEVER COMES NEXT — TOGETHER. Then he added, underneath: WE'LL FIGURE IT OUT.

I read at the words, at his handwriting on my archive, at the story we had been writing together without ever calling it that.

"The profile is done," I said.

"Almost." Rowan set down the pen and turned to face me fully. "There's one more thing. My turn."

He walked to the corner of the loft where my first hockey stick leaned against the wall. It was the stick I had bought at a thrift store months ago, trying to learn the physicality I needed for the role of Diego Santos. The same stick he had used to teach me, his hands over mine, his chest against my back.

Rowan picked it up and held it out to me. "Show me what you've learned," he said.

I took the stick, settling into the grip he had taught me—hands spread properly now, fingers relaxed, the shaft an extension of my arms rather than a foreign object. I had been practicing. Not for the role anymore—that choreography was set—but playing with the stick reminded me of him.

"Better," Rowan said, watching my form. "Much better."

"I had a good teacher."

"You had a distracted teacher." He moved closer, circling behind me the way he had that first time. "I spent half that lesson wondering how you tasted instead of how you held the stick."

"How I tasted?"

"I was right behind you, and I looked down at your neck and all I wanted to do was lick you." His hands settled over mine, adjusting my grip fractionally—more muscle memory than necessity. "It drove me crazy."

"You do realize that makes you sound like a vampire," I said. "You'd be a sexy vampire. Still, should I be worried?"

His chest was warm against my back. His breath stirred the hair at the nape of my neck. "Maybe you should. Maybe we both should be worried. We're not pretending anymore. Not teaching. Not learning.

"Rowan."

"Yeah?"

I turned in his arms, letting the stick clatter to the floor between us. His hands found my waist, steadying me, holding me in place. We were face-to-face now, inches apart, the air between us electric.

"I'm going to kiss you now," I said.

"I know."

The kiss started soft. His hands slid up my back, pulling me closer. I gripped the front of his shirt, feeling the heat of his skin through the fabric. The kiss deepened, opened, became something that couldn't be contained by standing upright in the middle of my loft.

"Elliot." His voice was rough when we broke apart. "Are you—"

"Yes." I didn't need to hear the rest of the question. I jumped up locking my legs around his waist, and my arms around his neck. "Whatever you're asking. Yes."

He carried me through the apartment to my bed. He gently laid me down. What came next wasn't graceful—there was fumbling with buttons and belts. A little awkward laughter when his elbow caught my ribs, a moment where we both froze and then dissolved into nervous giggles that broke the tension without diminishing the heat.

"I haven't done this in a while," Rowan admitted, his forehead pressed against mine.

"Neither have I."

"I'm nervous."

"Me too." I cupped his face in my hands, making him look at me. "We can stop. Anytime. If you want to stop—"

"I don't want to stop." He turned his head and pressed a kiss to my palm. "I just wanted you to know. That this matters. That you matter.

"You matter too."

The words felt inadequate, but they were true. And then we weren't talking anymore—just touching, discovering, learning each other in the way that only this kind of intimacy allowed.

He was careful with me. Attentive. Present in a way that made everything feel more intense, more real. Every touch was deliberate. Every sound was honest. There was no performance here, no masks, no hiding. Just two people, finally allowing themselves to be completely seen.

It felt fitting, somehow. That the story we had started as observer and subject would culminate here, in my bed, in the most vulnerable kind of visibility. Afterward, we lay tangled together, breathing hard, the sweat cooling on our skin.

"Okay?" Rowan asked.

"Very okay." I traced a pattern on his chest, feeling his heartbeat slow beneath my fingertips. "You?"

"Yeah." He pulled me closer, tucking my head under his chin. "Better than okay."

The city lights painted pale rectangles on the ceiling through my tall windows. We had been lying there for a while, not sleeping, just existing in the quiet aftermath.

"Championship in a week," Rowan said eventually.

"I know."

"Are you going to be there?"

"Of course. Where is it?"

He laughed quietly, the sound vibrating through his chest into mine. "San Francisco."

"Are you ready for that spotlight?" I lifted my head to look at him.

Rowan was quiet for a moment, considering the question seriously. "I think so. Big cities and large arenas just don't feel like home anymore. Home is here. Home is with you."

We lay like that, just resting in each other's arms. He gently ran a finger down my spine.

"Whatever happens," I said, "I'm glad you stopped running."

Ro's hand found mine, fingers intertwining. "I'm glad you chased me. Even when you were doing it for all the wrong reasons."

"I was kind of an asshole."

"You were kind of an asshole," he agreed. "But you stopped. You handed me the pen. No one had ever done that before."

We lay there in the dark. Everything was about to change. But here, in this moment, none of that mattered. There was just Rowan's heartbeat under my ear and the warmth of his body against mine.

"Go to sleep," he murmured, pressing a kiss to the top of my head.

"You first." I didn't close my eyes. Not yet. I wanted to hold on to this moment a little longer.

"Elliot."

"Hmm?"

"Thank you. For seeing me."

The words settled into the darkness between us, soft and true.

"Thank you for letting me," I said.

Chapter 33
The Scouting Report

Elliot

In the morning, Ro left the bed and headed to the gym to work out. He left me in a cold bed. I wanted him to keep me warm, those giant arms around me. Eventually, I dragged myself out of bed and looked at my phone to see what was happening in the world.

I started scrolling through X in bed, still half-asleep, when I saw the notification.

A retweet from someone in the theatre department—Marcus, one of the lighting techs who worked on The Penalty Box. The caption read: Wait . . . is this who I think it is?

The video was grainy, shot on someone's phone from the stands. But the footage was unmistakable: a hockey player receiving a pass at center ice, threading through two defenders with a move that was almost impossible, and burying a shot in the top corner of the net.

Ro. The semifinal. The goal that sent the Ospreys to the championship.

The video had been viewed over two hundred thousand times. And someone had cut out his team picture and put them side-by-side with an old headshot at the end of the video.

I sat up in bed, suddenly very awake, and started reading the comments.

Is that Chase St. Clair?

THE Ice Prince? No way

I thought he retired like 5 years ago

I heard he died of an overdose

Playing D3? What happened to him?

My sister went to high school with him. She says he just disappeared one day

That toe-drag is ELITE. This guy should be in the NHL

Wait I'm confused—the child actor? The Ice Kings kid? Playing D3 college hockey?

The thread goes on and on, hundreds of comments, people tagging hockey accounts and entertainment accounts and anyone they can think of who might care about the sudden reappearance of Chase St. Clair from the public eye.

My stomach dropped.

I called Rowan. Straight to voicemail. I tried again—same result. I texted him: Call me. It's urgent.

The message showed as delivered but not read. His phone was either off or he's ignoring it. God, I hope he doesn't think I had anything to do with this.

I'm already pulling on clothes, my mind racing through possibilities. He was heading to the gym. What would he do if he found out? Would he run? I couldn't imagine how he would process it. I think we both knew this could happen, but we never talked about what would happen if it got out.

My phone rang.

I answered without looking. "Rowan?"

"Not quite." The voice was smooth, accented, instantly recognizable from the one conversation we had in the theatre lobby. "But I'm glad you're thinking about him. Have you seen the video?"

Anders Holmström.

"How did you get this number?"

"That doesn't matter." His tone was casual, unbothered—the voice of someone who's used to getting what he wants. "What matters is that this is the moment. The opportunity we've been waiting for."

"We?"

"Ro. Me. Everyone who wants to see him succeed." I can almost hear the smile in his voice. "The video is everywhere, Elliot. By tonight, every hockey blog and entertainment site will be running the story. 'Ice Prince Returns: Former Child Star Playing Division III Hockey.' You can't put this genie back in the bottle."

I'm pacing my loft now, phone pressed hard against my ear. "What do you want?"

"I want to help. I have connections—PR people, media trainers, people who can spin this the right way. Ro doesn't have to be the runaway anymore. He can be the comeback story. The survivor who stepped away from the spotlight to find himself and is now ready to return on his own terms."

"That's not his story."

"It could be." Anders's voice drops, becomes more intimate. "Think about it. Controlled narrative. Sympathetic coverage. Maybe even a return to the entertainment industry—there's a project I've been developing, something perfect for him. He could have everything he walked away from, but better this time. Even his old agent is on board. Make sure you tell Ro that Chet says 'hi,' by the way."

I stop pacing. "And what do you get out of this?"

"The satisfaction of helping an old friend."

"Bullshit."

The word comes out sharper than I intended. There's a pause on the other end of the line.

"You don't know him like I do," Anders says, his voice cooling. "You've known him for what—a few months? I was there when he was fifteen. I was the only person he trusted. Then, when he was eighteen, I was his first lover."

"You were the person who photographed him without consent and sent that photo to the world. Publicly outing a teen who was barely navigating life."

"I loved him."

"In my opinion, you groomed him. Honestly Anders," I said his name with as much venom as I could muster, "I don't think you know what the fuck love is."

Silence.

When Anders finally spoke, it was low and cold. "When he's ready to stop playing pretend, he'll remember everything I did for him."

"He's not playing pretend. He's building a life."

"He'll come running back to me like the good lapdog he is," Anders paused. "You may hold the chain now, but I know how pleasant his bite can be."

I knew they'd had sex. Ro told me they'd been lovers. I'd seen the picture of Ro naked in a hot tub with Anders, but the thought of the two of them together made my stomach churn.

"Stay away from him," I growled.

"Well, tell your little doggie to heel," Anders said in a melodic voice that sounded more appropriate on a phone sex line. "Even better, tell him to beg. I used to love making him beg."

I hung up.

I found Rowan in the library.

It took me almost an hour to track him down. His apartment was empty, the arena was closed, the coffee shop where I worked was empty and the barista behind the counter hadn't seen him. Then she tried to get me cover for a guy who hadn't showed up. I passed. I started to panic, imagining him somewhere alone, spiraling, the exposure triggering everything he's worked so hard to overcome.

Finally, I realized the one place I hadn't searched was the first place I should have looked. The library. Third floor. Media studies section.

He was there.

Sitting at his usual table, hunched over nothing—no books, no laptop, just his phone lying dark and silent on the surface in front of him. He glanced up when I approached, and his face was pale, drawn, but not panicked. Not broken.

Just tired.

I threw my arms around him. "I've been going out of my mind with worry. I was terrified that you'd lef—"

"I wouldn't do that to you. Elliot, you've got to know that I wouldn't do that to you."

I let out a breath. Letting him go, I settled into the chair next to him.

He gestured to the phone on the table. "I turned it off an hour ago," he said before I could speak. "I should have called you first. I was lifting when it happened. My phone just started dinging nonstop. When I saw the guys staring at me strangely, I knew what had happened. I ran."

"Honey—"

"I couldn't stop checking. Every time I checked it out, there were more comments, more shares, more people who suddenly had all kinds of opinions about my life."

I reached out and grabbed his hand.

"Everyone's seen the video." He laughs, but there's no humor in it. "Five hundred thousand views last I checked. Probably more by now. Someone overlaid the Ice Kings theme music on one version. That one's really popular."

"Ro—"

A tear fell from his eyes. "Life was just starting to be perfect."

"Anders called." He met my eyes. "He called me this morning and had a whole pitch ready. PR teams, comeback narratives, some project he wants you to do. Says he can spin this into something positive."

"What did you tell him?" Ro's expression didn't change.

"Essentially, that he could go fuck himself." I'd thought about whether I should tell Ro everything Anders had said. I gave him the truncated version. "He basically admitted he was a controlling asshole, but we'd already pieced that together without his insight."

Something shifted in Ro's face—a softening, a release of tension he was holding. "Thank you."

"You don't have to thank me for that."

"I know. But still." He squeezed my hand. "What do I do, Elliot? The hiding is over. Everyone knows where I am, what I'm doing. By noon, there will be reporters calling the athletic department. Media requests. People showing up at practice."

"What do you want to do?"

The question hung between us. Not what should he do, not what's the smart play or the safe play.

Ro was quiet for a long moment, staring at our intertwined hands.

"I want to play in the championship," he said. "I want to finish what I started with this team. I don't want to run again."

"Then don't."

"But the exposure—"

"Will happen whether or not you run." I squeezed his hand. "The video is out there. Your name is out there. You can't un-ring that bell. The only choice you have is how you respond to it."

"Anders could help control the narrative—"

"Anders wants to control you." I leaned forward, making sure he's looking at me. "He doesn't care about your narrative. He cares about having access, having influence, having power over you again. That's what he's always wanted."

"I know." Ro's voice was quiet. "I know that. But part of me—the part that spent five years running—that part wants to believe there's an easy way out. Someone who can make this all go away."

"There isn't. There never was." I brought his hand to my lips, pressed a kiss on his knuckles. "But you don't have to face it alone. Not this time."

Ro turned to me, and I saw the war playing out behind his eyes.

"If I don't run," he intoned, "if I just . . . let it happen. Let people see who I am now. What then?"

"Then you play hockey. You finish your degree. You live your life." I shrugged. "The story will be whatever the story is. You can't control what people say about you. But you can control whether you let it stop you from being who you want to be."

"And who's that?"

"I don't know. That's for you to decide." I smiled. "But I'd like to be there while you work it out. If you'll let me."

The tension in Ro's shoulders finally eased. He didn't smile—not yet—but something in his expression shifted. The panic receded.

"Championship in six days," he said. "It's going to be a circus.

"Then fucking get me a whip and call me the ringleader."

The corner of Ro's lip twitched. "Kinky."

"Simmer down now, hockey boy. We need a plan. And we need a team to execute this plan."

"Everyone will be watching. Not just hockey fans. Everyone."

"Probably."

"And you'll be by my side."

"Where else would I be?"

Ro exhaled slowly, like he's releasing something he'd been holding for years. "Okay. Okay. I will not run. I'm going to play the game, and I'm going to be myself, and whatever happens after that . . . " He shook his head. "We'll figure it out."

"Together."

"Together." He said the word like he's testing it, feeling its weight. Then he said it again, more certain: "Together."

We sat there in the library for a while longer, holding hands across the table, letting the quiet settle around us. Eventually, we sketched out a plan. And it was simply crazy enough, it might work.

Chapter 34
The Viral Morning

Rowan

The rest of the day, I hid in Elliot's apartment. I just didn't want to deal with anyone. At some point, my phone died from so many messages coming in. I just let it die. I plugged it in overnight using a spare cable Elliot had. We slept in each other's arms. Well, he slept and drooled on my chest. I laid awake most of the night. Elliot's plan was insane. Just insane enough it might work.

We woke up to the sound of my phone vibrating. Not the single buzz of a text message or the brief pulse of an alarm. A continuous, insistent vibration that meant something was wrong—or at least, something has changed so dramatically that the world won't stop trying to reach me.

"Dear, God," Elliot groaned. "You could use that thing as a sex toy." He yawned. His hair was going in several directions. He kind of reminded me of a troll doll first thing in the morning. He rolled over and threw his arm around my chest and laid his head against me. "Are you going to look?"

"Maybe . . . "

"Just do it. Pull it off like a Band-Aid."

The lock screen was a wall of alerts. Missed calls from numbers I didn't recognize. Text messages from people I hadn't spoken to in years. Social media notifications—hundreds of them, maybe thousands. Voicemails from blocked numbers that had somehow gotten through, anyway.

I scrolled through the texts first, my stomach tightening with each swipe.

Rowan! It's Jake from Portland. Saw the video. Call me!

Is this still your number? This is Marie from Chet's office. We need to talk.

Dude, are you THE Chase St. Clair? I live in the apartment under you?

This is Sarah Cho from Sports Illustrated. We'd love to do a feature . . .

Ro, it's your mother. Please call us.

That last one hits different. I hadn't thought to warn my parents about what was happening. I sent her a quick text apologizing, telling her I was okay, and that I promised to call later. She sent back a thumbs-up emoji a minute later.

I kept scrolling.

Maddox.

Fuck!

Maddox: Guess you're not a serial killer after all. Lost that bet with Davies. You owe me $20.

Davies: DUDE! How did you not tell me? How did I not know? I think I drove my parents crazy watching your movies on repeat.

A number I didn't recognize caught my attention. "It's Okafor. Thanks for the shitstorm. Sterling was ready for this. Didn't tip his hand. Anyway, he wants me to reach out and see if you're alright. Just don't miss practice. The campus will have extra security on hand."

Of course, Sterling was ready for this. I probably should have called him yesterday.

"I'm going to class," I said, my voice flat.

"Are you insane?" Elliot asked, dropping his phone on the reclaimed wood desk. "The video has half a million views. The vultures are going to be circling the quad before the first class starts."

"I'm not running anymore, Elliot," I reminded him. "I have a journalism assignment due. And Professor Goodall is evil. She won't accept late work, not even for something like this. Besides, I'm not letting a viral clip dictate whether my life stops . . . even temporarily."

"Then I'm going with you," he declared, reaching for his jacket. "I'll be your shadow all day."

I turned, looking at him with a skeptical tilt of my head. "You have your own classes. Theatre theory doesn't attend itself."

"I'm going to protect you," he insisted, stepping into my personal space.

I paused, my gaze dropping to the contrast between us. I pondered my frame—honed by years of elite hockey and functional gym work—then at him, all cheekbones and lean, theatrical precision. A small, genuine huff of a laugh escaped me.

"Elliot, I appreciate the sentiment, truly," I said, my crooked smile surfacing. "But I'm a big-ass hockey player. I promise you, I'll be fine."

He bit his lip, the director in him clearly screaming that this was a bad scene. "Fine," he conceded, but he didn't stop moving. He reached into his bag and pulled out a heavy portable battery backup for my cell phone. "Take this. Your phone was dead half of yesterday, and I am not going through that panic again. You text me constantly. Every time you change buildings. Every time a 'fan' gets too close. Promise me."

I took the backup battery, sliding it into my bag with a resigned nod. "I promise."

"I'm still walking you to your first building," he said.

The walk to campus took fifteen minutes—a stretch of morning air that felt far too quiet for the storm I knew was coming. Elliot kept close to my side, his eyes scanning the environment for threats with the same hypervigilance I usually employed.

As we hit the quad, the atmosphere shifted. The space was busy with students crossing between buildings, but the normal rhythm of academic life stuttered as we passed. I kept my head up and my pace steady, refusing to skulk, but the whispers followed us like a wake.

"Is that him?"

"The hockey player? From the video?"

"I think that's Chase St. Clair. The actor."

"No way. What would he be doing here?"

Elliot tensed next to me with each whisper. He kind of reminded me of a wound-up cat. I almost expected him to hiss at people and try to gouge their eyes out. I found it adorable.

He walked me all the way to the steps of the media studies building, standing guard until I reached the heavy double doors. I glanced back, gave him a sharp, decisive nod, and disappeared inside.

I kept walking. The whispers followed me like a wake, spreading outward through the crowd. People stared now—not subtle glances but full-on stares, phones coming out of pockets, the particular attention that comes with sudden recognition.

"Hey!" A voice cut through the murmur. A girl—freshman, maybe, with bright-pink hair and an oversized sweatshirt—jogged toward me. "Hey, are you—I mean, I loved Ice Kings! When I was a kid, I watched it like a hundred times."

I stopped walking. The smart play would be to ignore her, keep moving, don't engage. But she was smiling, genuinely excited, and there's nothing predatory in her expression. Just enthusiasm.

"Thanks," I say. "I appreciate that."

"Can I get a picture? My little sister is going to freak out—"

"I'm sorry, I really have to get to class." I started moving again. "But thanks. Really."

She was clearly disappointed but didn't follow me. I made it another fifty feet before someone else approached—a guy this time, older, probably a senior.

"Yo, are you playing in the championship tomorrow? That goal in the semifinal was sick."

"Yeah. Thanks."

"Good luck, man."

"Thanks."

I kept walking. The interactions blurred together—some friendly, some just curious, a few felt vaguely hostile. Each one a small reminder that the bubble had burst, that the careful separation between Rowan Calloway and Chase St. Clair no longer existed.

But I made it to class. I sat in my usual seat, pulled out my laptop, and pretended to take notes while the professor talked about something I couldn't focus on.

And slowly, gradually, the stares become less intense. The whispers faded into background noise. Life went on, the way it always does, even when everything feels like it's falling apart.

My phone buzzed in my pocket as I stepped onto the concrete walkway leading toward the Oakridge Arena.

Elliot: Where are you?

Me: Just reaching the arena. Practice in ten.

Elliot: Wait for me. I'm two minutes away.

Me: Why? You have that seminar until four.

Elliot: Because there are three local news vans and a guy with a telephoto lens camping the player entrance. The only way I'm getting past that line is with you.

Elliot: I need my hunk of a boyfriend to convince the security guards that I belong inside. Apparently, this campus does employ campus security.

Me: Maybe I should tell them about this theatre kid who's been stalking me.

Elliot: Not funny! Two minutes.

I stopped at the edge of the parking lot, looking toward the side entrance where a small cluster of people with cameras were idling. The reality of the viral video hit me again. Five years of careful anonymity coming to an end.

I checked out my phone, then watched the ice. I had spent so long managing masks and guarding the "backstage" of my life that I'd forgotten how to just exist in the light. If I was going to walk into that locker room and finally tell the team the truth about Chase St. Clair, there was no point in keeping the rest of it a secret.

Me: Fine. Hurry up. We're going in together.

"Of course we are," Elliot's voice said right next to me, causing me to jump.

"I could have hit you," I said. "If you haven't noticed, I'm a bit jumpy today."

"No need to fear, your boyfriend/bodyguard is here."

"Boyfriend?" I asked.

"I figured that would play better in the media than personal sex slave."

My eyes went wide. "You wouldn't?"

"Try me, Mr. Hockey." He grinned. After a second, Elliot's face turned serious. "You ready for this?"

"Not in the least, but that doesn't mean I get to put it off."

"How do you want to do this?"

"What do you mean?"

"Well, we could walk in side-by-side. We could walk in with me riding your shoulders like a pony. Or we could walk in holding each other's hands."

Without thinking, I reached for Elliot's hand. It's not like the world didn't know I was gay. That ship had sailed when Anders gave the paparazzi access to my life. At least this way, I got to control everything. If I was finally going to open that fucking closet, I might as well let everything air out at once.

"Together then," I said.

We walked across the parking lot toward the player entrance, our hands linked between us. The news crews spotted us immediately.

"Mr. St. Clair! Can we get a statement?"

"Rowan! Are you playing in tomorrow's championship?"

"Who's your friend?"

A security guard I didn't recognize stood at the door, one hand up to stop us, the other reaching for his radio. "IDs please. Only authorized personnel."

I pulled out my student ID with my free hand, keeping Elliot's hand firmly in my other. The guard studied it, then my face, then back at the ID. His expression shifted—recognition, maybe surprise.

"You're on the roster," he said slowly.

"I am."

"And him?" He nodded at Elliot.

"He's with me," I said, my voice firmer than I felt.

Elliot produced his own student ID. The guard examined it.

"You're not on the approved list. I'm sorry, but—"

I cocked my head at the guy and was like, "Dude. Can we not?"

The guard glanced at the news crews pressing closer behind us, then stepped aside.

"Go ahead. But, Mr. Calloway, the coach said to send everyone straight to the locker room."

"Thanks."

We pushed through the door, the questions from the reporters cutting off as it closed behind us. The familiar smell of the arena hit me—ice and rubber and that scent of a hockey rink that I'd known my entire life.

"You okay?" Elliot asked.

"Ask me in an hour."

We walked down the corridor toward the locker room. I could hear voices inside—the team was already there, waiting. Of course they were. Sterling would have called them in early for this.

I stopped outside the door, my hand still in Elliot's.

"You don't have to come in," I said. "This might get—"

"Oh, I'm coming in. And miss what may be my one chance to see inside a college locker room," Elliot smirked. "Besides, we're doing this together, remember?"

I took a breath, squeezed his hand once, and pushed open the door.

The locker room fell silent the moment we entered.

Everyone was there. The entire team, dressed in various stages of their practice gear, all turned to stare at us. At me. At our joined hands.

The moment stretched.

Then Davies broke the silence.

"So, you're famous?" He was leaning against his stall, arms crossed, expression somewhere between amused and curious. "Cool. But, you're like old-person famous, right?"

Someone laughed—Chen, I think—and the tension cracked. Not completely, but enough to breathe.

"I'm not that old, Davies," I said.

"Whatever, Grandpa. I'm not carrying your celebrity ass in the championship." Davies grinned. I saw confusion cross Davies's face as he noticed Elliot and I were holding hands. "Wait. Hold on. Are you dating Caramel Guy?"

I blinked. "What?"

Elliot stepped forward slightly, a small smile playing at his lips. "I may have introduced Davies to the joyous world of caramel macchiato."

"You never told me that," I said.

"You never asked about my coffee evangelism," Elliot replied.

Davies was grinning now. "Dude changed my life. I didn't even drink coffee until he introduced me to the caramel macchiato. My girlfriend says I'm more tolerable in the mornings now."

The absurdity of it—standing in a locker room full of teammates who'd just learned I was a former child star, holding hands with the theatre major who'd been stalking me for months, discussing coffee orders—hit me all at once. I laughed. Actually laughed.

But not everyone was laughing.

Maddox appeared at my shoulder, his expression unreadable. The team captain who'd been suspicious of me all season, who knew something was off but couldn't prove it.

"Maddox," I said, the laughter dying in my throat.

He studied me for a long moment. "I knew something wasn't right. The way you moved. The hockey IQ. You don't get that from community college rec leagues."

"No. You don't."

"You should have told us."

The locker room went quiet again, everyone watching this confrontation.

I took a breath. Elliot's hand tightened in mine—support, not pressure.

"I couldn't," I said. "I know that sounds like an excuse, but I need you all to understand something."

I looked around the room, meeting the eyes of my teammates. These guys who'd accepted the walk-on, who'd worked with me, played with me, started to trust me.

"When I was fifteen," I continued, voice steady, "I left hockey for Hollywood. When I was eighteen, I walked away from everything—the movies, the endorsements, the life everyone thought I wanted. For the record, my name was never Chase St. Clair. That was a name my agent made up for me. When I ran, I went back to my name. Started over. Not because I hated acting or because something terrible happened, but because I had nothing left to give to that world. It had taken everything from me, and I was empty."

Kowalski was listening, his practical face thoughtful. Chen had stopped fidgeting with his tape job. Even Volkov, usually impassive, was focused on what I was saying.

"Hockey was the only thing that was ever just mine," I said. "Not something a manager set up or a publicist promoted. Just me and the ice and the work. When I came here, I didn't plan on playing. And then I read the article in the student newspaper and decided I needed the ice more than anything. I needed it to be about that. About the game. Not about Chase St. Clair or who I used to be or any of the mythology that follows that name around."

I gestured to Elliot beside me. "This guy spent months following me, building an archive of everything I'd left behind. And when I found out about it, I was furious. Terrified. Because I thought he was going to take away the one thing I'd built that was real."

Elliot's face colored, but he didn't let go of my hand.

"But he didn't," I continued. "He gave me the choice. Let me decide what story to tell, how to tell it. And slowly, I realized that hiding forever wasn't protecting me. It was just another kind of prison."

I looked at Maddox. "So yeah, I could have told you. Probably should have. But I needed to know that when I did, it would be on my terms. Not because someone exposed me or because the past caught up with me, but because I was finally ready to stop running. I won't lie. Yesterday when the video hit, I thought about running. But I wouldn't do that to you, to this team. I'm here because this is exactly where I need to be. No matter what kind of press shitstorm is headed my way."

The silence that followed was different from before. Not tense, but thoughtful.

Maddox nodded slowly. "You're better than I thought. Way better. That goal in the semifinal—I've seen NHL players who couldn't have made that shot."

It wasn't exactly an apology. But it was acknowledgment. Recognition. From the guy who'd spent the whole season questioning whether I belonged here.

"Thanks," I said.

Sterling's whistle cut through the locker room before anyone else could speak.

"On the ice. Five minutes. Time to stop this little revival meeting before someone speaks in tongues or cries." The room just kind of froze for a second. "I said, let's move."

We started to file out, Elliot releasing my hand as I moved toward my stall to finish gearing up. But Davies appeared beside him, grinning. He slapped him on his back hard enough that Elliot stumbled. I choked back a smile. Davies does not know how strong he is.

"So, Caramel Guy. You sticking around to watch practice?"

"If that's okay," Elliot said, having regained his balance and glancing at Sterling.

The coach was already heading toward the ice, but he called back over his shoulder: "Section 112. Don't distract my players."

Elliot smiled. "Wouldn't dream of it, Coach."

We gathered at center ice, and Sterling's expression was as impassive as ever.

"I assume everyone has seen the video," he said. "I assume everyone has opinions. Here's what I need you to understand: none of that matters."

He looked around the circle, making eye contact with each player.

"Five days gentlemen, we play for a championship. That's what matters. The name on the back of your jersey, the story in the papers, the people in the stands—none of it scores goals. The only thing that scores goals is what happens between these boards."

His eyes landed on Maddox.

"Maddox. Think your line is ready for the A spot?"

"Yes, Coach," Maddox said, shocked. Maddox shot Chen, Park, and Petrov a glance.

"You guys earned it," Chen said matter-of-factly. "The Bline is our best line. And as much as I would like to think the three of us are better than you three, I'm not that delusional."

"I still think I'm better," Petrov said. "But, I am delusional."

"Okay, then Maddox, Davies, and Calloway, you're the Aline. Now prove to me why you should be." He looked away, addressing the whole team again. "Everyone else: whatever questions you have, whatever feelings you have about this situation, put them aside until after the game. We've worked too hard to let anything distract us now."

He blew the whistle. "Skating drills. Let's go."

Chapter 35
Ranger Danger

Elliot

My phone had been ringing all day.

Not with calls from Rowan—those had stopped hours ago, his responses to my texts growing shorter until they disappeared entirely. No, my phone was ringing with numbers I didn't recognize, area codes from cities I'd never visited.

The renewed wave of interest in The Penalty Box had hit like a tidal wave that morning. Word of the viral video had turned our little campus production into a regional phenomenon. A critic from the Portland Tribune had been at the previous night's performance, writing a piece that used phrases like "raw emotional authenticity." A Seattle arts blog had called it "the most honest exploration of queer identity in sports I've seen on stage."

And then the San Francisco Chronicle picked up the thread, and suddenly my inbox was flooded with interview requests and inquiries from people whose names I recognized from the very theatre programs I'd dreamed about attending.

There was also a rumor—unconfirmed, whispered through the department like a secret—that someone from LA had been in the audience. Someone important. No one knew who, but the speculation was enough to make Professor Albright stare at me with something that might have been pride.

Three months ago, this would have been everything. The recognition I'd craved, the validation that my performance in Cameron Torres' script mattered. The fear of being forgotten that had driven me to build archives and hunt ghosts—finally silenced by proof that I'd been part of something lasting.

But right now, I couldn't think about any of it. Because Rowan had vanished.

I knew he'd had a meeting that morning with the university PR people. He'd mentioned it the night before, his jaw tight, his voice neutral in that way that meant he was already dreading it. "They want to talk about media strategy," he'd said. "Coordinated response protocols."

I'd watched his face shutter at the phrase. I didn't know then exactly what it meant to him, but I knew it meant something devastatingly familiar.

Davies's text came in at 4:47 p.m.: Hey, is Calloway with you? He missed practice. Sterling is PISSED.

I stared at the message, my chest tightening. Rowan didn't miss practice. Rowan would crawl to practice with broken bones before he'd give Sterling a reason to bench him.

Me: No. Haven't heard from him in hours. What happened?

Davies: No clue. He was in some meeting, then just disappeared. His SUV's gone.

I called Rowan's phone. Straight to voicemail.

I texted. No response.

I called again. Nothing.

My panic was building. What if it had finally been too much?

My phone buzzed.

Rowan: I'm at the place where we spent our first night together.

I read it three times, my mind racing. Our first night together. Not my loft—that came later. Not his apartment. Where had we—

The ranger station.

The lake. The team retreat. That freezing night when we'd huddled together in a dusty cabin, talking about ghosts and stories and the cost of being seen.

I grabbed my keys and ran.

The drive to the lake took twenty minutes. I probably did it in fifteen. Pulled into the parking lot at the main building.

The ranger station looked abandoned when I pulled up—no lights, no movement. But Ro's SUV was parked outside, confirmation that my guess had been right. I spent the next twenty minutes with a flashlight in the woods hunting for that ranger station he'd taken me to. I spent more time hunting for that blasted place than I had worried about him being missing.

I found him inside, sitting on the floor in the corner, his knees drawn up and his arms wrapped around them like he was trying to hold himself together. The early evening light caught the tracks on his face where tears had dried.

"Ro."

He glanced up. His eyes were red-rimmed, hollowed out. "You found me."

"You told me where you were." I crossed the room and kneeled in front of him. I placed my hands on his face and gently inched his chin until our eyes met. "What happened?"

The story came out in fragments.

The PR meeting had been a ambush. Three people he'd never met, arranged across a conference table like a tribunal. A woman from University Communications. Someone from the Athletic Director's office. A crisis management consultant the university had hired specifically for the situation.

"They kept talking about controlling the narrative," Rowan said, his voice flat. "Co-ordinated response strategies. Talking points for media inquiries. Donor events." He laughed, but there was no humor in it. "I've heard all those phrases before. Chet used to say them all the time, right before he'd hand me a script of approved answers and send me into another interview."

"Chet." His name was quickly becoming a four-letter word in my mind.

"Yeah." Rowan pressed the heels of his hands against his eyes. "Then, right in the middle of the meeting, I got a text from him. First time in five years."

He pulled out his phone and handed it to me. I read the message on the screen, my jaw tightening with each word.

Rowan. Heard through the grapevine you've resurfaced. Congratulations on the hockey—always knew you had it in you. Listen, I know we didn't part on the best terms, but I think it's worth having a conversation. The LA Reign has been making inquiries. Your name came up in their scouting meetings. I still have contacts. I could open some doors. Call me when you're ready to talk about your future.

"The LA Reign," I said slowly. "Professional hockey."

"The thing I've wanted my entire life." Rowan's voice cracked. "Dangled in front of me by the man who spent years turning me into a product. And the worst part—the part that makes me want to scream—is that some piece of me still wants it. Still craves the validation of making it to the highest level. Even a part of me still craves getting some kind of approval from that blasted man."

"But?"

"But I know how that story ends. I lived it once." He shook his head, his whole body rigid with tension. "The interviews that never stop. The personas that have to be maintained. The slow erosion of everything private until there's nothing left but the brand. I can't do it again, Elliot. I wouldn't survive a second time."

I sat with that for a moment, feeling the weight of his fear. The PR meeting, the talking points, Chet's perfectly timed reappearance—it was a coordinated assault on everything Rowan had built in his years of hiding. Whether intentional or not, the universe had conspired to remind him exactly what he'd escaped.

And he'd done the only thing he knew how to do. He'd run.

"Do you want to play professional hockey?" I asked.

Rowan looked at me like I'd asked if he wanted to breathe. "It's all I've ever wanted. Since I was six years old. But not like that. Not if it means going back to being a product. Not if it means letting Chet anywhere near my life again."

"Okay." I nodded slowly, something settling into place in my chest. "Then here's what's going to happen."

He blinked at the shift in my tone. "What?"

"I'm going to text Chet Finlay back from your phone and tell him to go fuck himself. If you want, I'll be creative about it—I can make it poetic." I held up the phone, still in my hand. "There once was a vulture named Chet, Whose soul was as black as it gets. He marketed pain, Now his life's down the drain, So go fuck yourself and your threats."

"Please, please send that," Ro asked. "I need that in my life."

I did and signed it, "Love Elliot."

"Done," I said with a certain sense of pride. "Then I'm going to call the university PR people and tell them that any media strategy that doesn't have your explicit, enthusiastic approval can also go fuck itself."

Rowan stared at me. "You can't just—"

"Watch me." I paused, meeting his eyes. "Unless you don't want me to. This is your call, Ro. All of it. But if what you need right now is someone to be the asshole so you don't have to be, I'm gladly volunteering."

"You'd do that?"

"I'd do anything." The words came out fiercer than I intended, but I didn't take them back. "I love you. I know what you're afraid of, and I know what you need. And right now, you need someone who will stand in your corner no matter what. If that means telling some powerful agent to go fuck off, I'll do it. If it means telling the university off, count me in."

Rowan's breath hitched. "That's . . . that's a lot."

"I know." I reached out and took his hand, threading our fingers together. "I've told you from the beginning, people accuse me of being extra." I squeezed his hand. "But I can point that extra energy in a targeted direction. I can be obsessive about protecting you instead of studying you. I can be relentless about making sure no one ever makes you feel like a product again."

He was quiet for a long moment, his gray eyes searching my face. I held still, letting him look, letting him see whatever he needed to see. The actor in me wanted to fill the silence, to shape the scene, to guide the moment toward the outcome I wanted. I forced that instinct down. This wasn't a play. This was real, and it had to be his choice.

"I missed practice," he said finally, his voice rough. "Sterling's going to kill me."

"Yeah. Davies texted me. I'll handle Sterling."

"You can't handle Sterling. Sterling handles everyone."

"Then I'll be very polite while he yells at me." I lifted our joined hands and pressed a kiss to his knuckles. "We'll figure it out. You don't have to do this alone, and you don't have to make any decisions tonight."

Rowan let out a long, shaky breath. Some of the tension drained out of his shoulders, like ice finally cracking after a long freeze.

"What about you?" he asked. "Davies mentioned something about reviews. Important people at your show."

"It can wait."

"Elliot—"

"It can wait," I repeated firmly. "You're more important than reviews. You're more important than any of it."

"You have a little over twenty-four hours before the DIII championship. The last weekend of my show doesn't start until Thursday. I've got time. Right now, you need me."

He searched my face for a long moment, looking for something—doubt, maybe, or calculation. Whatever he thought he would see, he didn't seem to find it. Instead, something in his expression softened, the hard edges of his panic giving way to exhaustion.

"Okay," he said. "Okay. But I'm not going back tonight. I can't face any of it yet."

"Then we stay here." I gestured at the dusty floor, the empty cabin, the failing light outside the windows. "It's not exactly the Ritz, but I've slept in worse places."

"You've never slept anywhere worse than this."

"I've slept in a dorm room, in the theatre building during tech week, in . . . I'm sure there's been somewhere else that is worse. Trust me, this is an upgrade."

That finally got a small huff of laughter out of him—not much, but enough. He shifted, leaning into me, his head dropping to my shoulder. I wrapped an arm around him and held on; his heartbeat slowed against my ribs.

Outside, the last light faded from the sky, and the lake settled into darkness. I listened to Ro's breathing even as the tension finally released its grip on him and he fell asleep.

Chapter 36
The Championship: First Period

Rowan

The locker room was quieter than it should have been.

Twenty players, fully dressed, equipment checked and doublechecked, sitting in their stalls like soldiers waiting for the order to advance. The usual pregame energy—the music, the chirping, the nervous laughter—had been replaced by something heavier. Something that felt like history.

Championship game. Winner takes everything. Loser goes home with nothing but the memory of how close they came.

I sat in my stall, stick across my knees, working through the taping ritual one last time. The movements were automatic now—wrap, pull, smooth, repeat. But for once, the ritual wasn't about managing anxiety. It was about preparation. About getting ready for the biggest game of my life.

The arena above us was already loud. I could feel the vibrations through the floor, the stamp of feet and the roar of voices bleeding through concrete and steel. This wasn't our home ice—this was the Golden Bay Arena in San Francisco, the Seismic Arena, home of the professional Tremors. The conference had chosen this neutral site for the championship, and the building was packed to the rafters. Standing room only.

Some of them were here for hockey. Some of them were here for the story.

I didn't care anymore. I was here to play.

Davies dropped onto the bench beside me, his leg bouncing with that familiar nervous energy. But there was something different in his face tonight—not fear, exactly. Anticipation.

"Big crowd," he said.

"Yeah."

"Lots of cameras. And I heard Tremors scouts are in the press box. Their GM too—Sofia Marquez."

The name hit me like a check I didn't see coming. The Tremors. Chet had mentioned the team that had been asking about me. That was a problem for another day.

"Yeah," I managed.

Davies was quiet for a moment. "You ready for this?"

I finished the last wrap of tape and tested the grip. Perfect.

"I've been ready for this my whole life," I said. "I just didn't know it until now."

Sterling entered the locker room, and the silence deepened into something absolute. He walked to the center of the space, turning slowly to look at each player. His face was carved from granite, unreadable, but there was something in his eyes I'd never seen before.

Pride, maybe. Or hope.

"Pacific Lutheran," he said. "You know who they are. Bigger than us. Faster than us. Favored to win by every analyst who's ever watched a hockey game." He paused, letting the words land. "They've won three of the last five conference championships. They have four players who've been drafted by NHL teams. On paper, we shouldn't be here."

Another pause. The silence was total.

"But we are here. We earned this ice. Every practice, every drill, every moment of discipline and sacrifice this season brought us to this room, on this night." His voice dropped, became something almost intimate. "I don't care what the papers say. I don't care what the odds say. When that puck drops, the only thing that matters is what happens between those boards."

He looked at me.

"You've earned this," Sterling said. "Now take it."

He turned and walked out of the locker room. The message was clear: time to go.

The tunnel was dark and narrow, the light at the end growing brighter with each step. The roar of the crowd built as we approached—not a single sound but a wall of noise, thousands of voices blending into something primal and overwhelming.

I walked with my teammates, stick in hand, helmet secure. The cage of the facemask framed my vision the way it always had, but tonight it didn't feel like a hiding place. It felt like armor.

We emerged onto the ice, and the noise hit me like a physical force.

The Golden Bay Arena was a cathedral of modern hockey—sleek, massive, intimidating. The stands rose steeply on all sides, packed with bodies. A sea of orange and navy for our fans, purple and gold for Pacific Lutheran. Tremors banners hung from the rafters, championship years stitched in gold, a reminder of what professional glory was. The faultline patterns in the arena lighting pulsed subtly across the ice surface, the building's signature design element.

Signs waved above the crowd—GO OSPREYS, CALLOWAY #28, CHAMPIONSHIP OR NOTHING. The Jumbotron cycled through player photos and sponsor logos and reminders to visit the concession stands.

And scattered through the press section, the cameras. Dozens of them, their lenses catching the light, recording everything for the audience that existed beyond these walls. The viral video had brought some of them here. The story of the Ice Prince's resurrection had brought others.

I spotted a luxury box near center ice. A woman with dark hair sat in the front row, flanked by men in suits. Sofia Marquez—the Tremors' GM. I recognized her from the sports pages. She was watching the warmups with the focused intensity of someone evaluating an investment.

Let them watch. Let them all watch.

I skated through warmups on autopilot, my body moving through familiar patterns while my mind cataloged the environment. Pacific Lutheran was on the other end of the ice, their purple and gold jerseys bright under the lights. They were big—Sterling wasn't exaggerating. Their defensemen could be linebackers, and their forwards moved with the kind of fluid speed that came from years of elite development.

They were good. Really good.

But I'd played against good before. I'd played against the best. And I'd survived things that had nothing to do with hockey.

We'd been given four tickets per player so our family and friends could get seats in the arena. I had a general idea where it was located, but couldn't find the section easily. Two of my tickets went to my parents, Elliot got my third, and the fourth ticket I gave to Davies, who had a large family and needed more seats.

Elliot was up there somewhere. Watching. Not with a notebook anymore—just watching. I may not have known where he was, but I knew he was in here somewhere. Just the knowledge that whatever happened tonight, I wasn't alone.

Then the horn sounded for the end of warmups, and I skated toward the bench, toward the game, toward whatever came next.

The puck dropped.

Davies won the faceoff—he'd been clutch on draws all playoffs—pulling it back to Hedman at the point. Sterling had us running as the Aline now, me and Maddox flanking Davies at center. The configuration that had carried us through the semifinals.

First shift, first read. I was on the left wing, tracking the play as it developed. Hedman moved the puck to Chelios, who fed it up the boards to Maddox. Maddox carried through the neutral zone, then dumped it deep.

We forechecked hard. I got to the puck first behind their net, cycling it low, drawing a defender. Davies was crashing toward the slot. Maddox positioned himself at the half-wall.

I fed Maddox. He had a lane—not much, but enough. Quick release, low to the ice.

The puck rang off the post with a sound that echoed through the arena.

Close. So close.

Pacific Lutheran cleared the zone and counterattacked with speed. Their top line moved the puck with crisp precision, their passes tape-to-tape, their movement coordinated in a way that spoke to years of playing together.

They entered our zone with speed. I backchecked hard, closing the gap on their forward, taking away the passing lane. The shot came from the point—hard, accurate—but Lindros was there in goal, glove snapping up to make the save.

Whistle. Faceoff in our zone.

My heart was pounding, but my mind was clear. This was hockey. This was what I knew how to do.

The first period unfolded in a blur of action—shifts and changes, chances and saves, the constant churn of two teams feeling each other out. Pacific Lutheran was everything the scouting report promised: fast, physical, skilled. But we weren't backing down. Davies was winning board battles. Maddox was breaking up plays. Lindros was making saves that kept us in the game.

And I was playing. Really playing. Taking the ice with confidence, making plays, trusting my instincts.

Midway through the period, the taunts started.

"Hey, Ice Prince!" The voice came from the Pacific Lutheran bench, loud enough to carry across the ice. "Shouldn't you be filming a commercial?"

I ignored it. Kept skating. Kept playing.

"Thought you retired!" Another voice, different player. "What happened, Hollywood? Couldn't hack it in the real world?"

The old Rowan would have flinched. Would have felt the shame crawling up his spine, would have played smaller to avoid drawing more attention.

But I wasn't the old Rowan anymore.

I took the puck in the neutral zone, skating hard through center ice. A Pacific Lutheran defenseman stepped up to challenge me—the same one who'd been running his mouth all period. I dropped my shoulder, protected the puck, and blew past him on the outside. He was left grasping at air while I drove toward the offensive zone.

The shot went wide, but the message was clear: your words don't touch me anymore.

At the eight-minute mark, the penalties started flying.

Maddox got called for a borderline interference—finishing a check half a second late. Two minutes in the box. Pacific Lutheran's power play unit took the ice, their top players fresh and hungry.

"Kill it!" Sterling shouted from the bench.

I was out there with Davies, Kowalski, and Hedman on defense, working the penalty kill. Pacific Lutheran moved the puck around the perimeter with surgical precision, probing for weaknesses. Their point man wound up for a one-timer.

I threw myself into the lane, blocking the shot with my shin. The puck ricocheted to Davies, who cleared it down the ice. Forty-five seconds killed.

They set up again. More passing, more movement. A cross-ice feed to their sniper in the circle. He one-timed it toward the net—

Lindros got a piece of it with his blocker, sending the puck into the corner. Hedman tied up their forward, and we survived another fifteen seconds.

The penalty expired. Maddox jumped back onto the ice.

But the reprieve was temporary.

Pacific Lutheran scored at the twelve-minute mark.

It was a good goal—a quick passing play that caught our defense in transition, a one-timer from the slot that beat Lindros before he could react. The Pacific Lutheran section erupted, their purple and gold waving like victory flags. The faultline lights in the arena pulsed once—even the building seemed to acknowledge the moment.

1-0.

The arena's energy shifted. Our fans went quiet, anxiety replacing anticipation. Down by one in a championship game, against a team that knew how to protect leads.

But I stayed calm. We stayed calm.

Sterling didn't panic. He made adjustments, sent out fresh lines, kept us focused on the process instead of the score. One goal wasn't a death sentence. One goal was just hockey.

Two minutes later, Pacific Lutheran took a penalty—their defenseman hooked Davies on a breakaway. Two minutes. Power play.

Sterling sent out the top unit: me, Maddox, Davies up front, Hedman and Chelios on the points. We set up in their zone.

The puck moved around the perimeter. Hedman to Chelios to me at the half-wall. I cycled low, drawing the penalty killers toward me. Davies was parked in front, screening the goalie. Maddox was at the far post.

I saw the lane. Fed Hedman at the point.

Hedman wound up for a slap shot. Their penalty killers reacted, one of them diving to block. But Hedman faked the shot and instead fed Chelios, who quickly moved it to Davies in the slot.

Davies one-timed it. The goalie got a piece, but the rebound kicked out to me at the side of the net.

I didn't think. Just buried it.

1-1.

The arena exploded—our half of it, anyway. The Ospreys' fans were on their feet, the noise crashing over us like a wave. Davies was screaming in my ear, grabbing my jersey, pulling me into a celebration that felt like validation.

"THAT'S what I'm talking about!" Davies shouted. "THAT'S the play!"

I tapped his helmet, accepted the congratulations, skated back to the bench. But inside, something was glowing. Not just the goal—the play. The vision. The patience to wait for the right moment.

The period wound down with both teams trading chances—and penalties. The refs were calling everything tight, trying to keep the championship game from boiling over.

Volkov went to the box for slashing. We killed it.

Pacific Lutheran's captain took a hooking call. Our power play couldn't convert, but we generated pressure.

Chen got called for a high stick—accidental, but the rule was the rule. Pacific Lutheran's power play set up again.

With three minutes left, I was back on the penalty kill. Blocking shots. Taking away lanes. Doing everything I could to keep us even.

Their one-timer came from the circle. I dove to block it, taking it off my thigh. The pain was immediate, but the puck deflected away. Maddox cleared it.

Penalty killed.

With two minutes left, I took a hit.

It came from the blind side—legal but brutal, a Pacific Lutheran forward catching me with my head down in the neutral zone. I went down hard, the ice cold against my back, my vision swimming for a moment.

The whistle blew. The crowd held its breath.

I got up. Checked myself over. The hit hurt but broke nothing. There was still hockey to play.

I skated back to the bench under my own power. Davies handed me a water bottle.

"You good?"

"I'm good."

The period ended thirty seconds later. 1-1. Everything still to play for.

The locker room was focused but not frantic.

Sterling stood at the whiteboard, drawing up adjustments, pointing out tendencies he'd noticed in Pacific Lutheran's play. Their defense pinched too aggressively on the forecheck. Their goalie had a weakness high on the glove side. Their top line was tired from playing too many minutes.

"They're fast. We expected that," Sterling said. "But we're smarter. We're more disciplined. And we want this more than they do."

He paused.

"I saw Sofia Marquez up in that luxury box. The Tremors' GM. Half the scouts in the Pacific Northwest are in the press section." He let that land. "They're not here to watch Pacific Lutheran. They're here to watch you—all of you—prove what Oakridge hockey is made of."

He looked around the room, making eye contact with each player.

"Twenty minutes of hockey have decided championships. Twenty minutes have defined careers." His voice dropped. "This is your twenty minutes. Make them count."

He walked out. The room was quiet for a moment.

Davies appeared at my shoulder. "Honest, you good? That was a rough hit."

"I'm good." I rolled my shoulder—sore, but functional. "Better than good."

"Yeah?"

I stared at him, this kid who'd been a nervous wreck at tryouts, who I'd taught to breathe through panic, who'd become something like a brother over the course of this season.

"For the first time in my life," I said, "I'm fucking amazing."

Davies grinned. "Then let's go win a championship."

Chapter 37
The Championship: Second Period

Elliot

I was hanging out with Rowan's parents. That wasn't awkward. I knew they planned on being at the game, but didn't know our seats would be together. I should have put two and two together since it was the family and friends section and each player got four seats. His parents were nice. They weren't hockey parents by any stretch of the imagination. Sadly, I think I had a higher hockey IQ than either of them, which was saying something.

The seats in the Golden Bay Arena were plusher. The sightlines were sharper. Honestly, everything was more professional than our home rink. This was where the San Francisco Tremors played. Where champions were made. Where Rowan might end up if the scouts in the luxury boxes liked what they saw.

The arena was louder than anything I'd ever experienced. The first period had ended 1-1, and the crowd had had fifteen minutes to build anticipation into something feverish. The noise crashed against me in waves—cheers and chants and the thunderous stamp of feet on concrete. The faultline lighting pulsed with the energy, the whole building seeming to vibrate with tension.

The teams took the ice for the second period. I found Rowan immediately, moving through warmup skates with that fluid efficiency I'd memorized. My chest was tight with something that felt like prayer. I wasn't religious—never had been—but sitting here, watching him prepare for what came next, I reached for something beyond myself. Please let him be okay. Please let him play the way I know he can. Please let this end the way it should.

The referee skated to center ice. The teams lined up. The puck dropped.

The second period began.

The game was different now.

Whatever restraint both teams had shown in the first period had evaporated. This was desperate hockey—physical, fast, unrelenting. Every puck battle was a war. Every shift was maximum effort. The ice was a battlefield, and neither side was willing to give ground.

Pacific Lutheran came out aggressive, pressing hard into the Oakridge zone. Their size advantage was more apparent now, their defensemen using their bodies to win positions, their forwards crashing the net with abandon. The Ospreys absorbed the pressure, bent but didn't break, and gradually pushed back.

Rowan was everywhere.

I watched him backcheck with ferocious intensity, closing gaps, taking away passing lanes. I watched him win a board battle against a player who had thirty pounds on him, using leverage and positioning and sheer will to come away with the puck. I watched him make a pass through traffic that shouldn't have been possible, finding Davies in the slot for a chance that went just wide.

He was playing beautifully.

Four minutes into the period, the Ospreys took a penalty. Morrissey got called for hooking—a desperate reach as a Pacific Lutheran forward blew past him. Two minutes in the box.

Pacific Lutheran's power play took the ice.

The next two minutes were agony.

I watched Rowan kill the penalty alongside Davies, with Hedman and Kowalski on defense. They threw themselves into shooting lanes, blocking shots with their bodies. Pacific Lutheran's top unit was surgical, moving the puck with precision that made my chest tight.

A one-timer from the circle—Lindros got his glove on it.

A cross-crease pass—Rowan dove to intercept, sending the puck down the ice.

With thirty seconds left on the penalty, Pacific Lutheran's point man wound up for a slap shot. The puck screamed toward the net—

Lindros made the save. The buzzer sounded. Penalty killed.

But two minutes later, the Ospreys went to the box again. Chelios—a retaliation slash after taking a hard hit in the corner. The ref's arm went up, and Chelios slammed his stick against the boards in frustration.

Pacific Lutheran didn't waste their second chance.

Their power play set up in the Oakridge zone, the puck moving around the perimeter with crisp precision. Rowan was out there again, exhausted from the previous kill, but still fighting. Still trying to close lanes.

The pass came across the slot. Their sniper in the left circle had a half-second of open ice.

He buried it. One-timer, top corner. Lindros had no chance.

2-1 Pacific Lutheran.

The crowd groaned—our half of it, anyway. The purple and gold section erupted. The faultline lights pulsed in celebration. I watched Rowan's shoulders tighten as he processed the shift in momentum.

But the Ospreys didn't fold.

Three minutes later, Davies stripped the puck at center ice, drove into the zone with Rowan on his wing, and fed a perfect pass across the crease. Rowan one-timed it glove side—exactly where Sterling had said the goalie was weak.

2-2.

The arena exploded back to life.

The game became a seesaw—both teams trading chances, both goalies making saves, the ice tilting back and forth with dizzying speed. And the penalties kept coming. The referees were calling everything, trying to keep the game from boiling over.

Volkov went to the box for tripping. Killed.

Pacific Lutheran's captain took an interference call. The Ospreys' power play couldn't convert, but they generated pressure.

Petrov got called for a high stick—accidental. Pacific Lutheran's power play set up again, hungry for blood.

I gripped the armrests of my seat, watching Rowan take yet another penalty kill shift. He'd been on the ice for what felt like half the period, burning through energy reserves that would be needed in the third. But he kept going. Kept fighting. Kept refusing to let his team fall behind.

Pacific Lutheran's power play moved the puck. Cross-ice pass to the far circle. One-timer—

Lindros stopped it with his blocker.

Rebound to the slot—

Kowalski dove to block the follow-up shot. The puck ricocheted off his shin and out of the zone. Penalty killed.

Up in the luxury box, I could see Sofia Marquez leaning forward, conferring with her scouts. Whatever she was seeing, it had her attention. She never smiled, but her eyes never left the ice.

With eight minutes left in the period, Pacific Lutheran scored again.

This one hurt. A broken play, a puck that bounced the wrong way off the boards, a shot that deflected off Hedman's skate and trickled through Lindros's pads. Unlucky. But the scoreboard didn't care about luck.

3-2 Pacific Lutheran.

The crowd deflated. The energy in the building shifted. Our side was running out of time, running out of margin for error.

I dug my fingers into the padded armrests and watched Rowan take the next faceoff. His body language hadn't changed—still focused, still determined, still playing like he had something to prove.

Seven minutes left in the period.

Then twenty more to decide everything.

It happened fast.

Rowan picked up the puck behind his own net, started the breakout with a burst of speed. He moved through the neutral zone, head up, reading the defense. A Pacific Lutheran forward was closing from the left. A defenseman was stepping up at the blue line.

Rowan saw a lane—not much of one, but enough. He accelerated, trying to split the defenders, trying to create something from nothing.

He didn't see the other defenseman.

The hit came from the blind side. Legal—shoulder to shoulder, no head contact—but devastating. The Pacific Lutheran player was huge, and he caught Rowan in full stride, all of that momentum reversing in an instant.

Rowan went down.

He didn't get up.

The whistle blew. The arena went silent—that particular silence that happened when everyone in the building held their breath at once. Thousands of people, watching and waiting and hoping.

I was on my feet without remembering standing. My hands were gripping the back of the seat in front of me, knuckles white, fingernails digging into the plastic. Every muscle in my body was locked.

Please get up. Please get up. Please.

The ghost of Henderson flickered through my mind. I knew the statistics, knew that serious injuries were rare, knew that players took hard hits every game and skated away fine.

Rowan wasn't moving.

The seconds stretched. The trainers reached him, crouched down, and examined him. The arena was so quiet.

I'll give anything. I'll do anything. Just please let him be okay.

Rowan moved.

First, his head lifted. Then, his arms pushed against the ice. Then, slowly, carefully, he was rising—first to his knees, then to his feet. He wobbled slightly, and one trainer steadied him, but he was standing. He was conscious. He was alive.

The crowd exhaled as one. Then the applause started—not the roar of celebration, but the sustained clap of relief, of respect for a player who'd taken a hard hit and gotten back up.

My legs gave out. I dropped into my seat, suddenly boneless, my heart pounding so hard I could feel it in my throat.

He's okay. He's okay. He's okay.

Rowan skated slowly toward the bench, the trainers hovering nearby. He was moving carefully—definitely hurt, definitely feeling the impact—but he was moving under his own power. When he reached the bench, Sterling leaned in to talk to him. I couldn't see Rowan's response, but I saw him shake his head once, firmly.

He wasn't coming out of the game. Of course he wasn't. But I still watched as a trainer walked him out of the arena.

Pacific Lutheran tried to extend their lead, pressing hard while the Ospreys were still recovering from the shock of seeing their player go down. But Lindros made two big saves, and Maddox cleared a puck off the goal line with a desperation dive, and somehow the score stayed 3-2.

The horn sounded. Second intermission. Twenty minutes of hockey left to decide a championship.

I pulled out my phone, my hands still trembling slightly.

Are you okay?

I sent the text and watched the screen, waiting for a response I knew wasn't coming. Rowan was in the locker room right now, probably getting checked by the trainers, probably listening to Sterling make adjustments for the third period. He didn't have time to read his texts.

But I'd needed to ask. Needed to reach out across the distance, to let him know I was here; I was watching. Even when we were separated by concrete and steel, I was with him.

The intermission crawled by.

People around me were talking—analyzing the period, debating strategy, expressing concern about the hit Rowan had taken. Rowan's parents talked to me, but their words weren't registering. I didn't think I would breathe again until I saw Rowan coming back out of the tunnel. A couple rows down, I saw some of the Ospreys' parents, their faces tight with the particular worry of people who loved someone taking risks they couldn't control. In the press section, the reporters were typing furiously, probably already drafting stories about the dramatic turn the game had taken.

I glanced at the luxury box. Sofia Marquez was conferring with her people. Even from this distance, I could see them gesturing, discussing. They'd just watched a strong player take a devastating hit and get back up. That had to mean something in hockey. That's all Rowan did. He took hits, and he stood back up.

I didn't talk to anyone. I just sat in my seat, Moleskine untouched in my pocket, phone dark in my hand, and waited.

The horn sounded. The teams retook the ice.

Rowan was among them.

The third period began.

Chapter 38
The Championship: Third Period

Rowan

The tunnel back to the ice felt like a descent into a cold, concrete purgatory. My ribs screamed from the hit—deep, throbbing pain that flared with every breath.

The head trainer pulled his hands away from my side, his mouth set in a grim line that usually signaled the end of a player's night.

"Ribs are badly bruised, Calloway. Maybe worse," he said, checking a mark on his clipboard. "You're breathing is shallower than I'd like. I'm calling it. You're sitting out the third to be safe."

"The hell I am," I rasped, the words catching on a sharp spike of pain in my chest. I shoved myself off the training table, ignoring the way the room tilted for a fraction of a second.

Sterling stood by the door, his shadow long across the concrete floor. He didn't move as I approached, his eyes tracking the slight hitch in my side. "You heard him, Calloway. We have depth on the bench."

"I'm playing, Coach," I said, stepping into his space until we were eye to eye. "I'm playing these final twenty minutes if I have to crawl across that ice."

Sterling searched my face. He stayed silent for a heartbeat, then gave me that single, definitive nod.

"Tape him up," Sterling commanded over his shoulder. "Tight. But Calloway, if you flinch or grimace on the ice, I'm pulling you. No arguments. Period. I will not have us lose because you couldn't be man enough to admit you're not able to skate."

"Yes, Coach."

I was battered and bruised, every breath a physical negotiation, but as I grabbed my stick, I knew nothing was broken that couldn't be ignored for one more period.

Twenty minutes. Down by one. Everything we'd built came down to this.

I took the ice with my teammates, and the pain receded to background noise. It was still there and would be there for the entire period. Pain was manageable. What mattered was what you did while you were hurting.

The Golden Bay Arena was deafening. The Ospreys' faithful had found their voice again, desperate belief replacing the anxiety that had settled in when we'd fallen behind. Signs waved above the crowd. My name—both names, Calloway and St. Clair—echoed from the rafters. The faultline lights pulsed with the crowd's vibrating energy.

I got down on the ground and stretched out my hips. Davies nearby.

"Davies, ever find the family and friends section?"

"Yeah. You know where the GM's box is, it's just south of there for our team."

I looked up in that direction while I lay on the ice like a frog, letting my legs dip from side to side. I found the section. Elliot was there, leaning forward, his entire body radiating tension I could feel from here. Oh, shit. He's next to my parents. Well, that's awkward.

Focus.

The whistle blew. The referee skated to center ice. Pacific Lutheran lined up, their purple and gold bright under the lights. Their defensemen was overconfident—up by one with twenty minutes to play, against a team whose best player had just taken a devastating hit. They thought they had this.

They were wrong.

The puck dropped.

The first five minutes were desperate, physical, both teams playing like everything depended on the next shift. Because it did.

Pacific Lutheran sat back, protecting their lead, content to let us throw ourselves against their defense and hope we ran out of time. It was smart strategy. It was also exactly what Sterling had predicted.

"They'll turtle," he'd said during intermission. "They'll clog the neutral zone and wait for us to make mistakes. Don't make mistakes. Be patient. Be smart. The chances will come."

I took every shift Sterling gave me, playing through the pain, pushing harder than I'd ever pushed. My ribs protested with every stride, every check absorbed, and every breath that I drew too deep. But I didn't slow down. Couldn't slow down.

Davies was playing like a man possessed, winning board battles, creating space, doing all the dirty work that didn't show up on the scoresheet. Maddox was using his captain's presence to keep the team focused, barking instructions, leading by example. Lindros was a wall in net, making saves that kept us alive, refusing to let Pacific Lutheran extend their lead.

The Ospreys were pushing, generating chances, building pressure. But Pacific Lutheran's goalie was good—really good—and the puck just wouldn't go in.

Six minutes into the period, and the Pacific Lutheran's top defenseman lost his mind.

Davies had just won a board battle, sending the puck up the ice, when the hit came—late, high, and vicious. The defenseman drove his elbow into Davies's head, sending him crashing into the boards with a sickening crack. Davies crumpled to the ice.

The whistle shrieked. Then another. The refs skated in fast, arms raised, signals flying.

I was already moving toward Davies, but Maddox got there first. I could tell Maddox was about to go apeshit on the guy's ass. Thankfully, Hedman stepped between them before it could escalate and get Maddox a penalty, too. The arena was chaos—our fans screaming for blood, their fans going quiet as the refs huddled.

Davies was upright, but his gaze was glassy. He sat with his mouth slightly parted, his eyes tracking something invisible in the rafters while the trainers barked questions he clearly couldn't hear. After a long moment, he gave a thumbs up and skated slowly toward the bench under his own power. The crowd applauded—that same relief applause I'd heard after my own hit.

The ref skated to center ice, microphone in hand.

"Pacific Lutheran, number forty-four. Fiveminute major penalty for elbowing. Game misconduct."

The arena erupted. Five minutes. A major. And their best defenseman was done for the night—skating toward the locker room with his head down while his coach screamed at the officials.

Five minutes of power play. This was our chance. This was the hockey gods giving us a gift.

Sterling sent out Chen to replace Davies. When I had time to see what was going on, Davies was on the bench with a trainer's flashlight shining into his eyes. We set up in their zone, the puck moving around the perimeter with practiced precision.

Five minutes was an eternity in hockey. We didn't need to force anything. We just needed to be patient.

Hedman to Chelios. Chelios down low to me. I cycled behind the net, drawing the penalty killers toward me, then fed it back to Hedman at the point.

Hedman wound up for a one-timer.

The shot screamed toward the net. Their goalie got his blocker on it, but the rebound kicked out to Maddox in the slot. He had an open net—

The goalie dove across, got a piece of it with his pad. The puck trickled wide.

Still 3-2. Still down by one. But we had over three minutes of power play remaining.

We kept pressing. Fresh legs came over the boards. Chen won a faceoff clean back to Chelios. The puck moved to me at the half-wall.

I saw Maddox setting a screen in front. Saw the goalie's view partially blocked. Saw the lane.

I didn't hesitate. Quick release, low to the ice, through traffic.

The puck found the corner of the net.

3-3.

The arena erupted.

I didn't remember the celebration—just bodies crashing into me, Chen screaming something unintelligible, the roar of the crowd washing over us like a wave. The faultline lights went crazy, pulsing in time with the goal horn. The pain in my ribs flared as someone pounded my back, but I didn't care. We were tied. We were alive.

Fourteen minutes to play.

Pacific Lutheran responded with fury.

The goal had woken them up, shattered the comfortable lead they'd been protecting. Even down a man with their top defenseman ejected, they weren't backing down. If anything, the ejection and my subsequent goal had ignited something—rage, desperation, the refusal to let their teammate's sacrifice mean nothing. They pressed hard, playing aggressive despite the disadvantage, making us work for every inch of ice.

Without Davies, our line felt incomplete. Chen had slotted in at center, solid but unfamiliar. The chemistry we'd built over months of playing together was gone, replaced by something functional but fragile.

With just over two minutes left on the major penalty, the refs' arms went up again.

Seibert took a tripping call—a desperation reach as a Pacific Lutheran forward broke toward the net on a partial breakaway. It was the right play, preventing a quality scoring chance, but it evened the sides. Four-on-four for the remaining two minutes of their major, then we'd be shorthanded.

Pacific Lutheran's four-on-four play was lethal.

The open ice suited their speed. They set up in our zone, moving the puck with crisp precision, probing for weaknesses. I was out there with Maddox, Hedman, and Kowalski, blocking shots, taking away passing lanes, doing everything we could to survive.

The shot came from the point—I threw myself into the lane, taking it off my already-screaming ribs. The pain was blinding, but the puck deflected away. Maddox cleared it down the ice.

The major penalty expired. Now we were shorthanded. Four-on-five for another thirty seconds.

They set up again. More passing, more movement. Cross-ice to their sniper in the circle. He wound up—

Lindros made a desperation glove save, snatching the puck out of the air. The crowd roared.

Seibert's penalty expired. Finally back to even strength.

But thirty seconds later, Pacific Lutheran scored anyway.

It wasn't a power play goal—just good hockey. A cycle down low, a pass to the slot, a one-timer that beat Lindros before he could react.

4-3 Pacific Lutheran.

Nine minutes left. Down a goal. Down Davies.

We'd just tied the game, clawed our way back, and now we were down again. The mountain had just gotten steeper—and we'd lost one of our best climbers.

But I'd been climbing mountains my whole life. What was one more?

The final nine minutes were a blur.

Pacific Lutheran was playing smart now, mixing defensive structure with timely counterattacks. Every time we pushed forward, they made us pay with chances the other way. Lindros made two more incredible saves. The crowd held its breath with every shot.

Under five minutes to play. Still down by one.

Sterling called timeout.

The team gathered at the bench, exhausted, desperate, hanging on every word. Sterling watched each of us, his granite face showing the first cracks of emotion I'd ever seen.

"We've got one card left to play," he said. "Under two minutes, I'm pulling Lindros. Six attackers. Maximum pressure."

He turned to me.

"Calloway. You're on the ice for that final push. Whatever happens, you're out there. Davies, you good to go?"

"Yes, Coach—"

"No, Coach," the trainer said.

"Chen—you're with him. Hedman and Chelios on the points."

I nodded. My ribs screamed. I didn't care.

"We've come too far to lose this now," Sterling said. "Give me everything you've got. Leave nothing on the ice. No matter what happens, I'm proud of every single one of you."

The timeout ended. The game resumed.

Four minutes. Three. The clock ticked down like a countdown to something I couldn't name.

Pacific Lutheran took a penalty—their exhausted defenseman held Chen's jersey as he tried to drive the net. Holding. Two minutes. Power play.

This was it. This was our chance.

The power play set up. Hedman had the puck at the point. I was at the half-wall, Maddox in front of the net, Chen in the opposite circle. Chelios was at the far point.

The puck moved. Hedman to me. I cycled low, drawing the penalty killers. Fed it back to Chelios.

Chelios wound up for a slap shot. It was blocked. The puck bounced to Chen.

Chen didn't hesitate. He ripped a wrist shot toward the net—

The goalie got a piece of it. Rebound into the crease. Maddox was there, hacking at it—

The whistle blew. The goalie had covered it.

Faceoff in the offensive zone. Under two minutes to play. Back on a power play.

Sterling gave the signal. Lindros skated to the bench. Six attackers, maximum risk.

The faceoff was critical. Chen lined up against their best center. The puck dropped—

Chen won it. Clean draw back to Hedman.

The next ninety seconds were the longest of my life.

We cycled the puck in the offensive zone, trying to create something, anything. Pacific Lutheran was packed tight in front of their net, blocking shots, clearing rebounds, doing everything they could to survive.

Sixty seconds left. The penalty expired, but we kept possession. Still six attackers. Still searching.

The puck bounced off a shin pad, squirted loose into the corner. I chased it down, fighting off a defender. Chen was in front of the net. Maddox was at the far post. The goalie was down, scrambling to find the puck.

Forty seconds.

I got the puck on my stick. Two defenders were closing. I had no angle, no shot, no play.

Except I did.

The lane opened for just a fraction of a second—a gap between the defenders, a sliver of net visible behind the scrambling goalie. It was the same lane I'd seen in the semifinal. The same choice I'd faced a hundred times this season.

I took the shot.

It wasn't pretty. Not the highlight-reel snipe that made the scouting reports. Just a quick release, low to the ice, threading the gap between defenders and finding the corner of the net.

The red light went on.

4-4.

Thirty-one seconds left in regulation.

The arena erupted—a sound so loud it felt like the building might collapse, the fault-line lights going crazy, the whole Golden Bay Arena shaking with the force of it. I was mobbed by teammates.

We didn't give up. We'd tied the game with less than a minute to play.

Overtime.

The intermission before overtime was surreal.

The Zamboni crawled across the ice, resurfacing the sheet for what could be another full twenty minutes of hockey before the last man was even off the ice. NCAF tournament rules—sudden death, five-on-five, a complete period if needed. No shootout. No gimmicks. Just hockey until someone scored.

The locker room was quiet. Not defeated—focused. We'd already proven we could come back, proven we wouldn't break. Now we just had to finish it.

Davies sat next to me on the bench like a lost puppy. He had an ice pack pressed to his head, his eyes still not quite tracking right. Davies had tried to argue to go back into the game, but the trainers did a onceover and informed him of the concussion protocol. No arguments. He'd tried to argue anyway, but Sterling had shut it down with a single glance.

"Win it for me," Davies had said, grabbing my arm as I walked past. "I didn't take that hit for nothing."

Sterling walked through the room, making eye contact with each player, that double-nod of acknowledgment that I understood meant more than words.

When he reached me, he stopped.

"How are the ribs?"

"Manageable."

"Can you play twenty minutes if you have to?"

"Try to stop me."

Something that might have been a smile crossed his granite face. "Chen's continuing to center your line. You and Maddox on the wings. Hedman and Chelios on defense. That's our unit for the big moments. As soon as any of you look tired, I'm sending in the Bline even if it's just for a minute to give your line a respite."

He moved on. I closed my eyes and breathed—carefully, feeling the pain with each inhale—and tried to find the stillness I needed for what came next.

This was why I'd come back to hockey. Not to hide. Not to punish myself.

This. The feeling of being exactly where I belonged, doing exactly what I was born to do, surrounded by people who had become family.

Whatever happened in overtime, I was grateful.

But I really wanted to win.

Overtime began.

The fresh ice gleamed under the lights, pristine and waiting. The arena was somehow even louder now; the crowd sensed that history was about to be made one way or another. Twenty minutes of sudden death. One goal to end it all.

Both teams were cautious at first, neither wanting to make the mistake that ended everything. The puck moved back and forth through the neutral zone, possession changing hands, chances scarce. Every shot attempt sent the crowd to their feet. Every save brought them back down, hearts pounding.

Three minutes in, Pacific Lutheran got a breakaway. Their fastest forward, alone against Lindros, the game about to end.

Lindros stacked his pads in a blur of motion, throwing his entire body across the crease in a move of pure desperation. The puck thudded against the leather—a dull, glorious sound that cut through the roar.

He kept it out.

We're still alive. The arena exhaled as one, the collective breath of thousands of people hitting the glass like a shockwave.

Five minutes in, we got our first real chance. A two-on-one, Chen and me against a single defender. I carried the puck, waiting for the defender to commit. He slid toward me, trying to take away the shot.

I passed to Chen. Chen shot. The goalie stopped it.

The game continued.

Twenty minutes. Nineteen. Eighteen.

The whistle shrieked at 11:47, the sound slicing through the roar of the crowd and freezing the game in its tracks. A defensive zone icing call—I'd put too much on the clear, and now we were trapped.

The officials signaled for an ice maintenance timeout. It gave us sixty seconds while the crews scraped the snow from the high-traffic areas.

I leaned against the boards, sucking air, feeling every hit I'd taken over the past three periods. My ribs screamed. My legs were getting wobbly. But the pain meant I was still alive, still playing, still in this.

Sterling appeared at my shoulder. "You good for the final push?"

"I'm good."

"We've got our timeout if we need it. I'm saving it for the last five minutes if we're still alive." He stared at me with those granite eyes. "Don't make me use it."

The whistle blew. Play resumed.

Both teams were exhausted now, running on fumes and desperation. Every shift felt like a marathon. Every change felt like a risk. Pacific Lutheran had adjusted to playing without their ejected defenseman, but the loss was showing—their pairings were jumbled, their minutes unbalanced.

Eleven minutes. Sterling pulled our line from the ice.

Ten. Sterling sent our line back out. The unit that had been on the ice for every big moment since Davies went down.

Eight minutes. We cycled in their zone for what felt like forever, the puck moving but never finding the back of the net. Maddox hit the post. Chen's redirect went wide. I had a half-chance from the slot that their goalie smothered.

Seven minutes. The crowd was standing now, unable to sit, the tension unbearable.

The puck came to me at center ice.

I carried it into the offensive zone, feeling the defense closing, looking for options. Chen was covered. Maddox was fighting for position in front. There was no obvious play, no clear chance.

But I saw something.

The defense was cheating toward Chen—expecting the pass to the center, the safe play. The goalie was positioned off-center, anticipating the same thing. The lane could exist for just a moment, if I could find it.

I drove toward the net.

The defender stepped up to challenge. I dropped my shoulder, protected the puck, and slipped past him with a burst of speed I didn't know I still had. The goalie came out to cut the angle, and suddenly it was just me and him, one-on-one, the championship hanging in the balance.

Time slowed.

I saw his stance—weight forward, glove low, expecting a shot to the blocker side. An opening high, on the glove side. I saw everything I'd ever learned about this game, every drill and practice and moment of dedication, crystallizing into this single instant.

I shot.

The puck rose, finding the gap between the goalie's glove and the crossbar. It hit the back of the net with a sound I'd remember for the rest of my life.

Goal.

I don't remember much of what happened next.

Bodies crashed into me—the whole team, it felt like, everyone on the ice and then everyone from the bench, a pile of joy and exhaustion and disbelief. Someone was screaming in my ear. Someone else was crying. The arena was a wall of sound so loud it seemed to vibrate through my bones, the faultline lights pulsing in celebration.

Davies lifted me off my feet, spinning me around despite my protesting ribs, shouting something I couldn't hear over the noise. Maddox was there too, his usually stern captain's face split into a grin I'd never seen before. Lindros was on his knees at center ice, his mask off, tears streaming down his face.

Sterling walked onto the ice—something I'd never seen him do—and there was something on his face that looked almost like a grin. He reached me through the crowd of teammates and put a hand on my shoulder.

"That's the player I knew you could be," he said. I could barely hear him over the noise, but I saw the words on his lips. "Welcome back."

The championship trophy appeared—where from, I had no idea—and suddenly it was being passed around, everyone touching it, everyone part of this moment. When it reached me, I lifted it over my head.

Chapter 39
The Win

Elliot

The puck hit the back of the net, and I lost my mind.

I was screaming before I knew I was screaming—a raw, wordless sound that tore out of my throat and joined the thousands of other voices exploding around me. The Golden Bay Arena shook with it, the concrete vibrating under my feet, the faultline lights pulsing in celebration, the air itself seeming to ripple with the force of collective joy. I turned and gave Rowan's mom a hug, which surprised both of us.

On the ice, Rowan disappeared under a pile of teammates. I could barely see him—just a flash of his number, 28, before bodies crashed together in the most beautiful chaos I'd ever witnessed. The goal horn was still blaring, the crowd roaring. Somewhere in the middle of it all was the man I loved, buried under a celebration he'd spent five years convinced he didn't deserve.

My eyes burned. I was crying, I realized—actual tears streaming down my face, and I didn't care.

He did it.

Rowan emerged from the celebration, his helmet off, his hair plastered to his forehead with sweat. Even from this distance, even through the chaos, I could see his face. The disbelief giving way to joy. The walls he'd spent five years building crumbling into something that looked like peace.

He glanced up.

He found me.

And something passed between us—something that didn't need words, didn't need explanation. Just recognition. Just love.

I had to get down there.

Leaving the family and friends section was like trying to swim upstream through a river of pure emotion.

Everyone was celebrating—hugging strangers, high-fiving people they'd never met, crying and laughing and shouting until their voices cracked. The aisles were clogged with bodies, everyone trying to get closer to the ice, closer to the team, closer to the moment.

I pushed through as politely as I could, murmuring apologies, using my elbows when I had to. The stairs were a crush of humanity, people packed so tightly I could barely move. But I kept going. I had to keep going.

"Excuse me—sorry—I need to get through—"

The journey that should have taken two minutes stretched into what felt like hours. Every step was a battle, every inch of progress hard won. Around me, the celebration continued unabated—strangers embracing, chants rising and falling, the particular delirium that came from watching something impossible happen in real time.

I reached the concourse level, and it was somehow even more chaotic. People streamed toward the exits, toward the ice level, toward anywhere they could get a better view of the ongoing celebration. Security guards tried to maintain some semblance of order, but they were outnumbered and overwhelmed.

The tunnel entrance to ice level was blocked by a wall of people and a line of security personnel. I pushed toward it anyway, desperation making me bold.

"I need to get through," I said to the guard blocking the entrance. "Please—I need to get to the ice."

"Sorry, sir. Players and staff only."

"But I—" I didn't know how to explain. I wasn't a player. I wasn't staff. I was just someone who needed to be down there, needed to reach the person who had changed everything.

"Hey." A voice from behind me. I turned to find a woman with a press badge, her camera slung around her neck. "You're the actor, right? The boyfriend?"

I hesitated. The exposure that came with being recognized, the scrutiny that followed—it was everything I'd watched Rowan struggle with. But right now, it might be the only way through.

"Yeah," I said. "That's me."

The woman turned to the security guard. "He's with the story. The Chase St. Clair story. You should let him through."

The guard was uncertain, but the chaos was intensifying around us, and he had bigger problems than one boyfriend trying to reach the ice. He sighed and stepped aside.

I was through the barrier before he could change his mind, jogging down the tunnel toward the ice. The noise grew louder with every step—the cheers of the crowd, the shouts of the players, the constant blare of the goal horn that someone had forgotten to turn off.

The ice was a sea of orange and navy.

Players were everywhere—hugging, crying, lying on the ice in exhausted celebration. Coaches and staff had flooded onto the surface, joining the chaos. The championship trophy gleamed under the lights, being passed from hand to hand, everyone wanting to touch it, to hold proof that this had happened.

I scanned the crowd, searching for number 28. For the dark hair and gray eyes and crooked smile I'd spent months studying, cataloging, falling in love with.

Where is he?

There—by the far boards, surrounded by teammates. Davies had an arm around his shoulders, shouting something I couldn't hear. Maddox was nearby, his usual stern expression replaced by something that was almost affection. Sterling stood at the edge of the group, watching with that granite face that somehow conveyed more pride than a smile ever could.

Rowan found me.

Across the ice, through the chaos of bodies and noise and celebration, his eyes found mine.

He broke away from Davies, from Maddox, from the cluster of teammates still celebrating around him. He skated toward the boards where I was standing—not fast, not desperate, just steady. Certain. Like he'd been skating toward this moment his whole life.

I met him in the player's bench.

Up close, I could tell he was exhausted. His face was flushed, his jersey dark with sweat, his hair a disaster. There was a bruise forming on his cheekbone from some hit I must have missed, and he was clearly favoring his left side where the second period impact still lingered.

He'd never looked more beautiful.

"Hey," I said. My voice came out rough, wrecked from screaming. "Nice goal."

Rowan laughed—that surprised, genuine sound I'd learned to coax out of him. "Thanks. I had good motivation."

"The championship trophy?"

"You." He reached over the boards, his gloved hand finding my face, cupping my cheek with a gentleness that contrasted with the chaos around us. "Watching."

"I'm always watching."

"I know." His thumb traced my cheekbone. "I'm finally okay with that."

And then he kissed me.

Not a hidden kiss. Not a stolen moment in a dark corner or an empty loft. This was center ice of a championship arena—the Golden Bay Arena, home of the Tremors, where the professional hockey world had gathered to watch a college championship game. Surrounded by thousands of people and dozens of cameras and his entire team, we kissed.

The kiss was everything. I gripped the boards with one hand and reached for him with the other, pulling him closer, not caring who saw, not caring about anything except this moment and this person and this impossible, perfect ending to a story I'd never expected to write.

When we broke apart, the arena had gone quiet.

Not silent—there was still noise, still celebration happening somewhere—but the people nearby stopped to watch. A handful of cameras were pointed at us. Phones were recording. I glanced up to see our kiss captured on the Jumbotron. They were already showing a replay of the kiss, and I could see our faces on the screen, could see the moment captured and broadcast for everyone to witness.

"Well, that just happened," I joked jutting my chin toward the Jumbotron.

"Not the first kiss of mine to be caught on camera," Ro said. "At least this time, I picked the time, the place, and the right guy."

"I love you," I said, refusing to let go of his neck.

"I love you more," Ro responded.

We kissed again.

"Well," he said. "I guess we're doing this."

"I guess we are."

"Any regrets?"

He was sweaty, exhausted, bruised, and beautiful. The ghost I'd hunted who had become the person I loved. The subject of my research who had become my partner, my equal, my home.

"Not a single one."

The moment broke when Davies appeared at Rowan's side, moving slower than usual, a trainer hovering nearby.

"We did it," Davies said, his voice rough, his eyes still slightly unfocused from the hit. But he was grinning—that huge, infectious grin. "We actually did it."

Rowan pulled him into a careful hug, mindful of the concussion. "Couldn't have done it without you. That hit you took—"

"Was worth it." Davies looked past Rowan, spotted me still standing at the boards. "Caramel guy! What are you doing over there? Get on the ice!"

"I can't just—"

But Rowan grabbed me under the arms, and before I could protest, he'd lifted me clean over the barrier and onto the ice.

I stumbled on the slick surface—I was wearing sneakers, not skates—but Rowan caught me, steadied me, pulled me close.

"You're insane," I said.

"You're on the ice with me," he countered. "Where you belong."

Around us, the celebration was expanding. The arena staff had opened the gates, and now family and friends were streaming onto the ice—parents in orange and navy scarves, siblings with phone cameras out, girlfriends and boyfriends picking their way across the frozen surface. Maddox's parents reached him first, his mother crying. Lindros was surrounded by what I assumed were three generations of family, all of them tall and blond and beaming.

Davies's mom appeared, rushing toward her son with the particular terror of a parent who'd watched her child take a devastating hit on national television. Davies let her fuss over him, let her touch his face and demand to know if he was okay, while the trainer explained the concussion protocol.

Then I heard it—a familiar voice cutting through the chaos.

"Robert, slow down, you're going to—"

A yelp. A thud. Laughter.

I turned to see Robert Calloway—Ro's father—flat on his back on the ice, his wife Susan clutching his arm and trying not to go down with him. They looked out of their element, two people who, despite their son's years playing hockey, had probably never set foot on a hockey rink in their lives. They attempted to navigate a championship celebration in dress shoes.

"Dad!" Ro skated toward them, catching his mother's elbow just as she started to slip. "What are you—I thought you were watching from the stands!"

"And miss this?" Susan's face was streaked with tears, her mascara running, and she didn't seem to care at all. "After everything we just watched? Not a chance."

Robert was back on his feet now, holding onto Ro's arm like a lifeline, his dignity bruised but his smile genuine. He looked at his son—really took him in—and something passed between them that I couldn't quite read.

"That was . . . " Robert shook his head. "I don't understand half of what just happened out here. The penalties, the overtime, the—" He gestured vaguely at the ice. "Any of it."

"That's okay, Dad."

"But I understand that." Robert pointed at the championship trophy, still being passed among the players. "And I understand that smile on your face. Haven't seen that smile in years." His voice caught. "It's good to see you happy again, son."

Ro pulled his father into a hug—careful, brief, but real. When they separated, Robert turned to me.

"Elliot." He extended his hand, his footing precarious but his grip firm when I took it. "I meant what I said. I don't understand any of this—the hockey, acting, how any of it works. But I can see what you mean to my son." He held my gaze. "Thank you for that."

Before I could respond, Susan had pulled me into a hug so tight I could barely breathe. She was crying openly now. Laughing and crying the way mothers do when their hearts are too full for just one emotion.

"Oh, Elliot." She pulled back just enough to cup my face in her hands. "I'm so glad we got to sit together tonight. Getting to know you during the game—watching you watch him—" She dissolved into fresh tears. "I'm just so proud. Of both of you. Of everything."

"Mom," Ro said, his voice thick. "You're going to make him cry too."

"Good!" Susan pulled Ro into the hug, so now she was holding both of us, all three of us slipping slightly on the ice but refusing to let go. "You boys deserve happy tears."

Robert stood to the side, fondly uncomfortable with all the emotion, occasionally grabbing Ro's shoulder for balance. But he was smiling. Really, genuinely smiling.

More teammates gathered around—Hedman clapping Ro on the back, Chen grinning and giving me a thumbs up, Volkov wrapping everyone within reach into a massive bear hug that somehow included both of Rowan's parents.

"Championship!" Volkov bellowed, his Russian accent thick with joy. "We are champions!"

Sterling appeared at the edge of the group, his granite face showing the closest thing to a smile I'd ever seen on him. He nodded at Ro, then took in the swarm of family surrounding them—parents who had no business being on the ice, a boyfriend in sneakers, a whole messy beautiful support system.

"Calloway," Sterling said. "You going to lift that trophy or just stand there hugging people?"

Ro laughed—actually laughed, bright and unguarded. "Yes, sir."

He skated toward center ice, and we followed—me shuffling carefully, his parents clinging to each other and occasionally grabbing passing players for support. The trophy gleamed under the lights. When it reached Ro's hands, he lifted it over his head, and the arena erupted one more time.

"And your MVP of the game, ROWAN CALLOWAY!" the announcer's voice boomed.

Confetti fell like snow. The faultline lights pulsed in celebration. Photographers captured the moment from every angle.

Susan was crying again. Robert had given up on dignity entirely and was cheering like he'd been a hockey fan his whole life. And I stood there on the ice in my useless sneakers, watching the person I loved hold a championship trophy over his head, surrounded by family and teammates and everything he'd spent five years convinced he didn't deserve.

Rowan passed the trophy to Maddox, then skated back to me. His face was flushed, exhausted, radiant with joy.

"Thank you," he said, low enough that only I could hear.

"For what?"

"For chasing me. For seeing me. For not giving up when I tried to disappear." He glanced at his parents, still wobbling on the ice nearby, still beaming. "For sitting with them tonight. For helping them understand."

I brought his hand to my lips, pressed a kiss to his knuckles. "Thank you for letting me catch you."

Chapter 40
The Morning After

Elliot

I woke up to sunlight and warmth as I snuggled against Rowan in the hotel bed. For a moment, I didn't move. I just lay there, feeling Rowan's back pressed against my chest, his breathing slow and steady in sleep. My arm was draped across his waist, and at some point during the night, our fingers intertwined. The morning light filtered through the tall windows of my loft, painting pale rectangles across the tangled sheets.

Last night felt like a dream.

The goal. The celebration. The kiss on the Jumbotron that probably made the front page of every sports blog in the country. The party afterward, surrounded by teammates and noise and the particular chaos of victory. Then slipping away to my hotel room. We'd known neither of us would be able to drive after the party, so getting a room had just made the most sense.

Rowan stirred slightly, his fingers tightening around mine.

"You're thinking too loud," he mumbled, voice rough with sleep.

"Sorry. I'll try to think more quietly."

He rolled over to face me, and even sleep-rumpled and exhausted, he's beautiful. The bruise on his cheekbone had darkened overnight, and there were shadows under his eyes from everything the championship took out of him. But he smiled—that crooked smile that still makes my chest tight every time I see it.

"Hi," he said.

"Hi yourself."

"How are the ribs?" I asked, reaching out to trace gentle fingers along his side.

"Sore. Worth it." He caught my hand, pressed a kiss to my knuckles. "How are you?"

"Still processing." I shook my head. "Yesterday was . . . a lot."

"Yeah." His expression shifted—something more serious surfacing beneath the morning softness. "It's going to be more, isn't it? Today. Tomorrow. The whole thing."

As if summoned by his words, a phone buzzes somewhere in the room. Then another. Then a third, different tone—mine, probably, wherever I dropped it last night.

The outside world demanded to be let in.

Rowan closed his eyes. "I don't want to look at that yet."

"We don't have to."

"Yeah, we do." He sighed, but didn't move. "Just . . . five more minutes. Five more minutes of this before we have to deal with all of that."

I pulled him closer, tucking his head under my chin, breathing in the smell of him—sweat and sleep and something underneath that's just Rowan. Five more minutes of quiet. Five more minutes of pretending the world outside this room doesn't exist.

The phones kept buzzing.

Five minutes became ten, then fifteen. But eventually, reality couldn't be ignored any longer.

Rowan sat up in bed, running a hand through his disheveled hair, and reached for his phone on the nightstand. I watched his face as he read the screen—watch the peace of the morning dissolve into something more complicated.

"How bad?" I asked.

"Depends on your definition of bad." He scrolled through what must be dozens of notifications. "Seventeen voicemails. Forty-three texts. Email inbox is . . . I'm not even going to count." He paused on something. "Oh. And Anders apparently got a new phone since I'd previously blocked him."

The name landed like a cold stone in the warmth of the morning.

"What do you want to do about him?"

"Nothing. Not today." Rowan set the phone down, faceup on the sheets. I can see the notifications still cascading across the screen. "He doesn't get to be part of this. Not anymore."

I reached for my own phone, finding it half-buried in my discarded jeans. The screen is similarly overwhelmed—texts from castmates, emails from people I don't recognize, social media notifications I'm afraid to open.

"The video of the kiss is everywhere," I said, scrolling through the previews without actually opening anything. "Someone already made a compilation set to music."

"What song?"

"I'm not going to tell you."

"That bad?"

"Let's just say it's very . . . sincere."

Ro laughed—a real laugh, surprised and genuine. "Great. That's exactly what I needed. A sincere musical tribute to my love life going viral."

But the laughter faded quickly, replaced by something more serious. He was looking at his phone again, at the wall of messages demanding his attention.

"The championship is going to be overshadowed by this, isn't it?" he said quietly. "The team won, and everyone's going to be talking about the Ice Prince kissing a guy on the Jumbotron."

"Is that what you're worried about? The team?"

"Partly." He picked up the phone, then put it down again. "They worked so hard. They deserve to be the story. And instead, it's going to be all about me, and you, and the whole circus that follows me."

I sat up, positioning myself so I can see into his eyes. "Rowan. The team just won their first championship in fifteen years. That's going to be the story. Everything else is . . . noise. Footnotes."

"You don't know that."

"No. But I know Davies spent last night telling anyone who would listen about the game-winning goal, not about who you kissed afterward. The team cares about the championship. The media might care about the rest, but the team knows what matters."

Ro's quiet for a moment, processing. "There's going to be interviews. Requests for statements. People wanting to know about . . . us. About everything."

"I know."

"I don't know how to do this, Elliot." He looked at me, and there was something vulnerable in his expression that cut through the morning softness. "I don't know how to give them enough without giving them everything."

"We'll figure it out," I said. "Together."

The word hangs between us. Together. It's what we said last night, on the ice, in front of everyone. But saying it in the chaos of victory differs from saying it in the quiet of morning, when the reality of what comes next is finally sinking in.

"Elliot." Rowan set down his phone and turned to face me fully. "I need to ask you something, and I need you to answer honestly."

"Okay."

"Do you want to be part of this? The media stuff, the attention, the whole . . . spectacle?" He gestured vaguely at the phones still buzzing around us. "Because I know what I'm asking. I've lived this before, and it's not easy. It's invasive and exhausting, and sometimes it feels like you're losing pieces of yourself to people who don't care about you; they just want content."

"I know what you're asking."

"And I need you to know that if you want to step back—if you want to keep our relationship private, or quiet, or whatever—I understand. I won't be hurt. I won't be angry." He took a breath. "I just need to know now, before we make any decisions about how to handle this."

I study him—really take him in, with the same obsessive lens I've used to track him for months. The person I observed from Section 112, who became the person I researched in my archive, who became the person I fell in love with somewhere along the way.

"You're offering me an out," I said.

"I'm offering you a choice."

"Then, here's my choice." I reached for his hand, intertwining our fingers the way they were when we woke up. "I'm not stepping back. I'm not hiding. I'm not going anywhere."

"Elliot—"

"You're part of my story," I said, squeezing his hand. "So, whatever comes next, we face it together. Unless you're the one who wants to step back?"

"No." The word comes immediately, certain. "I want you with me. I just needed to make sure you wanted to be there."

"I want to be here."

Something shifted in his expression—relief, maybe, or hope. He leaned forward and kissed me, soft and sweet and unhurried, a kiss that has nothing to prove and nowhere to go except exactly where we are.

"Okay," Rowan said. "So. How do we do this?"

We spend the next two hours in a hotel bed with our phones and my laptop, mapping out a strategy.

It's strangely familiar—reminiscent of the nights we spent at my desk, correcting the archive, building a true story out of speculation and research. Except now we're not just documenting the past. We're planning our future.

"First things first," I said, pulling up a document on my laptop. "We need to decide what we're willing to share and what's off-limits."

"Everything about Henderson is off-limits." Rowan's voice was firm. "That's not a story I'm ready to tell publicly. Maybe not ever."

"Understood. What about Anders?"

He hesitated. "I don't want to give him attention. But I also don't want him to be the one controlling the narrative if it comes out."

"So, we acknowledge the past relationship if directly asked, but we don't volunteer details."

"That works."

We continued like this, category by category. His acting career—he's willing to acknowledge it, even talk about leaving, but not in detail. The reasons for his disappearance—"personal reasons" remains the official line. Our relationship—we're together, we're happy, and everything else is private.

"What about the kiss?" I asked. "It's going to be the headline."

Ro winced. "I know. I thought about that last night, after. Whether I should have waited, done it somewhere more private."

"Do you regret it?"

"No." He said it without hesitation. "If people want to make a story out of me kissing my boyfriend in public, that's their problem, not mine."

Boyfriend. The word sent a small thrill through me. We hadn't used that word before—hadn't named what we are in such concrete terms.

"So, we acknowledge the relationship," I said, trying to keep my voice steady despite the flutter in my chest. "But we don't make it the focus. The focus is the championship, the team, your return to hockey."

"And your play?"

I hadn't thought about that. "What about it?"

"People are going to connect the dots. Someone's going to figure out that you based your character study on me."

He's right. The connection is obvious, especially now. "We can acknowledge the inspiration," I said slowly, thinking it through. "Without giving a blowby-blow of how I researched you. That stays between us."

"Agreed," he said with a chuckle.

By eleven, we were getting ready to check out of the hotel and had a rough plan. A unified message. A set of boundaries we're both comfortable with.

"This feels weird," Ro said, staring at the document on my laptop. "Planning how to be authentic. Isn't that a contradiction?"

"It's protection," I said. "There's a difference between being authentic and being available. You can be real without being exposed. You can share truth without giving away everything."

He considered this. "Where did you learn that?"

"From watching you." I closed the laptop. "You've been navigating this your whole life—managing what people see, protecting the parts of yourself that matter. The difference now is that you're doing it on your own terms. You're choosing what to share instead of having it taken from you."

Rowan was quiet for a moment. Then he reached out, taking my hand.

"I couldn't do this without you," he said. "I want you to know that. This morning, this planning, all of it—I couldn't face it alone."

"You're not alone."

"I know." He smiled—that crooked smile that started everything. "That's new for me. I'm still getting used to it."

We checked out of the hotel by noon and made our way north to Oakridge Falls. We made my apartment our war room to handle the onslaught of media requests and other messages. By midafternoon, we'd responded to the most urgent messages. A brief statement to the media requests: Rowan Calloway is grateful for the support and focused on celebrating the championship with his teammates. He will not be giving interviews at this time. A text to Davies confirming dinner plans with the team tonight. A voicemail to Sterling assuring him that Rowan's fine and will be at the trophy ceremony tomorrow.

The Anders calls go unanswered. That's a problem for another day.

We're sitting on the hotel bed, phones finally silent, the chaos temporarily contained. The afternoon light has shifted, painting new rectangles across the floor, marking the passage of time we've spent building something together.

"So, what happens now?" Rowan asked.

"Now?" I looked at him—the bruise on his cheek, the exhaustion still visible around his eyes, the peace underneath it all that I've only just started seeing. "Now, we take it one day at a time. Handle what comes as it comes. Figure out the next thing when we get to it."

"That's very Zen of you."

"I'm growing as a person."

Ro laughed. "Clearly." Then, more seriously: "Thank you. For all of this. For being willing to face it with me."

"Thank you for letting me."

We sat in comfortable silence for a moment. Outside the windows, the world continued—traffic sounds, distant voices, the ongoing hum of life that doesn't care about viral videos or championship trophies or the complicated intersection of public and private that we're trying to navigate.

But in here, in this room, there's just us. I leaned into Rowan, feeling his arm come around my shoulders, pulling me close.

"Ready for tonight?" I asked. "Dinner with the team?"

"Ready as I'll ever be." He pressed a kiss to the top of my head. "You?"

"I'm ready."

Chapter 41
The Decision

Rowan

It'd been a week since the championship. The press insanity had died down, somewhat. After a really long conversation with Elliot, I decided the best thing to do was face Anders head on since he wouldn't leave me alone.

Anders had chosen a restaurant in Fort Dick—neutral territory, about twenty minutes from campus. The restaurant was a nice steakhouse, but not the upscale places Anders was used to dining. When I walked in, he was already seated at a corner table. His appearance hadn't changed in five years. Expensive clothes, practiced ease, the particular confidence of someone who'd never doubted himself.

He stood when he saw me, and for a moment, we just stared at each other. Five years of silence. Five years of running. And here we are, face-to-face in a restaurant with a cartoon cow for a mascot.

"Ro." His voice was warm, familiar in a way that makes something in my chest tighten. "Thank you for coming." He leaned toward me like he was going to come in for a hug, but extended his hand instead.

"I almost didn't," I said, sitting down at the table, keeping my body language neutral.

"I know." He sat back down on his side. "But you did. That means something."

This isn't a confrontation. It's a conversation I need to have—not because Anders deserves my time, but because I need to hear what he has to say. Need to understand what I'd choose when I walk away.

Because I was walking away. I've known that since before I agreed to meet him.

But I wanted to make the choice from clarity, not fear.

The waiter appeared, took our drink orders, and disappeared. Anders watched me across the table with those ice-blue eyes that used to make me feel seen and now just made me feel studied.

"You look good," he said. "Different. More . . . settled."

"I am different."

"I saw the championship game. The overtime goal." He shook his head slightly. "That was elite hockey, Ro. NHL-caliber. You've still got it."

"I never lost it."

"No. You just hid it." He leaned back in his chair. "For five years. While scouts were asking what happened to the Ice Prince, while opportunities passed you by, you hid in the middle of nowhere. Then magically resurfaced playing DIII hockey under a fake name."

"It's my legal name."

"It's a disguise." There was no judgment in his voice. "But I understand why you did it. I understand better than anyone."

I didn't respond because I wasn't there to debate Anders Holmström. I was there to listen to whatever offer he was about to make, then make my own decision.

Anders read my silence correctly. He reached into the leather messenger bag beside him and pulled out a folder—thick, professional. I could already tell it held some kind of contract prepared by a team of people who got paid too much.

"The Blue Line," he said, sliding the folder across the table. "Canadian production. Biggest hockey movie since Miracle. They've been developing it for three years, and they've been looking for a lead the entire time."

I didn't touch the folder. "And they want me."

"They want Chase St. Clair. The comeback story." Anders's voice took on the particular intensity I remembered from when he was selling something. "Think about it, Ro. You disappeared at the height of your career. Everyone wondered what happened. And now, five years later, you resurface—not just as an actor, but as a championship-winning hockey player—even if it was just DIII. The narrative writes itself."

"The narrative you want to write."

"The narrative the world wants to hear." He tapped the folder. "Inside you'll find the offer. Lead role. Creative consultation on the hockey sequences. Seven figures, plus backend points. And a publicity team—of your choosing—that will make sure the story is told your way."

I picked up the folder, more to have something to do with my hands than because I cared about the contents. The pages inside were dense with legal language and financial projections. It was a serious offer. A lifechanging amount of money.

"What's the catch?" I asked.

"No catch."

"Anders. There's always a catch with you."

He was quiet for a moment. Then: "The catch is that it goes through me. I'm attached as a producer. The studio wanted someone who knows you, who can vouch for your . . . stability."

"My stability."

"You disappeared for five years, Ro. You understand why they'd want reassurance."

I set down the folder. "So, the deal is . . . I come back to acting, and you get to be part of my career again. Part of my life."

"Would that be so terrible?" His voice softened, became something almost vulnerable. "I know I made mistakes. The photo—what happened with the photo—I've never forgiven myself for that. But I was young, too. We were both young. And I've spent five years thinking about what I could have done differently."

"Have you?"

"I have." He met my eyes. "I'm not asking for anything personal; not even your forgiveness. I'm just saying that this opportunity is real, and it's yours if you want it. Whatever happened between us doesn't have to define what comes next."

The conversation continued through lunch—Anders painting pictures of premieres and press tours and the kind of visibility I had spent five years avoiding. He was good at this, I remembered. He was always good at making his ideas sound like your ideas, his plans sound like your dreams.

But something had changed in me. The words washed over me without the old pull, the old fear. I could see what he was offering now—the money, yes, but also the strings attached.

"Think about it," Anders said as we finished. "You don't have to decide today. Take the folder, read through everything, let me know when you're ready to talk next steps."

"I don't need to think about it."

Something flickered across his face—surprise, maybe, or the beginning of disappointment. "Ro—"

"I'm not interested, Anders. Not in the movie, not in the comeback narrative, not in any of it."

"You haven't even read the offer."

"I don't need to read it," I said, pushing the folder back across the table. "I know what it would cost me. And I'm not willing to pay that price."

After lunch, I couldn't leave Fort Dick fast enough. Anders had tried pitching me in several ways, but he never resorted to threats. When it was over, I thanked him for lunch and drove home.

I found Elliot in his apartment, sitting at his desk, surrounded by the familiar chaos of his creative process. He glanced up when I entered, and his face did that thing it did when he saw me—softening, brightening, becoming more alive.

"Hey. How was Fort Dick?"

"Informative." I crossed the room and dropped onto the edge of his bed. "Anders made his pitch."

Elliot set down his pen, giving me his full attention. "And?"

"I turned him down."

"Okay."

"I'm building something here. I don't want to run away from this just because Hollywood and professional hockey comes calling. Need to get my head on straight first."

"What is keeping you here, besides me of course?"

"This." I gestured vaguely at the room, at him, at everything. "Oakridge. Journalism. The life I've been building instead of the one I ran away from." I paused. "There's a summer internship. NPR's sports desk. Professor Grahams thinks I should apply."

"That's amazing, Ro."

"It's in Sacramento"

The words landed between us, carrying the weight of distance.

"I know," Elliot said quietly. "I Googled it after Grahams mentioned it was a possibility."

"You knew?"

"She asked me for a perspective on your work." He smiled. "I told her you were the most serious person I'd ever met."

I laughed—I couldn't help it.

"So," Elliot said, moving to sit beside me on the bed. "Sacramento for the summer. That's three months apart."

"Yeah."

"Then what?"

"I don't know." I took his hand, intertwining our fingers. "But whatever comes next . . . we'll face it head on . . . together. If you want to."

"Of course, I want to. Stop asking that."

Elliot leaned in and kissed me—soft, certain, a promise without words.

"I spent months watching you from Section 112," he said when we broke apart. "Trying to understand the architecture of your hiding." He touched my face. "You think a little distance is going to scare me away?"

"I just wanted to be sure."

"I'm sure." He pulled me closer. "I'm staying, Ro. As long as you want me to stay."

"I'm staying too." The words felt important. "I'm done running. I'm done hiding. I'm choosing this life. This future. You."

Chapter 42
The Curtain Call

Elliot

After six weeks, we were finally getting ready to put the show to rest. We'd had an amazing run and even extended two weeks because we kept selling out.

I sat in front of the mirror, applying the last touches of stage makeup, watching my reflection transform into Diego Santos one final time. After tonight, the character would belong to the audience—to their memories of the performance and their interpretations of the story. But right now, in this moment before the curtain rose, Diego still belonged to me.

"Five minutes to places!"

The call echoed through the green room, triggering the familiar cascade of lastminute preparations. I was nervous, but it was a different kind of nervous than opening night. That was terror—fear of failure, fear of being seen. This was something closer to grief. The particular sadness of an ending, even a good one.

My phone buzzed on the makeup table. I glanced at the screen.

Rowan: Front row. Center. Where I belong.

I smiled at the screen. He was here. Visible. Not hiding in the back row under a hoodie, but sitting in the front where everyone could see him.

Me: Don't distract me with your face.

Rowan: My face is very distracting. You should have thought of that before you started dating it.

I was smiling at my phone like an idiot when Professor Albright appeared at the door.

"Personal business can wait, Elliot. You have a show to do."

"Yes, sir."

He studied me for a moment—that sharp, assessing look that missed nothing. "How are we feeling?"

"Ready," I said, setting down the phone. "Sad that it's ending, but ready."

"Good. Sadness is useful. Channel it." He paused. "I hear your hockey player is in the audience."

"He is. Front row."

Something that might have been approval crossed his face. "Good. Use that too. The best performances happen when we have something real to play for."

The house lights dimmed, and the Black Box went dark. I stood in the wings, breathing deep, finding the stillness I needed. The stage lights came up, and I stepped into the light.

The performance flowed like water. Every beat landed exactly where it should. And throughout it all, I was aware of Rowan in the front row. His presence was a grounding force. Every time Lucas, as Tyler, spoke about the weight of the mask, I drew from the reality of the man sitting just feet away. I wasn't just playing Diego anymore; I was living the version of the story we had rewritten together in my loft.

The play built toward its climax—the final scene on the ice. The arena was gone, the crowds were gone, and it was just the two of us under a single, unforgiving spotlight. I reached out, my fingers finding Lucas's hand in a grip that was deliberate and visible. I let the silence of the theater stretch, thick with the shared breath of the audience.

"We're going to be okay. Right?" I asked. My voice was steady, but I let the vulnerability of the question hang in the air.

Lucas stared at me, his eyes shining under the gels. "I don't know."

"That's not the answer I wanted."

"It's the honest one," he said, squeezing my hand. "But I know we're going to try. And that's something."

I stared into the darkness beyond the stage, where the world usually waited to judge, to archive, and to categorize. Then I looked back at him.

"Yeah," I said, the words feeling heavy and true. "It's something."

We stood there for a heartbeat, connected and brave. I could see Rowan in the front row, his silhouette leaning forward, his gaze locked on our joined hands.

"I love you," I whispered.

"I love you, too."

The spotlight faded slowly, shrinking until it was just a tiny pinprick of light on our clasped hands. The speakers crackled with the final sound effect—the sharp, clean scrape of a single pair of skates on fresh ice.

Blackout.

Curtain call was usually routine, but that night, the applause was sustained and enthusiastic. People were on their feet. When my turn came, I stepped forward alone.

In the front row, Rowan stood with everyone else applauding, but his eyes were locked on mine. There was pride in his expression. Joy. Love.

I didn't plan what happened next. I touched my hand to my chest, over my heart, and then extended it toward him. A small gesture. A dedication. This was for you. All of it.

Rowan's smile widened. He was moving. He left his seat and walked toward the stage, and I realized he was carrying something—a bouquet wrapped in cellophane. How that hadn't made noise throughout the show was beyond me.

The audience's murmur became delighted recognition. Rowan reached the edge of the stage and held up the flowers. I knelt down to take them—a ridiculous gesture, theatrical in a way that would have made Albright proud—and our fingers brushed as the bouquet passed from his hands to mine.

"Congratulations," he said, loud enough for the people nearby to hear.

"You brought me flowers."

"That's what you do at plays, right? I Googled it."

The audience was laughing now—warm, genuine laughter. I kissed him before standing up, flowers clutched to my chest, and the applause erupted again.

The lobby afterward was chaos. I found Rowan by the trophy case talking to Davies and Maddox.

"There he is," Davies said. "The man of the hour. Dude, that play was intense. The hockey stuff was right."

Maddox nodded. "Decent staging on the locker room scenes. The board work was accurate." Coming from Maddox, that was a rave review.

They disappeared into the crowd to head to the afterparty, leaving Rowan and me alone.

"You brought me flowers," I said again.

"I did." He reached out, adjusting a stem. "They're probably going to die in like three days. I don't really understand the point of flowers as gifts. Here's something beautiful that's going to slowly decay in front of you."

I laughed. "That's very romantic."

"I'm working on it."

But I knew why he had brought them. Rowan was showing up in my world the way I had showed up in his.

"Thank you." I placed one hand on the back of his head drawing him down for a brief kiss. "For the flowers. For being here. For all of it."

Later, after the afterparty, Rowan and I walked back to campus together. The flowers were wilting, but I still carried them.

"You know," I said, "in the theatre, closing night is sad because something is ending. But it's also beautiful. The story belongs only in people's memories." I gestured with the bouquet, "Like these flowers will be in a few days."

Rowan was quiet for a moment. "I brought you dying flowers as a metaphor?"

"You brought me dying flowers as a gesture of love. The metaphor is just a bonus."

He laughed—that surprised, genuine sound I never got tired of hearing. We reached my apartment.

"The set strike is tomorrow," I said climbing the stairs. "Taking everything down. It's usually kind of melancholy."

"Do you want company?"

"You want to help strike a theatre set?"

"I want to be where you are." He shrugged. "Besides, I spent five years building walls. It seems fitting to help take some down."

I pulled him closer, kissing him at the door's threshold. Then slipped the key from my pocket and opened the door. Ro swept me off my feet before I could enter. He carried me inside the apartment. It still amazed me how easily he could carry me.

"Put me down," I squealed. He did when he finally placed me gently down on the bed and looked down at me from above.

"Tomorrow, then," I said. "The end of one story and the beginning of another."

"I like the sound of that." He smiled—that crooked smile that had started everything. "Especially the beginning part."

Chapter 43
The off Season

Elliot

Spring arrived in Northern California like a welcomed apology for winter.

The redwoods that lined the campus paths were greening now, their branches swaying in warm breezes that smelled of damp earth and blooming jasmine—nothing like the sterile, frozen scent of the rink. Students sprawled on the quad in shorts and T-shirts, studying for finals, throwing frisbees, and soaking up sunlight like they'd been starving for it.

I walked through campus with my bag slung over one shoulder, heading to my final journalism exam. I didn't even know if I'd recognize the person I had been when I first arrived here. That Rowan—the one who kept his head down and his hood up, who scanned every room for exits, who flinched at the sound of his own name—felt like a character from someone else's story now. A ghost I had finally stopped running from.

The arena was quiet when I passed it. No practices, no games, no crowds. Just an empty building waiting for the next season to begin. I stopped for a moment at the side entrance where I had walked in for tryouts all those months ago, terrified of being recognized, terrified of being seen.

Back then, I had been a man hiding in plain sight. I had walked through those doors terrified of being recognized, clutching my anonymity like a shield. I thought of that first day, meeting a creepier version of Elliot in Section 112—the observer who had pulled me out of the shadows. By putting me under his crazy microscope, he'd taught me to live.

This was the place where I had found the joy of skating again, stripped of the Hollywood lights and the predatory expectations. More importantly, I had found a family. I looked at the concrete ramp leading to the locker rooms and thought of the guys—Maddox, Davies, and the rest—who had challenged me, fought me, and changed my life forever. They hadn't just given me a jersey; they'd given me a place to belong.

The end-of-year team meeting was held in the athletic center conference room—a space I'd never been inside. Usually, the room was reserved for administrative functions and donor presentations. Today, it was full of hockey players sprawled in chairs designed for people in suits, everyone fidgeting with the restlessness of athletes who'd already been off the ice for too long.

Sterling and Okafor stood at the front, their expressions as unreadable as ever. But there was something softer in Sterling's posture today. The season was over. The championship trophy was displayed in the arena lobby. He'd earned the right to relax, even if he didn't quite remember how to do it.

"I'm not going to give a long speech." His voice carried through the room without effort. "You've heard enough of my speeches to last a lifetime. But I want to acknowledge what this season meant. Not just the championship—though that matters—but the way this team came together. The way you learned to trust each other."

He looked around the room, making eye contact with each of us.

"Some of you will be moving on. Graduating, transferring, choosing different paths. For those of you coming back, the work starts now. We're not defending a title. We're building a new team, with new challenges." His eyes landed on me. "Calloway. Stand up."

I rose, feeling a familiar flicker of the old anxiety that came with being singled out, but it was muted now. Manageable.

"This program's MVP," Sterling said. "A walk-on who turned out to be something more. The championship goal speaks for itself, but what the stats don't show is the leadership. The way he pushed his teammates to be better. The example he set."

Davies whooped, and someone else started a rhythmic clapping. I felt the heat rising to my face.

"The All-Conference team selections come out next week," Sterling continued, waving for quiet. "I'm not supposed to say anything, but I think we can expect to see your name on the list."

More cheering erupted. I caught Maddox's eye; he nodded.

"Before we break," Sterling said, his voice dropping an octave. "Davies. You have something to show the class?"

Davies didn't just stand; he surged. He fumbled a heavy, professional-looking folder onto the table. "I signed it this morning," he said. "Entry-Level Contract. Three years with the San Francisco Tremors."

The room went from silent to explosive in a heartbeat. Maddox let out a roar, lunging across the table to pull Davies into a suffocating headlock. The guys swarmed him, a sea of hoodies and shouting.

I stayed back, leaning against the wall, a slow smile spreading across my face. I knew exactly what that paper said. I knew the fine print of a UFA deal—the $850k base, the two-way split for the AHL, and the specific "slide" provisions for a freshman.

Davies finally broke free from Maddox's grip, his face flushed and his eyes suspiciously bright. He stared at me across the crowd.

"I didn't think I'd get here," Davies said, directed at the room but meant for me. "Last summer, I was sitting in my bedroom in San Jose thinking I was done. No draft calls, no scouts, nothing. I thought walking on here was just . . . a way to delay the end."

He took a shaky breath, tapping the folder. "I wouldn't even have known who to call. But someone put me in touch with an agent who gives a damn. Someone who told me that being undrafted didn't mean I was invisible."

He gave me a sharp, private nod—the only "thank you" I needed. He was a College Free Agent now. He'd gone from a walk-on who felt like a failure to a pro-prospect because someone had whispered the right name into the right ear.

"Ospreys on three!" Maddox yelled, slamming his fist on the table.

"ONE, TWO, THREE—OSPREYS!"

The meeting broke up into clusters—players making summer plans, exchanging numbers, promising to stay in touch. I was surrounded for a few minutes, accepting congratulations and deflecting praise until Sterling appeared at my shoulder.

"Walk with me."

We left the conference room together, moving through the quiet hallways until we reached his office. He didn't invite me in—just leaned against the doorframe, arms crossed.

"You've got something," he said. "You've always had it. The question was whether you were going to use it or hide from it."

"I think I'm done hiding, Coach."

"I know you are." He studied me for a long moment. "The NHL scouts are going to come sniffing around next season. You're old for a prospect, but not too old. If you have another year like this one, there'll be opportunities."

I'd thought about this. Late at night, in the quiet moments, I'd let myself imagine what it would be like to play professional hockey again. Not as the "Ice Prince," but as myself.

"I'm not ruling anything out," I said carefully. "But I'm also not making decisions based on what might happen. I've got another year here. A degree to finish. A life to live."

Approval crossed Sterling's face. "Right answer."

"It's the only one I've got."

"That's why it's right. Enjoy your summer, Calloway. You've earned it."

Maddox caught me in the parking lot.

"Hey," he called out. I turned to see the captain standing by his truck, which was packed to the window line with cardboard boxes and a stray hockey stick. He held his keys with a tightness I'd never seen on the ice—the restless grip of someone realizing they were about to drive away from the last four years of their life.

"I wanted to say something," he said, his gaze dropping to the pavement. "I gave you a hard time this year. At the beginning, I thought you were hiding something, and I didn't trust you."

"You weren't wrong, Maddox. I was hiding plenty."

"Yeah, but . . . " He shook his head. "I remember your ragtag collection of hockey equipment and discounted you without thinking twice. Even after Coach listed you on the roster, my ego prevented me from seeing what Sterling did. As your captain, I should have given you a chance to prove yourself on the ice. That's what I'd want if I were in your position."

It wasn't quite a formal apology, but coming from Maddox, it was a monumental gesture.

"We're good," I said, reaching out. "You pushed me. I needed the push."

"You pushed back. I respected that." He gripped my hand, but he didn't let go immediately. He looked past me toward the rink, then back at me, his expression turning serious. "It's your barn now, Rowan. Take care of it."

The weight of the statement sat between us. "What's next for you?" I asked. "Besides the oil changes at your dad's place?"

Maddox let out a short, dry laugh. "Yeah, I'll be at the dealership a few days a week to keep the old man happy, but I just got hired as an assistant coach for a Junior-B team near LA. It's closer to home."

"Coach Maddox," I said, testing the title. "Has a ring to it."

"It's a start," he shrugged, though his chest expanded just a fraction. "I'm going to build some credibility, put in the hours, and hopefully work my way up to something fulltime in the AHL or the show one day. But for now? I'm the guy who picks up the pucks after practice."

"You'll be the head coach in three years," I predicted.

"Don't bet the house on it." Maddox finally let go of my hand and climbed into his truck. "Don't let the team get soft over the summer, Rowan. If I come back for alumni weekend and see you guys playing like a bunch of figure skaters, I'm making you do suicides until you puke."

"Drive safe, Coach."

I stood in the parking lot for a moment after his taillights faded, processing the strangeness of it. Four months ago, I didn't have teammates. I didn't have a barn to protect. I had a lockbox full of guilt and a ghost I couldn't stop running from. Now, I had been handed a legacy, and for the first time, I had more reasons to stay than I had ever had for running.

Back at my apartment, I sat at my desk with a pen and a piece of paper. The skateboard was in front of me—that jagged piece of red and gold I'd been carrying for five years.

Elliot's words from Portland echoed in my mind: The only one still trapped on that ice is you.

I picked up the pen and started to write.

I've been trying to figure out how to put into words what your family's hospitality meant to me. That dinner—the pot roast, Emily's wedding stories, your mom calling me "honey" like I'd always been welcome—I didn't know how much I needed that until it was happening.

You told me to stop being a ghost. I'm trying.

I played in a championship this year. Division III, nothing like what we dreamed about when we were kids in those hotel rooms talking about the NHL, but it was real. I scored the winning goal in overtime. And somewhere in the middle of it—maybe because of what you said, maybe because I finally let myself believe it—I stopped running.

I'm enclosing the skate shard. I've carried it for seven years, telling myself it was penance. But you showed me that holding onto guilt isn't the same as honoring what happened. You turned something painful into something that helps kids fall in love with the game. That's what matters. That's what I want to do.

When I finish school, I'd love to learn more about the work you're doing with the junior league. The equipment, the ice time, all of it. I don't know exactly what that looks like yet, but I know I want to be part of something that gives kids access to hockey who wouldn't have it otherwise. If you're willing to show me the ropes, I'm willing to learn.

Thank you for dinner. Thank you for the truth. Thank you for being happy—genuinely happy—when I spent seven years convinced I'd destroyed your life.

Tell Emily congratulations. Elliot and I are still planning on being at the wedding. Thanks for the invitation.

Your friend,

Rowan

P.S. — Put the shard with your trophies. Or throw it in a river. Either way, it's yours now.

I folded the letter around the shard and sealed it in an envelope. This time, there was no money inside. Just a piece of the past, finally being returned to where it belonged.

On the last day of the semester, Elliot found me on the quad. He dropped onto the grass beside me, close enough that our shoulders touched. The campus was emptying out—cars packed with dorm gear, students hugging goodbye, the bittersweetness of an ending.

"So," he said. "Summer."

"Summer."

"I've been thinking about Sacramento." He pulled up a blade of grass, twisting it between his fingers. "If you get that internship, I could come down for a few weeks. See the sights. Watch you be a journalist."

"I'd like that," I said, and I meant it. "And if I don't get the internship?"

"Then we figure out something else." He reached for my hand, intertwining our fingers. "That's how this works, right? We figure it out together."

"That's how it works."

We sat there as the afternoon light slanted golden across the quad.

"You know what's strange?" I asked after a while. "I'm looking forward to things. Not just surviving them or getting through them. Actually looking forward."

Elliot squeezed my hand and leaned his head against my shoulder. "That's not strange, Ro. That's finally living."

Chapter 44
The Next Chapter

Elliot

The corkboard was empty.

I stood in front of it, holding the last photograph—a candid shot I'd taken during the university's trophy ceremony. It was a bizarre, beautiful collision of worlds. In the picture, the team was on the ice, but the jerseys had been replaced by sharp suits. Rowan stood at center ice, the blades of his skates biting into the surface, his formal trousers barely pulled over the laces. Hockey skates were not intended for formal wear.

The college president was shaking his hand, but Rowan's focus was elsewhere. He was hoisting the heavy silver trophy high above his head, his head tilted back, a genuine, unburdened laugh caught in the frame. His face wasn't hidden by a helmet cage or a hoodie anymore. The stadium lights hit him, illuminating the man who had stepped out of the shadows.

I looked at the bare corkboard one last time. For months, it had been a map of my obsession—a constellation of red ink, stolen moments, and clinical observations. I had spent so much time trying to decode the "Ice Prince" that I'd nearly missed the person right in front of me.

I didn't pin the photo back up. I didn't need to study it to remember how he looked in that moment.

I wrote three words across the back: Found. Seen. Ours.

I set the photograph in the box with the rest of them—all the articles, the forum printouts, the timeline cards, the notes in my handwriting and the corrections in his. The archive that started as research, became obsession, transformed into understanding, and finally served its purpose.

I grabbed my keys and headed for the door, leaving the almost empty room behind. I'd be back the next morning with a couple of Ro's teammates to finish moving my stuff to our apartment. For now, I needed to get this wrapped up and head to my coffee shop job.

For years, Rowan's face had watched over me from above my teenage bed. Now, I got the real thing. No reason to kiss my hand pretending it was Chase St. Clair when I had the real Rowan Calloway sleeping in my bed.

Rowan's apartment—our apartment now, I had to keep reminding myself—was waiting across town. Bigger, nicer, and increasingly full of my books and scripts and the accumulated chaos of a theatre kid who'd never learned to travel light. We'd been talking about it for a month, the practicality of paying two rents when we spent every night together. When Rowan got the call from San Francisco, the decision made itself.

I taped the box shut and added it to the stack by the door. Three years of my life in the loft, reduced to cardboard and packing tape. It should have felt sad. Instead, it felt like the start of something.

My phone buzzed.

Rowan: Made it to SF. The apartment they set me up with is tiny but clean. Miss you already.

I smiled at the screen.

Me: Miss you too. I'm surrounded by boxes and questioning all my life choices.

Rowan: How many boxes of books?

Me: . . . Seven.

Rowan: Elliot.

Me: Some of them are scripts! That's different.

Rowan: It's really not.

I pocketed the phone and looked around the loft one more time. The tall windows, the reclaimed wood desk, the bed where we'd spent so many nights tangled together. Good memories lived in these walls. But better ones were waiting somewhere else.

I grabbed my jacket and headed out to make another trip across town.

Rowan's apartment—our apartment—was slowly looked like two people lived there instead of one.

His minimalist aesthetic had been invaded by my maximalist tendencies: throw pillows on the couch, art prints leaning against walls waiting to be hung, a truly unreasonable number of coffee mugs taking over the kitchen cabinets. The bookshelf that used to hold his sparse collection of hockey biographies now sagged under the weight of my plays and novels and critical theory texts.

"It looks like a library exploded in here," Davies had said when he stopped by to help me move boxes. "Calloway's going to have a stroke."

"Ro already approved the book situation," I'd replied. "He said, and I quote, 'As long as I can still find my protein powder, you can have whatever you want.'"

"True love."

It was, actually. That was the thing I still couldn't quite believe, even after all this time.

The Tremors internship had come out of nowhere.

Rowan had been hoping for Sacramento, a more traditional journalism internship. When he hadn't gotten that one, he'd been disappointed but philosophical. "Something else will come up," he'd said, with the calm certainty of someone who'd learned to stop catastrophizing about the future.

Then Sofia Marquez called.

The Tremors' GM had watched Rowan score the championship-winning goal in her arena. She'd watched him kiss me at center ice. And apparently, she'd been thinking about him ever since.

"We need someone in our PR department who understands what it's like to be in the spotlight," she'd told him. "Someone who knows how the media machine works from the inside. Your background—the acting, the viral moments, the way you've handled your own story—that's exactly the perspective we're looking for. For now, it's a summer internship, but it will give you options in whatever you decide you want to do when you graduate."

It wasn't playing hockey. But it was being part of hockey, learning the business from the inside, building connections and skills that could lead anywhere. Rowan had accepted before he even hung up the phone.

"It's not what I pictured," he'd admitted to me that night, lying in bed with his head on my chest. "But maybe that's okay. Maybe what I pictured was always too small."

Now he was in San Francisco for the summer, learning the inner workings of a professional hockey organization, and I was here, surrounded by boxes, trying to figure out where to put my collection of vintage playbills.

My phone buzzed again.

Rowan: They asked me to help with the hockey camps.

Me: The kids' camps?

Rowan: Yeah. Apparently being a former child star who plays hockey is good marketing. Sofia wants me to do some demonstrations, maybe talk to the kids about balancing sports and other interests.

Me: Well, duh! Who wouldn't want to hire Chase St. Claire. That's amazing, Ro.

Rowan: I'm terrified. What if they ask about my movies?

Me: Then you tell them Ice Prince 2 was a cinematic masterpiece and anyone who disagrees is wrong.

Rowan: I hate you.

Me: You love me.

Rowan: Unfortunately true. Gotta go—team meeting. Talk tonight?

Me: Always.

I set the phone down and surveyed the chaos around me. Boxes everywhere, furniture half-arranged, my life in the process of merging with his. It should have been overwhelming. Instead, it felt exactly right.

Summer stretched ahead of us—him in San Francisco learning the business of hockey, me here finishing summer school credits and pulling espresso shots at the campus coffee shop. Not the most glamorous arrangement. But he'd come up on his days off, weekends when the Tremors didn't need him, and we'd have this apartment waiting. Our apartment. Our home.

I picked up another box and got back to work.

By evening, the apartment was starting to look habitable.

My books had found homes on the expanded shelving we'd installed last weekend. The art prints were hung—crooked, but hung. The kitchen was a reasonable compromise between his protein powder collection and my unreasonable mug habit.

I collapsed onto the couch with a beer and my script for the fall show.

Burning Daylight by Marcus Webb—a contemporary drama about a family unraveling after the death of the patriarch. I'd been cast as Daniel, the eldest son, a straightlaced accountant whose carefully constructed life falls apart over the course of the play.

"Playing a straight guy," I'd told Rowan when I got the callback, leaning against the doorframe of my loft. "A total stretch for my artistic abilities. I might need a dialect coach for 'bro.'"

Rowan had looked up from the hockey tape he was unraveling, a flicker of amusement in his eyes. "You've never even tried to fake it? Not even for a high school play?"

"Never," I said, popping a stray thread on my costume. "I've been the theatre department's resident queer since I was twelve. I skipped the 'straight-passing' phase entirely and went straight to 'theatrical lead.'"

"A rare luxury," he'd murmured, his voice softening.

"It wasn't a luxury, it was just the truth. I don't know how to do the mask thing, Rowan. I've spent my whole life being extra." I looked at him pointedly. "This role is the first time I've had to pretend I'm attracted to women. It feels like sci-fi."

"So, you're saying this is a genuine test of your craft?"

"Exactly. This isn't just a role. This is an exploration of a foreign culture."

"You're ridiculous."

"Maybe I should stalk Maddox. He seems straight."

"No," Ro said decisively. "No more stalking people to learn about them. If you want to know about someone's life, just ask them."

"So, what I hear you saying is, is that I should ask Maddox about what it's like to have sex with women?"

"That is so not what I said," he pinned me with a look.

"Fine."

I flipped through the script, mouthing Daniel's lines. The character was repressed, buttoned-up, the kind of man who expressed emotion through spreadsheets and scheduled phone calls. Nothing like me. Which was, of course, the point.

I smiled at the memory. That conversation had been a week ago, before Rowan had left for San Francisco. Now I was alone in our apartment, surrounded by his things and mine slowly merging together, rehearsing lines to an empty room.

"The numbers don't lie, Mom," I read aloud again, trying to find Daniel's voice. "Dad left us with nothing but debt and secrets. We can mourn him or we can survive him, but we can't do both."

My phone buzzed, interrupting my rehearsal. Not a text this time—a FaceTime request. Rowan's face filled the screen when I answered, slightly pixelated but unmistakably him. He was sitting on what looked like a tiny apartment couch, wearing a Tremors T-shirt I hadn't seen before.

"Hey, you," I said.

"Hey yourself." He shifted, and I caught a glimpse of a bare wall behind him. "How's the apartment?"

"Livable. I hung the art."

"Did you use a level?"

"I used my eyes. Same thing."

"It's really not." He was smiling though, that crooked smile that still made my chest do stupid things. "I'll fix it when I come up this weekend."

This weekend. Three days away. It felt like forever and no time at all.

"How was the team meeting?" I asked, settling deeper into the couch cushions.

Rowan's face lit up in a way I'd rarely seen before San Francisco. "Good. Really good, actually. They're planning the summer camp schedule—I'm going to help run drills for the twelve-and-under group. And I met Viktor Larsson today. The captain."

"Quake himself?"

"In the terrifying flesh. He's like Sterling but Swedish and bigger. I thought he was going to crush my hand when he shook it." Rowan held up his right hand, flexing it dramatically. "Are you ready for this, he asked me for an autograph. Can you even imagine? His kids are fans. He said they have Ice Prince 1, 2, and 3 on a loop in their house. I almost fell over."

"Did you give him the autograph?"

"Well, duh! One, he could break me. And two, when your boss wants your autograph, you give your boss an autograph. Then he asked about the championship game. Apparently, he watched the highlights. Said I had 'good instincts for pressure.'"

"That's high praise from a guy who could kill you with his bare hands."

"Right?" He was grinning now, fully animated. "And Logan Lieu was there—the fast winger. Super nice. He asked if I was nervous about the PR stuff. When I said yes, he said 'Good. Nervous people try harder.' Which I think was encouragement?"

"Hockey players are weird."

"The weirdest." He leaned back against his tiny couch, and even through the phone screen I could see something settle in him. Something peaceful. "I love it here, Elliot. I know it's not playing, but being around the team, learning how the organization works from the inside—it feels right. Like maybe this is what I'm supposed to do with my life."

"I'm proud of you," I said. "For taking the chance. For being there."

"I'm proud of you too. For staying. For slinging coffee for decaffeinated college students." His smile turned teasing. "For memorizing lines about spreadsheets."

"The spreadsheet monologue is actually really emotional."

"I believe you. Can't wait to see it."

"I can't wait to show you. As they say, accountants do it in the sheets. If you're lucky, maybe I'll let you see my pivot table."

Ro cocked his head to the side. Even across FaceTime, the eye roll was pronounced. "Really? Dirty Excel jokes?"

"Let's merge some cells!"

"Definitely not." We both started laughing.

We talked for another hour—about nothing and everything, the way we always did. His tiny apartment. My crooked art. The kids he'd be teaching at hockey camp. The dialect coach I definitely needed for saying "bro." By the time we said goodnight, my phone battery was at 9 percent and my face hurt from smiling.

"Three days," Rowan said.

"Three days."

"Love you."

"Love you too."

The screen went dark.

I plugged in my dying phone and looked around the apartment—Rowan's minimalist furniture slowly drowning under my chaos. Seven boxes of books. An unreasonable mug collection. Art prints hung at angles that would offend him when he got here Friday.

Three days. I could survive three days.

I picked up the script, but Daniel's daddy issues couldn't compete with the real-life drama of figuring out where to put my winter sweaters. Rowan had exactly three inches of closet space left, and I had approximately three closets worth of clothes still in garbage bags.

The red pen caught my eye—sitting on the coffee table where I'd tossed it during unpacking. The same pen we'd used to correct the archive.

I kept saying I was going to use it to write something new, but hadn't written a damn thing with it.

That seemed like a waste.

I grabbed my notebook, uncapped the pen, and stared at the blank page. Somewhere in San Francisco, Ro was probably organizing his sock drawer by color because that's the kind of psychopath I'd fallen in love with. And here I was, surrounded by boxes, about to do something deeply embarrassing.

Two people who learned to stop hiding, I wrote. Standing together in the light.

I looked at the words. Groaned.

"That's terrible," I said out loud to no one. "That's greeting card terrible."

But I didn't cross it out.

Instead, I turned to a fresh page and kept writing.

The Penalty Box

QR Code

Download the Full Play

The Penalty Box — the play that changes Elliot Vega's life — is a real, fully staged three-act drama. And it's yours, free.

The penalty for hiding is worse than getting caught.

Diego Santos and Tyler Mitchell are high school hockey teammates hiding a secret that could cost them everything — their team, their families, and every future they've been promised. When they're caught in a moment they can't take back, five people are trapped in a locker room where the only exit requires the truth.

Download your free copy at:

The Penalty Box is published under a Creative Commons license. You're free to read it, share it, or stage it. Theatre works best when it's accessible.

A Note to Readers (revised for the free download edition)

Thank you for reading *Romancing the Rookie.*

The play you just watched Elliot rehearse, perform, and lose himself inside is real. I wrote *The Penalty Box* as a complete three-act drama that could stand on its own — with its own characters, its own arc, and its own heart. You don't need the novel to read it, and you don't need the play to enjoy the novel. But if you've followed Elliot's journey, this is where it begins. This is the role that cracks him open, the production that draws him into the world of hockey, and the script that first makes him ask what it means to stop hiding.

A note on the playwright name: I've published this play under the pen name Cameron Torres. This name reflects and honors Diego Santos, one of the central characters, and the Latinx experience that's integral to his story. It's not an attempt to disguise my identity — it's a deliberate choice to center the voices and experiences depicted in this work.

The Penalty Box is licensed under a Creative Commons Attribution-ShareAlike 4.0 International License. That means anyone is free to stage, adapt, or share this play, provided you give appropriate credit, indicate if changes were made, and distribute your contributions under the same license. If you want to produce it, you don't need my permission — just my gratitude. If you do stage it, I'd love to hear about it.

This play was written with love for every young person who's ever felt like they had to choose between who they are and what they love. You don't. You never did.

— Jason S. Wrench (writing as Cameron Torres)

Content Advisory

The Penalty Box deals honestly with the experiences of closeted LGBTQ+ teenagers in competitive athletics. The following content may be difficult for some readers or audiences:

- Homophobic language, including an on-page slur directed at a main character
- Forced outing and the aftermath of being seen before you're ready
- Video recording of a private moment shared without consent
- Physical altercation between two teenagers
- Discussion of LGBTQ+ suicide rates and anti-LGBTQ+ violence (referenced in dialogue, not depicted)
- Parental grief and loss — both central families are navigating life after the death of a father
- Emotional pressure and manipulation, including a parent's fear weaponized as control
- Internalized homophobia and self-denial

If you or someone you know is struggling, help is available:

The Trevor Project — Crisis support for LGBTQ+ young people Call: 1-866-488-7386 | Text: START to 678-678 | thetrevorproject.org

Crisis Text Line — Text HOME to 741741

988 Suicide & Crisis Lifeline — Call or text 988

Link: https://dl.bookfunnel.com/xp5z95wro4

Goalie and the Geek: Tales from the Crease - Book 1

Chapter 1: Home Ice Advantage

Luke

Five days into preseason and I was already exhausted. I shouldered my goalie bag and pushed through the propped-open doors of Stony Creek Hall, the August humidity clinging to my post-practice sweat. The lobby, which had been empty for the last week while I got settled, was now a war zone on a Thursday afternoon. Parents maneuvered flatbed carts like battering rams, and the air smelled like floor wax, cardboard, and the frantic stress of a thousand goodbyes.

I dodged a dad carrying a futon and headed for the elevator. Move-in day. The one day I'd been dreading since I picked up my key a week ago.

I'd spent the last week in a quiet rhythm: wake up, two-a-days at the rink, lift, eat, sleep. Room 317 had been my sanctuary. I was guaranteed a single, one of the last on campus. That was the deal Coach Harper had swung for the transfer. Get in, steady the crease, keep the grades serviceable, and prove I could be the starter when the season kicked off in October. And so far, I'd been living up to my end of the bargain in practice. Admittedly, it was just the first week, but the team was good. Their previous goalie graduated, and I'd been recruited from a lower-division college the previous spring.

The elevator lurched open. Two first-years squeezed in with me, one holding a tower of plastic storage bins, the other juggling a mini-fridge. They stared at the massive goalie pad sticking out of my duffel, then at the Frost Demons logo on my dry-fit shirt.

"You guys start already?" Mini-Fridge asked.

"Preseason," I said, pressing the button for the third floor. "Been on the ice a week."

"Nice." He shifted the fridge, grimacing. "Heard the Demons needed a miracle in net this year."

I lifted my eyebrows but let the comment slide. People talked; I stopped caring about unverified opinions two teams ago. The doors opened on three, and I nudged the bag out into a hallway of buzzing fluorescent light and mismatched carpeting.

I headed for 317, anticipating the silence waiting for me. The rest of my day included a shower, a protein shake, and zero human interaction. I reached for my key, ready to unlock my fortress of solitude—and stopped.

The door was unlocked.

Actually, it was cracked open an inch.

My grip tightened on my bag strap. *I swear I locked it.* Routine was the only thing keeping me sane, and locking the door was step one. I pushed it open with my shoulder, ready to tell whoever was confused about their room number to get out.

But the room wasn't occupied; it had been colonized.

A guy my age stood by the far wall—average height, lean in that effortless way runners always looked, with brown hair that probably argued with a comb every morning. He wore a faded Harbor Commons T-shirt and shorts, and he was placing a stack of books onto a second desk that hadn't been there this morning.

Behind him, the room had transformed. My bed was still on the left, but a second bed had been jammed against the right wall. Two dressers. Two desks. One... roommate.

I dropped by gear bag on the ground. The thud made him jump. "Who are you?" I asked.

He turned, holding a mechanical pencil like a dart. His eyes scanned the goalie gear, then my face. "I'm guessing you're Luke." He looked at me, took a couple of steps toward me, and extended his hand, "Austen Lovell."

I didn't take it and watched as he lowered it looking at the scowl crossing my face.

"Yeah, I was guaranteed a single, which is what I've had for the last week. By myself." I gestured around the cramped space. "What is all this?"

"Furniture, mostly." He was annoyingly calm compared to my rising panic. "Housing sent me over about an hour ago. Apparently, the 'single' on your housing contract was a clerical error."

"A clerical error," I repeated flatly.

"That's what they called it when I showed up, and they didn't have a room for me in the system." He pointed to the new bed, which sat about three feet from mine. "I filed for a single too, if it makes you feel better. Neither of us won that lottery."

"But they told me there'd be space."

"And yet, here we are." He looked at me with a scowl that matched my own. "Trust me, this isn't my idea of a good time either."

Heat crawled up my neck. I'd planned for late dorm noise, forced fire drills, the weird smell common rooms developed after midnight. Not this. This was the equivalent to a breakaway before the puck even dropped.

I moved my gear bag by the unclaimed dresser. "Housing must've screwed up. I'll straighten it out."

Austen hummed noncommittally. "If you get a miracle out of them, tell me how you did it. I'll buy you dinner."

The words were casual, but his shoulders stayed tight. He flopped down on his bed, picked up a notebook, and started scribbling away. He was leaving space, letting me set the tone. Fine. Tone would be composed. Controlled.

I pulled my phone, thumbed to the contact sheet they'd emailed earlier, and found the number for housing services. I stepped into the hallway for privacy, closing the door enough to muffle my conversation but not enough to feel like retreating.

Four rings. "Northern Ridge Housing, this is Trish."

"Hi, this is Luke Carter. I checked into Stony Creek Hall, Room 317. I was assigned a single. And I got back from practice to find my room had been invaded along with new furniture."

A keyboard clacked. "Hmm. One moment."

I waited, eyes tracing the cinderblock wall, patches of tape peeled where old decorations had come off. Someone down the hall laughed too loud; a door slammed.

Trish came back. "Looks like the database still shows that room as designated for double occupancy because of fall semester overflow."

"But I was guaranteed a single. My coach guaranteed me a single. I'm on the hockey roster." I hated how that sounded—name-dropping the program—but eligibility had been the reason they'd rush-processed my housing application. Athletic department had pulled strings; that's what Coach Harper told me.

"I understand," Trish said pleasantly. "Unfortunately, we're beyond full capacity. The new dorm construction is behind schedule, so we converted several singles."

"Maybe a different dorm? There's gotta be somewhere on campus."

"Sorry. Right now, we're rearranging some rooms for three occupants and even housing a few first-year students in a local hotel until we iron out campus housing."

"So, what, I just—" I forced my shoulders down. Yelling at staff never helped. "Could you put me on a list? First open single, call me?"

"I'll add your name to the list," she said. "Earliest reassessment date is four to six weeks. Until then, university policy is shared space."

We'd be starting the season by then. Four to six weeks might as well be forever.

"Okay," I said because the alternative was nothing. "Thanks."

I slid the phone into my pocket and rested my head against the wall for a count of three. Plan B. Adapt. That's what goalies do when the play breaks down—square up, track the puck, trust the angle.

Back in the room, Austen hadn't moved. Still sat cross-legged on his bed, holding the mechanical pencil and writing in his notebook. He looked up, expression neutral. "Any luck?"

"I was put on a list, four to six weeks minimum before housing can do anything about this."

He nodded as if he'd anticipated this outcome. I exhaled through my nose and rubbed the crease between my eyebrows.

"Look," he said, without staring up, "I'm not trying to invade your space. This happened fast."

"Pretty sure it's happening to both of us." My tone wasn't sarcastic, more observational.

"I took the empty closet." I glanced at his side. Sweatshirts ordered from dark to light, shoes lined under the bed.

The one where I'd been storing my gear bag, which alone could eat half the floor. "I'll stack my duffel on my desk, for now." I picked it up and placed on the empty desk on my side of the room.

He tapped the pencil against the notebook twice. "Fair enough."

A bang erupted from the wall—metallic pipes protesting like they did every evening around this time. Austen flinched.

"AC unit," I said. "Maintenance hasn't fixed it. Clanks around two a.m. So, if you're a light sleeper—"

"Eight hours of partial differential equations tends to induce coma-level sleep." He shrugged. "I'll adapt."

"Math major?" He nodded. I thought of the intro sequence I'd dodged by choosing business. "Sounds intense."

"Let me guess. Business major?" A flicker of humor—almost a smile—crossed his mouth.

I didn't love how easily he'd clocked me. "That obvious?"

"Hockey player, business degree. It's a statistically reliable pairing." He said it without malice, just observation. "You're clearly not a first-year student, so I take it you transferred here to play hockey?"

"Yeah." I shoved the folder deeper, pretend casual. "Needed the right system."

He nodded like that translated. Maybe it did; I was told hockey in Cold Harbor was local currency.

"One more thing," I said. "The guy next door likes to play EDM at midnight. Thump the wall twice. He'll kill the bass. Still haven't seen him, so have no idea why he moved into the hall early. He's always gone before I am in the morning and comes home much later than I do at night."

"Midnight EDM, two thumps." He mimed knocking. "Noted."

I checked my watch—fifteen past five. Tomorrow's practice started at six sharp, meaning a 4:45 alarm if I wanted pre-ice stretch and coffee. A week ago this room had felt like a sanctuary. Now it felt like a penalty box built for two.

Austen stood, pocketed his phone. "I saw the fridge. Top shelf yours?"

"Yeah. Bottom's free." I'd already claimed my territory—protein shakes lined up beside the peas I used for icing.

"Got it." He grabbed a jacket from the hook he'd commandeered. "I've got a study group at eight. I'm out most nights till eleven, if you want private time."

"Study group? School hasn't even started."

He cocked his head. "You've been here for a week playing hockey and school hasn't started."

"Yeah, but that's practice. We're gearing up for the season."

"And we're gearing up for the school year." He reached for the doorknob, then paused. "Luke?"

"Yeah?"

"I don't mind sharing space. Just communicate, and we'll be fine."

"Copy that," I said, hand lifting in a small salute.

He disappeared into the hallway, footsteps fading. The latch clicked, and the room felt different—smaller, somehow, even with him gone. I sat on the edge of the mattress and braced my elbows on my knees.

Four weeks. I can do anything for four weeks. I closed my eyes, picturing the crease—painted blue, edges sharp. You don't control the team, the refs, the crowd, or the rink. You control the crease. This was the same. Control what's closet-sized and let the rest be noise.

A single had been the plan. Dad always said a plan kept you from sliding. He had plenty of plans, once, until the knee ligament shredded and he slid anyway. I shook off the thought, reached for my phone, and pulled up tomorrow's checklist: 4:45 alarm, medical clearance documentation, team physical at 5:30, dynamic stretch routine, on ice 6:00–8:15.

I set the alarm, resisted the urge to set three backups, then stood. Most of my stuff was already in place—had been for a week. The dresser drawers I'd organized on day one. The toiletries claiming half the narrow sink shelf. All of it now sharing airspace with someone else's things.

The AC rattled again, pipes banging like someone dropping pucks down the wall. I'd gotten used to the sound over the past week. Wondered how long it would take Austen.

I shot a quick text to Ryan O'Connell—left-wing enforcer, one of the few guys who'd reached out after the transfer.

Me: *Housing screwed me. Got a roommate now.*

Ryan: *Welcome to Cold Harbor luxury suites. Who'd they stick you with?*

Me: *Math major. Seems quiet.*

Ryan: *Could be worse. Could be Javier. He snores during video review.*

Me: *Good to know.*

I tossed the phone onto the pillow and surveyed Austen's side. His stuff was neat. Almost too neat. I mean, who arranges their sweatshirts arranged dark to light? I stared at his desk. Even his books were stacked by size. The precision should have been reassuring. Instead, it felt like someone had moved furniture in my head without asking.

Dinner. I should go eat. I grabbed my wallet, checked the knob out of habit—it still stuck sometimes, but I'd learned the trick—and stepped into the hallway.

The floor hummed with early-semester energy: doors open, people laughing, somebody blasting Mario Kart music. I'd at least avoided the move-in chaos by arriving a week early. I'd already found my footing. Devon, the RA, had given me the welcome packet and the sympathetic grin about the AC. Now, I was just another face in the crowd.

Outside, dusk had settled. Cold Harbor's campus lights glowed soft gold, and across the lawn, the science complex flickered with late-night labs. Ridgeway Hall, the math and science building, stood off to the right—windows lit sporadically. I imagined Austen sitting in a room of friends doing math problems on a whiteboard.

A gentle breeze took the sting off the summer evening. I jammed my hands into my shorts pockets and set off toward North Point Dining Hall.

Inside North Point, the grill line was short. I loaded a tray—chicken, rice, and whatever vegetable wasn't dripping butter—and claimed a table near the windows. Students buzzed around me, laughter bouncing off cinderblock walls. Groups formed and re-formed, tables claimed, inside jokes flying. The kind of chemistry teams tried to manufacture in locker rooms.

I ate methodically, fueling more than tasting. Between bites, I opened my planner: class list, rink schedule, workouts. Every block accounted for. The plan. Except now it had an asterisk—room shared, privacy compromised, mental space unknown.

Halfway through dinner, a text popped from Coach Harper: *Reminder—medical clearance forms due at 0530 tomorrow or you're off the ice.*

I replied: *Form signed, see you at five.*

Coach Harper wasn't big on emojis. Good. Neither was I.

I finished eating, bused the tray, and ignored the surrounding chatter about upcoming ski trips and fall singles mixers. Back outside, the air felt sharper. I retraced steps to Stony Creek Hall.

The lobby was quieter now, lights dimmed. Third floor was quieter too, though EDM bass thumped faintly behind my neighbor's door. I tapped twice, testing my own advice. The bass cut off mid-drop. At least that still worked.

Inside 317, the AC unit sputtered but hadn't started its percussion solo. Austen's bed was empty, desk lamp off. The clock on my phone read 7:43. Plenty of time before he came back.

I toed off shoes, left them by the door—same spot as always—and changed into sleep shorts and a T-shirt. Then, because routine mattered, I unrolled the yoga mat between the beds. Tighter squeeze now, but it still fit. Ten minutes of hip mobility drills, pausing for a second only when the floor creaked in the hallway and I thought my new roommate was coming home. But the door remained locked. Stretching ended with me on my back, lying on the yoga mat and doing goalie-specific visualizations my high school coach had taught me—crease, angles, shooter patterns. The exercises usually cleared my head. Tonight, they only underlined that I was practicing recovery breathing six feet from a stranger's pillow.

I stood, rolled the mat tight, and slid it under the bed. Considered reviewing the team's playbook again, but rejected the idea. Brain done. Instead, I turned off the overhead light, climbed under the covers, checked the alarm on my phone, and stared at the ceiling. The hairline crack spidering across cinderblock looked vaguely like a face—I'd named it Gary on night three. I blinked until it became patternless again.

Footsteps approached. Austen's key scraped the lock at 10:56. I checked without meaning to. The door opened; he slipped inside, closed it softly.

"Hey," he whispered, seeing me awake.

"Hey." My voice came out rougher than intended. "How was your study group?"

"Good." He hung his jacket on the hook—his hook now, I supposed. He went to his set of drawers and pulled out a pair of sweatpants and a T-shirt. The room was dark, but my eyes had already adjusted. I should have looked away. I didn't.

He slid out of his shirt first. Lean shoulders, the kind of definition that came from movement rather than weights. A runner's build, maybe, or someone who biked everywhere. His spine curved as he reached for the sweatpants, and I caught the shadow of muscle shifting across his back before he stepped out of his jeans.

I stared at the ceiling. Forced myself to count the cracks.

The rustle of fabric said he'd finished. I heard him grab something from the desk—toiletry bag, maybe—and the door opened again, light slicing across the floor.

"Bathroom," he said, half-whispered.

I nodded, not trusting my voice.

The door clicked shut. I exhaled slowly, rubbing a hand over my face. *What the hell was that?* I'd seen guys change in locker rooms a thousand times. This was no different.

Except I hadn't looked away.

A minute later, footsteps returned. The door opened, closed again softly. Darkness settled back over the room. Only the glow of my phone remained.

He pointed at the screen. "Alarm early?"

"Four forty-five."

"Got it." He fished wireless earbuds from the desk drawer. "I'll keep quiet."

He didn't need to; his presence barely registered sound. Mattress springs sighed as he lay down, and for a minute only the hum of the AC filled the room. Then—bang—metal pipes clanged like an unwelcome drum solo.

Austen chuckled under his breath. "Showtime, I assume?"

"You'll sleep through it by Wednesday." I flipped onto my side, facing the wall. "Took me till Thursday."

"Noted." Rustle of sheets. "Goodnight, Luke."

My brain cataloged practice drills: T pushes, butterfly recoveries, rebound smothers. Anything but the fact that my room had become our room, my silence had become shared silence, my sanctuary now came with a witness. The AC settled into a steady hum. Austen's breathing evened out, quiet and rhythmic.

Four weeks, I reminded myself. *Control what's yours.*

I closed my eyes. The mattress felt the same, but everything else had shifted. Somewhere between pipe hiss and dorm quiet, sleep dragged me under.

Alarm. 4:45. Phone vibrated against the nightstand—barely a nightstand; more like a plank screwed to the wall. I slapped the screen, silencing the buzz before it could wake Austen, then swung my legs over the edge. The AC ticked in post-performance cooldown, otherwise silent.

I dressed in low light—compression gear, hoodie, track pants—breathing through each motion. "*Tomorrow's routine starts with today's discipline.*" Dad's voice, years old, still coaching. I tied my laces, shoulders rolling loose. I grabbed my gear bag and tried to be quiet, but the heavy plastic pieces clanged against each other.

A rustle behind me. I looked over to see Austen rolling onto his side. I slipped out of the room as quietly as possible, angling my body to block the hallway's light from pouring into the room. I inhaled the cold dorm air mixed with stale pizza. One day in and my perfect fall plan had cracks, but the ice waited.

I jogged down the stairwell, bag over my shoulder, and stepped into the predawn dark.

Pucking Power Plays: Tales from the Crease – Book Three

Chapter 1: The Home Barn

Bogdan

The Northstar University men's hockey locker room smelled of fermented sweat, bacteria, mildew, with undertones of rotting cheese and maybe a dead skunk. The sweet smell of success, or at least the smell of twenty-six college males confined to a space really designed for twenty-two. We maxed our roster, so a few of the first-years who didn't get much playtime had to double up on lockers.

I rolled my shoulders, letting the pads settle, then checked the mirror above the trainer's table. Visor clean, jawline razor-sharp, white shield stitched to the royal blue of my jersey. My black captain's patch sat above my left pec, the number 17 across my back. Puck first; everything else follows.

Around me, the locker room cracked with pre-game noise—sticks knocking against benches, laughter pitched high enough to hide nerves. Evan, one of my first-line defensemen, taped his shin guards beside me, white cloth spiraling so tight it left indentations in his fingers.

"You good?" he asked without looking up.

"Never better." I flexed my hands, feeling the leather gloves creak. "Ridgewater thinks they're taking our ice tonight. Let's remind them whose rink this is."

Evan barked a laugh. "Pretty sure the scoreboard will handle that."

"No. We handle it."

Caleb, my left wing, whistled the intro riff to "Seven Nation Army," off-key but obnoxiously loud.

"That's practically whistling with the oldies," Evan said, before lobbing a roll of tape in Caleb's direction.

That had the opposite effect of what Evan was hoping for. Someone pounded a fist against a metal locker, amplifying the drumbeat. Energy spiked—electric, volatile. I loved this moment. The sliver of time when anything could still happen. We were amped. And we all looked great, now that we were out of our warmup jerseys and ready to teach the punks from Ridgewater how to play hockey.

Coach Keller shoved through the door, baseball cap low, jacket collar up. February wind sneaked in behind him, scattering tape rolls.

"Eyes up." His voice was an interesting, almost falsetto, which was always a huge contrast to the middle-aged ex-professional hockey player who stood six-foot-five and had to be pushing three hundred pounds. The first time I'd met him on my campus visit, I'd nearly laughed at the disconnect. Then he'd taken my parents and me to dinner with his husband, Dr. Cole Callahan, a history professor and former NFL linebacker who studied sport history—specifically the inclusion of marginalized groups in athletics. I'd walked into that dinner expecting a recruiting pitch. I'd walked out a history major.

I could have gone to more prestigious programs. But Northstar was known for being a progressive campus with a zero-tolerance policy for any kind of discrimination. When you're a bisexual kid trying to build something real in this sport, you pick the environment where you know the people around you will actually have your back. Not just on paper. In practice. I'd learned the hard way that not every locker room lives up to its stated values.

"Conference quarterfinal," Keller said, snapping me back to the present. "Lose and we bus home tomorrow. Win and we kick the Navigators into my golf season." He paused. "Scouts are upstairs. I know the Lakeview Sentinels and San Francisco Tremors are both in the barn. The San Francisco people are easy to spot. They look like they're dressed for the beach and not late February in Minnesota. Almost amazed they could find Ironvale on a map. Play your game, not theirs."

Laughter. Tension bled. Keller nodded at me. I rose, stick blade slapping the concrete.

"Northstar," I said, letting the word hang. Twenty-six pairs of eyes locked on mine. "We don't let anyone rewrite our story in our barn. They want center ice? Make them pay rent. They want the wall? Charge interest. They want the blue paint? Evict them."

Cheers. Fists against pads. I waited until the noise peaked, then cut it with a slice through the air.

"And Draisaitl?" I added, quieter. Silence snapped into place. "Draisaitl is mine."

Caleb hooted. "Daddy Bog's gonna spank the golden boy!"

"Keep it in your pants, Rourke," Keller muttered through a smirk. "Andro, lead 'em out."

I banged my stick twice on the floor, and the boys flooded the tunnel, skates clacking. Under the arena lights, Northstar jerseys glowed deep navy, almost black, like storm clouds gathering.

We gathered in the tunnel, waiting for the announcer to finish reading the starting lineup for the Navigators.

"—on the other defense, number 44, Finn Orr. At center, number 29, Niklas Draisaitl—"

The arena erupted in boos. I watched the six-foot-three blond German skate onto the ice. Same smug look he always had.

I'd known—and hated—Niklas Draisaitl since we were in our early teens, when his family had moved to the US from Germany. We'd been through 16U, 18U, and now Division I together, constantly facing off on different teams, and the media had thoroughly enjoyed comparing us our entire lives. Our stats, our families, our potential draft positions—the comparisons had gotten so relentless they were obnoxious. It didn't help that when I'd come out as bisexual in my senior year of high school, Draisaitl had come out as gay the very next month. Like he even had to make our sexuality a competition. *You're only half gay—me, full gay.* I heard him say in the back of my mind, in his thick German accent. Those words had never actually left his mouth, but I heard them anyway.

The hockey blogs had a field day with both of us coming out. There'd been rumors we were dating, which we'd both shut down. I'd tried to be civil about it, congratulating Draisaitl on his bravery. He'd told a blogger I wasn't his type—he preferred masculine men. It was an offhand quip, but it pissed me off enough that I may have dented a cinder block with my fist. Thankfully I just split my knuckles open and didn't break anything.

As for backlash, I'd heard the slur once, in 18U. A defenseman on my own team broke the guy's nose, and that was the last time anyone said it to my face. My teams always had my back. Anyone stupid enough to test that learned the lesson fast.

Now here he was, two inches taller than me and somehow always looking down his nose at me when we met. Such a prick.

The poor goalie's name couldn't even be heard over the PA.

Then the amp-up music kicked in, and the announcer's voice changed from reading a boring script to reading off the starting lineup of the home team.

"For the Northstar Paladins, starting on right wing, number 19, Marcus Sawchuk." Marcus skated out and raised his stick toward the crowd, drawing loud applause. "On left wing, number 22, Caleb Rourke." Caleb skated out, all business. He didn't even acknowledge the crowd. "On defense, number 4, Evan Bourque." Evan just skated out and glanced at the Jumbotron. "On the other defense, number 3, Jack Robinson." Jack lifted his chin at the camera guy as if to say *what's up*. "At center, your team captain, number 17, Bogdan Andro." I skated out and lifted both arms. The crowd was already chanting *Bog*. "And finally in goal, number 31, Trent Dryden."

Behind the opposite bench, Ridgewater stretched in crimson and white. Draisaitl kneeled at the red line, head bowed, helmet off. Blond hair caught the overhead lights—stupid perfect, like he'd scheduled a stylist between warmups. He rose, rolled his neck, and spotted me.

Niklas tipped his chin in a greeting that wasn't one. Mouthguard peeked between his teeth in something like a smile. Even from thirty feet, I could read the words on his lips.

"Ready, Andro?"

I shoved my visor lower. "Fuck yeah, I'm ready." I knew he couldn't hear me, but he got the message.

Starting lineups skated toward center before some minor celebrity singer whose career had passed years ago belted out the national anthem.

First faceoff.

I crouched opposite Draisaitl, shoulders square, weight balanced on toes. The ref's hand hovered over the puck. The crowd thundered—students banging on glass, cowbells, someone's air horn shrieking.

He was taller than me by two inches, so I had to angle my chin up slightly to hold eye contact. Heat rolled off him. His cologne hadn't burned off during warmups, so there was still a citrusy smell coming off him. The scent shouldn't have registered. It did.

Eighteen inches between us. Close enough that I could count his breaths. I noted his stance, his grip on his stick. Standard scouting.

His eyes flicked to my left hand, cataloguing tells. He licked his bottom lip—nervous habit or deliberate distraction, impossible to say.

"You look pretty today, little bog," he said through the plastic. "Too pretty to get sweaty playing hockey. Why don't you go sit on your bench, kick your skates up—"

"You'd like that? But since you're clearly into me, I'll send you a selfie with the cup."

He grinned. "Nah, I'll send you one." He winked.

Whistle. The puck dropped.

I snapped my wrist, won clean, slid the rubber back to Evan. Draisaitl's stick carved air. Frustration flashed across his face, gone in a blink. He pivoted, hounded my winger to the corner. Textbook recovery.

Shift ended. Both benches roared approval. Keller bumped knuckles with me as I slid past. "Stay on him."

I nodded but didn't sit..I had to watch Niklas's next shift, memorize it. He jumped the boards, legs long, stride fluid as cursive. Bastard made skating look effortless. He had the power of a professional hockey player with the grace of a figure skater. How he managed that at his height and size was beyond me.

Back over the rail and on the ice, we gained the zone. Draisaitl called for the puck, top of the circle. One-timer. Pipe. The arena gasped. Rebound popped, cleared by Evan.

Close. Too close.

Caleb slapped my shoulder. "He almost ate your lunch there."

"I don't share food." I spit water, eyes still on the ice. Still on Draisaitl.

Second faceoff, neutral zone. Niklas muttered something in German—probably a swear—then added, "Let's make this interesting. Loser buys post-game drinks?"

"As long as you bring your ID." I leaned into the circle, close enough to see the gold flecks in his irises. "Wouldn't want the bartender carding you for that baby face."

He chuckled. "My baby face, your pretty face. What a cute couple we'd make."

The puck dropped. Draisaitl exploded forward, tied me up, and Ridgewater won possession. He peeled off, torque in every push, thighs driving power I could almost feel through the ice. My ribs squeezed. Draisaitl took the shot, but Trent snagged it out of the air with ease.

The period wore on. Hits stacked. Sticks tangled. The scoreboard stayed empty until the final minute, when their winger deflected a point shot past Trent. Horn blared. Crowd deflated.

I skated to the bench, chest heaving. Keller set his jaw. "We answer early next period. Andro, get under Draisaitl's skin. He's too comfortable."

Translation: go break something.

Second period. I found Draisaitl behind Ridgewater's net, battling for a loose puck. I angled in, shoulder leveled, and drove him into the boards. Impact rattled through my frame—his body dense, unyielding, warmer than the arena air. The puck squirted free. Draisaitl grunted, hooked my elbow with his stick, used my momentum to spin us both around, then pressed his forearms into my chest to shove off.

His palm flattened over my heart. He landed on his edges, balanced, maddeningly graceful. "That's the best you've got, little bog?"

"Saving the good stuff." I chopped at his stick, forced a turnover. "Bring your credit card, Draisaitl—I'm not a cheap date!" I yelled back at him.

The crowd surged.

We forechecked like demons. Caleb roofed one. Tie game. The stands went nuclear. I ignored the noise, eyes only for Draisaitl gliding to center ice.

No trash talk this time; the grin was gone. Sweat darkened his hair, curled at his temples. The ref dropped the puck. Scramble. Skates kicked up snow. Our sticks clacked—his blade against mine, vibration singing up my arms. He won, barely, but I slashed the tape, nudged it loose, stole it right back.

"Scheiße!" followed me down the ice.

By the end of forty minutes, the score was still 1–1. Bodies were bruised and tempers were fraying. I sat between periods with thigh pads unstrapped, sipping electrolytes. Miguel, the trainer, dabbed an alcohol wipe over my knuckles where the skin had split on a cross-check.

"You hitting helmets again?"

"Visor caught me." I shrugged, flexing the hand. "Good pain."

Miguel arched a brow but taped gauze anyway. "Don't break anything important."

Third period opened with Ridgewater pressing. Our defense bent but didn't break. Trent kicked shots to the corner; boards rattled; blood sizzled in my ears.

Ridgewater called a timeout. I wheeled past center ice and brushed Niklas's hip with my stick. He looked back—an unreadable expression behind his visor.

The ref blew his whistle. Play resumed. Tension coiled tighter.

Nine minutes left. I intercepted a neutral-zone pass and charged the blue line. Draisaitl pivoted backward, defensive posture textbook, but I feinted inside then cut wide. He matched, kept stick length. Smart. I dumped the puck behind him, chased, slammed on the brakes. Snow dusted his shin guards. He tried to pin me; I slipped under, reverse hit, shielded the puck.

We tangled along the wall, arms wedged, hips knocking. His breath was too close. Everything about him was too close. The scent of his musk filled my lungs whether I wanted it there or not.

His thigh wedged between mine for leverage.

"You dance well for a control freak," he murmured, lips close enough that I felt the words more than heard them.

"I prefer to lead."

A grin, feral, visible even through his visor. "Prove it."

We battled, spun, puck trapped between skates. A Ridgewater defenseman joined, digging it free. Whistle—hand pass. Faceoff left circle.

Draisaitl and I leaned in again. Sweat dripped from my brow underneath my helmet onto the ice, freezing in tiny pearls.

Drop. I clamped the puck, kicked it back. Shot from the point sailed wide, rimmed around to neutral. Damn.

The minute hand crawled. We kept colliding—sticks, shoulders, words.

Regulation ended 1–1.

Overtime in playoffs was sudden death, but conference quarters used five-minute OT then a shootout. Stupid rule. Anything that lets a skills competition decide months of work deserves setting on fire.

Players hunched along the boards. Keller gathered us. "First shift decides it. Andro's line starts. Be ruthless."

Draisaitl's line started too. Naturally.

We circled center. The puck felt heavier in the official's hand. Crowd on its feet. Adrenaline sharpened every sense.

"Ready to go home early?" Draisaitl asked, voice quiet.

"Nice projection."

Faceoff. He lunged. I read it, slipped under, and the puck slid to my winger. We stormed the zone. Shot—pad save—rebound kicked wide. Ridgewater countered. Niklas blasted up ice, skating like he owned gravity. Pass across, return feed, my defenseman sprawled.

I dove, stick outstretched. Puck clipped the tape cradle of Niklas's blade. He snapped the shot anyway. It deflected off my shaft, fluttered, arced over our goalie, clanged off the crossbar, bounced out.

Whistle.

My lungs burned. Niklas stared at the empty air where the puck hadn't gone. "*Was zum Teufel?!*" He exhaled hard, shoulders lifting, dropping.

Next draw. He cheated—encroached early. Ref called him off.

"*Hurensohn!*"

Their second-line center took the drop; I won easy, sprung Evan, but he missed the shot.

Time drained. The buzzer cut through. Shootout.

The building went insane—half thrill, half dread. Players lined the benches. Coin toss decided we shot first. Keller pointed at me.

I rolled my neck, shook out my hands. Helmet off, gloves off, head clear. The ice stretched white and infinite between me and their goalie. I skated to the dot, picked up the puck, and cradled it on my blade. Sound fell away—crowd, coaches, everything except the scrape of my edges and the distant heartbeat in my ears.

Me and their goalie, a nice enough guy named Henrik Sawchuk. One chance.

I faked forehand, dragged backhand, roofed it. Net rippled. Water bottle flew. Students exploded.

Draisaitl shot third for them. He needed to score to keep it alive. He glided in slow, effortless—like he had all the time in the world, like pressure was a concept that applied to other people. At the hashmarks, he pulled a toe drag so smooth it looked choreographed, opened Trent like a book, tucked it five-hole.

Cheater. Beautiful cheater.

He pumped a fist, spared me a glance that asked, *Still even?*

Our fourth shooter missed. Their fourth missed. Fifth round. Caleb skated wide, snapped low blocker—goal. Pressure flipped. Their right winger, Luca Moretti, struggled and fired high. Crossbar again. Clang. Game.

Northstar's bench erupted over the boards. I flung my stick and yelled something wordless. Pandemonium. Our student section rattled the rafters like an avalanche contained by brick.

Glove taps, helmet smacks, hugs—chaotic communion. Amid it, I scanned for one face.

Draisaitl stood in the handshake line, helmet off, blond hair wet and messy. His eyes found mine across the swarm. He wasn't smiling. He wasn't frowning. He looked alive. And hungry.

We formed lines. Tradition demanded civility—congratulations, good luck, little nods hiding killer intent for next time. Player after player passed. My hand went numb from gripping and releasing.

Then Draisaitl.

He gripped my hand harder than necessary, palm hot and calloused against mine. His knuckles were raw from a scrum in the second period—we'd both taken our share of damage tonight. I squeezed back, felt his pulse in his fingertips—or imagined I did—then let go.

"Still want those drinks?"

"Only if we trash-talk the whole time."

"Wouldn't have it any other way."

We moved on. My palm tingled for the next hour.

Postgame, reporters lurked outside the dressing room. Cameras, recorders, manic energy. I fielded questions—faceoffs, momentum, playoff mindset.

Dan Holloway, regional pain in my ass, asked, "That showdown with Draisaitl in overtime looked personal. What did he say?"

"Nothing printable. Game moves fast. Emotions run hotter."

"Is this the central rivalry of the conference now?"

"Rivalry implies parity," I answered. "Scoreboard says Northstar."

He laughed. "Bold. See you in the semis."

God, I hoped so.

The locker room was loud and messy and perfect. Players sprawled on benches in various states of undress, exhaustion and adrenaline battling for control of every face.

"Dude, you smell," I said to Evan as he wrapped me in his sweaty arms.

"You love it," he said before grabbing my head and kissing me on the forehead.

"Eww," I cried, exaggeratedly wiping the kiss from my forehead. "Cooties!"

Keller appeared, expression a mix of satisfaction and something already forward-looking. "Good game. Don't get comfortable. Semifinals are in two weeks. Enjoy tonight, then we get back to work."

Two weeks. Enough time to heal the bruises, review the film, sharpen the details. Enough time to not think about Niklas Draisaitl.

I showered, changed, said my goodbyes. The arena emptied around me until it was just staff and echoes.

Hours later, I lay in the dark of my apartment, ice pack on my hand, phone buzzing with congratulatory texts. Team group chat. Family. Friends from high school I hadn't spoken to in months. Someone had already tagged me in a photo from the locker room celebration. I'd had exactly one beer—enough to be present, not enough to let my guard down. That was the rule. I aimlessly scrolled past all of them.

Nothing caught my attention.

I stared at the ceiling and replayed the game. Not the shootout, not Caleb's winner. The moments between. Draisaitl's ability to read my tells bothered me—I'd need to fix that before we met again. The faceoffs where he'd leaned in close enough that I could smell him. The wall battle where his thigh had wedged between mine and neither of us had pulled away faster than necessary. His incessant flirting. *Pretty. Little bog.* That stupid nickname, delivered with that stupid accent he somehow still had after living half his life in the US.

I'd known Draisaitl for half my life. I'd competed against him, trash-talked him, resented him, studied him like a text I couldn't stop rereading. And tonight, standing close enough to count his breaths, I'd noticed something I didn't want to name.

Puck first; everything else follows. That was my rule. My religion. And Draisaitl was the opposite of control—he was chaos in a crimson jersey, too loud, too tall, too present, too much.

I thought about the bet. Loser buys post-game drinks. He'd lost. He owed me.

I was almost asleep when my phone buzzed.

Unknown number.

Nice shot. Still owe drinks. —N

About the author

Jason Wrench

Jason Wrench is the author of *12 Days of Murder* (November 2021) and *Till Death Do Us Wed* (February 2022); the Up on the Farm series: *Finding a Farmer* (August 2022), *Bewitched by the Barista* (September 2022), *Sanctuary for the Surgeon* (January, 2023), and *Catching the Composer* (May 2023); *Wolf Island* (October, 2022); and the Love and Liquidation Series: *Boy Bands and Bullets* (November 2023), *A Choreographed Coup* (April 2024), and *Rhythmic Reclamation* (June 2024) all with Pride Publishing. He's also the author of *The Veil, Jekyll/Hyde, Life on the Naughty List, or What the Elf!* (November 2024), *Shattering Securities* (June 2025), and *Goalie and the Geek* (February 2026). And translated *Manor: A Novella by Karl Heinrich Ulrichs* (August 2024). And he's the man behind the cozy mystery pen name, J. J. Justice.

When he's not writing novels, he's a college professor at SUNY New Paltz in the Department of Communication. In that capacity, he's authored or edited twenty academic books, thirty-five plus research articles, and numerous chapters in other books.

In his downtime, he loves reading/writing, Broadway, coffee, and his puggle, Max (9-year-old) and Branch (8-year-old).

He's a member of the Romance Writers of America and the Textbook and Academic Author Association.

You can find his other works on his website: https://jasonwrench.com/.

www.ingramcontent.com/pod-product-compliance
Lightning Source LLC
LaVergne TN
LVHW041924090826
845145LV00015B/297

9781971739052